He Kissed Me Gently, and It Was All I Had Ever Dreamed of In My Wildest Imaginings.

———————

Fervently, I clung to him, exulting in the feel of his body quivering taut as a bowstring against mine, too young and naive to know how I tempted him.

Nicky brought his mouth down on mine again, harder this time, and more demanding, so he bruised me with his kiss. His tongue probed my mouth, searching out its every dark, moist crevice, until I could scarcely breathe. But my ragged gasps only spurred him on. His fingers slid sensuously up my spine to entwine themselves in my tresses, pulling me back, so I only dimly realized I was being deliberately compelled to lie upon the stone bench.

I had not intended things to go this far. I started to struggle against him, imploring him to take me back to the ballroom.

"Don't fight me, Laura," he muttered thickly. "You know you want this as much as I do."

And to my utter shame, much as I longed to deny it, some part of me thrilled to his touch as he slowly lowered his mouth, and his tongue scorched me with liquid fire.

Also by Rebecca Brandewyne

———

And Gold Was Ours
Desire in Disguise
Forever My Love
Love, Cherish Me
No Gentle Love
The Outlaw Hearts
Rose of Rapture
Upon a Moon-Dark Moor

———

Published by
WARNER BOOKS

Across A Starlit Sea

Rebecca Brandewyne

WARNER BOOKS

A Warner Communications Company

For Aunt Shirley,
who encouraged me to read.
With love.

The Family Tree

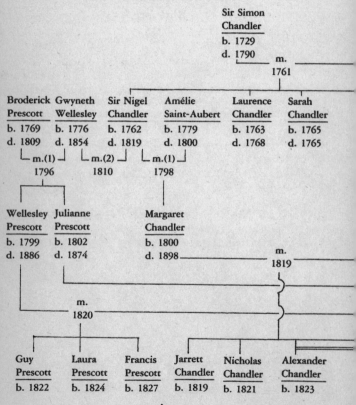

Sir Simon
Chandler
b. 1729
d. 1790
m.
1761

| Broderick Prescott b. 1769 d. 1809 | Gwyneth Wellesley b. 1776 d. 1854 | Sir Nigel Chandler b. 1762 d. 1819 | Amélie Saint-Aubert b. 1779 d. 1800 | Laurence Chandler b. 1763 d. 1768 | Sarah Chandler b. 1765 d. 1765 |

m.(1) 1796   m.(2) 1810   m.(1) 1798

Wellesley Prescott
b. 1799
d. 1886

Julianne Prescott
b. 1802
d. 1874

Margaret Chandler
b. 1800
d. 1898

m. 1819

m. 1820

| Guy Prescott b. 1822 | Laura Prescott b. 1824 | Francis Prescott b. 1827 | Jarrett Chandler b. 1819 | Nicholas Chandler b. 1821 | Alexander Chandler b. 1823 |

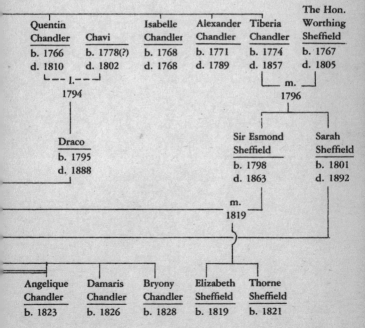

Margaret
Darnley
b. 1743
d. 1798

Quentin
Chandler
b. 1766
d. 1810

Chavi
b. 1778(?)
d. 1802

⌞ _ _ m. _ _ ⌟
1794

Isabelle
Chandler
b. 1768
d. 1768

Alexander
Chandler
b. 1771
d. 1789

Tiberia
Chandler
b. 1774
d. 1857

The Hon.
Worthing
Sheffield
b. 1767
d. 1805

⌞ _ m. _ ⌟
1796

Draco
b. 1795
d. 1888

Sir Esmond
Sheffield
b. 1798
d. 1863

Sarah
Sheffield
b. 1801
d. 1892

m.
1819

Angelique
Chandler
b. 1823

Damaris
Chandler
b. 1826

Bryony
Chandler
b. 1828

Elizabeth
Sheffield
b. 1819

Thorne
Sheffield
b. 1821

Contents

PROLOGUE
In Twilight Dim
1

BOOK ONE
Autumn, Aflame and Cruel
9

BOOK TWO
Scattered Hopes and Hearts
187

BOOK THREE
The Notorious
295

EPILOGUE
Across a Starlit Sea
361

Across a Starlit Sea

Age doth bring wisdom
And regrets, they say,
And memories, pale, unbidden;
Yet how wondrous bright I find
I see the past. Like silver stars,
It shines and shimmers in my mind—
In twilight dim, I think . . .

And I remember that certain autumn
'Neath a midnight sky aflame and cruel,
When the way of it had gone awry
And far too swift did judgment rule.

When, ill-gotten sprite of jest—
Oh, vile and hateful thing!—
With delight, you unleashed your devils,
Demons reckless in their need.
And swept our lives, like a raging storm,
To the winds and, without heed,
Scattered hopes and hearts like ashes. . . .

'Twas madness! Madness, wild and savage,
Drove us ruthlessly toward crime,
To acts born of wounded hearts turned
Icy hard as winter's rime.

But, still, how rapturous!
How splendid was my shame!
I cannot lie. Such wanton passion . . .
Oh, I blush when I recall
How eager my surrender
When love demanded all.
I've none but myself to blame.

Daring robber of my maidenhood,
Carnal thief of purity and youth,
How you stripped away my childishness
To expose a woman's naked truth—

Oh, worthy creature,
Wondrous rogue,
Sweet was the pain with which you pierced me,
Shot your arrow in my heart,
And stole away my innocence,
Then tore my love and me apart—
And, still, were not content.

Bitter fate you plotted even then.
How your spiteful eyes did gleam.
Naught but a pawn was I upon your board,
No chance against your scheme.

Thence come the follies of youth!
I can but weep now—and repent
That dreadful day of wickedness,
All those evil words I cried,
While one lay still and silent,
Though he knew full well I lied.
Oh, would I had not done it!

For vengeance wrought but vengeance.
Never together again shall we be,
As we were before one, twice accused, did sail
Far across a starlit sea.

So, in my age, I curse you,
You, who trod upon my dreams
And trampled all I e'er did cherish
Years ago. . . . Still, they were glorious,
Those halcyon days of wild abandon,
Misspent by us, the notorious.
Yes, long have I loved you now.

Across A Starlit Sea

In Twilight Dim
1898

Remember me when I am gone
away,
    Gone far away into the silent land.

—*Remember*
Christina Rossetti

The Cornish Moors, England, 1898

The others have long since gone—and I am alone now, alone with her who lies beneath the freshly turned sod of these wild, windswept moors she loved so well.

In the pale grey light of the slowly descending dusk, I kneel beside her grave, feeling the chill of the ground, sodden with mist and drizzle, seeping into my bones; but still, I cannot bring myself to leave her. In a vain attempt to keep her with me just a little while longer, my hand rests upon the moist mound of turf that covers her—

3

cruelly, I think, though she would not have agreed, for she belonged to these fierce Cornish heaths with all her heart and soul, and she was glad to be joined with them. But even now, when she is dead and buried, I cannot believe that she, who was so much a part of my life, is truly lost to me at last, that I will never see her again upon this earth. I had always thought she was ageless, and somehow I had expected her to endure forever, like the endless land and sea. I still feel that presently we will walk through the rusty wrought-iron gates of the cemetery together and ride back in the waiting carriage to Stormswept Heights, as we have done each Sunday for far more years than I like to remember.

Yet I know our parting will not be for long. Soon I will rest beside her, for I am an old woman now, though in my heart, I think I shall always be just eighteen, as I was when I came as a young bride to the Heights, as she had come before me. Yet my clearest memory of her is an earlier one, when we stood upon the rugged cliffs that edge the Cornish coast and she brought light into the darkest hour of my life.

Her name was Maggie Chandler, and though there were those who scorned her as a woman of scandal, she was ever my friend. We were bound together by both blood and marriage, but the strongest tie of all between us was the love born of our years of shared joy and sorrow at the Heights. We were Chandler women—not just in name, but in spirit, bold and brazen as the Chandler men we loved so passionately and with such reckless abandon, heedless of the consequences.

Yet she once told me that if she had her life to live

again, she would change nothing of it, for she had lived each precious moment to the fullest and had no regrets. At the time, I did not understand her, for she had known much hardship and suffering. But now I know it is these things that are truly the making of us; and if, as hers were, my memories are sometimes painful, I, too, have no regrets, for I have none but myself to blame for the choices I made, the rough waves I set sail upon in my youth and so was forced to cross, though there were many times when I would have turned back—if only I could have done so. But I could not. I was what I was, what we all were, and perhaps it was not within us to be other than that. I do not know.

I know only that, as the young often do, we seized life with a vengeance and made of it what we willed, a mosaic ill fashioned and much mended, and the cracks did ever show afterward. . . . But I do not complain. My pieces were as fragmented as the rest, as poorly placed, without thought of pattern or color; for what do the young, in their ignorance, really know of harmony and grace?

The twilight is fading into darkness now; the light from the early stars glows faintly, hazily, obscured by the mist and the gentle rain that falls upon the weathered granite headstones of those who were so much a part of my life, who sleep now beneath this rocky Cornish earth, as I will also in the end. Yet there is one who is not here; and as always, I am saddened when I think of him, for he is buried in a distant land across the sea—and my youth with him. But not my heart. I know that now.

Presently, I shall rise and walk through the gates of the cemetery to where my son Rhodes waits with the carriage to take me back to the Heights, the old manor house that is my home. How strange indeed are the twists of fate, for I never thought it should be his arm I leaned on in the winter of my years. Still, it is so, and I am glad, for a part of his father, whom I loved, lives on in him. In truth, sometimes when Rhodes's face is cast in shadow, I can almost imagine he *is* his father; and then the memories come rushing to engulf me, setting me atremble, for they are best forgotten.

Still, I do not forget. Indeed, with each passing year, the past seems to grow ever clearer to me, bright and sharp-edged as sunlight reflected by a spyglass. And so I linger a while yet here in the silence, an old woman, alone with my ghosts, as the old so often are; and as though it were only yesterday, I see us all as we were in our youth, rash and defiant, never dreaming of the grievous turns our lives would take. How brave we were then, I think, in those halcyon days gone by, those bittersweet days when, in our passion and folly, we thought the world could be had for the taking and we had only to reach out and make it ours.

And at last, the tears I could not shed earlier come, for it is not death, dear reader, that makes us weep, but the fears, the emptiness, and the memories it stirs in its callous wake. So it is of these I will speak—and be honest in the telling. But more than this, I will not do, for I, who am so much a part of this story, am not fit to judge the right or the wrong of it. That is only for God to decide, and it is to Him alone that I will answer for my sins, which are many.

Let me go back to my childhood, then, for that is the beginning of my tale—indeed, the beginning of all tales—for that is the time when the mold of each one's life is cast and, for good or ill, we shape our future.

BOOK ONE

Autumn, Aflame and Cruel
1832–1842

Chapter I

The Trunk in the Attic

A difference of taste in jokes is
a great strain on the affections.

—*Daniel Deronda*
George Eliot

Pembroke Grange, England, 1832

Long afterward, whenever I reflected upon the matter, I always thought a great deal of trouble and grief could have been avoided if only my parents had consulted me about my betrothal, for I would have told them it was not Jarrett Chandler I loved, but his younger brother Nicholas.

Unfortunately, since I had only just been born at the time, no one asked my feelings about my engagement, of course, and by the time I grew old enough to voice them, it was too late: I was already promised to Jarrett.

It might seem strange to you that in my day and age, such an unstylish arrangement was made for me, when it was usual then for a genteel girl just out of the schoolroom to make her debut in London during the Season and there, at balls and suppers held at elegant residences and fashionable establishments, to make the acquaintance of any number of eligible bachelors, in the hope of securing a husband, and thus her future.

But though my mother was the granddaughter of an earl, Lord Sheffield had been both a drunkard and a wastrel, whose estates had been grossly encumbered besides; and he had, long before his death, indifferently cast off Mama and her relations.

Her mother, my grandmother Tiberia Chandler Sheffield, was recently widowed at the time; my grandfather the Honorable Worthing Sheffield, the earl's son, had been killed in a carriage accident—the result of a foolish wager, I often suspected, though no one ever said so, no doubt wishing to spare Granny Sheffield's feelings. Even now, her face would soften with love and her eyes mist with tears when she spoke of him. Still, I personally thought my grandfather's death was no great loss, for though I never knew him, it was obvious to me that he was as lacking in character as the rest of his kin. He left poor Granny Sheffield and their two children (my mother, Sarah, and her older brother, my uncle Esmond) virtually penniless, so my grandmother, grief-stricken and having little notion of how to get on in the world, had had no choice but to pack up and return home from London to Highclyffe Hall, the Cornish baronetcy of her eldest brother, Sir Nigel Chandler.

My granduncle Nigel was a hard, cold man, and he was not happy to have the burden of Granny Sheffield and her children thrust upon him. Still, he had known his duty, and he had unshirkingly, if grudgingly, permitted them to take up residence at a nearby farm that was part of his estate. That was how my family came to live at Pembroke Grange.

Of course, all this happened long before I was born and does not in the least explain the peculiar circumstances of my betrothal, but I will come to that presently, as you shall see.

Some years later, Granduncle Nigel, a widower, remarried. His bride, Gwyneth Wellesley Prescott, was herself the widow of a sea captain, Broderick Prescott, to whom she had borne two children, Wellesley and Julianne. This brought the number of Granduncle Nigel's young dependents to a total of six, for he already possessed a daughter, Maggie, from his first marriage, and in time, he became the guardian, too, of his nephew Draco Chandler, the illegitimate son of his and Granny Sheffield's dead brother Quentin.

The children grew up together, for they were all close in age and in one way or another related; and eventually, their lives were further intertwined when Maggie eloped with Draco, Uncle Esmond wed Julianne, and Mama married Wellesley.

In the eyes of the world at least, Mama might have done better for herself, but her heart was set on Papa; and since he chose to follow Grandfather Prescott's seafaring ways, that was why I, who was the great-grand-daughter of both an earl and a baronet, was only the daughter of a mere sea captain and could not therefore be considered gentry. But I loved my father dearly and did not mind in the least his being in trade, except that, in the end, it was the cause of my tangled engagement.

Papa had made a fortune from the sea, and although my blue blood was so diluted as to be trifling, my dowry, which was substantial, more than made up the lack. Thus a Season in London, and even an aristocratic suitor, was not beyond me, for many a gentleman who had naught but an empty purse to show for his title might be quite interested in making a match. But neither Papa's business partner, Draco Chandler, Jarrett and Nicholas's father, nor Papa had any use for the gentry, and because they saw no reason to exchange their riches for rank, they determined that Jarrett and I should wed.

I admit it did indeed seem quite the thing to unite the Prescotts and the Chandlers by marriage, as well as by blood, and since Jarrett was the eldest of the Chandler sons and I was the only Prescott daughter, we were, I suppose, the obvious match. But still, I couldn't see why my older brother, Guy, couldn't just as easily have taken my place and married one of the Chandler daughters, for there were three of them; and any one, I felt sure, would have made him a suitable wife.

It just wasn't fair, I decided crossly when I learned of the matter, that I should be the sacrificial lamb upon the wedding altar (although I daresay no one except I thought of it in quite that light)—especially when it was not Jarrett, but Nicholas I loved.

Still, I said nothing of this to my parents, for even as a child, I sensed my revelation would prove upsetting to them. Naturally, Papa believed he had had my best interests at heart when he had consented to my betrothal, and his feelings would have been hurt had I openly disapproved of his choice for me; and Mama, particularly, could not abide conflict. Whenever there was a disagreement in our house, her gentle mouth would settle into an almost grim line that spoke of her distress far more eloquently than words.

Such episodes did not occur often, however, for in general, our house was a happy one. Papa was a jovial man who showered us all with careless affection and numerous presents from his long voyages to faraway places; and Mama was the sweetest of creatures, ruling us all, including Papa, with a firm but kind and loving hand. Guy took after Papa in both looks and disposition, being blond-haired, blue-eyed, and something of a rogue; while my younger brother, Francis, had Mama's soft brown hair, hazel eyes, and quiet, reflective personality. I was the odd man out, I always thought, for I had dark brown hair streaked with gold, eyes I fancied were the color of topazes, and a passionate nature that Granny Sheffield declared could have come only from the Chandler side of our family.

"You are an atavism, Laura," she often said to me. "You resemble my mother, your great-grandmother Margaret Darnley Chandler, in appearance. But I'm sadly afraid"—she would *tsk* and shake her head—"your character is that of my father, your great-grandfather Sir Simon Chandler, who—though I *did* love him, truly, I did!—was a most fierce man and had quite a wicked temper. Indeed, I fear there is a wild streak in all the

Chandlers, for although, thankfully, I was spared the burden of such a volatile temperament, my brothers Nigel and Quentin were Sir Simon made over—especially Nigel. No one ever defied *him*, you know—except Maggie and Draco, who dared to elope to Gretna Green, for Nigel hated Draco and would never have permitted him to marry Maggie. Such a dreadful scandal, there was! Nigel tried to hush it all up, of course, but even so, there was always talk afterward. . . . You really must learn to restrain your emotions, Laura dear, lest one day they prove your undoing.''

I would always bite my tongue when Granny Sheffield admonished me, for her stories fascinated me—I never tired of hearing them—and if I defended myself against her, she would frown at me and cease telling her tales.

For some reason, her likening me to Great-grand-mother Chandler intrigued me; and sometimes, astride my Welsh pony, Calico Jack, I would ride over to High-clyffe Hall to study my great-grandmother's portrait, which hung in the long gallery at the manor. She did indeed have the same hair and eyes as I, though I concluded dejectedly that she was much more beautiful. My dark brown eyebrows were straight and had a tendency to swoop down like wings on the end; my nose was not as finely chiseled as hers; my mouth was far more generous; my chin was stubbornly set, and my shape was sturdy rather than graceful.

Perhaps I shall grow prettier in time, I would muse as I gazed at her picture, *like the ugly duckling that turned into a swan*, and I would wonder if Great-grandmother Chandler had been as plain as I when she was a child.

Since it was I who resembled her, I felt strongly that the painting should belong to me, and I hated to think of it hanging at the Hall. Sometimes I actually considered stealing it so I could look at it whenever I wished; but common sense prevailed, and I contented myself with occasional glimpses of it at the Hall, for I did not go there as often as I might have.

Years ago, after Granduncle Nigel had been murdered by a vicious smuggler, Uncle Esmond had inherited the baronetcy. He was a solemn, reserved man, with a faint air of sadness about him. I often overheard him referred to by the servants as "henpecked," and I suppose it was true; for both my aunt Julianne and her mother, my grandmother Gwyneth Wellesley Prescott Chandler (now the Dowager Lady Chandler, who had stayed on at the Hall after Granduncle Nigel's death), were dissatisfied with their lot in life and blamed Uncle Esmond for the highly annoying state of their circumstances. Being inclined toward the studious rather than the industrious, he was not cut out to manage a large estate, and the Hall, which had once been very grand, had suffered a gradual decline under his ownership.

I pitied Uncle Esmond and heartily disliked Aunt Julianne and their two children, my cousins Elizabeth and Thorne, who thought they were better than the rest of us because they were gentry and the Prescotts and Chandlers no longer were. Lizzie and Thorne looked down on the Chandlers especially, because they had Gypsy blood in them, that of Uncle Draco's Romany mother.

I despised Thorne even more than I did Lizzie, for he was the sort of sly, horrid boy who delighted in putting a toad in one's bed or a spider down the back of one's dress as a joke. Although I was only eight years old at the time, there is one such incident in particular that I recall with crystal clarity, for it was then that I fell in love with Nicholas and ever after hated Thorne vehemently.

It was May Day, and all the Prescotts, the Chandlers, and the Sheffields were gathered at Pembroke Grange for the traditional celebration.

We Cornish are a clannish lot, descended, for the most part, from the Celts, and despite the advances of civilization, we still cling stubbornly to a great many of our ancestors' superstitions and pagan rites. So, although, of course, on Beltane, as May Day was once known, we no longer made sacrifices to the Goddess Ceridwen or drove our cattle through the ritual flames to receive the Earth Mother's blessing, we still danced about the Elizabethan maypole and, with the coming of dusk, lighted the ceremonial bonfires as the Druids and other ancients had done.

Unfortunately, May Day that year of 1832 was a dreary one, the sky leaden, the distant horizon dark with massing thunderheads that promised rain. Papa optimistically predicted the weather would hold off long enough for our alfresco luncheon; but, alas, despite all our hopes to the contrary, it was not to be. We had no sooner sat down to eat than it began to drizzle, ruining the bright, trailing ribbons of our maypole. The servants hurried to gather up the many dishes from the long, white-cloth-covered tables arrayed upon the lawn; and we were forced to move our party indoors.

Our house was set in northern Cornwall, upon the vast, sweeping moors that stretched to the sea, cutting a stark, harsh line against the horizon, for the heaths here were barren of trees, although alders, birches, oaks, and ashes could be found in the deep, sheltered combes. Only the tors, great, misshapen hills of granite, rose to serrate the sky above the commons.

Pembroke Grange dated from the late seventeenth century, which meant it was newer than Highclyffe Hall, which was some few miles to the southwest of us and had been built during the reign of Queen Elizabeth. Uncle Draco's manor, Stormswept Heights, which lay beyond the baronetcy, at the edge of the cliffs overlooking the ocean, had stood since the thirteenth century. Our house was neither as daunting as the stern, austere Hall nor as intriguing as the mysterious, towered Heights. It was also smaller and of simpler design than its two rivals. But unlike them, it radiated warmth and cheerfulness, and this give it a charm the others lacked.

It was constructed of Bath stone, pale yellow rock that, over the ages, had weathered to a beautiful cream shade that reminded me of fresh buttermilk. When the sun shone upon the rectangular blocks, they reflected its rays with a rich, mellow glow that faded gently at dusk. The Grange was quadrangular in shape, the bare, angular lines of the front softened by a wide porch with pillars that supported a balcony with an ornate stone balustrade above. Long, narrow casement windows with muntined panes of lead glass were set at regular intervals along both the first and second stories. The mansard roof was of black slate, its length broken by a plain pediment rising above the balcony. On either side of the pediment were three dormer windows, so the top floor provided a pleasing contrast to the bottom two. Four tall chimneys rose from the roof's peak.

Rolling green lawns dotted with the sparsely branched, narrow-crowned elms native to Cornwall, as well as other trees that had been planted through the years, sloped away from the front and sides of the house. Flower beds, now blooming with spring blossoms, curved prettily about the walls. To the back were the more extensive gardens, a riotous profusion of color and foliage. It was here that Mama had her herb garden, to which she gave special care, for she loved all plant life and had an uncanny knack of making it grow.

Inside, our house was a virtual rabbit warren, for although the rooms themselves were both spacious and neatly laid out, there was throughout the whole a great number of odd alcoves, nooks, and closets—the caprice of some architect, I had no doubt—which gave the Grange a wondrous, whimsical character and made it a delightful place in which to play.

Though our maypole was lost to us, we children were too adventurous and inventive a lot to have our spirits dampened for long; and after dining, we enthusiastically embarked upon the time-honored game of hide-and-seek.

It was on the third rousing round that I hit upon the idea of secreting myself in one of the old trunks in the attic. Nicholas was the current seeker, and since he and my brother Guy were the best of friends and he was often at our house, he knew its many hiding places well. Therefore, I would have to be especially clever if I were to elude him.

While Nicky closed his eyes and started the count to one hundred, the rest of us children rushed off, an occasional whisper or giggle punctuating our stealthy scattering in all directions. Fast as I could, I scampered upstairs to the attic and breathlessly slipped into one of the storerooms. My mouth was dry with nervous anticipation at the prospect of discovery; my heart pounded furiously with excitement in my breast.

The attic was dark and shadowed—only the pale grey light filtering through the grimy dormer windows illuminated the storeroom—and the air was close and humid from the spring rain. For a moment, I stood uncertainly, glancing about through the swirling cloud of dust I had stirred up with my intrusion at the hodgepodge that surrounded me. I seldom came up here, for the attic always scared me just a little. The part that was not the servants' quarters was filled with old furniture, knickknacks, clocks, china, musical instruments, books, toys, clothes, and other discarded paraphernalia for which the family no longer had any use; and although there was nothing the least bit unfamiliar about any of it, still, it all seemed somehow menacing to me, as though since its banishment to the attic, it had taken on a life of its own. This eerie sensation was especially strong now, in the gloomy half-light, with the rain pitter-pattering upon the roof and trickling down the glass panes of the windows, and briefly, I was tempted to scurry back to the safety of the house below. In the end, however, my desire to outwit

Nicky proved stronger than my fright, and screwing up my courage, I forced myself to advance into the storeroom.

To my dismay, the first thing I observed were three cracked porcelain dolls staring hard at me from a set of shelves upon which they were wedged. Their wide, round eyes appeared to have a faint, maniacal gleam; their pearly white teeth looked small and sharp between their parted, painted lips. In an absurdly morbid moment, I imagined the dolls suddenly coming to life and flinging themselves upon me, intent on doing me some injury, and shivering, I turned away, gasping as I bumped into a dressmaker's mannequin topped by a bedraggled, veiled hat. My heart leaped to my throat before, realizing I had been deceived by its womanlike form into thinking it was someone lurking in the attic, I steadied the now tottering mannequin, then squeezed between it, a scarred desk, and a battered rocking horse to make my way quickly, before my pluck should fail me, toward a large trunk shoved into the elongated niche of one of the dormer windows.

To my relief, the storeroom was lighter and less stuffy here. I could feel the coolness of the spring rain emanating from the glass panes of the window as I squatted carefully upon the floor so I wouldn't dirty my dress or stockings as I investigated the chest. It was surely big enough for me to hide in, I decided, wondering what it might contain. I turned the key in the rusty lock, opened the hasp, and lifted the heavy lid on its creaking hinges, wincing at the noise, then grimacing with disgust at the dust I disturbed and at the musty smell of disuse and faded lavender sachets that assaulted my nostrils from within. I gasped softly as I caught sight of the carefully folded costumes inside, delight momentarily sweeping away my fear of the attic. How beautiful they were! Except in paintings of my ancestors, I had never before seen the like, and the game of hide-and-seek was forgotten as I touched the old garments gingerly, enchanted by them.

What fun it would be to dress up in them, I thought, and wondered to whom they had once belonged.

There were gowns of shimmering silk and satin, jackets of soft velvet trimmed with ornate gold lace, pelisses adorned with swansdown and fur, hats like scrumptious confections, delicate hand-painted fans, rich leather gloves, shoes decorated with bows or buckles and heels studded with jewels, and more. I could have whiled away the afternoon, trying on all the finery. But there was no time for me to examine it more closely, for even now, the sound of approaching footsteps reminded me of my purpose in being in the storeroom. Hastily, I snatched up a bunch of the clothes, along with various other odds and ends, and tossed them out onto the floor. Then I climbed into the trunk and pulled the lid down over my crouched form, leaving a crack through which I could see and breathe.

As the door opened and a silhouette drew near, my breath caught in my throat; the thudding of my heart seemed to shatter the silence as I waited expectantly, thinking it was Nicky and hoping to escape detection. Then softly I exhaled a sigh of relief, for as a shaft of dim light illuminated the intruder's face, I saw that it was only Thorne, who, like me, was searching for a place of concealment.

While I watched, he inspected a few likely spots; but evidently, they didn't suit him, for scowling, he continued to move about the storeroom, poking into this and that.

I wished he would go away, for I felt certain it was only a matter of time before he noticed the trunk and unearthed me, and I thought that even if it cost him the game, he was sure, simply for spite, to reveal my location to Nicky.

Even so, I have to confess I took a rather mean satisfaction in spying on Thorne, for believing himself unobserved, the sweet, angelic expression he normally wore upon his face to mask his thoughts and emotions had slipped to expose the wicked, deceitful nature that, deep down inside, I had always suspected him of having. Still, the transformation was so startling that even I was shocked.

Despite my loathing him, in all honesty, I am forced to admit Thorne was truly the most beautiful boy I had ever seen. He was of medium height and slender but strong build; his head was capped by a riotous crown of golden curls; his blue eyes were like sapphires in his thin, pale face; his every gesture was as delicate and graceful as a swan's. Everyone, even I, agreed he looked exactly like a young Greek god stepped from a Renaissance painting.

Thus it was awful to see his face so repellently distorted, his eyes wily and narrow, his tenderly curved lips twisted into an ugly sneer as he muttered angrily to himself at his inability to pinpoint the perfect hiding place and kicked at the clutter that barred his path. I was so disturbed by the sight of him that I knew I should never forget how he appeared in that moment, and some instinct cautioned me to stay still and silent as a frightened mouse, in the hope that he would not find me.

But at last, to my dismay, his eyes fell upon the chest, and as he crept toward it furtively, I knew with certainty that he had become aware of my presence. Like a cat pouncing, he jerked open the lid I held down over me, his movement so swift and sudden that he nearly wrenched my arm out of its socket in the process.

"Well, well, well. What have we here?" he asked tauntingly. "If it isn't my little cousin Laura."

"Go away, Thorne!" I demanded, rising and glaring at him as I rubbed my aching shoulder and armpit. "I was here first, and if you linger about, Nicky is sure to catch us both!"

"That just goes to show how much you know about it, you stupid twit," he scoffed. "My being here shan't make any difference one way or another, for any fool could tell you're hidden in there. Why else should all those old things be scattered upon the floor in such a haphazard manner? Really, Laura! You must have been standing in the wrong line when God passed out brains, for you've no more sense than a goose!"

"That's not true!" I rejoined tartly, indignant. "After all, *you* came up to the attic, looking for a place to hide, didn't you?"

"Yes, but you will notice that *I* was careful to cover my tracks with all this junk up here, while *you* not only threw that bundle of stuff out of the trunk, but left a trail of footprints leading right up to it in the dust. Why, you might as well have given Nicky a map to your where-abouts, you dunce!''

To my consternation, I saw that this was indeed the truth, and I was so incensed at Thorne's pointing out my foolishness to me that I nearly burst into tears. Biting my lower lip to still its trembling, I gazed about the attic unhappily, my pleasure in the game quite spoiled as I wondered how I would ever find another place of con-cealment in time; for even now, from below, there came the muffled sounds of Nicky's shouts and laughter and my cousin Lizzie's squeals of rage as he ascertained where she was hidden. Thorne grasped my predicament at once, and to my surprise, his face softened as he took pity on me.

"Look, Laura," he said more kindly, "I don't want to be found any more than you do, so we've got to act quickly. Tell you what: You scrunch back down inside there, and I'll pile those telltale costumes in on top of you and brush away your footprints. That way, even if Nicky *does* think to snoop in the trunk, he won't see you. Then I'll crawl into the space under that desk and pull a blanket or something down over the opening."

At first, my spirits were raised by Thorne's suggestion, for I knew it had merit. Then, remembering his cunning expression earlier, intuition warned me not to trust him.

"Fat chance, Thorne," I retorted, shaking my head. "I'm not such a fool as that! It's a trick—I know it! Why should you want to help me?"

"Oh, for heaven's sake! You are the most exasperating—'' He broke off abruptly, choking back whatever hateful words he'd meant to say. Then, smiling that saintly smile of his, he continued his attempt to persuade me. "I just told you, Laura: I don't want to be caught either. After all, what's the point in playing the game if not to win? And if Nicky finds you, you're just vindictive enough to blab that I'm up here as well, since obviously it's too late now for either of us to search for another hiding place—and you like him better than you do me anyway. So, of course, it's to my advantage to help you. Anyone could see that. You would, too, if you weren't so friendly with Nicky and so suspicious of me—although I don't know why you should be. After all, we're *first* cousins, and Nicky is only our *second* cousin.''

"Well, all right, then, since you put it that way,'' I said finally, for despite my misgivings, Thorne's words did indeed make sense to me, and besides, there wasn't any time left to go on arguing with him. With each passing moment, the third round of our game was drawing closer to an end, for now I could hear that Nicky had ferreted out two of his younger siblings, the twins, Alexander and Angelique.

"Get down in the trunk, then,'' Thorne urged. "Go on—and hurry! I still have to hide myself, too, you know.''

At last, reluctantly (for although I had agreed to his scheme, I still could not entirely dismiss my qualms about it), I again curled myself up inside the chest, wrinkling my nose with distaste and trying hard not to sneeze as rapidly Thorne crammed the garments in on top of me, sending dust motes flying. Then, with a loud thump, he closed the lid and walked away, his retreating footsteps echoing oddly in the silence. I thought I heard a faint, gleeful laugh, too, but I supposed that it came from downstairs and that Nicky had just discovered either Damaris or Bryony, his youngest sisters.

The trunk was dark and oppressive without the lid cracked. Further, now, with all the clothes heaped upon me, there was not nearly as much room inside as there had been, and I was having difficulty breathing beneath the layers of costumes. Either a feather or a strip of fur—I could not tell which—was tickling my nostrils as well, so I was once more tempted to sneeze; and awkwardly, I squirmed about, trying to wriggle into a more comfortable position and half hoping that, despite Thorne's precautions, Nicky would soon find me. I was beginning to think secreting myself in the trunk had not been such a good idea after all, and now, as the minutes ticked by, my doubts about trusting Thorne grew, too. Of course, he was hiding beneath the desk, mute and motionless as a statue, in case Nicky and the others who had already been caught should come into the attic, but surely, I thought, I should at least be able to hear him breathing.

"Thorne," I called softly to reassure myself. "Thorne, are you there?" Apparently, he couldn't hear me, for despite my repeated whispers, there was no reply, and finally, I decided to risk a quick peek at the storeroom. I pushed against the lid of the chest, but it didn't budge, and fighting down my rising panic, I cried out, "Thorne! Stop this nonsense, and answer me! Thorne! I can't breathe! Do you hear me? I can't breathe! And I can't get the lid open! You've got to come help me!''

But still, there was no response, and at last, to my utter chagrin, I realized my cousin had maliciously locked me inside the trunk and left me.

Chapter II

A Knight in Shining Armor

See, the conquering hero comes!
Sound the trumpets, beat the drums!

—*Joshua*
Thomas Morell

A cavalcade of emotions swept through me at Thorne's treachery.

At first, I was not, in truth, scared so much as infuriated, for in the beginning, it simply did not occur to me that, no matter how vile he was, my cousin would not soon return to release me. So, now, since I supposed he was, despite his silence, still skulking nearby, chortling soundlessly at my distress, my anxiety faded, and I ceased my futile outcries and attempts to escape, recognizing that they would no doubt only cause him to prolong my torment.

The sooner he sees he isn't going to get a rise out of

me, the sooner he'll be back, I thought grimly, *to set me free—and have a big laugh at my expense! Oh, just wait until I get my hands on that miserable cur! I'll wring his scrawny neck!*

I planned my revenge as, chewing on my lower lip, I fumed that I, who should have known better than to trust him, should prove the butt of Thorne's jest. My wrath mounted as I schemed how I would even the score between us once I was no longer imprisoned.

I knew from past experience that it would prove useless to tattle on my cousin. He would only lie to protect himself, shrewdly, albeit unfairly, casting all the blame for what had happened upon me; and although Uncle Esmond, nevertheless suspecting the truth, would attempt to discipline him, Aunt Julianne would intervene, just as she always did, to rescue him before justice was meted out. After a litany of sharp, scathing remarks about Uncle Esmond's shortcomings, Aunt Julianne would indignantly insist he should know her "darling" son couldn't possibly have committed the offense of which he was accused. Then, billowing with outrage, she would sail from the room, sniffing and pointedly ignoring Uncle Esmond as though he were a dirty ragman and shielding Thorne conspicuously, as though to protect him from some contaminating disease, as she whisked him away, effectively extricating him from any consequences he might otherwise have suffered. After that, as always, Uncle Esmond, wishing to avoid further unpleasantness, would sheepishly allow the matter to drop.

"He needs a whip taken to his breeches, Thorne does," Granny Sheffield would then remark reprovingly under her breath, as though addressing nobody in particular, "else he'll grow up to be a black sheep like my brother Quentin and no doubt end up on a gibbet."

At that, poor Uncle Esmond would flush scarlet as a pimpernel and mumble some defensive excuse that deceived no one about why my cousin was never punished.

Unfortunately, Papa and Mama were not so remiss in their duty toward their own children; my revenge against Thorne must be carefully plotted, lest I be soundly chastened for it. Slowly, as I hunched uncomfortably in the trunk, my head and knees jammed against its hard sides, an uncharitable plan began to take shape in my mind.

Once, when she was a young girl, Aunt Julianne had, with a hatpin, jabbed in the rump a pony not going fast enough to suit her. As a result, the pony had bolted into the wooded park surrounding Highclyffe Hall, and a low-hanging branch had knocked Aunt Julianne from the saddle, sending her flying and causing her to sprain her ankle severely upon landing.

Now I could not help but think of Thorne's handsome but high-strung New Forest and how violently it would surely react if I were to employ one of my hatpins upon it in a like manner. My cousin did not ride well, being too sharp and close with the reins, too rash and cruel with both whip and spurs, and I felt certain he would be unable to control his difficult, skittish pony, provoked by my quickly concealed but well-aimed hatpin, and so would be ignominiously unseated.

How ridiculous he will look, sprawled upon the ground, angry and humiliated beyond measure, and how I shall laugh at him then! I contemplated with relish the notion of Thorne's comeuppance, for I had no doubt he was taking just as mean a delight in the nasty prank he had played upon me.

This last thought sobered me, however, for it made me realize several interminably long minutes had passed, and still, my cousin had not returned to liberate me.

Where can he be? I wondered, exasperated. "Thorne," I shouted imperiously, peremptorily banging one fist against the lid of the trunk. "Thorne, open up! You've had your fun, but enough is enough, so let me out now before I scream the attic down about your ears!"

Still, there was no answer, and abruptly, with a sick, sinking feeling at the pit of my stomach, I became certain that the storeroom was empty, that my cousin had gone and forgotten all about me or, worse, had never had any intention of coming back to begin with. Sudden fear tingled up my spine at the realization, for I knew without a doubt that it meant he would not tell anyone where I was either, because then he must reveal the wicked turn he had done me.

I was as stunned as though I had fallen hard and had the wind knocked out of me. I did not know what to do. It was inconceivable to me that anybody, even Thorne, could have done such a horrible thing, and initially, I could not believe it.

Surely, I must be mistaken, I thought; but now, deep down inside, I knew better, and inexorably, the cold fist of dread that had seized hold of me began to tighten its grip, so once more my breath came raggedly and my heart throbbed erratically in my breast.

You must think, Laura, I chided myself sternly in a

futile attempt to combat my escalating panic. *You must think what to do.*

Deliberately, I forced myself to take several slow, deep breaths and to huddle quietly in the chest until the racing of my heart had lessened. Then, pushing aside the asphyxiating costumes, awkwardly twisting myself about again, and feeling for the trunk's lock, I at last managed to locate and inspect the keyhole. I could see naught save darkness, however, and my spirits lifted a little, for that meant my cousin had not taken away the key. Now, if I could only find something with which to turn it from the inside, perhaps I would be able to free myself.

I groped around in the chest until finally I scraped my knuckles across the sharp point of some small, stiff object. After a few moments of blind scrutiny, I perceived that it was the tip of a long, slender plume, perhaps that of a pheasant, and eagerly, I tugged the quill from the top of the discarded felt hat it embellished.

Then, cursing the blackness of the trunk's interior and the pile of garments that greatly hampered my movements, I fumbled once more for the keyhole. Carefully, I inserted the end of the feather into the lock and painstakingly started to manipulate the key as best I could under the circumstances. Minutes later, a tiny, narrow beam of dull grey light split the darkness inside the chest as, with a loud clank that rang in my ears like a death knell, the key tumbled out onto the storeroom floor.

I could have wept with vexation and despair, for certainly, I had no means of retrieving the lost key, and now I must face the fact that I was truly a captive without hope of escape.

Although I had no way of knowing just how much time had passed, by now, it seemed as though I had been shut up in the trunk for hours. It had grown hot and muggy inside. Sweat from the stifling atmosphere and my exertions ran down my forehead, beaded my upper lip, and dampened my palms. My clothes were sticking to my body, so I felt clammy all over; and despite my trying to remain calm, still, I could scarcely breathe for the anxiety that gnawed at me.

Outside, the hushed spring shower had burgeoned into a wild storm. I could hear the muffled tattoo of the pouring rain pelting the dormer window and a loose shutter battering against the side of the house. The noise echoed in the elongated niche of the attic, so it sounded as though some ominous entity were beating on the trunk, demanding to be let in. The cloying, fusty fragrance of the lavender sachets tucked among the costumes had grown so overpowering that now I felt dizzy and ill; the blackness of the chest's interior appeared to be wrapping itself around me like a tangible thing, making my skin, moist with perspiration, crawl.

Without warning, I was overcome by a terrible sensation that I was suffocating. Like a wild, trapped animal, I began to hammer my fists frenziedly against the lid of the trunk, shrieking distraughtly for help. But although I screeched until I was hoarse and exhausted, it soon became clear to me that no one could hear my screams; and finally, gasping frantically for air, I slumped down amid the contents of the chest, uncaring that the sharp heel of a shoe now dug painfully into my back.

Tears of fury and fright I could no longer hold at bay

streamed from my eyes. I cursed Thorne with a vengeance, and myself, too, for being such a gullible and willing victim of his duplicity; and anguished, I wondered now if I would die up here in the attic, locked inside the trunk, with no one the wiser as to what had become of me.

On a dismal winter's eve, when the wind moaned eerily across the moors and we children gathered before the fire in a hearth, I had heard my Chandler cousins whisper many a strange ghost story about Uncle Draco's enigmatic house, Stormswept Heights, some of which were chilling accounts of how murder had been done there and two bodies sealed up in a priest's hole, undiscovered for centuries until Uncle Draco and Aunt Maggie had renovated the old, ruined manor.

Now these terrifying tales returned to haunt me, and it came to me how like a crypt the trunk was, dark and airless and firmly secured against the world of the living; and I wondered if it would prove my coffin, if, years from now, someone would come up to the storeroom, unearth my bones, and bury me in an unmarked grave in the potter's field at the cemetery, as Uncle Draco and Aunt Maggie had laid to rest the two skeletons they had found.

Fueled by my fear, my vivid imagination ran wild, so I had worked myself into a state of hysteria by the time that suddenly, to my vast relief, the key grated in the trunk's lock and the lid was yanked open wide to reveal Jarrett and Nicholas, their dark Gypsy faces looking threatening as thunderclouds. Thorne, hanging by the scruff of his neck, his collar drawn tight around his throat, his feet dangling just above the floor, was squealing with outrage and struggling like a fish on a hook to wrench himself from Jarrett's strong grasp.

"All 'ee, all 'ee outs in free, Laura," Nicky said gently, a smile momentarily softening the resolute set of his lips as he gazed at my scared, tearstained face. Then, more soberly, he asked, "Oh, Laura, are you all right?"

"Nicky! Oh, Nicky!" I sobbed, casting myself into his outstretched arms. "I've been so afraid. . . . I—I couldn't breathe! I thought I was going to—to *die* in there!"

"There, there, poppet. It's all right. It's all right now." He hugged me close and patted my back soothingly as his quiet reassurances, tinged with the Gypsy lilt of his father, washed over me. "So, come on. Dry those tears, else you know your eyes will grow all red and puffy, and then everyone will want to know what happened to upset you so. There'll be the devil to pay then, that's for sure. That's my good girl." He grinned as, trying bravely to suppress my sniveling, I gave a small, woebegone hiccup. "Here." He grabbed a rather dirty lace handkerchief, stiff and yellowed with age, from the trunk and pressed it into my hand. "Blow your nose. That's right. There. Feeling better already, aren't you, poppet?"

Then, certain I was indeed beginning to regain my composure, Nicky doubled up his fists and, seething, rounded on Thorne.

"I'll tell you what, you slimy little worm," Nicky spat, punctuating his words by jabbing the incoherently protesting Thorne in the chest several times, "we're all sick and tired of your hateful mischief-making, and we're not going to take it anymore, see? Why, Laura might have smothered in there, you filthy beast! To say nothing of the fright you must have given her! What were you planning to do if I hadn't grown suspicious about her disappearance and prized the truth out of you, Thorne? Just leave her there? By God, you're a bloody monster, that's what! Well, this is one time you're not going to get off scot-free, and that's a fact. Aunt Julianne isn't here now to save your hide, as she usually does, and she won't be able to hear you yelling for help up here in the attic either. So you're at my mercy, just as poor Laura was at yours, and for once, you're going to get the beating you so richly deserve, you spoiled-rotten brat!''

"Hold on, Nicky." Jarrett spoke as though to an unruly puppy, staying his brother with an upraised hand. "Think a minute. Is it really worth all the trouble we'll both be in later if you teach this contemptible fool a lesson? Father's sure to be wroth—you know how he despises scenes—and Thorne is bound to run straight to Aunt Julianne afterward, whining his lies and excuses. I say we leave well enough alone for now. Laura isn't hurt, and there will be a better time and place to deal with this mama's boy." His lip curling with disgust, he gave Thorne a brief, rough shake.

Then his eyes fixed upon Nicky's intently, and for a moment, between the brothers, there was a current of tension I did not understand; for it was only with age that I learned to decipher the looks that serve as substitutes for words unsaid, words that if spoken can, like Pandora's box, loose dark, ugly things, with never a hope of shutting them up again. Yet even in my ignorance, something in Jarrett's demeanor reminded me unpleasantly of his autocratic father, and I shuddered at the similarity.

Now, despite a man's having several sons, as Uncle Draco did, it is the centuries-old law in England that only one of them, the eldest, may inherit and so become, in his time, the head of his family and thus the man to whom each of the family must answer, though the man himself answers to no one save God and the king. Jarrett was such a one as this. I think Nicky must have recalled it, too, for a livid flush suddenly mottled his skin, and a curse hissed like a biting wind from his lips into the silence.

"I'll not be dictated to, Jarrett," he asserted bluntly. "Not by anyone—least of all you! And you needn't shoulder any blame for me either; *I'm* certainly not asking you to. Go on back downstairs if you're afraid," he gibed, "and turn tattler like Thorne! See if I care! It won't do you any good anyhow. Father can't stand squealers, so you won't score any points with him that way, if that's what you're thinking—always trying to make yourself look better than me in his eyes. Well, go on, if you've a mind to. Otherwise, stand aside—and keep the hell out of my way!"

At that, Jarrett's mouth tightened grimly. I do not know what he would have said, for just then, without warning, Nicky tore into Thorne like a rabid dog, jerking him from Jarrett's grip so abruptly and forcefully that Jarrett reeled back and toppled over the rickety rocking horse from the impetus. Nicky and Thorne themselves were sent sprawling in a tangle of flailing limbs upon the storeroom floor.

Though both boys were eleven, Nicky was much larger and heavier than Thorne, who was small for his age and who, having always hidden behind his mother's skirts, knew practically nothing about fighting. I was therefore not surprised to see him floundering about as helplessly as a beetle suddenly pitched on its back, and his clearly horrified expression and squeaks of alarm at his inability to flee from the ensuing battle were enough to send my despondent spirits soaring.

My tears gone at last, I shouted, "Punch him in the nose, Nicky!" as gleefully and indecorously as I had once seen a coarse, frowzy barmaid do during a fracas that had broken out in the village. "Smash his weaselly face in!"

"What a common, bloodthirsty wench you are, Laura," Jarrett observed coolly at my unladylike exhortations as he righted himself and fastidiously brushed off the dust that now clung to his garments. "I shall have to remember that." Then, his voice hard, he called, "That's enough, Nicky. I'm warning you: You know how Father feels about brawling, and I don't intend to get a thrashing just because *you* couldn't control your temper."

"Butt out, Jarrett, or I'll make you sorry you didn't!" his brother shot back threateningly through clenched teeth as he landed a solid blow to Thorne's jaw. Then, between grunts of pain and exertion, he growled, "This . . . snotty whelp is finally getting what's . . . long overdue him, and you're not going . . . to stop me from giving it to him!''

At that, Jarrett's black eyes darkened with some unreadable emotion, and his jaw set in a stern line, so that, for a moment in the shadowed half-light, he appeared far older than his thirteen years and so like his father that once more I shivered as though a goose had just walked over my grave.

He will be a dangerous man to cross someday, I thought with a perception both startling and incongruous for an eight-year-old.

But, then, everyone I knew, except Aunt Maggie and Papa, was afraid of Uncle Draco, so perhaps it was not so strange, after all, that I should sense Jarrett would grow up to resemble his father not only in looks, but in disposition as well.

While Jarrett and I watched, the conflict in the attic raged on as ruthlessly as the storm that pummeled the roof and flayed the dormer windows. Thorne, now sporting a black eye and cut lip, was definitely getting the worst of it. Still, I must admit he had not proved slow to learn and was defending himself however he could, so Nicky, who was unused to such girlish and therefore (at least according to boys) underhanded tactics as scratching, biting, and pulling hair, was not unscathed. His face bore the deep red gouges of Thorne's fingernails, and his left arm exhibited a perfect imprint of Thorne's even white teeth.

Although not very tidy to begin with, the storeroom was now chaos. Furniture and gimcracks everywhere had been overturned and smashed; a fragile wooden chair with which Nicky had bashed Thorne over the shoulders had splintered into several long, jagged pieces that lay scattered about menacingly, providing, along with the razor-sharp fragments and sprung metal workings of a demolished china clock, a real hazard as the boys staggered, tumbled, and grappled their way across the floor, trouncing each other with a fury so strong that it seemed even to permeate the churned-up clouds of dust eddying through the air.

Now Thorne managed to wiggle free and scramble to his feet, but before he could take two steps, Nicky grabbed him by the shirt, ripping it in half as he spun Thorne about. Then, head bent like an attacking goat, Nicky rammed Thorne in the stomach, sending them both flying with such impact into a cheval mirror that the crazed glass cracked before the heavy oval frame teetered on its stout legs, then crashed to the floor so loudly that I was certain all in the house must have heard it.

Evidently, Jarrett thought so, too, for he snapped, ''For God's sake, Nicky! You'll have Father and everyone else up here in a minute!''

But Nicky paid his brother no heed, and the heated scuffle continued. Grabbing a warped bamboo birdcage, Thorne whacked Nicky over the head with it so hard that the stuffed nightingale inside was jostled from its perch and flung through the tiny door that swung open wildly before the cage collapsed in a jumbled heap around Nicky's neck. Tearing away the offending bamboo collar, he snatched from its shelf one of the porcelain dolls that had so plagued me earlier and brutally hit Thorne in the face with it, accidentally decapitating the doll in the process. The disembodied head bounced and rolled across stacks of rubbish before, miraculously undamaged, it came to rest upon a mice-eaten cushion, its sightless eyes staring up at me as though horrified at the grisly violation that had been done it.

Yammering like a squashed cat, Thorne stumbled back, then fell to the floor, twitching and writhing in agony, his hands glued to his injured face, a shockingly crimson tide of blood gushing between his ashen fingers from his nose and assorted gashes in his cheeks.

"Jesus Christ!" Jarrett exclaimed, then, speedily taking advantage of the momentary lull in the fray, seized hold of Nicky, who, cursing and panting, wrestled him determinedly until finally Jarrett caught him around the chest in a bone-crushing clench and pinned his arms to his sides. "Back off, you fool! Back off!" Jarrett ordered fiercely, giving Nicky a savage shake. "We'll all be lucky if you haven't killed that blubbering idiot."

Of course, it was at that moment that wretched fate must cause the storeroom door to open and Uncle Draco to appear, followed by Aunt Maggie, Papa and Mama, and Uncle Esmond. At the sight of my forbidding Gypsy uncle, along with so many other authority figures whose word I had been reared to respect as law, I inhaled sharply, and my heart plummeted to my toes, for I knew with certainty that the proverbial piper had arrived to extract payment for our dreadfully unruly behavior. Jarrett and Nicholas were like two soldiers caught in flagrant disobedience of military regulations, snapping suddenly and uncomfortably to attention; and even Thorne, except for a few muted whimpers, ceased his caterwauling as, in the abrupt, tense silence, Uncle Draco's glinting black eyes took in the deplorable state of both the attic and us children.

His gaze pierced Jarrett and Nicholas censuringly, roamed over me only cursorily (much to my relief), and at last assessed Thorne expertly, if quite distastefully. He did not go at once to my cousin's aid, although it was plain that Thorne, still bleeding profusely, was in great pain. No doubt, under other circumstances, Papa would have taken charge of the matter, seeing to Thorne first before delving into the events that had brought about his hapless condition; but as far as this particular incident was concerned, it was obvious from Papa's immobile, condemnatory stance that he intended to let Uncle Draco deal with us as he saw fit. Aunt Maggie, who was bold enough to have interceded for Thorne, disliked him intensely and so made no move in his direction either; and though inclined to rush to my cousin's side, even Uncle Esmond and Mama hung back as, in his low, deceptively silky voice, Uncle Draco demanded, "What's going on here?"

Naturally, none of us children dared to reply—or even to look at him, we were all so afraid of him. But, then, as I have said, almost everyone I knew was scared of Uncle Draco.

He was a tall, powerfully built man, who, although he was nearing forty, had not a trace of fat on his large, muscular frame. Over the years, he had easily bested more than one man in a fight, for he was responsible for keeping not only his vast estate, Stormswept Heights, in order, but the dangerous Chandler china-clay mines and their often explosive workers under strict control as well. Nor was there a hint of grey in his shaggy black hair that shone like jet and that he was rumored to trim with a dagger that had belonged to one of his Gypsy ancestors. His face, dark as bronze, looked as though it had been chiseled from granite, and because it had been weathered over the years by the harsh Cornish elements, fine lines splayed from his eyes and deep grooves bracketed his full mouth, giving his strong features a striking but austere appearance. His aquiline nose had been broken during his youth, too, and thus further marred what might otherwise have been a pleasing countenance. Still, some thought him handsome in a rugged, brutish fashion, although there were many others who swore he had a "damned Tyburn face" and direly predicted that, for all his success in life, he would nevertheless wind up on the gallows someday.

Now, as timidly I risked a surreptitious glimpse at him through my eyelashes, I could see that his thick, swooping brows were drawn together in a frown known to make even the most courageous of men quail, and I trembled that I should be a target, albeit a small, insignificant one, of his infamous temper.

"Well?" Uncle Draco spoke again, curtly, coldly, so I hastily lowered my eyes and began to fidget with the end of one of my long braids. "I was under the impression that I had asked a question, and as I am not a man who likes to be kept waiting, I suggest one of you be brave enough to answer."

Jarrett, who was the oldest among us and thus disposed to take the lead, cleared his throat awkwardly. But before he could respond, Aunt Julianne, who was what is politely termed ''pleasingly plump'' and so doubtless had had difficulty climbing the two steep, interminable flights of stairs to the attic, huffed and puffed her way onto the scene.

''My God! Thorne! My baby!'' she wailed upon spying her precious son bleeding and prostrate upon the floor. ''What have they done to you? What have those heathens done?''

She flashed us all an angry, accusing glance and would have dashed at once to my cousin's assistance had not Uncle Draco's next words brought her up short, an occurrence I viewed with considerable surprise, as I had never before known Aunt Julianne to take orders from anyone.

''Stay where you are, Julianne,'' Uncle Draco commanded sharply, ''and get hold of yourself, for I cannot abide histrionics. 'Tis only Thorne's pride, I suspect, which is seriously wounded. Your estimable boy will live. His cuts are not deep enough to leave permanent scars; and though I presume his nose is broken, I've never heard of anybody dying from that, so I doubt that Thorne will be the first, though he shall certainly be sore for several weeks. Besides, if he chooses to indulge in fisticuffs, he must learn to take his lumps as other men do and not expect to be cossetted like a baby afterward.''

''Broken!'' Aunt Julianne shrilled, the word apparently dominating her consciousness to the exclusion of all else. ''You think his nose is broken! Oh, my poor, beautiful boy—his face ruined—and still, you stand there doing nothing! You fiend! How dare you? What do you know about a young boy's delicate sensibilities? *You* certainly never possessed any, Draco, but were always a cruel, heartless devil,'' she raved on in tones that suggested she was auditioning for the role of tragedienne in some drama. ''And your sons are like to follow in your footsteps, it seems.''

''And glad I am of it, too,'' Uncle Draco drawled dryly, ''for I've no stomach for any spineless jackanapes who must use a woman as a buckler to protect himself from the consequences of his ill-considered actions. Now, let us get to the bottom of this contretemps before Thorne bleeds to death. From the amount of blood he is losing, that appears to be a slight but distinctly more realistic possibility than his expiring from a few negligible lacerations and a trifling realignment of his nose.''

Although, indeed, blood still trickled down Thorne's sickly white face, I felt certain nevertheless that Uncle Draco had made this last remark merely to agitate Aunt Julianne; for a sardonic smile curved his lips as she gasped and, pressing her embroidered handkerchief to her brow, began to fumble in her bodice for her vinaigrette, which she was prone to produce whenever things didn't go as she wished.

''Oh! I feel faint,'' she moaned. ''Esmond! Are you going to stand there and let your detestable cousin prevent me from ministering to our son?''

''My dear,'' Uncle Esmond remarked with a rare spark of spirit and wit, ''I have never known anyone to stop you from doing anything you had your mind set on, so

I cannot think why you should have need of my intervention on this occasion.''

"I always knew that when push came to shove, you would desert me," Aunt Julianne sniffed, glowering at him in denouncement, a martyred expression upon her fleshy face.

"Enough!" Uncle Draco growled, startling us all and promptly squelching Aunt Julianne, although her double chin quivered and her ample bosom heaved with pique at this new affront. "I want an explanation for this unseemly affair, and I want it now. Jarrett?"

At last, the sorry tale was told, the upshot being that Jarrett and Nicholas received a severe lecture but, mercifully, were spared a whipping, since Uncle Draco felt they had acted in my defense; and I was soundly rebuked by Papa for being such a fool as to fall prey to Thorne's chicanery.

As usual, Thorne himself avoided parental punishment, but he did indeed, as Uncle Draco had surmised, have a broken nose, which, when healed, quite spoiled his good looks; and thereafter, he held a grudge against Nicky and went out of his way to harass him whenever he could.

In this, Thorne did not often succeed, however; for now, in my eyes, Nicky had taken on all the glow of a knight in shining armor, and I began tagging after him like a faithful watchdog, constantly on the alert against any threat to his well-being. Though he adamantly insisted he didn't need the protection of a mere girl, Nicky was secretly delighted at finding himself the object of my hero worship, and he swaggered with pride when I continued to trail after him stubbornly. Jarrett, on the other hand, was not amused, and shaking his head with disgust, he nicknamed us "the Prince and Briar Rose" and often inquired mockingly as to whether we had tangled with any more "Thornebushes" lately.

Chapter III

The Passing Years

And yet time hath his revolution;
there must be a period and an end
to all temporal things . . .

—*Oxford Peerage Case, 1625*
Sir Ranulphe Crewe

Now that I am old and, with the telling of this story, looking back on the years, I know how swiftly the days of one's youth are ended, never to come again; and I mourn the loss of what the young, in their ignorance, make such haste to waste so carelessly, as though time is infinite and passes too slowly. How ironic it is, I think now, that youth is so eager to grow up—while age yearns only to turn back the hands of the clock. Yet honesty compels me to admit I was in my girlhood, and am now, no different from the rest.

When I was young, I could not wait to pin up my long

golden-brown tresses, let down the hems of my frocks, and dance the night away at some ball. Now I curse the silver that threads my hair, the layers of skirts that hamper my movements, and the cane I must use to walk. How unfair it is, I think, that my mind, sharp as ever, and my heart, yet full of emotion, should be trapped now in this old body with its brittle bones and aching joints.

But that is the way of life, as I have come to learn, and to regret, and so to believe that perhaps it is a kindness that youth is spared, after all, the knowledge of age.

Indeed, how blissfully oblivious was I in my girlhood of that which bore no consequence to me—for I knew little of life beyond northern Cornwall, of the events even then shaping England's future, and thus my own, as the world forged relentlessly ahead, only rarely disturbing the boundaries of my existence.

Wars raged on several fronts, in Portugal, Spain, the United States, Mexico, South Africa, and other distant places that were nothing more to me than names on the maps I studied during my geography lessons. No one I knew had gone for a soldier or was likely to do so.

A cholera epidemic that had decimated Russia spread to Scotland, and then on to New York, infecting and killing thousands of people before, in desperation, a Scottish physician, Thomas Latta, injected a patient with a saline solution, pioneering a new treatment for the dreaded disease. But I, growing and thriving in Cornwall, could not even conceive of an illness so deadly and on such a widespread scale.

In England, Parliament abolished slavery in the colonies, established an anatomy act to halt body-snatching for medical research, and passed a factory act forbidding the employment of children younger than nine years of age. A national consolidation of trade unions was organized, with members pledging to strike for an eight-hour workday, and a league was founded to oppose the unfair, and therefore despised, Corn Laws. But I was not enslaved, forced to steal or toil to put bread in my mouth; and so I was far more interested in the latest fiction published, such as the *Sketches by 'Boz,'* a series of stories penned by a London court reporter, Charles Dickens, the first of which appeared in 1833, in the December issue of a periodical.

Even the death, in 1837, of King William IV and the ascension of his eighteen-year-old niece Victoria to the throne of England held no meaning for me, for though I was astounded by the news that a girl only five years older than I should be named a queen, I did not then know how a coronation in London could possibly have any effect upon me, so I paid scant heed to the incident that, in later years, would betoken a milestone in English history. Nor did I take any particular notice of Victoria herself, though I might have spared myself and others much grief if I had; for she was to become, with age, a childishly stubborn woman possessed of stern, unforgiving morals that would one day reach out to haunt not only me, but those I loved, tearing us apart in a way I never dreamed.

But I get ahead of myself. I must continue now about my girlhood, which, as has no doubt become obvious, passed happily enough for the most part, but unexceptionally, so I was often bored with the routine of my days and, feeling as though I were only marking time, waited expectantly, yearned impatiently, for *life* to begin.

Then, at long last, just when I felt I would burst from all the pent-up emotions burgeoning inside me, there came the morning when, at seventeen, having learned to write a graceful hand, to speak both French and Italian fluently, to sing and to play the pianoforte, to dance the waltz and the quadrille, to paint a watercolor landscape or still life, and to embroider a dainty stitch, I was pronounced "finished" and removed from the aegis of my tearfully departing but proud governess to enter the real world.

Now, in the twilight of my years, when one tends to color one's memories to suit oneself, I should like to think that, by then, I had acquired a modicum of sensibleness and restraint; but in truth, it was not so. Instead, I was as foolish as any other girl my age, my head stuffed full of the romantic notions to be found in many a popular novel, some of which were forbidden me, but which I obtained and read and sighed over in secret just the same.

Reluctantly do I confess these things, knowing I shall be thought by some as making excuses for my behavior in the months that followed. But this is not so, dear reader. I tell you these things only so you will know my state of mind then, and understand, if not approve or forgive—for indeed, that is too much to ask—how I came to act as I did before my innocence and youth were stripped from me. No doubt some will say I received no less than I deserved; and perhaps they will speak the truth, for I have ever thought that it is we who are our own worst enemies, that through our sins—our spite, ignorance, greed, and lust—we bring upon ourselves that which we most fear in life. So I blame no one but myself for all that happened, what shall be told to you by and by, and I make no excuses.

Now I know how it all began—and how it ended— and if I had it all to do again, perhaps there is much I would do differently. But we are not granted that opportunity; good or ill, we cannot change the past. And so hindsight is useless, as I have come to recognize and accept. Still, even now, knowing what came after, I cannot help but remember how thrilled I was when I stood finally upon that momentous brink of womanhood, poised to step irrevocably into its bittersweet realm.

There was to be an informal coming-out party at the Grange to celebrate my emerging from the schoolroom, followed, despite my engagement to Jarrett, by a formal debut ball at Papa's town house in London, Mama stating sweetly but firmly to all that, betrothed or not, every girl was entitled to at least one Season in her life.

I fairly floated through the days, my head awhirl with countless trips to the milliner, the dressmaker, the glover, and the shoemaker, where I was outfitted from top to bottom with ensembles brightly colored and cleverly tailored to make the most of my tall, dark, willowy figure, so unsuited for fashionable pastel frills and furbelows. But in the end, I had no care for what was modish, because my own costumes, daringly dramatic, were so flattering that whenever I gazed at my reflection in a mirror, I scarcely recognized myself.

Can that strange, exotic girl really be me? I wondered over and over, marveling at the change wrought in me.

Though I had not, as once I had hoped, grown into a ravishing beauty, nevertheless, my blossoming womanhood and new wardrobe had brought to the surface some primitive and arresting quality previously hidden deep inside me, so now I saw I was striking in an unusual way and felt a hitherto unknown confidence that I might attract a man's eye and hold it if I so desired. Granny Sheffield, however, was inclined to view me askance and to admonish me even more often than usual about bridling my wild, turbulent self. But I refused to be curbed and so disregarded her counsel.

My penchant for the romantic and the exciting superseded my common sense, and fancifully, I imagined that I resembled a hunting hawk, barely tame, longing to break free of its bonds: that the rich gold streaks in my dark brown hair shimmered like a soaring falcon's feathered wings stretched wide beneath the Cornish sun, that my topaz-colored eyes gleamed like its piercing amber orbs, that my skin glowed like the soft, honeyed down of its breast, and that I moved with its lissome grace, my long skirts swishing and trailing behind me like jesses.

For despite my wishing I were otherwise, I was, in reality, no more unfettered than the captive bird to which I likened myself. I was merely being given a chance to spread my wings before, after my Season in London, I must return home to marry, eventually, Jarrett, the man to whom I had been promised—and so belonged.

But to that prospect, I nonchalantly paid little heed, for in truth, it had never seemed quite real to me; thus it dampened my enthusiastic spirits not at all. With gay abandon, I flung myself into the preparations and training for my maiden flight.

Clemency, my abigail, spent hours brushing, crimping, arranging, and pinning my hair until finally she was satisfied as to which of the several styles currently in vogue most became me. Thereafter, I appeared with my tresses dressed à la this or that, and tossed my head so my curls danced in what I envisioned was a highly enchanting manner, although it sometimes resulted in a disarray that brought a *tsk* of annoyance from Clemency, which I studiously ignored.

Since I have promised to be honest in my recounting of this tale, I must admit I was not fond of my maid. She was four years older and, I suspected, a great deal more worldly than I, though she never rattled off her knowledge as many abigails do, to give themselves airs or to sate their mistresses' curiosity regarding those delicate matters that ladies of good breeding either profess to know nothing about or of which they are truly kept ignorant. Instead, Clemency was closemouthed as a sphinx. It was her sly, slanted green eyes that implied she was privy to secrets about which I could only guess, and I often thought uncomfortably that, behind my back, she gossiped about me and laughed at my naïveté.

Even had she not given me such a disconcerting impression, however, I would have known from her tainted background that she had not led nearly so sheltered a life as I, for Clemency (through no fault of her own, I must confess) was a notorious woman. She was the bastard daughter of an Irish immigrant, Mick Dyson, the unscrupulous smuggler who had, before I was born, cold-bloodedly murdered my granduncle Nigel.

At the time, Dyson was the head foreman at the Chandler china-clay mines, Wheal Anant and Wheal Penforth. By night, however, he was the leader of a ruthless gang of wreckers, who, with a false signal light, would lure ships to their destruction on the rocky Cornish coast. There, Dyson and his nefarious crew would brutally kill all aboard and steal the vessels' cargo, which was then concealed in abandoned regions of the mines until it could be safely disposed of for a tidy profit.

Somehow (it is thought to have been through a disgruntled laborer at the mines) Granduncle Nigel, then the local magistrate, became aware of the Irishman's horrible activities. So, one bitter October night, suspecting himself on the verge of arrest otherwise, Dyson held up Granduncle Nigel's coach and shot him straight through the heart.

That might have been the end of the story except that, upon Granduncle Nigel's death, Uncle Draco inherited the mines, and he, too, soon grew distrustful of their head foreman. After spying upon the Irishman and learning of his foul enterprise, Uncle Draco, together with Papa, conceived a clever plan whereby Dyson and his band were exposed and apprehended. After that, of course, all except one of them were justly hanged for their crimes.

The accomplice spared was Dyson's lover, a woman named Linnet Tyrrell, who had been reared in the miners' rows, the sprawling stretch of hovels that housed the families of the rough men who worked the mines. Because she was carrying Dyson's child when she was brought to trial, Linnet evaded the gibbet and was sentenced instead to be transported to an Australian penal colony after the birth of her baby.

In due time, her daughter, appropriately christened Clemency, was born, and because a harsh penitentiary in a savage land was no place for an infant, the authorities took her away from Linnet and sent her to live with her mother's family in the miners' rows.

Although blameless for her parents' deeds, Clemency was branded by the scandal just the same. As she grew up, the old busybodies in the village fastened a sharp eye on her, eagerly watching and waiting for any hint of wantonness or wickedness in her behavior; and when there was none, they swore sullenly that blood would yet tell and prophesied darkly that she would come to a bad end.

So, despite the fact that, in later years, Mama took pity on her and employed her at the Grange, I knew Clemency's life had not been an easy one; and I would have felt sorry for her had she not coolly rebuffed my initial overtures of friendship, making it plain that she felt herself the equal of a queen and had accepted the job as my maid only to learn everything she could about the speech, manners, and so forth of those whose ranks she was fervently determined to join one day.

She was, like me, I suppose, pretty after an odd fashion, for her hair, red-gold as a fox, and her triangular face and high cheekbones combined to give her an intriguing, vixenish appearance that certain men seemed to find appealing; and although she was always neatly and presentably dressed, still, she never failed somehow to manage to look as though she had just tumbled out of bed—or was ripe for tumbling into one.

Even Papa had been known to spare her a second, if somewhat penetrating, glance, and more than once, I overheard him insist to Mama that Clemency was a girl bound to cause trouble sooner or later and ought to be sent packing before that day arrived. But Mama would only smile and shake her head at Papa's grumbling and, chiding him gently, remind him of Clemency's adverse lot and that we must be kind to those less fortunate than ourselves.

So Clemency stayed on at the Grange, and Papa kept his sea-eagle eye trained upon my older brother, lest Guy should somehow develop the misguided notion of succumbing to my abigail's charms.

Finally, after several hectic, last-minute preparations, the evening of my party at the Grange was upon us. How well I remember it even now, after all these many long years. It was 1841, a beautiful spring night.

Earlier that day, it had rained, and now from the dark, moist earth wafted that clean, fresh scent of newly washed grass and loam, mingling headily with the sweet fragrance of budding heather and gorse, which was carried by a soughing wind from the sweeping moors to the Grange.

With each gust, too, came the salty smell of the distant sea spraying spindrift against the gnarled fingers of black rock that cleaved the shingled beach. A thin grey veil of mist floated on the breeze, making it damp and cool. The night air echoed with the piercing cries of the sea gulls along the coast and the lyrical but forlorn call of a lone curlew upon the heaths.

In the inky sky above, the full moon and stars shone, their silvery glimmer softly diffused by the mist. Glowing beams filtered through the branches of the trees in the park surrounding the Grange, dappling the dewy ground with sparkling prisms of light, so it seemed to me, looking out through my open bedroom window, as though a thousand diamonds lay scattered upon the lawn below. Droplets glistened upon the petals of the flowers that filled the gardens with winding ribbons of color, and with gentle plops, bright beads of water dripped from the rustling green leaves of the stirring trees.

The Grange itself was like a beacon in the night, ablaze with lamps and candles, so it appeared as though the pale cream house radiated a golden aura. Torches flickered on either side of the front door, and the ornate brass knocker hanging upon the stout oak portal gleamed where struck by the erratic light.

From the open French doors of the ballroom that gave way to the terrace beneath my window, I could hear the noises of the servants as they scurried to and fro, making certain all was in readiness; crystal and china clattered, and the discordant clamor of the musicians tuning their various instruments reverberated through the air.

A knock sounded upon my door, drawing me from my reverie. The oval knob turned, and Clemency entered my chamber.

"'Tis time for you to go downstairs, Miss Laura," she announced, her green eyes glittering like bits of glass in her piquant face, her cheeks unexpectedly flushed.

I wondered if she was as excited as I that we would have guests here tonight at the Grange, or if her high color was due instead merely to some passing flirtation with one of the footmen. If I asked her, she would not answer me truthfully, I knew, but would make some vague, evasive reply, as usual, mocking me all the while with her scornful, sloe eyes. So I did not question her, but said instead, "Yes, I know. I was just coming."

She nodded aloofly, as was her way, and left me. Turning to my cheval mirror, I glanced once more at my reflection to reassure myself that my appearance was all I could wish. Then I smiled with delight at the image I presented.

Earlier, Clemency had arranged my hair, deftly parting it in the middle, twisting it up, and then curling it so it fell on either side of my face in two masses of ringlets. These, she had intertwined with gold satin ribands and tiny white orchid blossoms to match my dress.

This was not, of course, as fancy as my debut ball gown, but I was well pleased with it all the same. It was of oyster-white silk overlaid with a delicate cobwebbing of lace, the heart-shaped bodice cut modestly low to reveal a hint of my full breasts and fitted with short, off-the-shoulder sleeves that were fluted and puffed so they resembled scallop shells. At the top of each sleeve was a large gold bow edged with dainty tatting. A wide, trailing gold sash encircled my waist. From this, the folds of the skirt fell in the smooth contours of a bell to the floor, where the flounced hem was threaded with a slender gold ribbon. About my neck, I wore a simple strand of pearls. Gold slippers adorned my feet.

Now, pulling on my long white lace gloves and retrieving my gold fan and reticule, I exited my bedroom and walked swiftly down the corridor to the stairs, at whose foot, in the hall below, Papa and Mama were waiting expectantly for me. They gazed up at me with pride and approval as I descended the steps, Papa's low, admiring whistle bringing a blush to my cheeks and a softly scolding "Welles!" from Mama, although she was forced to turn away to hide her smile at his antics. Gaily, I took my place between my parents just as the crunch of carriage wheels on the gravel drive outside informed us that the first of our guests had arrived.

Moments later, Sykes, our butler, admitted Uncle Draco and Aunt Maggie, along with Jarrett, Nicholas, and the twins, Alexander and Angelique. My cousins Damaris and Bryony, no doubt pouting because they were not yet out of the schoolroom and so, like my brother Francis, were too young to attend the party, had been left at home. At the same time, my brother Guy came tardily down the stairs.

The hall rang with a jovial flurry of talk and laughter as greetings were exchanged, while Sykes and two of the footmen deftly but unobtrusively whisked away hats, cloaks, malacca canes, and gloves. Though Mama had intended to form a receiving line, this notion was quickly abandoned amid the men's jocular shaking of hands and rowdy clapping of shoulders, the women's affectionate hugs and swift kissing of cheeks in the continental fash-

ion. Still, I had too newly crossed the threshold of adult-
hood to disregard my duties this night, and so I politely
traded pleasantries with Uncle Draco and Aunt Maggie
before wishing them an enjoyable evening and turning
eagerly to my cousins.

I had not seen them in a good while, for previously,
my lessons had not permitted me much time for social-
izing; nor had my cousins sought me out of late, as they
had used to do. These days, Jarrett, Nicholas, and Alexander were kept busy by their father at the Chandler
china-clay mines, at the P & C Shipping Line, which
Papa and Uncle Draco had founded some years ago, and
with other family interests, while Angelique, a year older
than I, had already made her debut and been away in
London the past Season. So, now, despite the fact that
we had grown up together, it was almost as though I
were seeing my cousins for the first time; and to my
surprise, I scarcely recognized the handsome men and
the beautiful woman who stood before me.

Although born to a life of ease, waited on hand and
foot by a staff of servants since infancy, my Chandler
cousins were neither soft nor indolent. Instead, like the
fine black horses raised by Uncle Draco at Stormswept
Heights, they were all dark, alert, high-spirited animals,
intelligent of mind, elegant of form, indelibly stamped
in the brazen Gypsy mold of their father, so even a
stranger should have known at once that they were their
sire's get. Sleek and supple, with tossing heads and flash-
ing eyes, they were hot-blooded and hot-tempered, bold,
mettlesome creatures prone to take the bit between their
teeth and run with it, although they were, withal, amiable

to those who knew how to manage them. But these were few and far between, and so my cousins were notorious for their wild, willful behavior, curbed only by their father's hard, restraining hand and their mother's cool, authoritative voice.

There were those who thought my Chandler cousins were too arrogant by half for the children of a parvenu Gypsy bastard. But if they were aware of this, they did not show it, taking stubborn pride in their heritage instead. Heedless of the fact that they and their exploits were frequently grist for the gossip mill, they were frankly amused by the open scorn or secret envy of duller, tamer souls unblessed with Uncle Draco's stamina and Aunt Maggie's grit. To offend one of them was to offend them all, for though they might, and often did, fight tooth and nail among themselves, each trying endlessly to best the others, they hung together fiercely against all outsiders, Gypsy blood evidently indeed thicker than water.

Now, like restless, caged beasts, they paced and posed, filling up the hall, so it seemed as though it would not hold them, as though the high ceiling were too low, the spacious walls too close, too confining for them. For a moment, as I watched them, I was reminded of the herds of wild horses and ponies that roamed the moors, with no man's mark notching their ears.

Yet there was one among my Chandler cousins that I would claim as mine, if I could: Nicholas. The brightness of my knight's shining armor had not dimmed with the years. As I had loved the boy in my childhood, so did I love the man now, devotedly, unswervingly, though I was promised, and always had been, to Jarrett.

So alike, yet so different, the two brothers were—Jarrett like the moon over the sea, I thought, cold and remote; Nicholas like the sun upon the moors, warm and scintillating, so that now, as he looked at me, I felt like a budding flower avidly unfurling its petals to him, yearning fervently for him to pick me as his own. Nevertheless, mindful of my obligations, I first extended my hand to Jarrett.

Though we had, as I have said, been affianced since my birth, still, somehow I had never imagined myself marrying him. He was my cousin, yes, but for all that, we had never been very close. In some ways, I felt I scarcely knew him; and since it is difficult to envision oneself wedding a stranger, I had, since learning of my betrothal, carelessly thrust the disagreeable knowledge to the back of my mind, then conveniently forgotten about it, having some vague notion that, in time, everyone else would forget about it, too. Indeed, if I had thought of Jarrett at all over the years, he had intruded only upon the fringes of my girlish daydreams—and never as more than a dark, nebulous figure, unbidden, unwelcome, unreal.

But now, without warning, as his fingers closed firmly around mine, the strength of him sent a quiver like an arrow up my arm to my shoulder blades, a tremor such as I had once felt after striking a stout stick hard against the trunk of a Cornish elm; and I realized, startled, that he was flesh and blood after all—and somehow disturbingly solid.

His proud, aristocratic bearing was his mother's, and like Aunt Maggie, who had been born gentry, I suspected

Jarrett had that backbone of steel that is inbred rather than acquired. Otherwise, at twenty-two, he was his father made over, tall and powerfully built, although he was more slender than Uncle Draco, with a lithe, sinewy grace and a compelling magnetism I found oddly disquieting, for it reminded me of the peculiar, mesmerizing effect a wild predator has upon its prey an interminable heartbeat before closing in for the kill.

His exquisitely tailored black silk jacket with its long tails clung to broad shoulders and muscular arms developed by grueling manual labor at the mines and at dockside warehouses, for Uncle Draco did not believe in coddling his sons. The frothy lace jabot of Jarrett's crisp white cambric shirt spilled down a massive chest that tapered to a belly firm and flat beneath his expensive grey-and-black paisley waistcoat, from which hung a sterling-silver watch chain adorned with a single fob and seal. His black silk pantaloons hugged thick, corded thighs and calves.

His hair was black and gleaming as jet, disheveled now from the wind, swept back in shaggy waves from his swarthy, satanic face. Though favoring Uncle Draco in looks, Jarrett's features were leaner, more refined, like those of a wolf, I thought uneasily, with my propensity for likening people to animals. Beneath his swooping black brows, his eyes shone like obsidian shards in his bronzed visage. Set above a generous, sensual mouth, his patrician nose was straight and finely chiseled. His cheeks were angular, hollow; the thrust of his jaw was imperious, determined.

Had he lived in another time, I felt sure he would have

been a pirate, for despite his impeccable clothes and polished manner, I sensed something primitive and savage lying just beneath the surface of him, something dark and somehow unnerving. As I had foreseen years ago, Jarrett had indeed become a man one would not wish to cross, a man accustomed to demanding—and getting—what he wanted. The perception troubled me, and I shivered as his eyes raked me casually, almost insolently, from beneath half-closed lids, then riveted on my face. He bowed over my hand, brushing his lips lightly across its back. The feel of his mouth against my skin was like an electric shock passing through me, and suddenly, it was all I could do to refrain from wrenching my hand from his like a gauche schoolgirl.

"You're looking very well, Laura," he drawled in his father's low, velvety voice, his eyes burning like dark, twin flames as they assessed me. Was there a flicker of interest there? I shrank from the thought. "Very well indeed. I must confess I never guessed when you were all flying braids and gangling limbs that you would someday grow into such a remarkable beauty."

My cheeks stained with color at his words, and I discovered I could no longer meet his gaze. I had never before known him to look at me as he did now, and I was made distinctly ill at ease by his appraisal. I felt as though I had suddenly run a long way and were now breathless, my heart beating too fast in my breast.

Bewildered by the perturbing sensations, I abruptly snatched my fingers from his grasp, barely resisting my urge to crush my hand to me and rub it vigorously in an effort to halt its tingling. Though I was mortified at my rudeness, still, I did not apologize, for when I glanced again at Jarrett, I had the distinct impression that he was laughing at me.

Impudent knave! I thought.

He had not changed a bit since our childhood, when he had used to taunt me about my hero worship of Nicky, but was as provoking as ever. In fact, I decided crossly, he was long overdue a smart set-down.

But aware that we were not alone, that this was neither the time nor the place to begin a quarrel, especially one from which I was not certain I would emerge victorious, I stifled the cutting words that rose in my throat. What had Jarrett done, after all, at which I could point an accusing finger? Complimented me on my appearance and kissed my hand? Why, I should look a fool to voice a complaint about such, for how could I explain that my agitation stemmed not from this, but from the confusing emotions he had unwittingly churned up inside me? I could not, and so, swallowing hard, I turned away, uncharitably wishing him in perdition.

He was nothing at all like Nicholas, whom I loved, Nicholas, whom I had adored since childhood, Nicholas, whom I wanted to marry. Despite being promised to Jarrett, I had set my heart firmly on having Nicky, blithely trusting, like a hermit crab appropriating a too-small shell, that somehow all would come out right in the end.

But now, for some reason, I found I could no longer ignore the fact that it was, after all, Jarrett who was my fiancé and that I had never protested this arrangement. He had every reason for supposing I was ready and willing to be his bride; and since he himself had raised no objections to that prospect, I could only assume he found it, if not desirable, at least acceptable. Regardless of how he felt about the matter, however, he certainly did not look like a man who would lightly step aside for another; and I could not understand how I could have been so cowardly and deceitful as not to have revealed my true emotions to both him and our parents before now.

Worse still was the painful recognition that even if, by some chance, Jarrett should prove amenable to releasing me from our bond, I did not know if Nicholas cared enough to ask, then, for my hand. He had never told me he loved me.

But had he not, through the years, dropped by the Grange at every opportunity, even when he knew Guy would not be there? And had he not then inquired of Sykes if I were at home and cared to entertain my wayward cousin? And did he not call me his "dear Laura," and had he not, just this past Christmas, kissed me under the mistletoe when no one was watching—a far from cousinly kiss? He must love me. He must! And yet . . . a niggling doubt assailed me, for how often had I heard him vow that he was born to be footloose and fancy-free, to cast his fate to the four winds and go where they blew him?

"Let Jarrett be the one to tie himself up to the old apron strings—no offense intended, dear Laura," Nicky would say, grinning at me, "since, after all, they'll be *your* apron strings. So I daresay he shan't mind a bit. But I've a mind to see the world myself—although I must admit it *would* be nice to have someone along to do the cooking and keep my shirts clean."

"I'll wager I should be a marvel with a skillet and washboard," I had once jokingly replied, though in my heart, I had been in earnest.

And his black eyes suddenly glinting speculatively, he had said, "Yes, I'll bet you would be at that," before he had laughed and chucked me under the chin.

On such as this had I built my hopes and dreams.

Now, as Jarrett strode toward the ballroom, Nicky sauntered up to take his place, eyes dancing with frank appreciation as they roamed over me. A crooked grin split his charming countenance before, with a smart click of his heels, he bowed gallantly over my hand and kissed it lingeringly, with a flourish that set my heart aflutter.

A less handsome version of Jarrett, there was nevertheless something wildly enchanting about Nicky. He was gay and dashing, a reckless blade determined to live each moment as though it were his last. Because of this, he was more often than not the primary target of his father's temper, his mother's despair, and the cap of many a matchmaking mama's daughter. Even my haughty cousin Elizabeth had, much to Aunt Julianne's rage and chagrin, thus far rejected numerous proposals of marriage (including one from an eccentric but very rich old duke) because she was, I believed, secretly enamored of Nicky.

"By Jove! You look stunning, Laura!" he declared, favoring me with that special look that made a woman feel as though all other women paled into insignificance beside her. "But, then, I always knew you would someday. Jarrett had best have a care what he's about, else I'll be stealing you out from under his nose."

I glowed with pleasure at his words and thought, *Oh,*

Nicky, if only you would, and wished he could read my mind.

I hoped he would stay and talk to me, but instead, whistling a merry tune, he jammed his hands into his pockets and nonchalantly strolled after Jarrett, pausing only to lift a glass of champagne from the silver tray being carried through the hall by a passing footman.

Trying hard not to lose my sparkle, I next greeted Alexander Chandler, who, being smitten by the daughter of an earl in neighboring Devon, had only cousinly interest in me. After that, I held out my hands to his twin, Angelique, knowing from her clever, discerning eyes that she had sensed my sudden dejection and was speculating curiously about its cause.

"Don't you look divine, Laura!" she exclaimed, enveloping me in a crush of sweet heather scent. Then, her black eyes alight with lively suspicion and inquisitiveness, she drew me a little aside from the rest and whispered baitingly, "Nicky is positively green with envy of Jarrett, I expect. I only hope they shan't come to blows over you!"

"Why should they?" I asked, my voice even enough, although, still, I could not prevent a guilty flush from stealing over my face or refrain from surreptitiously glancing about to see if anyone else had heard her. To my relief, nobody had, for which I was profoundly thankful. Naturally, under the circumstances, I did not care to wear my heart upon my sleeve.

"Hmph!" Angelique sniffed, then smiled with delight at correctly surmising the reason for my distress. "I'm not blind, Laura, and trying to pull the wool over my eyes won't make me that way either. I've seen how Nicky looks at you when he thinks no one is watching —and how you look at him. Twins are very intuitive, you know. I've long suspected you were head over heels in love with him—and frankly, if that's so, I think you're an inordinately silly goose!

"Still, 'tis none of my business after all, and certainly, I've never been one to stick my nose in where it wasn't wanted. Nevertheless, you *are* my cousin, and I've always liked you, which is more than I can say about some of our relations. So I'm going to give you some . . . shall we say . . . friendly words of advice. After that, I promise to hold my tongue, so you needn't worry that I shall bandy about what I've guessed. Twins know how to keep a secret better than most, because they tell each other lots of things they don't share with anyone else.

"Listen, then, and mark my words well: Jarrett's worth ten of Nicky, and he's nobody's fool besides. What he might do if he ever found out about your pining after Nicky, I shouldn't like to imagine. Suffice to say that there'd be trouble—and bad blood between them ever after, regardless of how it all turned out. So if it's Nicky you want, Laura, then the only decent thing to do is to break off your engagement to Jarrett before it's too late."

"Oh, hush, Angelique, hush!" I uttered, my voice rising. "I don't want to hear such things!" Abruptly, I bit my lip to quell my outburst. Then, on a lower note, seeing that it was pointless to try to hide the truth from her, I confessed, "Still, I know you're right. Somehow I've just got to work up the courage to tell Papa and Mama I don't want to marry Jarrett, no matter how much it will hurt their feelings—or how furious it will make Uncle Draco.''

"Oh, pooh!" Angelique tossed her head disdainfully, so her glossy black curls shook. "I shouldn't stew about *that*, if I were you. Papa's not really such an ogre as everyone thinks. 'Tis just that he's had to fight like a dog to get ahead in the world and so has become adept at barking and biting. You know that Grandfather Chandler hated him and put him to work mucking out the stables instead of giving him a proper place at the Hall.

"Honestly, Laura! It truly *is* Jarrett's reaction you ought to be fretting about! Why, just think what an idiot he should look if you cried off and then turned around and set your cap for Nicky! Gracious! Jarrett would probably be so angry that he'd spit in a pew—and his temper is as bad as Papa's, maybe even worse, because Jarrett holds everything inside him until he finally just explodes.''

"Well, that's hardly very reassuring, Angelique," I pointed out with some alarm.

"All the more reason, then, why you'd better watch your step! Because once you make your bed, you have to lie in it, regardless of how hard or lumpy your mattress is. You'll see—or, then again, maybe you won't, because Nicky will never wed you, Laura, no matter what you may think to the contrary. He's not the marrying kind. I've heard him say so repeatedly. So if you're smart, you'll take my advice, and put him out of your heart and mind. 'Tis for the best. Really, it is. Because, otherwise, in the long run, he'll only wind up making you miserable.''

After that, her black eyes speaking volumes, Angelique turned and made her way to the ballroom, where the others were now gathered. Silently, I watched her go, recognizing that she had indeed spoken to me out of love and friendship, and that she was, too, a year older than I and so was doubtless far more experienced in these matters. Still, I denied her wisdom and rejected her words, for I did not want to believe her. Angelique was wrong about Nicky, I thought. Though he was her brother, she simply did not know him as I did.

Determinedly shrugging off her warnings, I took Papa's arm in mine and, smiling, my head held high, made my grand entrance through the open ballroom doors.

Chapter IV

Waltzes and Wisteria

What shall be the maiden's fate?
Who shall be the maiden's
mate?

—*The Lay of the Last Minstrel*
Sir Walter Scott

Even now, when I am grown too stiff and frail to dance even a few steps across a beckoning floor, all I knew and felt that night of my coming-out party is pressed like a flower into the pages of my memory.

I drank and danced, then drank and danced some more, until my head spun from the dry, unaccustomed, pale gold champagne and the smooth, sophisticated compliments of my many partners, young and old. My coming-out party was a success—*I* was a success—and I was giddy with my triumph.

The ballroom, which had been especially swathed in

yards of vibrant-hued fabric—iridescent silk, rippling satin, striped muslin, cloudlike gauze, and cloth of gold and silver—and otherwise exotically decorated to resemble a palatial Arabian tent, was filled to overflowing with guests who had come from all over Cornwall, from Devon, Somerset, and Dorset, and in some cases, from as far away as Bristol, Oxford, and London, for Papa's acquaintances were many and varied.

Lords and ladies hobnobbed with the upstart nouveau riche, into which category fell men like Papa and Uncle Draco; for it was into hands such as theirs that the reins of power and pelf the gentry had so long gripped tightly were beginning to slip as the common man everywhere rose up to demand his rights.

I saw Angelique twirl past in the arms of an earl, and I thought of how her father, Uncle Draco, a Gypsy bastard, had started with nothing and clawed his way up out of the muck in which society would have seen him mired. So Papa, the son of a mere sea captain, had done also. It had not, however, been a battle just or honest or easily won, for the gentry did not hesitate to use whatever means they could to keep their foot firmly planted upon the common man's neck, and those means were countered accordingly by men who obstinately refused to be kept down. As a result, in the bygone days of their youth, neither Papa nor Uncle Draco had scrupled over smuggling a case of brandy or French perfume past the excisemen, or at drastically undercutting their competition in order to secure a contract, even if it had meant suffering an initial loss. Now they could buy and sell many of those present tonight.

Yes, the world was indeed changing, the elite system of the aristocracy decaying and crumbling about them, while a new breed and class sprang up to take its place, men like Papa and Uncle Draco—and the sons who would follow in their footsteps. For it was Jarrett and Nicholas, Guy and Francis, and others like them, to whom the future would belong, young men reared in the mold of enterprise and reformation, unafraid to reach out and grasp the world with both hands and bend it to their will.

Strong, determined hands, they would have, these young men, hard and self-assured, like Jarrett's hands upon me as he guided me expertly around the ballroom floor to the waltz the musicians were playing.

Unlike previous partners, he spoke little. No pretty, practiced phrases issued from his lips; nor did he otherwise flirt with me, as all the rest had. Nevertheless, Jarrett, with his silent, intense demeanor, had flustered me as no other man tonight had succeeded in doing.

Though he held me no closer than was proper, he seemed so near that I fancied I could hear his heart beating. I could smell the sharp, spicy scent of bay rum that emanated from his smooth, dark skin, and feel his breath, warm as a kiss, upon my face. He danced divinely, with such a fluid grace and poise to his movements that I was certain he never made a misstep or trod on his partner's toes; and had I not felt so inexplicably tense, as though I must be on my guard every moment with him, I should have delighted in losing myself in his arms as he swept me about the ballroom.

As it was, I danced badly, awkward as a schoolgirl,

my eyes glued to the black-pearl tiepin in his cravat, my tongue tied up in knots, my face and hands hot with humiliation at my ineptitude. I knew I was capable of doing far better; Mr. Rutledge, Mama's own dancing master before becoming mine, had taught me well. I had no doubt Jarrett found me clumsy and boring, and though I had no interest in him, my vanity was piqued at the idea that I should be thought ungainly or dreary by any man. Angry at him for undermining my only recently acquired confidence, I missed my footing and stumbled, nearly falling. Immediately, Jarrett's arm tightened around my waist, pressing me to his chest, crushing my cheek against the foamy folds of his jabot. His heart drummed in my ear, a strong, steady rhythm that contrasted sharply with the sudden, wild, birdlike fluttering of my own.

He held me thus for no more than an instant; yet somehow it seemed like forever, one of those odd moments out of time, in which things appear to mist and fade in one's mind, so it was as though abruptly I viewed my surroundings through a vignette, with all my senses narrowed, focused acutely on Jarrett.

"Got your balance now, Laura?" he asked, his voice husky, his breath falling light as a caress upon the top of my head.

"Y-yes," I replied. "It was—was stupid of me, tripping like that."

"Well, 'tis very crowded in here, especially with Old 'Peacock' hogging all the space. Absolutely no one is safe when *he's* on a dance floor, you know; doubtless, he jostled you." He glossed over my misstep smoothly, so I should suffer no embarrassment, and for that, I was grateful.

The tumult inside me lessened; involuntarily, I smiled at his use of our childhood nickname for blustery Colonel Pennock. He was a stout old soldier who was accustomed to performing military maneuvers on an open Indian plain and who, unfortunately, did not allow his current vicinity's restrictions to hamper his enthusiastic movements. For the first time, Jarrett's eyes twinkled.

"You should smile more often, Laura," he declared. "It lights up your face like the morning sun upon the moors."

I blushed, glad that, just then, the music ended and he was forced to release me. It seemed he did so reluctantly, but perhaps I only imagined this. Certainly, after escorting me to a chair, he took his leave quickly enough when hailed by one of his friends. I felt an incomprehensible pang of regret as I watched him head toward the small drawing room, which had been set aside for gaming. All the Chandler men had a passion for cards and dice; and I suspected, curiously disappointed, that I should not see Jarrett again this night.

But the baffling feeling was forgotten in the gush of ardor that, like water through a broken dam, surged through me when Nicholas arrived to claim me for the next dance, sweeping all thoughts of Jarrett aside. With aplomb, Nicky held out his hand to me; eagerly, I seized it, not even bothering to consult my program, so the gawky boy whose name was plainly written upon my card, but whom I had not even observed approaching me, was left standing awkwardly to one side. I saw the tips of the boy's ears redden with indignation and embarrassment and his prominent Adam's apple bob convulsively in his throat, as, having stolen a march on him, Nicky whirled me onto the ballroom floor.

"Poor Onslow," he drawled with amusement, causing me to glance over my shoulder to where I had been seated and to spy guiltily the flushed boy I had so rudely ignored. "A most appropriate surname, wouldn't you agree?" He *tsk*ed with feigned pity. "For he's as slow on the uptake as ever. I went to prep school with him, you know. We used to think it was the day he accidentally got smashed over the head with a cricket bat that did him in, but I fancy he was always a trifle thick-witted. I say, he rather looks as though he's swallowed an unripe persimmon, doesn't he? Was it his dance after all, then, Laura? Funny. I could have sworn it was mine."

"Liar," I accused, turning back to him, but I smiled ruefully as I spoke the word, for the insult done to the hapless Onslow was just as much my fault as it was Nicky's.

He only laughed.

"Yes, I'm afraid I must confess I am indeed," he admitted without a trace of conscience or regret, "and apparently a rather bad one at that. But, then, it really wasn't very kind of you to point a finger at me, Laura. I wanted to dance with you, and as I was somewhat dilatory in getting my name placed on your program, due to the matter of a small wager in the card room, what else could I do? There was nothing for it but to cut some other fellow out, and poor Onslow seemed a likely candidate, too plodding to cause a scene. Not quite the gentlemanly thing to do, I agree, but, then, I didn't really think you'd mind. He's ruined a hundred ladies' slippers with those big, bumbling feet of his."

"A hundred?" I lifted one eyebrow skeptically.

"Well, at least a dozen, then," he amended, grinning. "But let's not talk about him—such a dull subject! Let's talk about us instead."

" 'Us?' " I inquired archly, my pulse quickening, my mouth suddenly so dry that it was difficult for me to swallow.

"But of course," Nicky rejoined lightly enough, but his eyes darkened as he gazed down at me, and his arm tightened about my waist. "Have we not always been companions in crime, like Don Quixote and the fair Dulcinea?"

"Or the Prince and Briar Rose?" I suggested teasingly, recalling Jarrett's childhood nicknames for us.

"Yes, though, in truth, I would liken you to a paradise tree myself, Laura, all brown and gold, and trimmed with satin and lace. What delightful surprises do you hold in store, I wonder?"

"That, dear Nicholas, is something you shall have to discover yourself," I declared boldly, made reckless by the champagne I had drunk and the daring expression in his inviting black eyes.

"Shall I?"

"Yes, indeed."

"Saucy wench! I do believe you're flirting with me."

"Perhaps I am."

"Even so, one should not issue challenges one is not prepared to keep," he asserted, his voice low, his face grown serious now.

"I . . . never do," I whispered provocatively.

"Indeed? Well, we shall see."

"Shall we?" I asked.

He did not answer, but drew me nearer instead, looking at me in a way that made my heart pound and the blood rush to my head. Drowning in the fathomless depths of his eyes, I fell silent, too, my every nerve stretched so taut that I felt as though the slightest brush against my skin would be like a bolt of lightning coursing through me. My feet seemed hardly to touch the floor as, exhilarated, I surrendered myself to his dashing lead, twirling around and around until I was dizzy and breathless, uncertain whether it was the dance or Nicky himself who made me feel so.

We moved together as though we had been made for each other, I thought dreamily, through a haze of champagne and a rainbow of colors that spun and shimmered beneath the blaze of hundreds of candles melting in the crystal chandeliers of the ballroom, casting their glow upon strings of dangling prisms that bent and reflected the light. How like those brilliant beams, I was, molded by Nicky to fit his sinuous body as we stepped and swayed to the music. His arms felt so right about me that I was sure it was in them I belonged, and now, more than ever, did the fact that I was affianced to Jarrett dismay me. I resolved that, tomorrow morning, I would tell my parents what was in my heart and ask their permission to break off my betrothal. Surely, they would agree that I could not wed Jarrett when it was Nicholas I loved.

Lost in my reverie, I did not even realize that we were no longer in the ballroom, that Nicky had, without my protesting, skillfully guided me out through the open French doors to the terrace. It was only when I felt the night air, cool and damp against my skin, that, startled back to reality, I took notice of my surroundings and saw we had left the bright lights of the ballroom behind.

On the edge of my consciousness, I perceived that, here and there, couples seeking a breath of fresh air circumspectly strolled within plain view of the ballroom, and at the east end of the terrace, a knot of men enjoying cigars had gathered, talking and laughing amid wafting clouds of smoke. But all this seemed somehow far removed from me, and I scarcely spared it any attention. It was as though I were ensorcelled as Nicky and I continued to dance, my skirts brushing lightly against the stone balustrade as we waltzed along the moonlit terrace toward its darker, deserted west end.

Moments later, the last strains of the music died away, and we were alone in the silence. Still, buoyed up by the champagne I had drunk, I said nothing as Nicky seized my hand so firmly in his that I could not have pulled away even had I wanted to, which I did not. Swiftly, he tugged me down the steps into the gardens. Deeper and deeper into the flowers and foliage glistening with mist and dew, we followed the twisting fieldstone paths until finally we came to my favorite place, a small, secluded arbor, where I had often whiled away the hours of my childhood, reading.

Here, a lovely Chinese wisteria tree grew, a cutting of which Papa had brought home to Mama several years ago from some botanical garden in the Far East and which she had planted in this sheltered spot. With her green thumb, she had carefully nurtured the fragile tree until it had taken root and begun to grow and thrive. Now it was hung with a profusion of cascading, grapelike blossoms, deep lavender in color, which filled the night air with their rich, sweet perfume. A shower of delicate petals loosed from the tree by the breeze strewed the soft, mossy ground and the stone bench to which Nicky now led me. With his handkerchief, he chivalrously dusted off the seat, and I sat down upon it, arranging my skirts about me prettily.

The arbor was a place of enchantment in the darkness, and I reveled in the spell it cast upon me. Above, the full moon shone like a lustrous pearl; the stars glittered like diamonds scattered across the black-velvet sky. Moonbeams dripped through the slender branches of the wisteria tree to dapple the earth with gleaming pieces of silver that might have been stolen from a pirate's sea chest.

The night wind sighed, gentle as a baby's breath, and the leaves of the trees and shrubs sang a melodious lullaby to the flowers. In harmonious counterpoint came the dulcet coos and calls of the night birds that stirred and preened, ruffling their feathers for warmth against the coolness of the spring air. Somewhere upon the moors, an owl hooted, a hawk screamed; and nearby, some tiny, frightened creature skittered through the tangle of creeping vines that covered the soil like a plush green carpet. The chirruping of the locusts as they rubbed their gossamer wings together was a tranquil drone, almost hypnotic in the stillness, punctuated by the rhythmic croaking of frogs crouched on lily pads in the pond at the center of the gardens. The occasional rippling and splashing of the water as its serene surface was disturbed by its amphibious inhabitants was echoed soothingly by the soft swish of the surf breaking against the rocky shore in the distance.

Yet all this faded into insignificance as Nicky settled himself beside me, his black silk pantaloons scraping slightly against the stone bench, a discordant note that jarred me from my quiet contemplation of the night, so I became abruptly and distinctly aware of his closeness. My body trembled like that of a startled doe, alert and poised for flight; for though I welcomed his proximity—indeed, had brazenly encouraged it—now I grew unexpectedly nervous as some niggling sense of propriety returned to me and I thought of the unpleasant consequences bound to result if we were discovered here alone in the gardens. Still, I made no move to go back inside, for despite my anxiety, I was filled with keen-edged excitement, too, anticipatory as a child about to receive some long-awaited treat; and whatever the cost, I would not have it snatched from me.

Slowly, casually, Nicky encircled my waist with his arm. His skin felt light as a feather against mine. Yet such was my desire for him that my every pore seemed to be intensely, painfully, sensitive to touch, so his embrace was like a white-hot brand pressing against me, searing me so with its heat that I felt almost agonizingly faint. His fingers rested just beneath my breast, in a careless caress, it appeared; but still, I was all too aware of how his thumb lay at the rim of my nipple, causing it to tingle and throb, a strange quickening sensation that spread like a fever through my body, making me shiver and yearn passionately for some unknown cure.

Unconsciously, I leaned against him, my tongue flicking out to moisten my lips, which felt parched as the strawlike Cornish grass in summer, an unwitting invitation Nicky did not hesitate to accept. His grip upon me tightened; his eyes bored into mine as he caught my chin with his free hand and tilted my eager face up to his.

"Laura," he murmured. "Laura."

He kissed me then, gently, and it was all I had ever dreamed of in my wildest imaginings. Fervently, I clung to him, exulting in the feel of his body quivering taut as a bowstring against mine, too young and naive to know how I tempted him, how it was only with the greatest of difficulty that he held himself in check; for he was too clever and experienced to risk demanding too much of me before he felt certain he had sufficiently aroused me to the point that further advances would not startle me into fleeing.

Reluctantly, he broke the kiss, drawing a little away from me, his black eyes lingering on my parted mouth in a way that made my heart race, my breath come too quickly.

" 'Weave a circle round him thrice,' " he quoted softly. " 'And close your eyes with holy dread/For he on honeydew hath fed/And drunk the milk of Paradise.' "

"Have you, Nicholas?" I asked, my voice barely a whisper.

"Yes, oh, yes," he breathed. Then he burst out, "Oh, Laura, you don't know how long I've wanted you! It seems like I've waited forever for you to grow up!"

"And now I have," I said, triumph shooting through me at the words, a gloriously powerful feeling such as I had never before felt.

Hard on its heels came happiness and relief at the knowledge that he *did* love me—and always had. Closing my eyes, I offered my lips up to him as reverently as a sacrifice. Needing no further urging, he brought his mouth down on mine, harder this time, more demanding, so he bruised me with his kiss. But I did not care. I was too caught up in the emotions he was unleashing inside me, the joy and love for him that filled my heart to overflowing.

Savagely, his tongue forced my lips to open so he might ravish the sweetness within. His teeth grazed my mouth, drawing blood, coppery tasting upon my tongue, as he kissed me fiercely, again and again, as though he could not get enough of me, would devour me with his lips. His tongue probed my mouth, deeply, greedily, searching out its every dark, moist crevice until I could scarcely breathe, panted for air.

But my ragged gasps only spurred him on. As though he had long coveted it, his hand swept down to take possession of my breast through the thin material of my gown. Slowly, expertly, he rotated his thumb across my nipple until the responsive peak stiffened and strained against my bodice, tangible evidence of my desire for him. Sparks of delight radiated from its center, setting me aflame. A low moan issued from my throat, and involuntarily, my body arched against his, instinctively seeking the caresses that would bring it fulfillment. In answer to my body's silent appeal, Nicky's fingers slid sensuously up my spine to entwine themselves in my tresses, pulling me back, even as the palm that cupped my breast began to exert subtle pressure upon it, pushing me down, squeezing and kneading all the while, so I only dimly realized I was being deliberately compelled to lie upon the stone bench.

His lips slashed across my cheek to my temple and the strands of my hair, then sought my mouth again before trailing down my throat to the hollow between my breasts. Tantalizingly, his tongue darted out to lick away the sweat that beaded the narrow valley. I inhaled sharply, half rising in protest against him, but like a bee sucking nectar from a flower, he buried his face in my chest, weighing me down, oblivious of my sudden demurring.

Without warning, an overwhelming uneasiness now began to pervade my body as he stretched himself atop me, his lips crushing mine, his hands roaming where they willed. I became uncomfortably aware of the coarse edges of the stone bench digging into my bare shoulders, abrading my tender skin. But although hurtful, the raw ache was blunted by the far more potent thrust of Nicky's bold, rigid maleness insinuating itself between my thighs, rubbing against me suggestively through my skirts.

In my champagne-clouded mind, a dull but insistent alarm rang; for in truth, I had not intended things to go this far. I was, after all, gently bred, and although I had been blessed—or cursed, some said—with the Chandler wild streak, I was not so brash and foolish as to surrender my virginity to a man who was not my husband.

Trying valiantly to clear my befuddled senses, I started to struggle against him, imploring him to take me back to the ballroom. But to my shock, Nicky ignored me, crudely plunging his hand deep inside my bodice to fondle one naked breast instead. I was stunned and horrified, for surely, he would never have dared to take such a liberty had I not previously led him on, behaving as no lady ought if she wished to keep her virtue and reputation intact. Now, genuinely frightened and understanding all too clearly the dreadful wrong I had done, I began to fight him earnestly, desperately, begging him to let me up. But Nicky paid no heed to my pleas.

"Don't you love me, Laura?" he asked, his mouth against mine, his fingers taunting my nipple roughly, almost cruelly, evoking a humiliating mixture of pleasure and pain within me.

"Yes, of course, I do! You know I do!" I exclaimed, aggrieved that he should doubt me.

"Then show me," he goaded purposefully. "Show

me! Let me love you as you were meant to be loved—
or are you nothing but a liar and a tease after all?'' he
snarled, his eyes suddenly growing hard as flint in the
moonlight.

Stung by his vindictive words, I bit my lip uncertainly,
afraid of giving in to him, but just as afraid of losing
him if I did not. Before I realized what he was about,
he took advantage of my momentary indecision to yank
my sleeves down over my elbows, exposing my breasts
to his avid gaze.

''Ahhhhh,'' he sighed, his hands fastening upon my
soft, heaving flesh. ''What a beautiful, bountiful feast
you offer me, Laura—and I am a man starving. . . .''
Gasping, I tried to push him away, to cover myself, but
he caught my arms easily, pinioning them above my
head. ''Don't fight me, Laura,'' he muttered thickly as
I writhed beneath him in a wasted effort to free myself,
for he was much stronger than I. ''You know you want
this as much as I do.''

And to my utter shame, much as I longed to deny it,
some part of me did, some terrible, treacherous part of
me thrilled to his touch as, his insidious eyes never leaving my face, he slowly lowered his mouth to one nipple
and seized it between his teeth. A scalding sensation
flooded through me as his tongue scorched me with its
liquid fire. I gave a muted cry—but of passion or fear,
I did not know.

''Laura? Laura, is that you?''

''My God!'' Nicky swore at the sound of the voice
we both recognized at once. His head jerked up abruptly;
his nostrils flared like those of a wily animal scenting

danger. "'Tis Jarrett!" He scrambled off me so frantically that he nearly fell, running one hand hastily through his hair in a futile attempt to comb it into some semblance of order. "For Christ's sake, Laura!" he hissed. "Hurry up and compose yourself! Jarrett has sharp, jealous eyes and a devilish temper, and he'd kill any man he found trifling with you!"

His words echoed Angelique's warnings earlier about Jarrett's explosive disposition. Now, certain there must be some cause, after all, for both of them to insist Jarrett was wicked in a rage, I sat up, as terrified as Nicky, my hands shaking so badly that I could hardly control them as I fumbled rapidly to order my appearance. Shuddering with panic at the sound of Jarrett's calling me impatiently, at the ominous approach of his footsteps as, in search of me, he entered the gardens, I snatched up my sleeves and tugged at my bodice like a madwoman to straighten it. Then my trembling fingers flew to my hair, where, in my haste, I jammed a loose hairpin in so hard and at such an awkward angle that it punctured my scalp. I winced with pain, tears stinging my eyes. But there was no time to feel sorry for myself; every second was precious. Spying my gold fan and reticule lying upon the clammy ground beside the stone bench, where they had fallen earlier during my impassioned tussle with Nicky, I bent to retrieve them, scrubbing frenziedly at a small, damp grass stain on my bag, which seemed to stand out like an enormous, condemnatory blot.

"Damn!" Nicky cursed as he grappled with his askew cravat. "Why must you be *Jarrett's* fiancée? Brother or not, he'll murder me! Isn't there any other way out of here?'' he asked, looking around wildly at the arbor, which was enclosed on three sides by a tall hedge. ''Lord in heaven, *hurry up*, Laura!''

''I'm hurrying as fast as I can!'' I spat, indignant and overwrought. ''Besides, 'tis all *your* fault anyway! If only you'd listened to me when I first entreated you to take me back inside, none of this would be happening now! Oh, God, Nicky! Why don't we just tell Jarrett the truth—that we're in love with each other, and always have been? Surely, he'll understand. Surely, he'll release me from my engagement to him then, and we can be married.''

To my horror, Nicky stared at me as though I were insane.

''Are you mad, Laura?'' he cried heatedly, stabbing me to the core with his unthinking confirmation of my suspicion. Then, seeing the stricken expression upon my countenance, he recovered and coaxed more gently, ''Don't be a fool, darling. Now is not the time or the place to make such an announcement. Surely, you can see that! Jarrett's bound to be angry—if for no other reason than because his damnable pride will be wounded—and doubtless, he'll start an argument. There'll be trouble then—perhaps even a brawl—you know there will be! And people will hear us, Laura. They'll come to investigate! Then just think of the scandal that will arise—and at your coming-out party, too! Surely, you don't want that, do you, darling?''

''No. No, of course not,'' I said, biting my lip.

''Then let's just keep quiet for the time being, all

right, Laura?'' At my reluctant nod, Nicky chucked me carelessly under the chin. ''There's my good girl,'' he declared approvingly. ''Now, give me a kiss, darling, for I believe 'tis best, after all, if we're not found alone here together, and so I'm going to do my damnedest to get through that hedge, one way or another.''

My emotions churning like a backwash, I moved toward him. His lips swooped down upon mine; his tongue shot deep into my mouth. Firmly, possessively, his hand closed over my breast, his thumb gliding across my nipple, deliberately recalling to my mind all we had shared this night, as though he might somehow leave his mark upon me. Despite my fear, desire once more leaped within me, and I clung to him fervidly, not caring that, in his ardor, he bent me back so far that I would have fallen had he not held me so tightly. For a long, risky moment, we dared to embrace thus, our bodies tense with craving. Then at last, loath to part from me but hearing Jarrett drawing perilously near, Nicky released me.

''Remember to keep our secret yet a while, dear Laura,'' he uttered softly. ''It won't be for long, I promise you.''

Then somehow he forced aside the spindly branches of the hedge, shouldering a path through it into the darkness. The limbs jarred by his intrusion crackled and snapped aside, then sprang shut behind him as he disappeared; several tiny leaves, jostled by his passing, floated to the earth in his wake. Heaving a sigh of relief,

I sat down upon the stone bench and began to fan myself as calmly as I could. It was not a moment too soon, for just then, Jarrett appeared.

"Laura," he said, stepping from the shadows, his black eyes hooded and unreadable in the moonlight, so I could not tell what he was thinking, though I felt he scrutinized me keenly. "What are you doing out here? Did you not hear me calling you?"

"No," I lied, praying the darkness would hide my guilty blush. "It was so—so warm in the ballroom, and so crowded. I simply had to get away for a moment, so I came outside for a breath of fresh air, and it was such a—such a beautiful night that I walked on into the gardens. I'm afraid I—I was daydreaming. This is my favorite spot, you know; I often came here as a child to while away the hours. . . ." I gave a little laugh. "Goodness! I must have lost all track of time. What will my guests think? I had best go inside at once."

"Yes." Jarrett's voice was as cool and even as always, as it would not have been, surely, if he suspected me of trysting with a lover. His eyes strayed to the fallen leaves of the hedge, but he did not remark upon them, and again, I exhaled with relief, certain he noticed naught amiss. "Aunt Sarah sent me to fetch you. 'Tis time for the midnight supper, and I'm to escort you to the dining room. Come."

He held out his hand to me, and hesitantly, I laid my palm in his. His fingers closed about mine like an iron band, and without warning, a twinge of apprehension ran through me, as though I had, with a stick, tauntingly prodded some dangerous beast. I shivered, wishing I had a shawl, as though its flimsy folds might offer me some protection—but against what, I did not know.

In silence, we returned to the house, the alluring scent of wisteria drifting on the wind to my nostrils, the bittersweet taste of forbidden passion lingering on my lips, and my hand cold as ice in Jarrett's own.

I did not see Nicholas again that night or, indeed, for many long weeks afterward, as you shall learn. Still, sometime after supper, I could not prevent myself from once more slipping out furtively to the gardens, in the fruitless hope that he would be in the arbor, longing and waiting for me to come to him. I do not know why I sought him out, especially in light of how, earlier, despite my resistance, he had almost had his way with me there. But such was my pride, my vanity, my foolishness that I believed his love for me was so strong that he could hardly contain it. Too, I blamed myself for teasing him, tempting him, when I ought to have known better. Though I had chafed at such restrictions previously, now I understood all too well why young ladies of good breeding were always so stringently chaperoned. When blood ran hot and high, it was all too easy for things to get out of hand.

Lifting my skirts, I wended my way swiftly along the fieldstone paths of the gardens, panting a little for breath, for one is not meant to run in tightly laced stays. Now and then, I cast a glance over my shoulder to be certain I was unobserved, so it happened that I did not see my cousin Thorne until, turning ahead again, I bumped squarely into him, nearly knocking us both down. Instinctively, his arms caught hold of me, steadying us both.

"Thorne!" I cried, startled, my hands fluttering to my breast, where my heart now thumped erratically. "Heavens! What a fright you gave me!"

"Running *from* a rendezvous, Laura—or *to* one?" he inquired acerbically as he released me and, frowning with annoyance, fastidiously straightened his elegant jacket and cravat, which I had accidentally disarranged.

"Neither, of course," I stated coldly, drawing myself up to my full height and giving him a hard, disdainful stare, silently refusing to disclose any explanation for my being in the gardens.

Thorne was clever; whatever excuse I made, he would guess I lied, and it would never do for him to suspect about Nicky and me. He would hold his knowledge over us like a cudgel and find some way to bludgeon us with it to his advantage, for he had never got over his hatred of Nicky, nor did he particularly like me. Still, I thought, actually, Nicky had done Thorne a favor, for over the years, my cousin had grown from a beautiful boy into an extremely handsome man, his broken nose giving his face character and a masculinity it would otherwise have lacked. He was now, as in our childhood, of medium height and slender but strong build; his gestures were markedly graceful, almost delicate, in a way that always caused me somehow to feel a slight but distinct sense of disquiet in his presence, as though there were something wrong with him that I could not quite put my finger on. I attributed my reaction to his wicked, deceitful nature that, deep down inside, I felt certain had not changed with age, but was only more cunningly concealed, and I took great pains to avoid him whenever possible.

Now, however, before I could make good my escape, I was halted by the murmur of a man's baritone voice from the arbor just beyond, the one with the Chinese wisteria tree, where I had been headed before my collision with Thorne. My body went unexpectedly rigid at the sound; my heart jerked like a puppet whose strings have been suddenly wrenched. Was it Jarrett who had spoken? Or was it . . . no, surely, it was not . . . Nicholas? No, of course not. I was imagining things. It could be anyone, anyone at all. And even if it was a Chandler whom I heard, so what? There was no reason to assume it was Nicky. How foolish! Why, it might be Alexander, or even (though I admitted this seemed most unlikely) Uncle Draco, I tried to reassure myself, for all the Chandler sons sounded like their father, and the voice was low, indistinguishable.

The man's voice was answered by a woman's throaty laugh, which I did not recognize, followed by silence, a kiss, another husky laugh (male this time), and then the unmistakable rustle of a gown as it slid along smooth, female skin. My stomach twisted itself into knots at the sound; and I knew at once that had Thorne not been at my side, I should have crept stealthily as a Peeping Tom to the arbor to spy upon its inhabitants. As it was, I could only torment myself by guessing at their identities.

"Well, well," Thorne drawled dryly. "It seems one of our arrogant Chandler cousins is engaged in a . . .

diverting bit of sport. I wonder who he has found to amuse him? What do you say, Laura? Shall we go quietly around the bend and take a peek?''

"No, of course not!'' I snapped, mortified, though his suggestion was no more than what had already crossed my mind. Still, my heart sank at his identifying, too, the voice as being that of a Chandler.

"But, why, Laura? Come, come. Are you not dying of curiosity to know who the estimable Nicholas is . . . entertaining in the Prescott arbor?''

"What makes you think 'tis Nicky in there?'' I queried, more sharply than I had intended.

"A simple but logical deduction, Laura, which is therefore why it has doubtless escaped you,'' Thorne asserted sarcastically. "Jarrett is, of course, affianced to you, and whether that counts for anything with him or not, he's certainly not foolish enough to be tumbling someone else at your own coming-out party. Now, Alexander, on the other hand, is betrothed to no one, so presumably he is free to do as he pleases. However, since he is positively dotty about Lady Vanessa Dubray, who's far too decent even to be caught dead without her chaperon, I think we can safely count him out, too. And since somehow—though I confess I find the idea *most* amusing—I just can't see our tyrannical but fiercely faithful Uncle Draco rucking up Aunt Maggie's skirts in your parents' bushes,'' he continued vulgarly, "that just leaves dear old Nicholas, doesn't it?''

"How crude you are, Thorne,'' I observed. "Frankly, I don't know who is in the arbor—nor do I really care!'' I lied. "What I *do* know, however, is that I refuse to stand here any longer like a gossiping old busybody with nothing better to do but listen to your ugly speculations!''

I would have flounced off in a huff then, but quick as a snake striking, Thorne's hand flew out to clamp cruelly about my wrist, effectively detaining me.

''Why, Laura,'' he uttered, smirking, ''I do believe you know I'm right and can't bear the thought that I am.''

It was a shot in the dark—it had to be—but still, I blanched.

''I don't know what you're talking about, Thorne,'' I said angrily, curtly yanking my arm free and massaging the spot he had bruised with his fingers.

''Don't you?'' he asked.

''No! And I don't think you do either. In fact, I believe you must be drunk, or mad, or both, for 'tis quite obvious your wits are excessively addled!''

With that, I turned on my heel and left him, his soft, jeering laughter ringing like a hyena's in my ears, so I knew he had not been fooled one whit by my heated words of denial. I was too upset to care. It just couldn't be Nicky in the arbor! It just couldn't be! I thought, on the verge of tears.

Still, despite myself, the reasons Thorne had so spitefully given me for concluding that it was indeed Nicky gnawed at me, leaving a festering wound; and so the remainder of what had been, up until now, the most wonderful evening of my life was ruined. My heart ached; my previous gaiety and triumph now tasted as dry and bitter as ashes in my mouth. As soon as I could after returning to the ballroom, I informed Mama that I was exhausted, and that I had a splitting headache besides.

"I'm not surprised, Laura," she told me, her eyes filled with concern and understanding, as, with one hand, she smoothed a loose strand of hair back from my face. "I felt the same way the night of my debut ball at your granduncle Nigel's town house in London, so tired from all the excitement that I couldn't have danced another step, even if I'd wanted to—which I didn't, since none of my partners meant anything to me, except your father." She smiled gently, fondly, at the memory, so that now, shamed by the thought of her honesty and goodness in contrast to my own duplicitous, immodest behavior this evening, I could no longer meet her gaze. "Why don't you go on upstairs to bed, Laura. You really *do* look done in. Don't worry about anything here. I'll make your excuses to our guests and send Clemency up to you straightaway."

Swallowing hard, I nodded and turned away, grateful Mama could not see into my heart. Slowly, I climbed the stairs to my room. But though I waited and waited, Clemency did not come up until later, much later, so I had already undressed, got into bed, and nearly cried myself to sleep when she finally did arrive. To my surprise, she was flushed and out of breath, as though she had been running; her green eyes sparkled with elation, and a sly, secretive smile of satisfaction curved her lips.

She must have been flirting with one of the footmen

again, I decided wearily, *and has doubtless made a conquest of the poor, besotted dolt.*

In light of my own dispiritedness, I could not bear the smug look upon her pointed face, and dully, I sent her away, not even bothering to question her about her tardiness in attending me. As she exited my chamber, however, I noticed bits of something pale and airy, like lavender confetti, drift from her hair, strewing the carpet in her wake, and despite myself, roused by curiosity, I rose to see what it was.

I did not sleep for a very long time after that, but sat, staring numbly at the fragile wisteria petals I held crushed in my hand—torturing myself with questions for which I did not truly want to know the answers.

Chapter V

The Fox Hunt

What men or gods are these? What maidens loth?
What mad pursuit? What struggle to escape?
What pipes and timbrels? What wild ecstasy?

—*Ode on a Grecian Urn*
John Keats

A fortnight later, Papa and Mama whisked me away on my first trip to London, for my formal debut. I should have looked forward eagerly to this had I not been so downcast; but as it was, I had no chance to see Nicholas before I left, and so, tortured by painful suspicion and with a heavy heart, I climbed into our well-sprung carriage and took my place upon the plush velvet seat.

Despite my wishing it were otherwise, deep down inside, I now felt sure somehow that it had indeed been Nicky in the arbor the night of my coming-out party, and

I could hardly stand to look at Clemency as she settled herself beside me, for it was she who, I surmised, had been with him. Why else should she have had wisteria blossoms in her hair that evening? There could be no other reason except that, sometime during the night, she had gone to the arbor, for there was only one Chinese wisteria tree in the gardens.

I thought of her grandiose schemes to get ahead in the world, and I felt sick inside when I remembered her exultant smile upon entering my bedroom. What had it portended? Had Nicky, wanting to get even with me for teasing him, as he had accused me of doing, held her, kissed her, perhaps even made love to her? Had he whispered sweet promises in her ear, as he had in mine? I knew I could not bear it if he had; but still, a tiny voice inside me whispered mockingly that it would be no more than I deserved for tempting him when I'd had no intention of giving in to him. Had I not been warned on numerous occasions about the hazards of a woman's permitting a man to take liberties with her? If Nicky had sought solace from my maid, surely, I had no one to blame but myself! Nevertheless, the thought did not lessen my heartache, and my fingers itched to scratch the cool, complacent expression from Clemency's face.

Huddling in the corner of the coach, as far away from her as possible, I eyed her sharply through my lowered lashes.

Surely, I must be mistaken, I told myself for the hundredth time, in a futile attempt to reassure myself. *Perhaps it was indeed only one of the footmen with whom she dallied in the arbor.*

Still, if such were the case, I could not think why she should have looked so jubilant that evening, for I knew that, while she was not above amusing herself by playing the coquette, she was far too ambitious to waste herself on a mere servant, who would be of little use in furthering her high-flown aspirations. But Nicky was another matter entirely. While he might not be Uncle Draco's heir, his position and income were not to be sneered at; and though I could not imagine his father permitting him to wed Clemency, I felt certain my worldly-wise uncle would raise few objections if Nicky chose to take her as his mistress.

And so, my heart like an apple worm-eaten with doubt and jealousy, I had for once checked my impulsive emotions and said naught to Papa and Mama about wanting to break off my engagement to Jarrett. I would wait, I had decided, and speak with Nicky before determining a course of action. How horrible it would be if there was, in truth, no basis for my speculations and, in a fit of unreasoning pique, I stupidly cast aside the man I loved. But how much worse, I had thought, if I foolishly scorned Jarrett's suit and then discovered Nicky was only trifling with my affections after all. I should not only hurt and embarrass my parents terribly and needlessly, and rouse Uncle Draco's ire for naught, too, but I should be the laughingstock of northern Cornwall. I was not so reckless and senseless as that!

If Nicky could set to rest my fears—and I devoutly prayed he could—I would willingly face the gossip sure to ensue at my rejecting Jarrett for him. Otherwise, torn with anguish, I knew I would have no choice but to put aside what was in my heart and become Jarrett's wife.

I did not like London, which, to one who had been reared on the sweeping Cornish coast, seemed a place of cinders, clutter, and confinement. In the teeming city, on the dirty, narrow streets lined with town houses and packed with people and conveyances, I was sometimes reminded unpleasantly of the afternoon when Thorne had locked me in the stifling trunk in the attic and I had thought I would suffocate.

Further, I did not care for society, which certainly opened its doors wide enough to permit me and my dowry to enter, but which, even so, could not refrain, I felt, from sniffing my skirts suspiciously for the vulgar smell of trade.

Though, like any girl, I had secretly hoped to be the toast of the Season, this ambition was unrealized, for I was not what was commonly acclaimed as beautiful; and although there were many young bucks eager enough to fly in the face of convention and pronounce me "arresting," it was clear to me from their pockets, which were, for the most part, sadly to let, that it was not I, but my fortune that prompted their remarks.

I was greatly insulted by the fact that they thought me so simple and unperceptive that I would believe that their flattery was genuine, and I must confess I took petty revenge by flirting with them all, raising their false hopes to the point that two of them, their straits more desperate than the rest, actually came to blows over me.

I would have found this most gratifying had Nicholas

been present to witness it, for I must admit I would have liked to make him envious of a rival, as he had me; but he came to London only once during the Season, when sent up by his father on business. The evening of his arrival, he joined us at Almack's, but as I had nothing left on my program but a lively country dance, we had no opportunity for private conversation; and when next I had a moment to spare, I discovered he had already gone. Thus I had no chance to learn whether he was indeed angry with me over what had happened in the arbor the night of my coming-out party and had comforted himself with Clemency.

I was, of course, hurt and disappointed by his departure, but not really surprised, for Almack's, often referred to as "the Marriage Mart," was primarily an establishment that catered to young misses who had just emerged from the schoolroom and were now in search of a husband. Since no strong drink was served and the gaming stakes were strictly limited, I supposed Nicky had not found the entertainment very appealing.

Nevertheless, I thought he might at least have stayed for my sake, and I could not help but compare his behavior to that of Jarrett, who arrived a few days later and was punctilious about escorting me both to Covent Garden and the theater in Drury Lane before taking his leave of the city. Nicky certainly could use some lessons in manners from his older brother! Even if he *were* wroth with me for teasing him, he ought to have considered my feelings in the matter, too; and in my heart, my doubt about whether he truly cared for me after all took firm root and began to grow.

* * *

With the coming of summer, my Season ended, and I returned home to Cornwall, a trifle more worldly and sophisticated than when I had left, but, I'm afraid, little wiser.

It was good to be home. I had missed the moors and the sea, and now, every morning, I rode out upon my fine, spirited horse, my coming-out gift from Papa and Mama. I had christened the gelding Black Buccaneer, for he was one of Uncle Draco's stock, all of which were descended from a single, fierce stallion, Black Magic, and a wild, moorish mare. In honor of the magnificent stud, which had had to be destroyed because of a broken leg, all the true-black get produced of his line had the word "black" prefixed to their names. Uncle Draco seldom parted with these colts and fillies, selling only those that bore traces of white upon their coats or that were other colors. Being a true black, Black Buccaneer was obviously an exception to this rule. However, since I hadn't wished to annoy Uncle Draco, I had continued his tradition of names, calling my gelding after the pirates of yore, as I had my childhood pony, Calico Jack; for I was fascinated by Papa's tales of them and intrigued to think the ships of some of my ancestors had flown the Jolly Roger from their masts.

With the exception of Uncle Draco's stock, there were few horses in northern Cornwall to touch Black Buccaneer in speed, and I loved racing over the commons, with the exhilarating rush of the wind against my face and streaming through my hair, and the salty tang of the ocean's spume in my nostrils.

Sometimes I dismounted to climb the green-and-grey tors, where massive slabs of granite, which resembled the megaliths of Stonehenge and other such ancient rings of stone, stood, forming eerie shapes against the stark horizon. There were upon the tors rocks that looked like ruins of temples built by pagans to the old gods. Tall slabs eroded by the ceaseless elements leaned into one another as though pushed over by some giant hand; others, which had fallen to the ground or had the earth wrested away to expose their flat tops, lay at the centers of the rest like sacrificial altars waiting for blood to be spilled upon them.

To the north, Brown Willy towered like a misshapen obelisk over the other, smaller tors, while Brown Gelly crouched to the south, a lumbering mass. Kilmar Tor, looming over that part of Bodmin Moor that was called East Moor, was a titanic, maimed fist clawing its way up from the ground, knuckles reaching for the heavens. Below the crag, Trewartha Marsh stretched its way across the heaths that now, with the onslaught of summer, were patched like a crazy quilt in hues of green and gold. Heather and bracken filled the air with their sweet scent, as did the stunted shrubs of flowering broom with spindly branches grown sideways from the lash of the wind that blew always upon the commons.

The breeze was gentle now, causing scarcely a ripple in the grass or the springs and streams to be found here and there upon the moors. But in autumn and winter, it moaned like a sorrowful ghost or shouted like a mighty god, its shrieks wending through the cracks and crevices of the granite to send chills up one's spine before its echo faded, only to begin again. Then the grass and gorse would shudder and flatten as though trodden upon by some colossal foot; the stagnant, slate-colored pools that dotted the marshes would churn and bubble and turn black as the night sky over Cornwall, and the bog islands buoyed up by the murky water would tremble.

These last were dangerous places, where, amid the grass now yellowing beneath the hot summer sun, tufts with browning tips and sprouting tangled gold strands grew to deceive the unwary, the unsuspecting. Here, a man might step forward and find instead of ground beneath his feet only a thin layer of weeds and slime, and he would fall through it into the black, peat-tinged water and drown. It was easy to spy the treacherous pools now, but in autumn and winter, even I, who had been born and reared in northern Cornwall and knew every inch of this bleak, rugged terrain, did not care to be upon the heaths when the sky darkened and the fog rolled in from the sea to cover the grim, uncompromising land with a thick blanket of white. But for now, I roamed where I willed, Black Buccaneer my only companion.

From the tops of the tors, one could see the ocean shimmering in the distance, reflecting the azure of the endless sky, and the long, gnarled fingers of black rock that dipped into the sea, where the ruins of Tintagel Castle rose at the end of the narrow causeway linking it to the jagged headland. There, Uncle Draco and Aunt Maggie had played together in their youth; and there, too, off the shore, Papa had anchored his first ship, the *Sea Gypsy*, and his men had rowed their smuggled cargo to the slender strip of shingled beach, to be carried up the steep, winding tracks that cleaved the cliffs, where Uncle Draco or his lunatic caretaker, Renshaw, would be waiting with a string of pack ponies to transport the stolen goods to Stormswept Heights.

Papa and Uncle Draco had nearly been caught once, by Uncle Esmond, who was the local magistrate. But luckily, they had managed to conceal their own activities, while exposing the far more heinous crimes of the murderous Mick Dyson and his ruthless band of wreckers.

Farther east, like a chain of white mountains, the chalky residue heaped high upon the earth scarred by the excavated pits of Uncle Draco's china-clay mines, where Dyson had once concealed his ill-gotten gains, stretched across Bodmin Moor. At their edges lay vast greenish pools, formed when tons of dirt and granite were hewn from the ground and the china clay itself was washed into the deep pits and separated from the quartz.

It was a dangerous operation, and so I avoided the mines whenever I could, even though I knew I might catch a glimpse of Nicholas there. I had not seen him since returning home. Kept busy with his work, he had not come to the Grange, nor could I think of a plausible excuse for seeking him out at the Heights. Once or twice, I considered taking my brother Guy into my confidence and enlisting his aid; but even though Nicky was his best friend, I could not help but feel that Guy would be shocked to learn I was hankering after Nicky when I was engaged to Jarrett. So, in the end, I said naught to my brother, wishing to spare myself a chastening lecture.

My only consolation was that, as summer wore on, Clemency appeared to lose her previous buoyancy, and I was able to hope that if it had indeed been she and Nicky in the arbor that evening, he had merely been indulging a passing fancy born of his pique at me and had no real interest in her. This cheering notion helped to mitigate some of my earlier doubt about the sincerity of his affections, and now I longed for nothing more than to put matters aright between us.

This, I hoped to have a chance soon to accomplish, if not before, then at Uncle Esmond's fox hunt, which took place every year at the end of summer. It was an event much looked forward to by family, friends, and acquaintances alike, and those who received invitations came from miles around for both the sport and the ball that followed. It would be my first time to attend, but I knew that Nicky hadn't missed the fox hunt since his sixteenth birthday, and I was determined Black Buccaneer and I would be ready to keep pace with him.

This was the primary reason for my early morning jaunts, during which I went carefully over the surrounding terrain so I would be aware of any possible obstacles that might lie in my path during the chase; for I had no wish to be ignominiously unseated, as my cousin Elizabeth, who was not an adept horsewoman, often was. It would not suit my plans at all for me to appear a fool before Nicky, and so, no matter what course the fox chose to run, I intended to be prepared.

In dogged pursuit of my quarry, I never dreamed my way would be blocked by a barrier so solid and insurmountable that even I could not overcome it.

* * *

Summer lingered fitfully that year of 1841, as though loath to take its leave, though, here and there, the leaves of the trees had already begun to turn crimson and saffron, and the crisp, chilly scent of autumn permeated the air. On the morning of Uncle Esmond's fox hunt, the earth, after the previous night's rain, was soft and muddy beneath the hooves of the fretful horses; the trees were damp with mist borne on the cool wind from the sullen sea in the distance, and droplets glistening like dew beaded the shoulders of the scarlet- and black-coated riders who had passed under low-hanging branches in the park encompassing Highclyffe Hall to assemble at its fore.

Now that most were present, the front lawn was alive with cacophony and confusion; the excited barking of the foxhounds straining impatiently at the leash rang out sharply amid the shouted greetings and laughter of the milling crowd gathered, despite the leaden sky, for the meet. Horses snorted and nickered, stamped and shivered in the wet, and occasionally nipped or kicked at one another, while their riders fought to keep a tight rein upon them, hampered by the jarring crack of whips as the huntsman and whippers-in struggled to control the dogs. Footmen bearing sterling-silver trays heavily laden with refreshments scurried to and from the house, while inside, those guests not participating in the event helped themselves to a lavish breakfast from the dining-room sideboard.

Uncle Esmond, the master of the hunt, looked resplendent in his black velvet cap, scarlet jacket, white cravat, and white silk breeches, although I thought he seemed ill at ease as, mounted upon his elegant bay gelding, he moved among the arrivals to welcome them. It was well known throughout the countryside that he did not truly care for fox hunting and, after Granduncle Nigel's death, had reluctantly resumed the tradition at the Hall only at the insistence of Aunt Julianne and my grandmother Prescott Chandler. He was joined in his aversion to the sport by Mama, who did not ride to the hounds at all, and by Aunt Maggie, who rode but refused to be in at the kill and who, much to Uncle Draco and Papa's chagrin, frequently suggested to Uncle Esmond that he set the dogs upon a drag scent so there would be no brutal end to the chase.

I must admit I shared her sympathy for the fox and thus was not looking forward to its demise. This was my first hunt, and I knew, therefore, that if I were up at the death, I would doubtless be blooded, an unpleasant ceremony but one not without its own rewards—or so my cousin Angelique had assured me. Despite her claims to the contrary, the prospect remained unappealing, and deliberately, I pushed it from my mind, determined it should not spoil my day.

Earlier, Papa, Mama, and Guy had disappeared into the throng, leaving me to my own devices, but so far, I had been content to stay a little apart from the rest, watching them and searching covertly for Nicholas. Now, however, as I spied Angelique hailing me from atop her beautiful mare, Black Orchid, I nudged Black Buccaneer toward the circle of riders congregated about her, certain Nicky would be found nearby. My heart leaped when I saw that my assumption was correct, and adroitly, as I approached the small, boisterous bunch, I managed to maneuver my horse between his and Angelique's. Not one to miss such a stratagem, Angelique's lip curled faintly with wry amusement as she caught my eye; then she shook her head slightly at me in the way that one does when washing one's hands of a matter. At first, I thought she would make some embarrassing remark; however, much to my surprise and relief, she held her tongue, introducing me instead to her escort, Lord Oliver Fairhurst, Earl of Greystone, whom I had not previously met.

He was a dark, handsome, cynical man, for whom, I suspected, she had set her cap, and as, like all the Chandlers, she was relentless in pursuit of her ambitions, I supposed she would catch him. Nodding to each other, Lord Greystone and I dutifully exchanged the appropriate platitudes; then, shortly thereafter, he and Angelique, obviously intent on each other, drifted away, freeing me to turn my full attention to Nicky at last.

At the back of my mind, I surmised that leaving me alone with her brother had been Angelique's design all along, and briefly, I wondered why she had previously warned me against becoming enamored of him and now seemingly sought to further the entanglement. But then I thought of the strong sibling rivalry prevalent among the Chandlers; and I decided Angelique was not, for her own entertainment, above adding a few lumps of coal to simmering fires between her two older brothers, regardless of how much she loved them. It was a game my Chandler cousins played, as though they were animal cubs who must constantly test their wits and skills upon one another to ensure they would be fully prepared when the day came that they were cast out to fend for themselves, to survive or die in a world that was not kind to its inhabitants.

Abruptly, I thrust Angelique from my mind. I did not care what her motives in assisting me had been. It was enough that she had done so.

From beneath my lashes, my eyes devoured Nicky greedily, as though I must hoard in my memory every detail of his image, to console me when he was not present. I thought there had never been a more dashing figure than the one he cut this morning astride his black gelding, his black top hat perched rakishly upon his head, his black jacket and white breeches hugging his lithe form like a second skin, a spill of frothy lace at his throat and wrists, knee-high black leather boots gleaming upon his feet. He sat his saddle easily. One hand grasped his mount's reins lightly, expertly; from the other, his quirt dangled casually, so his demeanor seemed one of facility, of grace. Nevertheless, I, who knew him well, sensed a subtle tenseness, a discord in him that I believed sprang from excitement and desire as his eyes met mine; and of its own volition, my body started to tremble, my heart to beat wildly in my breast.

"Hullo, Laura," he said quietly, his low voice like a caress to my ears as he reined his horse, Blackjack, nearer to mine, deftly edging us away from the rowdy group that surrounded us, as though to gain for us a few moments of privacy before the hunt.

Hope stirred within me at the gesture, for it meant that even if he had not forgiven me for teasing him the night of my coming-out party, at least he did not despise me for it.

"Hullo, Nicky," I answered softly, feeling, despite my gladness at his proximity, yet a trifle shy and uncertain with him now that I was not fortified with Dutch courage, as I had been that evening in the gardens.

"You're in rare good looks this morning," he observed. "Black becomes you, Laura." His eyes roamed appreciatively over my new, somber but exquisite silk bowler hat and riding habit, de rigueur black like his, for only the master, huntsman, whippers-in, as well as a few privileged others, were permitted to don velvet caps and scarlet coats. "You should wear it more often. Are you ready for the hunt? Your first, is it not?"

"Yes, I've been practicing for weeks so I shan't take a tumble," I admitted. "Still, I hope the course won't prove too difficult."

"Oh, I shouldn't worry about that, if I were you," he reassured me. "You've excellent form, and besides, you can always ride around any jumps that are too high. Unlike *some* of our relations I could mention"—his eyes slid with disgust toward Elizabeth, who, a short distance away, had arranged herself prettily beneath a Cornish elm and was flirting shamelessly with the company of young bucks she had collected about her—"you've too much sense to risk Black Buccaneer's breaking a leg. Father would never have sold him to Uncle Welles for you otherwise."

"Yes, I know."

After that, a little silence fell between us, somehow taut and awkward as a tightrope, as though we were strangers groping for a common ground. It disconcerted me, this perfectly ordinary conversation, this uncomfortable lapse, for it was not at all what I had expected. From beneath half-closed lids, I could see a muscle working in Nicky's jaw, and I longed fervently to ask if he was still angry with me, if it had indeed been he and Clemency in the arbor that night. But what one fantasizes doing and what one actually does in reality are often two very different things, as I have come to learn; and to my dismay, now that I had Nicky to myself, I found I was not brave enough to blurt out the questions that plagued me. So I chewed at my lower lip and said nothing, nervously smoothing a wrinkle from the long skirt of my riding habit instead, then fiddling studiedly with the trailing ends of my reins, no longer able to meet his penetrating gaze.

I could not help but remember what had passed between us that evening in the gardens, and I blushed with mortification to recall it. Yet I could still feel his mouth upon mine, his hands upon my body, his lips pressed to my burning flesh, and perversely, there was within me, too, an unspeakable wish to know these things again.

Perhaps Nicky thought of them also, for suddenly, he cleared his throat and slid his fingers beneath the circle of his stock, back and forth, once, twice, as though it were too tight. Then, becoming aware of the fidgety motion, he ceased it and dropped his hand to his side.

"Would you care for a stirrup cup, Laura?" he asked finally, breaking the stillness between us. At my nod, he beckoned curtly to one of the servants, who approached with a tray upon which the traditional farewell libations offered to departing riders were artfully arrayed. "Will you have mulled wine or brandy?"

"Wine, please," I said.

Nicky grasped a steaming mug and thrust it into my hand, then selected a glass of cognac for himself. The footman moved away. Silent once more, we sipped our drinks. The wine tasted good upon my tongue; its spicy heat and fragrance pervaded my nostrils, settled warm and sweet in my empty belly, taking the chill from my bones. A few more swallows, and lassitude began to slog a sluggish course through my body, so I was all the more startled when, without warning, Nicky snarled a crude oath and impulsively hurled his snifter to the ground. It bounced once, miraculously intact, and for a moment seemed suspended in midair, a delicate glass ball tossed by a careless juggler, sparkling like a prism as a stray shaft of dull light caught and illuminated the crystal. Fleetingly, the tiny rainbow it cast flitted like a butterfly across the lawn, then darkened and disappeared as the brandy sloshed forth in a spray of amber to fall like flecks of liquid gold upon the grass. The snifter cracked, a single shard flying away from the whole as it rolled across the yard. Nicky's horse, frightened by his abrupt, unexpected action, whinnied anxiously and tossed its head, white-eyed; it danced and sidestepped; one hard, solid hoof stamped upon the fragile crystal, smashing it to splinters, completing its ruin.

Speechless, I stared at Nicky, not knowing what had brought about his display of temper, but fearing instinctively that I was the cause.

"Damn it, Laura!" he swore, his voice throbbing with

emotion. "We are cousins . . . lovers—not chance acquaintances who must mouth polite banalities to each other for lack of anything else to discuss!" His face was dark and harsh with wrath; his jaw was set—perhaps as much against himself as me—for briefly, he glanced away, as though warring inwardly with himself, before turning back to me. "Damn Father for keeping me so busy all summer that I've scarce had a minute to call my own!" he growled. Then, both his visage and tone softening, he said, "I've missed you, Laura."

Though the day was yet miserably grey, for me, it was suddenly as though the sun shone on the horizon. My heart swelled to bursting with happiness and relief, and I thought what a fool I had been ever to doubt him, who loved me so. Now, seeing how tenderly he caressed me with his eyes, I was stricken with shame and remorse at how, faithless and eaten up with jealousy, I had allowed my ugly suspicions to run rampant in my heart and mind, had tormented myself and cursed him, the beloved source of my anguish, for naught. I did not need to ask my questions now; I had my answers as surely as though he had spoken them aloud.

Driven by my own insecurity and Thorne's malicious words, I had falsely accused and condemned Nicky, who had been innocent of the crime with which I had charged him. I felt sure of that now. It had not been he who had dallied with Clemency in the arbor beneath the Chinese wisteria tree; it had not been he who had pressed her down upon the stone bench there, but some other—Jarrett or Alexander, I guessed; I did not know or care which.

"Oh, Nicky," I breathed, my heart in my eyes, "I've missed you, too."

His smile was as bright and beautiful to me as a rainbow after a storm. But there was no time to say more, for just then, the hunting horn blew, the two notes that issued from its copper tube low and melodious but somehow strangely carrying, so they echoed hauntingly through the morning air.

Setting his heels to his big bay's sides, Uncle Esmond trotted down the long drive that wound through the park, scattering gravel in his wake. At his heels were the huntsman and the hounds, fifteen couples, as they were counted, loosed now from their leashes, yelping with anticipation, haunches swaying, long tails held aloft and waving like gay banners. Close behind the pack rode the whippers-in, whips snapping to keep the dogs moving forward in line, and the terrier men, bearing the fox terriers that would be sent down after the prey should it bolt into a den or hidey-hole. A few days before the hunt, such refuges were temporarily plugged by the earth stoppers, but there was always a chance one had escaped their notice. Singly, in pairs, or in clusters, the riders, grooms, and second horsemen followed.

"I'll lay you a bouquet against a kiss that I beat you to the finish, Laura!" Nicky laughed as he called the brazen challenge over his shoulder, having quickly wheeled his gelding about, while I, taken unaware, was leaning over to deposit my empty mug upon a passing servant's tray.

The mulled wine had done its work.

"You're on!" I shot back recklessly, eyes sparkling, cheeks flushed as I galloped after him, uncaring that the footman, though his impassive face gave no evidence of it, could not have failed to hear the proffered wager or my scandalous reply.

Swept up in the excitement of the gamble and the chase, I did not realize other ears had listened, too; nor did I spy the rider who cantered after me determinedly from the shadowed shelter of the trees, in pursuit of quarry that, in his mind, bore more resemblance to a jackal than a fox.

Once beyond the gates of the manor, the dogs spread out to draw the covert, in this case a thick tangle of broom upon the moors, where it was thought the fox would be found. After scant minutes of sniffing, the hounds picked up the scent. However, this was hardly as surprising as one would have thought, since it was widely rumored that, every year, Aunt Julianne bribed the head gamekeeper to smuggle a bagman there early the morning of the hunt to assure that her guests were not disappointed. The dogs commenced to bay, and the huntsman cheered and blasted his horn to signal their find.

"Tally-ho!" Uncle Esmond cried, somehow mustering at least a tolerable appearance of enthusiasm for the sport. "Tally-ho!"

The chase had begun. By this time, the sky had lightened, though it was still the shade of old pewter and marred by a patina of darker, scudding clouds that threatened further rain. But the mist had lifted only slightly; here and there, it drifted ghostily across the heaths, white and moist, and lay curled like waves of foam in the hollows of the land, hiding treacherous terrain.

The air reverberated with the barking of the hounds, the jingle of bridles, the labored breathing of horses and riders alike, the muffled thudding of hooves sinking into the sodden ground. Black, peaty soil oozed and sucked at its trespassers, rapidly becoming a mire as the pack and field streamed across it. Clumps of mud churned up by the foremost riders flew, daubing the lathered mounts and soberly tailored riding habits of those who followed.

Tears stung my eyes as the cool wind lashed my face and tore at the hair neatly coiled at my nape. More than one strand jerked free of its confining pins as I jockeyed for position alongside the rest, skirting slate-colored pools and sailing over stones and patches of bog I knew the deceptive mist concealed; for there was no part of these moors I did not know by heart, had not explored all summer so I should be certain of my path now. Exhilarated, I laughed aloud as I cleared a low, natural wall of granite and felt Black Buccaneer come down solidly beneath me, his powerful muscles surging against my calves pressed close to his left side.

The field was starting to thin and spread now, like an army of marching ants, as the better, surer riders pulled away from the others. I could see Papa and Uncle Draco in the lead, their spirited stallions racing neck and neck as they drew near to, and then surpassed, Uncle Esmond, which was quite rude, since he was the master of the hunt. They jeered good-naturedly at him, too, I had no doubt, when they overtook him. But he did not appear to mind, jauntily saluting them with his riding crop instead, thus acknowledging their superior skill. I had no hope of catching them, of course, I knew; but I was resolved to best Nicholas at least, who was some yards ahead of me and, much to my discomfiture, speedily lengthening the distance between us. Spurred on by the thought of his winning our bet, I set my jaw firmly, urging Black Buccaneer to a faster and, on the slick ground, more dangerous pace.

Sighting the fox at last, the huntsman gave the traditional hollo, a high-pitched yell, which was followed by another mellifluous sounding of his horn; and the pack and field pressed on eagerly. The fox was approximately seventy-five yards ahead, I judged, running this way and that as it dodged among the cover of the twisted gorse, only an occasional flash of copper fur revealing its whereabouts. But the dogs were hard on its track, frenzied by the sight and scent of it, and I knew it would have to be very clever to escape from them. I had little expectation that it would succeed; but to my secret delight, several minutes later, at a rivulet just beyond a small rise, the wily creature did indeed give them the slip. The gurgling water brought the hounds once more to their noses, but although they sniffed the soaked earth zealously in all directions, it was plain that they could no longer detect the scent.

While the dogs continued to mill about, baffled and perturbed by the apparent vanishing of their prey, the lead riders reluctantly reined in their mounts to confer with Uncle Esmond, the huntsman, and the whippers-in. A short distance away, the field also dutifully came to a halt to await the master's verdict, and thus I was able finally to pull up alongside Nicky, earning a gleeful chortle for my pains.

"Lucky for you the pack lost the scent, Laura," he declared. "You'd never have caught up with me otherwise."

"Hmph!" I snorted indignantly. "That's what you think! Why, a few more minutes, and you'd have been eating my mud!"

He grinned.

"We'll see, Laura. We'll see."

"That, we will," I retorted, patting Black Buccaneer's sweating neck proudly. "At least this time, we'll start out even. That was hardly sporting of you before . . . issuing your challenge when you were already halfway down the drive!"

"But, darling, I never play fair—not in love *or* war," he insisted, his voice, despite its bantering tone, holding a curious note, so that, for a moment, I half wondered if he spoke in earnest.

"I'll remember that," I told him.

"See that you do, Laura, my pet, for I shouldn't like you to say I didn't warn you—especially once you've lost our wager and must pay your forfeit."

There was an odd glint in his eyes now, I thought, hard, supercilious even, it seemed; but perhaps it was only my imagination or a trick of the light or mist, for when next I glanced at him, it was gone and he was smiling at me in a way that brought a blush to my cheeks. So I paid no further heed to his words, believing he had been jesting with me after all.

Before I could reply, however, Uncle Esmond and the

others concluded their deliberations and began to move off, evidently having elected to take the pack eastward and fan out across the commons, in the hope of relocating the fox's scent. While the whippers-in called the hounds to order, the huntsman signaled the master's judgment to the riders, and as the urgency of the chase had momentarily been curtailed by the evasiveness of its quarry, the field set forth at a leisurely gait, so Nicky and I were able to continue our dialogue as we trotted along.

"I hope Uncle Esmond knows what he's about—carting us all off in this direction," he commented glumly, "for I should certainly hate to spend the rest of the day slopping around in this muck for naught."

"Yes," I agreed. "We really didn't have much of a run before the fox got away, did we?"

"No—and Aunt Julianne is looking none too happy about it either. Poor Uncle Esmond. I'm afraid *he'll* be the one thrown to the dogs if the pack doesn't find the scent again—and soon."

This was the truth, I thought, for despite the smile she had pasted on her face for the benefit of those watching, it was obvious to me that Aunt Julianne was berating Uncle Esmond under her breath as she bounced along in her saddle at his side. She resembled, I reflected with some amusement, a plump robin in her tight scarlet coat, her breast puffed up with indignation as she twittered and pecked at Uncle Esmond, as though he were a worm bent on escaping from her.

Fortunately for him, however, his decision to search eastward did indeed prove propitious, for scarcely a quarter of an hour passed before the hounds began to bay triumphantly once more and, some minutes later, flushed the fox from a dense stretch of heather and bracken. A coppery streak, the animal fled for its life across the moors, a hundred and fifty yards clear or more, I estimated and privately hoped it would manage to elude the pack yet again, although, as the lead dogs were in hot pursuit of it, I had to admit this did not seem likely.

"Gone awaaaaay! Gone awaaaaay!" Uncle Draco and Papa shouted in unison at the top of their lungs, spurring their horses to a gallop as once more the huntsman's resonant horn blared.

A daredevil grin splitting his face, a startling whoop issuing from his lips, Nicky roweled Blackjack's sides sharply, causing the gelding to bolt ahead so suddenly that I, caught off guard, was left dawdling in its wake. Mud slung up by its churning hooves flecked my face and riding habit before, gathering my wits, I bent low over Black Buccaneer's neck to croon in his ear, exhorting him forward.

Hard on Nicky's heels, I rode, the mist like spindrift against my cheeks, the wind slicing at me like the keen edge of a knife. But I did not feel the precursory cold of autumn's onslaught. Instead, my excitement was such that I was flushed with heat, actually perspiring. I could feel my riding habit sticking to my skin; damp tendrils of hair clung to my face as I raced across the heaths, drawing ever nearer to Nicky. He would not outstrip me this time; about that, I was determined.

Now, over a brambly hedge, we flew, neck and neck, slipping and sliding in the sludge as we landed. To my immense satisfaction, Black Buccaneer was the first to recover, leaping ahead to a drier, firmer tract, while Blackjack continued to flounder about haplessly. Alternately cursing and cajoling the horse, Nicky jerked it up and steadied it, while I, giddy from the crisp air, the mulled wine I had drunk earlier, and the thrill of the chase, crowed with jubilation as I passed him by.

There was no holding me back now. I felt as though I were indomitable, a goddess, as I pounded across the commons. Tall grass and weeds flattened without protest beneath Black Buccaneer's trampling hooves; clumps of spiny gorse were as nothing in my path, for my hands had never been surer upon the reins as I intuitively, unerringly, guided the gelding over or around all that would have barred my progress. A small, smug smile twisted one corner of my mouth, for Nicky was a good three lengths or more behind me now. Still, only in the dimmest recesses of my mind did I register that fact and savor it, all my concentration otherwise riveted on the hunt as I continued to speed on rashly over the marshy ground.

The fox was still well ahead in the distance, scrabbling in a zigzag pattern through the brush, the pack surging after it vociferously, a tide of white and tan that dipped and swelled across the vast sweep of the moors. The field followed like an armada in its wake, spreading, shifting, driving forward relentlessly. Time and again, I saw horses stumble and go down, pitching their riders from the saddle; but still, I plowed on as though the hounds of hell pursued me, for I knew that Nicky, even more daring than I, would be doing his best to narrow the gap between us, and I did not intend that he should catch me.

I suppose I should have realized how foolhardy our behavior was, and to be honest, I must confess that, deep down inside, I did—though, in truth, the accident, when it happened, was none of our doing. But even so, I could not help but think afterward that had Nicky and I each not been so bent on winning our gamble, had we not ridden so carelessly that morning, maybe the mishap would never have occurred; and so, in the end, perhaps we have no one but ourselves to blame, after all, for the disastrous consequences that followed and were ultimately to prove a turning point in our lives.

The calamity struck so quickly that, later, it was hard to believe something so crucial could have taken place in the blink of eye—especially when, at the time, it seemed actually to transpire over hours, not seconds, to unfold somehow in slow motion, so that, even now, my memory of it is blurred and disjointed. But that is often the way of ghastly events, as I have since learned, as though the sudden shock of such to one's senses is so great that the brain must delay it in order to comprehend it all and, even then, rejects much of what would otherwise be too painful to endure. And so it is that, of the incident that changed my life forever, I remember only bits and pieces, a confusing mélange no clearer in my mind now than the day of the hunt.

It is often when we are at a pinnacle that we are brought low, and so it was with me. My emotions had reached a feverish peak; I felt as though I were soaring as Black Buccaneer thundered across the heaths, faster and faster, until it seemed as though we outran even the wind. Now a slope lay ahead, but such was my feeling of invincibility

that I did not check the gelding, but urged it on relentlessly instead. Up, up, we staggered, so swiftly that we
could not stop at the top of the knoll, but went skidding
down the steep embankment on its far side, Black Buccaneer reared back on his powerful haunches to retard
our impetus, head thrashing as he fought the bit between
his teeth, eyes white, nostrils flared. As we careened
down the slant, I could see Nicky from the corner of one
eye as, hard on my trail, he came over the crest, my
cousin Elizabeth perilously close behind him, so close,
in fact, that, to my horror, the forelegs of her flaxen-
gold mare clipped Blackjack's back fetlocks just before
he hit the slippery earth. Hooves flailing, he began to
plunge wildly down the incline, straight on a collision
course with Black Buccaneer—and me.

I think my heart stopped in that moment.

It was like a dream, a terrible nightmare. I seemed
suddenly to have gone deaf, so heavy was the silence
that enveloped me, a silence that was not silence at all,
but the sounds of the world cut off by the roaring in my
ears, the hammering of blood in my skull. My eyes refused to focus properly; my vision was as obscured and
narrowed as though I peered through a long, dark tunnel,
at whose end I saw nothing but Nicky and his horse,
lurching toward me, and Lizzie, her eyes wide, stricken
with disbelief, her mouth ludicrously agape, her mare
toppling beneath her. . . .

Instinct alone drove me to yank Black Buccaneer up,
so sharp and short that as we reached the bottom of the
rise, he bucked savagely, nearly unseating me before I
managed to get him under control and out of Blackjack's

way. Then helplessly, fighting back a sob of terror, I watched as Nicky, his knitted brow beaded with sweat, his teeth gritted tightly, struggled furiously to regain command of his own gelding. At last, much to my relief, he somehow scrambled on down the acclivity, unscathed. But harrowingly, Lizzie's mount, unable to retrieve its footing on the slick grade, started to roll, flinging her violently from the saddle in the process. Her bowler hat knocked from her blond hair, she and the mare tumbled heavily down the hill, a blur of flopping limbs and hooves, flying petticoats and reins, coming to rest in a trickle of muddy water that wended its way through the jumble of rocks littering the base of the precipitous mound.

An ominous scowl darkening his visage, Nicky wheeled his nervously prancing horse about, yelling dreadful, ungentlemanly things at Lizzie all the while, while I, dazed and shaking uncontrollably, approached to see if either of them was hurt. Thankfully, Nicky, though understandably incensed, was unharmed; and though Lizzie was trembling as fiercely as I and her posterior would doubtless be bruised for a week, I suspected it was really her pride that was squashed flat as her bowler hat, the casualty of her mare's clumsily but safely righting itself.

"You stupid idiot!" Nicky bellowed at her. "You could have caused us all to break our bloody necks with that inane stunt!—to say nothing of how the horses might have been injured! By God! I ought to slap you silly, Lizzie!"

But though obviously frightened by the near catastrophe, Lizzie was not one to be cowed, no matter the situation.

"You just try it, Nicky!" she goaded as she glared up at him, her pale blue eyes narrowed not only with anger, but humiliation at his contempt. "You'll be sorry, I promise you."

"Stow it, Lizzie," I interjected frostily. "I saw what happened, and *you* were the one responsible for it. It would serve you right if Nicky *did* hit you—and I shudder to think what Uncle Draco would do if he ever found out how you endangered not only us, but the horses as well with your foolishness."

Although she turned ashen at the thought of Uncle Draco's infamous temper, still, Lizzie refused to be quelled. Snatching up her ruined hat, she jumped to her feet, a cunning, vindictive expression distorting her classically but coldly beautiful face.

"I might have known you would side with Nicky, Laura!" she spat, grabbing her mare's dangling reins and mounting up. "He always was your hero. Still, I don't think the family would be any too pleased if they ever learned he's become more to you than that. So, run on along with your tales to Uncle Draco, because I'll be more than happy to entertain him and Jarrett, and everybody else, too, with a few choice stories of my own!"

With that parting shot, she cantered off before either I or Nicky could respond. Filled with trepidation, we stared after her, each of us, for our own reasons, wondering anxiously whether she really knew anything concrete about us or had merely been guessing and making idle threats.

"Do you suppose she truly means to let the cat out of the bag about us, Nicky?" I asked at last, cringing inwardly at the thought, knowing in what light Lizzie would paint us, how disgusting and tawdry she would make us appear.

"No," he answered tersely. "It was a bluff, just a bluff, that's all. She's petrified of Father; she wouldn't dare to say anything to him—even if she *does* know something to tell. She's shrewd enough to know we'd simply deny whatever she said, and besides, Father would be so angry upon learning how she jeopardized us and the horses today that he wouldn't believe her anyway; he'd just think she was lying to even the score."

"Maybe," I agreed slowly. Yet despite his comforting words, I was afraid, for Lizzie was passionately in love with Nicky also; I knew that for certain now. I had seen her bitter hatred and jealousy of me in her eyes, and I sensed that, in the hope of winning him for herself, she would stop at nothing to drive a wedge between him and me. "But—but . . . even if she doesn't speak to Uncle Draco, what about Jarrett?" I queried. "*He* surely won't be as likely to turn a deaf ear to her spiteful fabrications. Oh, Nicky!" I burst out. "How much longer are we going to have to hide what's between us? Sooner or later, we're going to have to tell Jarrett and everyone else the truth about us and get on with our lives, you know. What are we waiting for? I'm not ashamed of loving you—and I despise being made to feel as though I should be!"

"I know, darling, I know. But . . . try to understand, Laura: Jarrett *is* my brother, and you *are* his fiancée. You can hardly expect me to feel very good or decent about taking you away from him—'' He broke off abruptly, a muscle pulsing in his rigid jaw. After a moment, he continued more evenly. "Look, Laura, this is scarcely the place for this conversation. Let's go somewhere else. I'm not in the mood now to finish the hunt, are you?''

"No." I barely managed to choke out the word, so stricken with sudden shame and remorse was I at my belated recognition that Nicky had his own devils to contend with as far as our relationship was concerned.

How unutterably selfish I had been, wrapped up in my own misery, not to have grasped this previously. I cursed myself roundly for a fool, wanting to crawl into a hole and die over my self-centeredness. Of course, Nicky would balk at hurting Jarrett, his brother, just as I shrank from the idea of wounding my parents with the knowledge of our love. Nicky was as emotionally racked about us as I was, I realized finally, understanding now why he hesitated to lay claim to me publicly, why he had doubtless avoided me all summer as well. He must be eaten up with guilt over his betrayal of Jarrett.

For the first time, I was unable to assuage my own culpable conscience with excuses for our behavior; I was forced to face the unpalatable fact that with our secret love, Nicky and I were committing an unpardonable wrong against our families—though I think the heart cannot help where it lies.

I did not know what to do. Had I been stronger, nobler, I would have given Nicky up; but I was a woman in love, with all the attendant frailties and failings, and so, even now, I could not bring myself to forsake the man I felt was as necessary to me as the air I breathed.

By this time, except for a few stragglers, the field had passed us by. In silence, we rode toward a small coppice that stood in the sheltered hollow of land spreading before us. Here, protected from the ruthless, relentless Cornish elements, evergreens grew, along with elms, birches, rowans, ashes, and other deciduous trees. Many of the latter had begun to turn scarlet and amber; the colors punctuated the green like bright splashes of paint flung from an artist's palette to spatter a canvas. Drying leaves that had already fallen from branches crackled and crunched beneath the horses' hooves in the stillness as we entered the grove, and the rich scent of the first hints of decay that autumn brings wafted to my nostrils from the moist loam underfoot. Wisps of mist drifted across the ground, and an odd raindrop or two, the beginnings of the shower that had threatened all morning, sprinkled through the trees to plop softly upon the earth. From far away, the muted barking of the pack reached our ears; but other than this, all was as hushed as though we had left our own world behind us upon penetrating the woods.

Each of us lost in unhappy reverie, we did not speak as we guided the geldings through the trees, pausing only to brush aside an occasional low limb that hindered our path. Wet leaves scraped my bowler hat and shoulders; a twig snagged the bedraggled chiffon streamers billowing gently from my hatband. I pulled them free, then nudged Black Buccaneer on. His bridle jangled; his breath was a white cloud of warmth that hung in the air like steam as he snorted and twitched, his tail flicking away some irritant.

The heat I had felt earlier had left me now. From the gloomy sky, in spasmodic spurts, the rain had started to fall in earnest, and the chill of the dreary morning, grown late now, seeped into my bones, making me shiver, my teeth chatter. Nevertheless, I did not suggest returning to the Hall, for I did not know when I might have a chance to be alone with Nicky again.

Presently, we came upon a tiny glade, scarcely wider than the breadth of the horses side by side. There, by unspoken agreement, we halted, the mantle of our mutual distress weighing heavily upon us as slowly we dismounted. For a long moment, we could not seem to meet each other's eyes; it was as though neither of us knew how or where to begin to redress our relationship, knowing what our love would cost so many. Was the price too high to pay? I must admit I knew it was. But still, I did not draw away when at last Nicky took me in his arms.

"Laura, dear Laura," he murmured, smoothing back from my face a strand of hair that had come free of its pins. "What shall we do about us, I wonder?"

"I don't know," I whispered, aggrieved. "I don't know. I want so much for us to be together, yet when I think of the sorrow it will cause so many who are dear to us, I am so torn."

"Shall we part, then—never to hold each other like this again, never to touch each other, to kiss each other, to make love together? Even worse, knowing that we must constantly be reminded of each other, that we will spend the rest of our days gazing at each other from across a room someplace, that our lives are inextricably intertwined because of the closeness of our families? How could we stand that, darling?''

''I don't know, though some painfully honest part of me tells me that if we were more honorable, that is what we would do. But— Oh, Nicky, to live without you . . . for us to be so near and yet so far away from each other— The thought alone makes me feel sick inside! No, I do not think I could bear that! Oh, Nicky, what are we to do?''

''Wait and hope, I suppose, that this tangled skein will somehow unsnarl itself . . . in time. Till then, we must snatch whatever we can together, Laura, even if it is only bits and pieces of the whole I know you long for. 'Tis better than nothing at all, at least. Do not deny us that, darling.''

His voice had dropped to a low, hoarse pitch; beneath his hooded lids, his eyes glowed like embers as they surveyed me. His strong, slender fingers stroked my jaw lightly, briefly, before he caught hold of my chin, tilting my face up to his. Beneath the brim of my bowler hat, rain glistened on my lashes and penciled my cheeks as, tenderly at first, his mouth met mine, teeth nibbling my lower lip, tongue darting forth to taste me, tease me, setting me aquiver with desire. I moaned in my throat, a whimper that spoke far more eloquently than words of the wanting, the need that rose, quick and keen, within me at his touch; and the pressure of his mouth upon my own increased, gradually growing more insistent as I wrapped my arms around his neck and began to kiss him back, fervidly, as though with my lips alone, I could somehow exorcise the demons that lay between us.

How I clung to him, reveling in his body's warmth, which radiated through my riding habit wet with rain. His hands traveled down my spine to cup my buttocks, crushing me to him, so I could feel the proof of his craving for me pressing against my thighs; but such was my yearning for him that, unlike that night in the gardens, I did not pull away, apprehensive lest he should think I sought but to taunt him once more. The quirt he still carried swung from his fingers; its tip brushed my long skirt, gliding across a sensitive place at the back of one knee, sending an electric spark through my body.

His heart pounded against mine, seeming to mimic the rhythm of the pattering rain; and in my mind, the world spun away, so I knew naught but Nicky. How long did he hold me thus, kissing me, fondling me, arousing me? I did not know. I was oblivious of passing time, of the rain that spilled down upon us, drenching us, plastering our clothes to our skin, even as we stood plastering ourselves to each other, breast to breast, thigh to thigh, as though to prevent all those who would if they could from coming between us. Even the steadily loudening sounds of the pack and the field, evidence that they had come about and were now headed in our direction, did not pierce my consciousness; nor did the faint snap of a twig and the dull rustle of dead leaves nearby.

So I was all the more startled when Jarrett suddenly appeared, a black specter, it seemed, astride an ebony horse, looming up out of the mist and drizzle, his jet eyes blazing. He had every right to be angry, of course;

I could not deny that. But until now, despite both Nicky's and Angelique's warnings about Jarrett's temperament, I had never really thought he would care that it was his brother I preferred, for I was not yet old enough, experienced enough, wise enough to know that much of a man is his pride.

How much had he seen? I did not know. I knew only that at the sight of him, Nicky and I sprang apart as though we had been shot, and a small wail of fright involuntarily emanated from my throat. My hand flew to my mouth to stifle the cry; but to my dismay, I found myself guiltily scrubbing my lips instead, as though subconsciously I believed that if only I could somehow wipe away Nicky's kisses, it would be as though I had never tasted them upon my lips, and Jarrett would stop staring at me like Lucifer himself.

He had followed us here—he must have! I thought—and in my sinking heart, I knew, even without his saying so, that Lizzie, spurred on by her caustic animosity and envy, had indeed carried out her threat to tell him all she knew or suspected about Nicky and me.

Jarrett's dark Gypsy visage was murderous, even more terrifying, if that was possible, than Uncle Draco's in a rage; and for a horrible, crazy moment, I half feared he would kill us, perhaps would jab his spurs to his stallion's sides and ride us down before we could escape. A muscle throbbed in his set jaw, and upon his reins, his hands, gloved in black leather, were convulsively tightening and loosening, as though it were all he could do to keep from putting them about our necks and choking us to death.

I don't think I have ever been as afraid as I was then.

"Well, well"—he spoke curtly, his cold, flinty voice like a shard of ice in my heart—"I set out this morning to catch a jackal, and though I truly *had* hoped to be disappointed in my hunt, it seems I have succeeded after all."

"Look, Jarrett," Nicky began brashly, "I don't know what that rancorous cat Lizzie told you—"

"Nothing that did not but confirm what I had already suspected for several months," his brother cut him off harshly, "so save your breath, Nicholas. I neither want nor need to hear your explanations and excuses. Ever since childhood, you have always coveted what was mine; but in truth, even I did not think you would go this far." He paused. Then he bent his dagger gaze upon me, stabbing me to the core. "And you, madam," he drawled so scornfully that I flinched, "are you naught but a dishonorable dolt fallen prey to whatever flattery and lies my brother has doubtless beguiled you with, or do you detest me so much that you deliberately sought to help him turn the knife in the wound?"

"No, no, I—I, that is . . . we—we never meant to hurt you, Jarrett," I stammered. "Nicky and I l-l-love each other—"

"Love?" Jarrett lifted one eyebrow jeeringly, devilishly. "Nicholas doesn't know the meaning of the word, madam; nor, I suspect, do you—" He clamped his mouth shut abruptly, as though it were all he could do to restrain himself from unleashing the violence I sensed lay coiled taut as a spring just beneath the surface of his glacial demeanor. "By God!" he declared, "I ought to slay you where you stand, Nicholas! But for our dear mother's sake, I will not; nor will I administer to you the thrashing you so richly deserve! But be warned: Brother or not, the next time you seek to trifle with what is mine, I shall not be responsible for my actions. Now get on your horse, and get out of my sight!''

I thought surely that Nicky would not obey, that he would declare his love for me then and there, and defy Jarrett to do his worst to us both. Childish, romantic notions of the two of them battling each other for me flitted through my mind, puffing up my ego; for what woman's vanity is not secretly flattered by the idea of men coming to blows over her? I imagined Nicky, my conquering hero, sweeping me up and carrying me off, while Jarrett lay vanquished, even the memory of him soon forgotten. But to my utter shock and anguish, Nicky did none of these things. Instead, wordlessly shaking off the hand I laid imploringly upon his arm, ignoring my tortured calling of his name, he simply strode over to his gelding, mounted up, and rode off without a backward glance, leaving me to face his brother alone.

I could not believe it.

Such was not the act of a lover, a defender, surely, but the callousness of one indifferent to my fate, of one who did not care that I was but a woman, vulnerable, helpless against whatever reprisals Jarrett might choose to take against me.

Tears scalded my eyes; a broken sob issued from my lips. Such was my agony, my stupefaction, that it was as though my brain stopped functioning, my heart ceased to beat. I felt frozen, dead inside. Even time itself seemed to hang suspended, as, in that unbearable moment, all my hopes, my dreams came crashing down about me like delicate sand castles smashed by the sea; for now I saw with cruel clarity that all I had ever envisaged had been built from as little substance, erected on a foundation no more secure than a shifting beach, with only the illusion of solidity. Nicky had played me for a fool as surely as Thorne had that day in our childhood when he had locked me in the trunk in the attic. I was aghast at my idiocy, my gullibility. I did not know how I could have been so obtuse, so disposed to make excuses for Nicky's behavior, so eager to believe his lies.

"You see, Laura"—Jarrett spoke quietly, an odd note of pity for me in his voice now—"it is as I said: Nicholas wants you only because you belong to me. He does not love you."

No! It's not true! Even in the depths of my torment and realization of my folly, I repudiated the statement hotly, striving desperately to shore up the crumbling walls of my fantasies, as though I could somehow make them whole again. *It just can't be true! Jarrett just said it to wound me and turn me against Nicky!*

But still, mercilessly, doubt after doubt battered me in waves as, unbidden, images I had staunchly thrust to the back of my mind now rose to haunt me: of Nicky goading me to give in to him, while deliberately refusing to commit himself to me—oh, God, had he ever actually said he loved me, or had I only read into his words all I had longed to hear?—of his cowardly forcing his way through the arbor hedge, deserting me that evening in the gardens, even as he had now; of Clemency's sly, sloe eyes, of her smug smile, and of a scattering

petals. . . .

"No!" I cried out in protest, pride, if noth..

constraining me to push the unwelcome scenes awa

"No! You're wr-wr-wrong, Jarrett! Nicky *does* love me!

He just—just didn't wish to—to hurt you any further,

that's all!"

Jarrett laughed shortly, unpleasantly.

"Why, you poor, besotted little goose!" he scoffed, shaking his head with incredulity at my assertions. "Nicholas would cut off his right arm if he thought that by doing so, he would do me some injury. He has never learned that brothers make better friends than competitors. You do not believe me? No, I can see that you don't—or won't. But, then, what woman ever *does* believe ill of the man she loves?" he sneered.

Then, inhaling sharply, as though, still, it were all he could do to curb his turbulent emotions, he continued pitilessly, ignoring the tears that streamed down my face.

"It seems I have been sadly remiss in my duties where you are concerned, Laura. Because of our long-standing betrothal—to which you have never voiced any objections, I might add—I took you for granted, a mistake I shan't make again, I assure you."

With that, Jarrett dismounted and started to walk toward me slowly, determinedly, like a wolf stalking its prey, a strange, mocking smile, which did not quite reach his eyes, playing about the corners of his lips.

"If it was kissing you wanted, Laura, you ought to have told me so," he insisted softly.

...shivering with cold and dread and something I could not name, I cowered from him, edging surreptitiously toward my gelding, misliking the look of resolution on his face, the way his eyes glittered when they raked me, coming to rest on my pale, weeping countenance. I had no idea what he might do to me, alone here, as we were now, in the coppice; but I was suddenly quite sure I did not want to find out. He had never before seemed so tall, so lithe, so menacing—capable of anything, abuses my mind now conjured distraughtly from its dregs, lurid fears that lurk deep inside every woman; because despite the whispered stories we might hear, none of us ever really *knows*, unless actually the victim of such, precisely how horrible, how degrading the crimes men commit against women can be.

I had little cause to think Jarrett would spare me from punishment; to the contrary, I had every reason to suppose he would, at the very least, berate me for my faithlessness. Perhaps he would even beat me—or worse. I shuddered at the thought, drying my tears, self-preservation now uppermost in my mind.

Once I was far enough away from him that I reckoned I could make good my escape, I lunged for my horse's bridle and tried awkwardly to leap into the saddle. But with a rapidity I would not have believed possible, Jarrett erased the distance between us, catching me around the waist and jerking me back from the gelding so strenuously that my bowler hat sailed off my head. Vehemently, I struggled against him—to no avail. I could not pry myself from his iron grip, and finally, gasping for breath, my sopping hair straggling from its pins, I abandoned my futile attempts to elude him.

"That's better, much better, Laura," Jarrett muttered in my ear, his warm breath sending a tingle down my spine. "I like a woman with spirit, so I'd hate to have to break yours. Besides, much as the prospect holds a certain undeniable appeal, I'm not going to . . . how shall I put it? . . . force myself on you, my sweet, so there's no need for this Sabine conduct."

But despite his reassurances, I was all too aware of his steely arms wrapped just beneath my heaving breasts, of the hard, rugged length of his body flattened against my own soft, slender one; so I placed no faith in his words.

"Let me go, Jarrett," I begged. "Please. Let me go."

"Only if you promise not to try to run away again."

"Yes, all right, I promise," I agreed, biting my lip, worried he should guess I lied.

Perhaps he did. Yet even so, he released me, and the moment he did, I hitched up my skirts and took to my heels. I did not get far. Cursing under his breath, Jarrett gave chase, and within no more than a few strides of his long, muscular legs, he caught up with me, grabbing my arm and wrenching me about so savagely that I stumbled in the mud and fell to my knees.

"Let me go!" I snapped once more, attempting to wrestle away from him. "Don't touch me!"

But he was not to be duped a second time, and after grappling with me for several minutes in the rain and mire, he yanked me to my feet and shoved me up roughly against the trunk of a tree. The sudden blow knocked the wind from me, and for a time, I simply stood there, feeling the rain pummel my face and the coarse bark of the Cornish elm grate against my skin through my soiled riding habit. But then, as Jarrett began to move toward me, I recovered my wits, and raising my hand, in which I somehow still bore my riding crop, I struck out at him blindly, slashing him upward across his left cheek.

I shall never forget the impact of the quirt against his smooth, dark skin—vicious, sickening. Stunned, I blanched, gasping with horror at my action as I watched the blood that gushed from the wicked gash, to be just as quickly washed away by the rain before welling again to the surface. Jarrett stopped in his tracks, a peculiar half-smile twisting his lips as his hand went to his face and his fingers came away covered with vermilion. The rain splattered upon them; pinkish droplets dribbled to the ground.

"So, you dare to show your talons to me, my fierce falcon, do you?" he asked. "You are braver than most, then, for I would have killed a man for that," he averred—but calmly enough, so one could almost have thought he spoke in jest; but I did not mistake the wrath smoldering behind the words. Then, his voice hardening with intent, he vowed, "But on you, Laura, I shall take my revenge another way."

Before I realized what he meant to do, he snatched the riding crop from my grasp, broke it over his knee, and tossed the pieces into the brush. Then he advanced on me purposefully. I turned to flee, but in a flash, his arms slammed home on either side of me against the tree trunk, so I could not evade him. Trapped like some feral animal, I panicked and, crying out, doubled up my fists to beat hysterically against his broad chest. But he only laughed and, seizing my wrists easily, pinioned them behind my back. Then, in a cruel, unconscious travesty of Nicky's actions less than an hour ago, he clenched my chin between his viselike fingers and compelled my demurring face up to his.

"Now, Laura," he uttered in a tone that made gooseflesh prickle my nape, "since you are *my* fiancée, I think you owe me what you were only too willing to give to Nicholas earlier, don't you?"

Before I could respond, Jarrett ground his mouth down on mine—so hard that his teeth grazed the tender flesh of my lower lip and I tasted blood, coppery, bittersweet, upon my tongue. It was a kiss I was to remember the rest of my life—not only because of the sardonic man who took it from me so savagely, but because of my reaction to it as well. I wanted to die a thousand deaths, for even as I writhed helplessly against his demanding mouth, his imprisoning hands, to my everlasting shame, as Jarrett's tongue plunged deep between my lips, an atavistic thrill such as I had never before felt shot through me like a lightning bolt, making my head spin and my body burn like a catherine wheel set aflame. No one— not even Nicky—had ever kissed me like this; and in that prophetic moment, I knew instinctively that all those before Jarrett had been only fumbling boys, that here, at long last, was a man who could—and would—take me and break me and make me irrevocably his own.

The thought terrified me, and instantly, I rejected it.

I did not want to belong to Jarrett, had never wanted to belong to him. It was Nicky whom I loved, Nicky whom I went on loving even now, despite his betrayal of me; for the heart is not a candle that, once lit, can be extinguished at will, but a fragile, foolish thing, all too easily wounded, all too slow to heal. Why, then, was my traitorous body melting against Jarrett's, molding itself so pliantly, so indecently, to his—a man who had ruthlessly stripped away the chimeras of my heart and mind because he could not brook the thought that I loved him not, though, even now, he himself spoke no word of loving me? I did not know.

Mortified, I believed I must be a wanton, or mad. Granny Sheffield had warned me about the Chandler wild streak, predicted often enough that it would prove my downfall. Why hadn't I listened? Desperately, I tried again to escape from Jarrett. But the effort was wasted, for he only laughed, as he had previously—low, mockingly—and tightened his grip upon me.

"Did you really think I would let you go, Laura?" he asked huskily, studying me intensely from beneath shuttered lids. "Did you really think I would let you throw yourself away on the likes of Nicholas? You are mine. You have always been mine—whether I want you or not . . . though I *do* want you, you know. I should have made that clear to you from the very start."

I trembled to hear his words, for I had never truly imagined he desired me, had never before thought, as I did now, of him holding me, kissing me, pressing me down, and—

"Please, Jarrett . . ." I breathed.

But he swallowed the entreaty with his mouth, and such was his onslaught upon my senses then that all thoughts of further resistance were driven from my mind, swept away by the tide of passion that rushed through me at his kiss, leaving me defenseless in its wake. I felt as though I were drowning in a deluge, could no longer think, could only feel as he plundered my lips over and over, hungrily, possessively, seeming to drain the very life and soul from my body and then to pour it back in.

Time passed. I scarcely knew how much as I stood there in the grove, enfolded in Jarrett's embrace, his mouth claiming mine, his hands roaming where they willed, while the rain drummed its steady tattoo upon us. I knew only that, like a ship tossed upon stormy waves, my head rocked with the exquisite emotions he was wakening within me, that my knees shook so, that I would have fallen had he not held me so tightly. I felt small and weak as a child in his powerful arms, yielding to his kisses, his caresses, without rebellion now, my body seeming to have a volition all its own, acquiescent, even—to my deep-felt disgrace—eager to accept what he offered as expertly, remorselessly, he brought me to a feverish pitch, showing me how foolish I had been indeed to think only Nicky could make me feel so.

It was the beginning of the end of my innocence and youth, taken all too soon from me—I realize now—for I was still a child in so many ways. Although I understood that a child who plays with fire must learn the flames burn, I wished the man who taught me that had been kinder with his lesson. But whatever gentleness there was in Jarrett was layered between a casing of arrogance and a core of pride, as I was to discover in time, and it was never easy to reach; for a man such as Jarrett, the son of a Gypsy bastard obliged to scrap for all that should, by rights, have been his since birth, is not given to exposing his vulnerabilities. They were there, of course, if one looked closely enough. But this, I did not do, afflicted, as I was, by heartache and impotent ire that all I should have dreamed of was as diamonds turned to dust, with none but I caring that it should be so. That because I was a woman, I was, like all women, the chattel of men, with no power of my own to wield in any matter that counted. That, for all my satin ribands and French-perfumed ringlets, my silken gowns and carefully cultivated graces, I was, in truth, little more than a likely bone two dogs might quarrel over merely because each was determined the other should not have it—or at least not until it had been licked clean and the marrow sucked dry. That because I was a woman, I could be held captive, as Jarrett held me captive, kissed against my will, as Jarrett kissed me, my body made to respond, as Jarrett made it respond, even as my mind cried out at the thwarting of its dominion.

And then, just when I thought that, any moment, Jarrett would be forcing me down upon the soggy earth to have his way with me—I being quite incapable of preventing it—he suddenly, to my surprise, ceased his assault upon me, thrusting me away, holding himself very still, his head cocked a trifle, listening. Briefly, I wondered what was amiss, for I heard nothing but the harsh rasp of his ragged breathing, and of my own, and the thrumming of my heart. But then, above the cadence of the rain, there reached my ears the ring of urgent, victorious baying through the woods, the sound of some animal skittering through fallen leaves, the noise of the pack scrambling frenziedly through the undergrowth.

I had forgotten the hunt, and now it was upon us.

Without warning, the fox broke from the cover of the trees into the glade, hard-pressed, panting, its copper fur soaked with rain and mud, its dark, gleaming eyes haunted. Startled, it drew up short at the sight of us, then glanced about wildly, as though in search of a hiding place. But we lay ahead of it, the hounds behind, and even had there been some route to freedom, the valiant creature was exhausted and could run no farther. Now, dismissing us as the lesser threat, its masked face revealing its knowledge that it was but a heartbeat from death, the poor beast turned to make its defiant stand against the salivating dogs bursting from the brush to attack it.

The fox yipped a warning, then, with a last battle cry, bravely met its fate head-on. The shriek echoed piercingly through the coppice before it was abruptly silenced as the lead hounds tore into the animal ferociously, the impact sending them all rolling, a blurry ball of blood and fur. In seconds, the rest of the pack swarmed forth, snarling and ripping even at one another in their furor to ravage the prey they had sought all morning. Those who could not reach it yapped and howled, pacing about frantically, trying to jump over the other dogs or tunnel beneath them to get at the fox, buried now under a tide of undulating white and tan crested with bloody foam.

The hideous sight nauseated me; with difficulty, I

choked back the vomit that rose in my throat as swiftly, guessing my reaction to the brutal scene, Jarrett crushed me to his chest, shielding my face so I should see no more. But he could not shut out the abominable growling of the hounds, the gnashing of their teeth, the grate of rending fur and flesh.

Then the huntsman and the whippers-in were there, dismounting and wading through the pack, vigorously snapping their whips and shouting at the dogs to drive them away from the now mutilated carcass of the fox. Once a circle had been cleared around the corpse, the huntsman knelt and, with the sharp knife he carried at his waist, sliced off the head and tail of the dead creature. Then he kicked the remains to the greedily waiting hounds, who quickly reduced their reward to a few strips of fur stained with crimson. After that, holding aloft his bloody trophies, the huntsman approached Uncle Esmond and the other lead riders who were up at the death, Uncle Draco and Papa among them.

Grimacing with ill-concealed revulsion, Uncle Esmond bent down from his saddle, gingerly taking the mask and brush from the huntsman; then he looked about to see who was present and in need of a blooding ceremony. His eyes lit upon one of his guests, a young woman the same age as I, Lady Siobhan O'Halloran, the daughter of an impoverished Irish duke. After nudging his bay toward her sorrel, Uncle Esmond leaned over to rub her delightedly smiling countenance with blood from the gruesome stump of the fox's tail. Then, verbally applauding her skill as a horsewoman, he presented her with the beast's disembodied head. Heedless of the gore that still dripped from it, she displayed her prize proudly as she received the congratulations of those nearest her.

After that, much to my consternation, not knowing we had not completed the hunt, Uncle Esmond brought his horse alongside Jarrett and me, smeared my unwittingly upturned face also with blood from the brush, then gave me the grisly tail.

The blood felt warm and sticky upon my skin, trickling down my cheeks in little furrows from the rain. It was all I could do not to gag, to manage a shaky, sickly smile as Papa, Uncle Draco, and the rest crowded around me, petting and praising me over my false triumph. My head swam, my stomach roiled. I wanted nothing more than to get rid of the soft, furry, blood-streaked brush I clutched tremulously in my hand; yet I dared not throw it away, knowing how shocked and offended the rest would be by my action. So I held on to it, thinking that if I didn't get away from those who flocked about me, I would retch or faint.

Thus, regardless of whatever else I might feel toward him, I knew I should be eternally grateful to Jarrett for what he did then. As though sensing my desperate need to escape, he somehow smoothly extricated me from the throng, retrieved my bowler hat, and got me on my gelding and back to the Hall, relieving me of my wretched prize in the process. I neither knew nor cared what he did with it; it was enough that he had understood my abhorrence of it and the sport that revered it as a trophy. It was enough that he had not left me alone to fend for myself, as Nicky—faithless Nicky—had.

And so when, just before entering the manor, Jarrett

drew me aside and kissed me again, leisurely, thoroughly, like a man sure of his rights, I found I could not bring myself to object. Such was his confidence, his conceit, that he had known I would not—not then or even later, much later, when, at the hunt ball, linking his arm securely as a slave chain about my waist and smiling down at me like a conqueror anticipating his spoils, he formally, publicly, announced our betrothal.

Chapter VI

Interlude at Pembroke Grange

> The hope I dreamed of was a dream,
> Was but a dream; and now I wake,
> Exceeding comfortless, and worn, and old,
>   For a dream's sake.
>
> —*Mirage*
>   Christina Rossetti

To say I was stunned by Jarrett's presumption is an understatement. I could not credit it, for never in all my wildest imaginings had I dreamed that he would go so far, that his arrogance and audacity were such that without my prior knowledge or consent, he would actually take such a drastic step to bind us together forever.

"How did you dare?" I spat at him under my breath, quivering with dismay and outrage at his impudence.

"In time, you will learn I am capable of much that has never crossed your mind, my sweet," he rejoined with cool amusement, observing me insolently from beneath hooded lids, without a trace of conscience or regret. "Now, be a good girl—and smile, Laura. After all, I *am* considered quite a catch, you know. There are any number of women here tonight who hoped our childhood engagement would ultimately come to naught."

Oh, how I longed for my quirt! I should have done much more than just gash his handsome, mocking face with it, I fumed as I studied the red weal that marked his left cheek; I should have beaten him senseless! But as it was, my hands were tied. I could hardly openly spurn his suit. That would not only ruin the ball, but cause a scandal, too; and of course, it was now patently obvious to me that any private protest would avail me nothing. So, somehow I forced myself to swallow the angry words that rose in my throat, and to smile, as Jarrett had commanded—and all the while, I heartily wished him in Hades, where he surely belonged!

Gazing about, I saw I was not the only one affected by his declaration. Of all those present at the Hall to witness it, however, there were two whose faces in that moment I shall never forget: Nicholas and Elizabeth. At the news, Nicky's dark head jerked up as though manipulated by some invisible puppeteer, and from across the ballroom, he cast at me such an embittered and accusatory glance that I could not mistake the fact that Jarrett's words had proved a severe blow to him—though I was not, by now, so foolish as to suppose this was because of any love he bore me. Lizzie, on the other hand, smirked and preened like a cat who had just caught a plump pigeon, then shot me such a smug stare that my fingers itched to snatch her blond hair out by the roots. If she had just kept her malicious, meddlesome mouth shut, I thought heatedly, I should not now be so disconsolate; though grudgingly I admitted I owed her a debt of gratitude for causing Nicky's true feelings toward me to be revealed. Still, it did not make me like her—or Jarrett—any better; nor could I take any pleasure in how cleverly, no matter how underhandedly, I had been outmaneuvered by my disagreeable but bold, resourceful fiancé.

Yet such was Papa's proud, beaming expression, the look of happiness on Mama's glowing countenance, and Uncle Draco's pleased approval that I did naught but mutter, "Be very sure that I shall get even with you for this, Jarrett," before allowing myself to be drawn into the circle of well-wishing family and friends who soon surrounded us, laughing and chattering excitedly.

I never knew how I got through the remainder of the night. I drank and danced and smiled until my face felt frozen with the effort, and somehow pretended I was ecstatic over my betrothal, when, in reality, I yearned only to go home to the Grange, to retire to my bedroom and cry my eyes out with pain and fury; for the man I had been determined to wed had deceived me, and the man who was equally resolved to marry *me* had made all thoughts of breaking off our engagement impossible now that he had publicly announced it.

Truly, this had been, I reflected dismally, the worst day of my life. Surely, nothing further could possibly happen to hurt and humiliate me any more than I already had been.

But that was before Papa called for our carriage so we could depart from the ball, and upon searching for Clemency, I discovered her upstairs in one of the Hall's guest bedrooms, locked with flagrant abandon in Nicky's arms.

I was only seventeen, but I might as well be dead, for my life was over, I thought with all the passion of youth for grand tragedy; and I cried myself to sleep that night, pressing my face into my pillow so none should hear me weeping and come to investigate the cause of my woe. Papa, a man of the world, would understand, I believed, how my life had gone so awry, but still, he would be injured by my lack of faith in his choice for me; and Mama, so good and kind and earnest, would be deeply shocked by all that had brought about my despair. She would be terribly disappointed in me, I knew, and blame herself for my wanton behavior, thinking she had somehow failed me; and that, I could not bear, for she was all I could have wished for in a mother. It was I who had let her down, and since I could not now change what I had done, I could only hope she never learned that I had not lived up to her expectations.

This was why I had not dismissed Clemency as my maid, for what reason could I give for not wanting her about me anymore? If I told the truth, my own indiscreet conduct was bound to be exposed as well, for Clemency's attitude toward me upon my finding her with Nicholas had been so impertinent that I was certain she knew of my own clandestine meetings with him and would not hesitate to reveal all should I cause her to lose her place at the Grange. Inwardly, I cringed at the remembrance of Nicky's hard, supercilious smile when I had found them together, of Clemency's glowing green eyes, sly and slitted as a cat's with satisfaction and disdain; at the thought of how, even now, she must be laughing up her sleeve at me, secure in her knowledge that there was nothing I could do about it.

Yet despite my discomposure, now that my eyes had been so cruelly opened about Nicky, I could not help but feel almost sorry for my abigail, too, for I felt sure his intentions toward her were no more caring or honorable than they had been toward me. Jarrett was right: Nicky did not know what love was, else he could not have plucked my heartstrings so carelessly, so callously, and reacted so indifferently to my anguish. I saw that now —now, when it was too late—and cursed my stupidity, my naïveté, which had brought about my sorrow and delivered me so absolutely into the very hands I had sought to avoid.

Still, if I were honest, I knew I should consider myself fortunate that despite the circumstances, Jarrett had wanted me, had not denounced me as a trollop and a cheat; and deep down inside, I *was* thankful his desire for me had spared me the ignominy I should otherwise have suffered. Yet even so, I could not fear him any less. Before today, despite his being my cousin, he had been as a stranger to me; when I had thought of him at all, it had been as a dark, nebulous interloper in my dreams. I had never really believed we would eventually be married.

Now I had been given a glimpse of his carnal, satanic nature, of what I must endure once he was my husband, and I shuddered at the inevitability of becoming his wife.

I had been reared at the Grange, a farm, and upon occasion, I had witnessed the mating of our cattle, our sheep; so I was not ignorant, as so many brides of my straitlaced Victorian age were, of what happened between a man and woman sexually. Thus I had never been particularly frightened of physical intimacy; indeed, when I had thought Nicky loved me, I had exulted in his kisses, the touch of his hands upon my body. Even when he had nearly had his way with me that evening in the gardens, I had not recoiled from the act itself, only from the notion of surrendering my virtue without benefit of a wedding ring.

But I dreaded the prospect of sharing a bed with Jarrett, knowing that he would not be content with just taking me whenever he chose, but would force me to respond, whether I wished to or not, just as he had today in the coppice, and that I would be powerless to prevent it. I sensed also that there were depths to his sensuality about which I could not even guess (my enlightenment in such matters not extending beyond the rudiments); and I suspected that, as a consequence, the physical side of our marriage would not, as I had been led by whispered tales to assume was the usual case, be limited to diligent but infrequent couplings with the sole aim of begetting an heir. My vivid imagination ran wild, painting in my mind all sorts of vague but sordid pictures of what I might be subjected to as Jarrett's wife, fueling my trepidation so, that I should not have been at all surprised had he suddenly sprouted horns and a pointed tail, and called on me, wielding a pitchfork.

Surely, he is the devil incarnate, I would think time and again after his carriage had deposited me at the Grange; for true to his word, Jarrett neglected his duties toward me no longer, but arrived every other day, it seemed, to escort me riding or to some luncheon, party, or rout. Since we were affianced, I could hardly refuse his invitations, for what excuse could I make for avoiding him? No pretext would serve, and I dared not tell Papa or Mama the truth: that Jarrett's kisses far too often exceeded the bounds of propriety, leaving me breathless, bewildered, and strangely aching inside; that his cool, cynical remarks flustered or enraged me, for he seldom spared my sensibilities, but spoke to me most improperly, as no gentleman ought, taking satisfaction in my blushes, amusement in my anger.

Papa, had he known of Jarrett's behavior, would doubtless have felt obligated, for my sake, to challenge him to a duel, which was not only against the law, but would have caused an unmendable rift between the Prescotts and the Chandlers; and Mama would have been mortified, for she had led a very sheltered life, and even Uncle Draco always behaved with the utmost decorum toward her, so she supposed the baser stories told of him to be nothing more than vicious rumors put about by those jealous of his success.

So I suffered Jarrett's unwelcome attentions in silence, perversely morose because despite his wanting me, he said naught of loving me, even a little, which would have been some comfort, at least, to my battered heart. As the months passed, I faced my approaching wedding day with less and less courage, certain I should find no joy or tenderness in my marriage.

But the formal written announcement of my betrothal to Jarrett had been mailed to London for insertion in the *Gazette*; my trousseau had been ordered, and the date had been set. Come winter, I would be Jarrett's bride. Even had I been able to do so, it was far too late now to alter the course my life had taken. As Angelique had once warned me, I had made my bed, and now I must lie in it, regardless of how uncomfortable I might find it.

Glumly, I gazed down at the engagement ring on my left hand, a large topaz surrounded by small diamonds. Its shape was appropriate, I thought, for it resembled a teardrop; though Jarrett, when placing it on my finger, had told me he'd bought it because it was the color of my eyes. How ironic, I reflected bitterly, that something so lovely should be nothing to me but a symbol of my distress. Often, I yearned to wrench the ring off and fling it away; but it remained where it was, to gleam at me mockingly—like Jarrett's eyes when he looked at me.

Autumn had come and gone—and come again since that fateful day of Uncle Esmond's fox hunt. Through my bedroom window, I could see the leaves of the trees in the park, turned red as rubies and gold as the topaz set in my ring, encompassed by a swirl of diamondlike mist, a beautiful but somehow dismal scene, cold as the windowpane against which I pressed my face. I shivered at the smooth, chilly touch of the glass and drew away, my breath leaving a white cloud upon the square, so my

·vision was briefly obscured and I did not spy Jarrett as, mounted upon his splendid stallion, Blackfire, he trotted up the gravel drive to the Grange.

It was not Clemency who came to inform me that he had arrived, for of late, she had taken to disappearing without a word of warning, so I seldom knew where she was, though I suspected her of sneaking out to meet Nicky at some trysting place, and my heart ached at the thought.

I had not seen Nicky since that night of the hunt ball, and I did not wish to—or so I tried hard to convince myself; for though I now hated him with a passion for his duplicity, some small part of me went on loving him, went on hoping, albeit futilely, I knew, that there had been some horrible mistake, that he really did love me, that he had not just lusted for me out of some depraved desire to wound Jarrett's pride and masculinity.

But now, looking back, I could see that Nicky had always chafed at Jarrett's being the eldest and their father's heir, though Uncle Draco had never unduly favored any of his three sons and had made handsome provisions for Nicky. Still, that had never been enough for him, I realized now; though until that morning of the fox hunt, I had never guessed how acute his resentment of Jarrett truly was, to what lengths he would actually go to get back at his older brother for any real or imagined slights he felt he had suffered. Now, however, I knew the grudge he bore Jarrett was as deep-seated as Thorne's against Nicky himself, for Thorne had never forgiven Nicky for their childhood brawl that day in the attic.

Thinking of this, I shuddered slightly as I descended the stairs to the hall below, for all of us, through our shared great-grandfather, Sir Simon Chandler, had Chandler blood in us—and perhaps the Chandler wild streak also. Certainly, *I* had been cursed with it, I thought, and I knew only too well to what ruin it had brought me. What other disasters might it portend should it afflict my cousins as well? I did not know. But as I reluctantly opened the small drawing-room doors and stepped inside to greet Jarrett, I somehow felt strangely as though the proverbial goose stood poised to walk across my grave; and for a moment, I would have given anything to stop time from its relentless onward march.

Involuntarily, my breath caught in my throat at the sight of Jarrett's tall, dark figure, for each time I saw him, I was struck afresh by how handsome he was, as though I had never really looked at him before. The pale, thin scar that now marred his left cheek, where I had slashed him with my riding crop, did nothing to detract from his good looks, but, rather, oddly enhanced them, making him appear more rakish and demonic than ever.

"Hullo, Laura," he said, his black eyes glinting as he turned from the window through which he had been staring before my entrance.

Striding forward, he grasped my hands and pressed his lips to them lingeringly.

"Hullo, Jarrett," I replied, sternly quelling the urge I had to snatch my hands away.

Really, I thought, it was just ridiculous how my heart leaped when he touched me, as though it weren't sorely bruised at all, but only sleeping, waiting to be wakened;

how all my bones seemed to be dissolving inside me, so I felt as though I must be trickling down into a pool of quicksilver at his feet and was slightly surprised to find myself still standing. Even worse were the sensations that flooded my being when, after loosing my hands, he tipped my face up to his, brushing my mouth with his own before his tongue parted my lips and he kissed me more insistently. My traitorous body swayed against his, though I did try to restrain it, longing to escape from him and the confusing emotions he aroused within me. It was useless to protest, however, for past experience had taught me Jarrett would not be denied, but would release me only when it suited him.

When at last he freed me, I could feel the hot blush that rose to color my cheeks, and swallowing hard, I turned away, knowing even so that he was surveying me intently in that strange fashion of his, his eyes hungry and speculative, as though he were waiting for something. But for what, I knew not, for his lids were half closed, so I could not tell what he was thinking.

Now, as I sat down nervously upon a nearby chair, he slipped one hand into the pocket of his dark green, well-tailored jacket and withdrew a package wrapped and beribboned in silver.

"I brought you a wedding present, my sweet." He spoke lightly, so I marveled that the kisses that made me feel so giddy and unlike myself seemed not to affect him at all. He handed me the gift. "Go ahead. Open it," he urged.

My fingers trembling slightly, I stripped away the paper to reveal a black velvet box, whose lid, when I slowly raised it, gave way to a black satin interior upon which reposed an exquisite set of delicate pearl jewelry.

"Oh, Jarrett!" I gasped. "How gorgeous!"

"The set belonged to my grandmother Amélie Saint-Aubert Chandler," he explained. "It passed to my mother when she married my father—one of the few possessions Grandfather Chandler couldn't legally keep from her when he cut her off without a penny for making such a 'dreadful misalliance,' as he termed it," he drawled dryly. "Mother said it was only fitting that you, as my bride, should have it; it's to wear with your wedding gown."

"I shall treasure it always," I declared.

"Shall you, Laura?"

"Of course."

"Even though 'tis me for whom you will wear the pearls?" he inquired, casually, it seemed, though I thought I sensed a sudden tenseness in him nevertheless.

It was the first time he had really ever, even indirectly, sought to probe my feelings for him, and I did not know how to answer, what he expected me to say.

"Y-y-yes, of course," I stammered uneasily, flushing.

Jarrett was silent for a moment; then he uttered softly, "Never lie to me, Laura. I won't tolerate it, you know." He paused, then gave a short, harsh bark of laughter. "Admit it, my sweet: You'd sooner run into the path of a coach traveling at breakneck speed than marry me!"

"Well, if you know that, why do you want to wed me, then?" I asked, snapping shut with a bang the lid of the black velvet box, my delight in the pearls quite spoiled now by his surliness. "There are other women—"

"And I've had my share of them—make no mistake about that," he informed me arrogantly, insolently. "A man is permitted to sow his wild oats after all. But it was always you I meant to have in the end, Laura."

"But . . . why? Why me, Jarrett?"

Swiftly, maddeningly, his lashes swept down to veil his thoughts from me. Languidly, he reached into his waistcoat, removing a solid-gold case, from which he extracted a cheroot and a small box of matches.

"Because you were promised me," he responded coolly, lighting the cigar and inhaling deeply, then shaking the match until the flame died. He blew a cloud of smoke into the air, then tossed the match into the fireplace. "Now, let us cease this game of Twenty Questions, my sweet, for it is beginning to pall.

"I came not only to deliver your wedding present," he continued, smoothly changing the subject, "but good tidings as well. It appears romance is in the air, for the twins are to be married, too—Alex to Lady Vanessa Dubray, and Angel to Lord Greystone. They're planning a double ceremony to be held sometime next summer; the announcement's to be made at the Heights a fortnight hence. I shall call for you at seven o'clock that evening—if that is convenient," he added as an afterthought, grinning hugely as he observed my pique at his high-handedness.

"Very well," I consented tartly, scowling at him.

Then, happy that at least the twins had achieved their hearts' desires, I said warmly, "I will be pleased to offer them both my congratulations."

"I'm sure you will, for Angel, especially, has always liked you, Laura, and is looking forward to your becoming her sister by marriage. I believe she thinks you will prove a spirited accomplice to her many madcap schemes. I suspect she does not yet realize Lord Greystone will be master of his own house—as I shall be of mine. . . ." His voice trailed away as his eyes roamed over me impudently, meaningfully, so I turned scarlet once more and my gaze fell before his. An amused smile of satisfaction tugged at his lips as he went on.

"It might, in addition, interest you to know that our estimable cousin Thorne intends to tie the knot as well," he disclosed. "Frankly, for a number of reasons—none of which I shall sully your maidenly ears with, my sweet—I didn't think he had it in him. But apparently he has indeed come up to scratch, and that Irish witch Lady Siobhan O'Halloran has accepted his proposal— for all the good it shall do her! If Uncle Esmond's purse holds tuppence more than that of her father, the duke, I shall be surprised. But, then, perhaps she has other causes for stooping to a mere baronetcy—her appetites are not at all modest, I should venture to guess—or perhaps I do Uncle Esmond an injustice. After all, he *does* own the Grange, so I expect Uncle Welles keeps him afloat."

"I don't know," I stated truthfully. "But I would assume Papa pays him only a peppercorn rent."

"Laura . . . Laura." Jarrett shook his head wryly, grinning at me again. "How fortunate you are indeed to be wedding me, for 'tis quite obvious you know precious little about business and even less about people. If our dear grandmother Prescott Chandler and Aunt Julianne aren't wringing every last shilling they can out of poor Uncle Welles—and maybe even Father, too—why, I'll give my best suit to the ragman!''

"Yes, well, perhaps you *are* right about that," I agreed, beginning to chuckle at the mental image Jarrett had conjured.

Neither Grandmother Prescott Chandler nor Aunt Julianne would ever be accused of thrift; though the Hall itself was inclined toward shabbiness these days, both women, despite their frequent complaints of penury, were always elegantly coiffed and extravagantly gowned. For the first time, I wondered how many of the bills shoved in Papa's desk drawer were for his mother and sister, and I thought perhaps he had just cause to look so sour when the chits arrived.

At the idea that even his fearsome father might not be proof against the monetary demands of our formidable grandmother and petulant aunt, Jarrett burst into laughter, too; and soon we were making such a to-do that dour old Sykes, the butler, felt duty bound to intrude upon us to be certain "young Mr. Jarrett," as he called him, had not forgotten we were not yet married.

Such was the expression of censure upon Sykes's face that after he had politely but sufficiently assured himself of my well-being and closed the doors behind him, Jarrett and I erupted into laughter again; and when he finally took his leave of me, I was in better spirits than I had been for many a long day.

Chapter VII

Shells Upon the Sand

> She knew treachery,
> Rapine, deceit, and lust, and ill enow
> To be a woman.
>
> —*Progress of the Soul*
> John Donne

I shall never forget the night of the twins' engagement party, for that was the night I lost my innocence forever—though my youth was to endure one last, terrible blow before it, too, became but a bittersweet memory.

But once more, I get ahead of myself, for that loss came two months later, though still far too soon and sudden in my life. But I have only myself to blame for that, as well I know—and as you shall learn in time and say perhaps it was naught but my just deserts; though had my innocence not been stripped from me in the manner it was, I think I should not have been driven to the desperate act that ended my youth as well. At least it comforts me to believe that, to think I am not so hard and unscrupulous as some considered me afterward. They could not know—for how could I tell them?—what led me to commit the cruel, callous crime that nearly destroyed another's life and broke a mother's heart.

It is this last, more than anything else in my life, that I regret with all my heart and would undo if I could. I did not deserve forgiveness for it, though I *was* forgiven and, God help me, loved by her whom I had so deeply injured.

That was the hardest cross of all to bear.

Yet I would have borne its weight a thousand times again for her sake, for in the end, older, wiser than I, she was my salvation, and how does one repay a debt such as that? She was worthy of far more than I gave her, I know, though she would not have thought so, for she took what life handed her and made of it what she must, and with that, she was ever content.

Yet even so, I will not spare myself, but will speak —and be honest in the telling—of the great wrong I did her, who lies dead and buried now beneath the wild, windswept moors she loved so well, though she lives ever in my heart. And perhaps with the recounting of my sin, I can at last forgive myself for it, as she forgave me so many years ago.

So, listen now, for you shall be privy to what I never told another soul, save her.

It was still autumn, that night of my lost innocence,

chilly and bleak as autumn is always in northern Cornwall. The full moon was ghostily ringed, as it is sometimes on a dreary eve, and the faint, far-off stars in the leaden sky were veiled by the mist drifting in from the sea. Breakers crashed against the jagged black rocks lining the coast; spume rose white as death in the air, and the wind, scented with spindrift, whispered across the heaths, stirring the spindly limbs of straggling gorse. In the courtyard of the Heights, the boughs of the two ancient Cornish elms that towered over the old house rustled, forked tips scraping the pitched slate roof eerily, though the grating noise only occasionally pierced the din and laughter that echoed up to the massive rafters of the great hall within.

It was not a night one would have chosen to be out and about. Yet here was I, forest-green velvet cape hugged close about me against the wind's icy fingers, in thin morocco slippers, stumbling across the dewy grass of the manor's sprawling lawn, then sliding and sinking upon the steep, narrow, muddy track that wended its way perilously from the edge of the yard, down sheer, rugged cliffs to the rocky shore far below.

I scarcely knew what I did, acted purely on instinct, driven by the mad thing that had seized hold of me and now clawed at me mercilessly with sharp talons, so I ran faster and faster, as though I could somehow flee from it. But its malevolent grip upon me was supreme, and it would not be cast off. So I staggered on, blinded by tears, gasping for breath, a painful stitch in my side and in my heart an ache that would not be eased.

They had laughed at me.

I could have borne anything but that: the way their eyes had glittered with sudden malice, the wickedly meaningful looks they had given each other as, upon ascending the stairs from the great hall, they had spied me at the top of the landing; the scathing remarks they had deliberately begun to exchange about me, as though I were not there, but were merely an elongated shadow cast against the wall by the flickering candles; the exaggerated surprise and guilty dismay they had pretended when, cheeks flaming, I had stepped forward into the light to confront them.

But not their laughter.

I should never forget the sound of it: Nicholas's low, derisive snicker, Elizabeth's shrill, arch titter. It rang in my ears even now as I rushed on; I could not seem to shut it out.

I do not know why it should have affected me so. I despised them both—now more than ever after their cruel, childish behavior toward me. It had just been such a shock to see Nicky's hand at Lizzie's elbow, their heads bent together conspiratorially, their eyes conveying those unspoken thoughts only the nearest and dearest share, the mutually perverse enjoyment they had taken in baiting me.

I had not known they'd grown so close. I had believed Nicky amusing himself with Clemency, whom he would never wed, regardless of what she might think to the contrary. I had been unaware that Lizzie, a suitable prospective bride—albeit one who was two years older than Nicky and who, having reached her twenty-third year unwed, was considered by most a permanent fixture on the spinsters' shelf—had finally succeeded in drawing his attention to her, perhaps knew even now, as I had once known, his kisses and caresses.

The idea that she, who had so spitefully started into motion the chain of events that had caused me such turmoil and anguish, might actually attain for herself the man I had once loved galled me bitterly. She did not deserve to have him!

By now, I had reached the bottom of the precipitous path, and as my feet struck unevenly the shingle that littered the beach, so I nearly lost my balance, I slowed my pace to a walk, breathing hard. The turbulent emotion that had impelled me into my wild, headlong flight from the house had left me now; in its wake was naught but a sense of sadness, of emptiness, and a vague feeling of foolishness at my impetuosity. I thought I must look a fright, my hair windblown, the hem of my cloak and frock wet from the grass, my morocco slippers soiled with mud. How I should explain my rumpled state upon returning to the twins' engagement party, I could not imagine.

But though I guessed Jarrett, at least, must have missed me by now and wondered at my disappearance, I did not go back, but continued to meander along the shore, slightly relieved now to have escaped the crush of the crowd gathered at the Heights.

I came at last to a small cove, long a favorite spot of mine, and there, I sat down upon a boulder sheltered from the wind, spreading my green and gold skirts about me in a vain attempt to dry them, huddling in the warmth of my mantle as I stared out over the ocean. The dark, shifting waves were alight with a million pinpoints of winking silver, the reflection of the dim stars overhead, so it looked as though someone had scattered diamonds carelessly in the sea. The murmur of the water sluicing between the long fingers of rock soothed me, and for a while, I was content to sit, lost in reverie.

By the soft, hazy light of the moon, I noticed that upon the beach was scattered a handful of shells that had been washed up by the ocean and stranded, and idly, I studied them, marveling at their beauty and grace. Each was different from the rest; some were curved in intricate spirals or folded layer upon layer, like a Chinese puzzle box; others were open and simple, without hidden secrets, colors and patterns vulnerably exposed. But tough or fragile, all the shells were small and helpless against the powerful waves that continued to buffet them, so they tumbled helter-skelter across the sand and, striking the shingle, were cracked and chipped, forever scarred, some irretrievably shattered, others finally coming to rest in an imperfect mosaic.

What stories would those shells tell, I wondered, could they but speak—of life and what had brought them to this pass? They were silent, unable to reply, but even so, in my heart, I felt I knew the answer, for were we not all as shells upon the sand?

It was the crunch of footsteps upon the shingle that startled me back to reality, frightening me as, for the first time, I realized how alone and defenseless I was here upon the beach. As every tale I had ever heard of the smugglers and, even worse, the wreckers who frequented the isolated coast of northern Cornwall rose to haunt me, my breath came shallowly, quickly, and my heart beat too fast in my breast. It had been unwise, perhaps even dangerous of me, I recognized now, to leave the party, unaccompanied by even so much as my maid. Once more, I had allowed my reckless impulses to get the better of me, and perhaps now again, I would pay for it.

Trembling, I stood, glancing about frantically for some hiding place. But before I could crouch behind the boulder that appeared my only near refuge, a tall, dark figure detached itself, specterlike, from the mist and came toward me, black greatcoat swirling about it like a shroud, the diffuse moonlight illuminating its visage erratically, one moment revealing it, the next casting it in shadow, so it appeared to have a demon's face.

Strangely, I felt no alarm then, only relief, for I mistakenly thought it was Jarrett who approached; and though he often caused my heart to flutter with trepidation, and something else I could not name, he was not likely to rob, brutalize, kidnap, or murder me, as I had feared might prove my fate. It was only when the silhouette drew closer that I realized it was Nicky; and even then, I was not afraid—not at first—just angry that he had obviously followed me, when it was solitude I had sought.

"What do you want, Nicholas?" I asked sharply, stung by his effrontery in seeking me out.

"Why, you, of course, my pet," he rejoined flippantly, grinning at me; but his eyes were hard, feral even, and instinctively, I drew the edges of my cape together, as though it might somehow shield me from his jackal-like gaze. "Did you believe that had changed?"

"You must think me a very great fool indeed," I uttered coldly, staring at him with undisguised contempt, "to stand there and tell me that. How dare you come here to insult me further, Nicky? Was not your and Lizzie's laugh at my expense enough for you?"

"That was indeed uncalled for, I admit," he confessed. "But, then . . . did you not deserve it, Laura? After all, it was not *I* who led *you* on—and then accepted Jarrett's proposal!" He voice had lost its bantering tone, grown raw with feeling, and now he broke off abruptly, as though trying to master his emotions. Then he swore bitterly, "For Christ's sake! Did you think that I would not be hurt by that—that I would not want to hurt you back? Surely, you of all people should understand and forgive that, my pet, for *you've* certainly never been slow to stick someone with a knife and twist it in the wound, have you?" Once more, Nicky clamped his mouth shut; a muscle throbbed in his jaw as he tried again to regain his self-control.

After a time, more evenly, he said, "But, there. I did not come here to argue with you. If the truth be known, I am as much to blame as you that things went so awry between us. I should have spoken up and brought my desire for you into the open so Jarrett would have been forced to step aside; I see that now. But I could not bear to quarrel with my brother, to let bad blood come between us—though I should have . . . for your sake." He paused, then asserted softly, "It's still not too late, you know. You're not married to him yet. Come away with me, Laura!" he urged. "I love you. I have always loved you."

God help me, I had yearned for so long to hear him say those words that I almost believed him. Then I remembered the wisteria petals trailing like lavender confetti from Clemency's hair; how he had deserted me so uncaringly in the coppice that day of the fox hunt, leaving me to face Jarrett alone; how I had found him trifling, bold as brass, with my abigail at the Hall; and how, tonight at the Heights, he and Lizzie had heartlessly made me the butt of their invidious mirth.

"Jarrett is right, Nicky," I sneered. "You don't know the meaning of the word. Certainly, you consoled yourself for my loss quickly enough with Clemency—and now Lizzie—and with God only knows how many others as well!"

"They mean nothing to me," he insisted, still trying to win me over.

"Nor do I. Good night, Nicholas." I spoke crisply, firmly.

Clutching my cloak to me, I started toward the track that led to the cliffs above, only to come to a halt as, without warning, Nicky deliberately moved to bar my progress.

"Stand aside," I demanded, wroth yet distinctly apprehensive now, too, "and let me pass. We have nothing more to say to each other."

"Oh, but I think we do, Laura, my pet," he jeered, smiling unpleasantly, in a way that made my skin crawl. "I think we have a great deal more to say to each other."

His breath was hot against my face, and smelled strongly of whiskey. He was drunk, I thought, and therefore unpredictable; perhaps he would even do me some harm! His even teeth gleamed white in the moonlight, sharp and carnivorous, it seemed; and some primitive sense warning me, I whirled away from him and began to race down the beach, feet skidding hazardously upon the rough, damp shingle. With a short, nasty laugh that rang in my ears like a death knell, Nicky gave chase and, a few moments later, caught hold of me and flung me violently to the ground, knocking the wind from me. Briefly, I lay stunned as he towered over me, his black eyes glinting, appraising me lasciviously, his lips curled in a twisted half-smile, his face filled with a terrible threat and triumph.

He wanted me; that was true. He wanted to have me, whether *I* wanted *him* or not, because I belonged to Jarrett. Shivering uncontrollably, I bit the back of one shaking hand to stifle the sob of terror that rose in my throat, for I knew now, horrified, that Nicky had come here with the sole intention of raping me!

I tried to scramble away from him, but he fell upon me like a ravaging beast, his fingers ensnarling my hair agonizingly as he yanked my head up so savagely that I thought my slender neck would snap. Viciously, he ground his mouth down on mine, teeth cutting my tender lips, as, whimpering with fear and pain, I struggled against him fiercely, my hands tearing at his in an attempt to dislodge them. But his fingers were like a vise crushing my skull, and my efforts to pry them loose were futile. Insistently, his tongue forced its way deep into my mouth, sickening me, gagging me, shutting off my breath, so I panicked and fought him even harder, fists beating him wildly about the head and shoulders until he jerked away, cursing, to fend off my attack.

Like a person strangling, I gasped for air, feeling its coldness rush into my lungs so rapidly that I thought they would burst, while Nicky went on grappling with me, trying to grab my flailing arms and pin them to my sides. At last, much to my dread, he managed to secure a grip on my left wrist, and nearly wrenching it from its socket, he contorted it behind my back.

"Move and I'll break your Goddamned arm, Laura— I swear it!" he threatened, giving my wrist another excruciating tug, almost dislocating my elbow.

Tears scalded my eyes, and I bit my lip so hard that I tasted blood to keep from crying out, for I sensed he would derive a perverse satisfaction if I screamed.

"Please, Nicky," I begged, unable to believe this was the same man I had once loved and hoped to wed. "Please, don't do this."

But he paid no heed to my entreaties, cutting them off callously as his mouth took possession of mine once more. I thrashed my head, trying to avoid his encroaching lips, but he hauled on my wrist warningly, so I was compelled to accede to his demands as his tongue pillaged my mouth ruthlessly.

His free hand moved to my throat, working impatiently at the ribbons that tied my mantle. Once he had the knot undone, he flipped back the edges of the cloak to reveal its gold lining and my bare shoulders and bosom above the heart-shaped bodice of my dress. Then his fingers encircled my throat, tightening there briefly before trailing down to squeeze my breasts through the velvet of my gown. I moaned in protest and writhed beneath him in another attempt to liberate myself—to no avail. Crudely, he plunged his hand into my bodice to fondle my breast. His thumb flicked at my nipple. Upon finding it unresponsive, he raised his head and spat an obscenity, incensed at how I recoiled from him, for he had been sure he could arouse me in spite of myself.

"Damn you!" he snapped, glaring at me ominously. "There was a time when you weren't so repelled by my touch! There was a time when you liked it, lusted for it, my pet."

To my everlasting shame, I knew that was true—but not now. Not when I knew that he didn't love me, that he wanted only to spoil me for Jarrett.

"Please, Nicky. Please, don't do this," I pleaded again. "You're drunk. You don't know what you're doing. I know you wouldn't do this if you did. Please, if you ever cared about me at all, let me go."

For a moment, I thought he would relent, and involuntarily, a small sigh of relief issued from my lips. Then his jaw set purposefully, and I knew, hideously, that I was lost.

"Not until I've had what I came for, bitch!" he growled, then bent his head to kiss me cruelly once more.

But this time, I was ready for him. With my unrestrained hand, I snatched up a fistful of sand and threw it with all my might into his eyes. Howling with pain and fury, he toppled back, releasing me at once as his hands flew to his face to scrub at the grit that blinded him. Wriggling my legs from beneath his imprisoning thighs,

I scrabbled forward, lurching to my knees, then gaining my feet. Unsteadily, panting for breath, I started to run.

I had not gone more than a few yards when Nicky overtook me, catching me by my long hair, straggling from its pins and streaming out behind me in the wind, and jerked me back vehemently, his dark visage murderous with rage. As I slipped and tripped upon the shingle, he spun me about, then backhanded me brutally across the face, so I sprawled in a crumpled heap upon the beach, dazed and unbelieving that he should treat me thus. I had never expected it of him, had never fully realized until now how his jealousy of Jarrett had festered within him like a putrefying sore grown gangrenous; I had never dreamed he would unscrupulously cast aside his gentlemanly upbringing and honor to injure his brother. Jarrett had known him far better than I.

Sobbing, I attempted to rise, but instantly, Nicky's weight flattened me, expelling, with a loud *whoosh*, all the air from my lungs, so I gasped again raggedly for breath. Sharp pebbles gouged my skin. My head reeled from the blow he had dealt me. Before I could stop him, he grasped the top of my bodice and rent it in two; then he tore away the lacy, off-the-shoulder straps of my chemise and ripped the thin fabric down to expose my naked breasts to his leering eyes. Once more, I clawed at him, scratching his face, leaving deep red gashes as I tried vainly to fight him off. When that failed, I attempted pathetically to cover myself. But he wrested my arms from my breasts and slapped me again hard. Then, petrifyingly, he threatened to kill me if I offered any further resistance.

After that, I lay still and submissive beneath him, tears trickling silently down my cheeks as he laughed devilishly and pressed me down into the sand, his black greatcoat, beaded with mist, winding like a cerecloth around me, blotting out the heavens above.

BOOK TWO

Scattered Hopes and Hearts
1842–1845

Chapter VIII

Clash of the Titans

When shall we three meet again
In thunder, lightning, or in rain?
When the hurly-burly's done,
When the battle's lost and won.

—*Macbeth*
William Shakespeare

The Cornish Shore, England, 1842

To my dying day, I shall always believe that somehow my mind reached across time and space to touch Jarrett's, for as though in answer to my prayers, dear reader, he came.

Without warning, like an angry raven, he swooped to pluck Nicholas from my cringing body, powerful fist colliding with an audible crack against the side of his brother's face before Nicky even had a chance to realize

189

what was happening and defend himself. The jolting impact sent him sprawling, and for a moment, he lay as stunned as I had earlier. Then he shook his head to clear it, and his eyes narrowed, gleaming with rage and speculation as they acutely snapped into focus. Gingerly, he touched his hand to one corner of his mouth; his fingers came away streaked with blood. At the sight, his lips curved into a twisted smile that did not quite reach his eyes.

"Rather an underhanded blow, that, wasn't it, Jarrett?" he gibed.

"By God, I warned you, Nicholas," Jarrett hissed through gritted teeth as he advanced toward his brother threateningly, "and this time, you're going to pay! Get up, you bastard!"

"With pleasure, brother," Nicky rejoined, springing to his feet. "With pleasure. I've waited a long time for this, and I mean to savor it to the fullest! And just to make it more . . . interesting, why don't we forget the London Prize Ring rules—shall we?—and say no holds barred."

Jarrett shrugged indifferently.

"It's your funeral," he declared.

"Always so sure of yourself, aren't you, Jarrett?" Nicky drawled sarcastically. "How I'm going to enjoy grinding your face into the dirt, brother!"

Warily, the two men began to circle each other, dancing on booted feet, lunging, feinting, tossing a jab here, a punch there, to test each other's skill and mettle; for neither was a novice at pugilism. Both had, over the years, spent considerable time, when in London, at

Gentleman Jackson's boxing saloon in Bond Street. Finally, however, Nicky closed in to start the conflict in earnest, and as he did so, Jarrett slugged him hard in the stomach. With a loud "*Oof*," Nicky doubled over, groaning, and Jarrett smashed his clenched fists down on his brother's neck, so Nicky fell forward, facedown into the sand.

"Get up!" Jarrett goaded again, his lip curled with contempt. "Get up, you bastard, and fight like a man!—or is it only helpless women you victimize?"

"Victimize? *Victimize*?" Nicky laughed scornfully as he rocked to his knees, then stood. "Jesus Christ! You think I was '*victimizing*' her, you fool? Is that it? Brother, are you ever barking up the wrong tree! Hell! She was so hot for me that for a minute, I was half afraid I wouldn't have hose enough to put the fire out!"

"So help me, God . . . I'll kill you for that, Nicholas!" Jarrett's voice was soft, deadly, as he suddenly tore into his brother so ferociously that neither heard the broken whimper of denial that emanated from my throat at Nicky's lies.

As the two men started to pummel each other mercilessly, I somehow managed to wobble to my feet, shaking all over with shock at what had been done to me. My hair was hopelessly entangled; my mouth was bruised and swollen; the tender skin of my back was abraded from the coarse shingle; and purplish blue shadows marred my wrists and breasts, where Nicky had drunkenly mauled me. With trembling hands, I clutched the shreds of my bodice to my bosom in a wasted effort to cover my nakedness. Then, shivering with cold and fear and shame, I retrieved my cape and wrapped it tightly about me, as though it could somehow protect me from further hurt.

Jarrett and Nicky fought on furiously, neither giving any quarter as they staggered, tumbled, and grappled their way across the sand, their black greatcoats flapping like bats' wings in the wind until each man impatiently stripped his off and flung it aside. The ugly sound of the devastating blows the brothers exchanged reverberated sickeningly in my ears, so I felt as though I would faint or retch. Yet I did neither, for my eyes were morbidly enthralled by the vicious battle taking place before me, and I was unable to tear them away.

All the pent-up emotion the two men had felt toward each other since their childhood was now released and given full rein. Jarrett, snarling and cursing, pounded his brother's dark head savagely against the shingle, while Nicky, sweating and grunting and straining to free himself, grabbed Jarrett's throat and choked him determinedly until each man was forced out of self-preservation to break away from the other.

Now, rolling to his feet, Jarrett jerked Nicky up so violently by the lapels of his evening jacket that the silk fabric ripped. Then, employing the rapid jabs and fancy footwork that the Jewish prizefighter Daniel Mendoza had made famous, Jarrett hit his brother repeatedly in the face, blackening one of his eyes and bloodying his nose before Nicky landed a solid whack to his ribs, sending him reeling.

As Jarrett labored to recover his balance, Nicky took

advantage of the momentary lull in the fray to seize a heavy piece of driftwood that had washed up on the sand. Swinging the improvised club so it *whoosh*ed menacingly through the air, he strode toward his brother purposefully.

Half crouching, arms spread wide, Jarrett maneuvered with a dancer's grace, shifting and leaping to avoid the bludgeon Nicky wielded; and all the while, the brothers laughed and taunted each other vilely, so I was certain I witnessed a clash of demons or madmen, and I thought of the Chandler wild streak and shuddered.

From my vantage point, I could see the Heights perched like an aerie above us, looming over us like some ominous bird of prey from its nesting place upon the cliffs. The torches that had been ignited and placed in the exterior iron sconces for the twins' engagement party flickered eerily in the wind, seeming to blaze across the sky, so it was as though the very heavens themselves were aflame, consuming the two men silhouetted against the horizon.

In beautiful but macabre motion, they approached and retreated and sidestepped, jumped and whirled and dropped, as though executing the movements of some intricate ballet. Their brawny muscles bulged and rippled like those of jungle animals stalking and then springing upon their prey, or of young pagan gods, titans, each of whom would rule the world—and see the other driven from it, if he could. They were so much alike, and so similarly dressed, that sometimes it was difficult for me to tell them apart; and it was only when the far-off, wavering torchlight or a swirling spray of silver moonbeams illuminated their faces that I was certain who was who.

Somehow Jarrett had succeeded in grasping the opposite end of the driftwood, and now he and Nicky were engaged in a strenuous tug-of-war for possession of the makeshift club. The two men were equally strong, however, and seeing there was nothing to be gained by the struggle for control of it, Jarrett abruptly loosed his end, so Nicky tripped and nearly fell. But he caught himself just in time, lashing out at his brother rashly. Adroitly dodging the reckless swipe, Jarrett pivoted, one corded leg deftly coming up and around, kicking his brother so brutally in the back that Nicky arched spasmodically with pain, the bludgeon flying from his hands before he slowly sank to his knees. After that, his face filled with wrath and disgust that Nicky would stoop to its use in a bareknuckle brawl, Jarrett picked up the driftwood and hurled it into the ocean.

Nicky scrambled after it, but before he could reach it, Jarrett caught hold of him; and as though in a dream, I saw the two men, as they continued to wrestle with each other, stomp upon the shells I had so admired earlier, crushing them to bits. Blood spattered upon the shards, staining them with crimson before the sea rushed in and the splintered shells were swept away, nothing more now than flotsam on the waves.

Nearer and nearer, the brothers edged dangerously to the ocean, to my terror, suddenly plunging headlong into the madding, whitecapped surf, the pale mist enveloping them like a pall. I gasped, frozen with fear and incredulity as, for one ghastly, heart-stopping moment, they vanished beneath the dark water; then I exhaled with relief as they bobbed once more to the surface, locked in mortal combat. The sea was black as the night, lathered like a cake with icing by the white mist; and I could not differentiate between the two men as one shoved the other's head under the foaming waves again and again, while the ebony firmament glowed red as fire behind them from the distant torchlight. Each time the one man hauled the other up, the drowning brother gagged and rasped for air, slinging water in every direction as he shook his head to clear his eyes and nose, his arms flailing wildly, before the other pushed him down relentlessly once more; and at last, to my utter horror, I realized I was watching murder done.

"Stop it! Stop it!" I shrieked and sobbed hysterically over the roar of the ocean as I ran desperately toward the two men. "For God's sake! Stop it! You're killing him! You're killing him!"

The churning froth of the surf surged and sucked about my knees, almost dragging me under as I stumbled toward Jarrett—for it *was* Jarrett who held Nicky down—and tried frantically to loosen his steely grip on his brother. For a dreadful interlude, I thought I should not succeed. But then, to my relief, my screams must have penetrated his consciousness, for finally, Jarrett came to his senses, pulling Nicky up for good; and between us, we managed to half lug, half carry him to shore, where he collapsed upon the beach, coughing and sputtering saltwater from his lungs.

He was stone-cold sober now; but still, incredibly, he was unrepenting of his abominable behavior toward me, and churlishly, he knocked away the hand that Jarrett, unnerved by and deeply regretting what had nearly happened just now, stretched out to him in apology, friendship, and, most of all, love. If only Nicky had taken Jarrett's hand then, had bridged the black chasm that yawned between them! How very different all our lives might have been!

But instead, he stood unsteadily and, backing away from us, flicked his eyes lewdly over my ashen form, making me shiver as I remembered his hands forcing me down, roaming freely, roughly, over my body, hurting me. Then he grinned, an insolent smile that did not soften his flinty eyes.

"I wish you joy of her, brother," he taunted, laughing mockingly, "for though you may have won the battle, you still arrived too late to defend the citadel, you know. I'd already breached its walls—and, oh, how willingly did they yield!" he crowed jubilantly as I stared at him disbelievingly, shocked and appalled by this heinous revenge, though, unbeknown to me, the worst was yet to come.

"What do you mean, Nicholas?" Jarrett asked, his voice low and sharp, his glittering eyes narrowing, the expression that darkened his visage making my blood run cold. "Stop spouting metaphors and spell it out for me, why don't you?"

"All right, then," Nicky agreed. Then, each monstrous word falling lethally into the sudden silence, he said coolly, "I thought you knew. I had her maidenhead, Jarrett—just before you came."

Chapter IX

A Wilder Shore of Love

All which I took from thee I did but take,
  Not for thy harms,
But just that thou might'st seek it in My arms.

—*The Hound of Heaven*
Francis Thompson

"That's a lie!" I shouted hotly. "You bastard! That's a lie!"

To my distress, Nicholas only shrugged, unruffled by my fervent denial of his words.

"If you say so, Laura," he concurred. "But, then, of course, you *must* say so, mustn't you?" he pointed out glibly, shrewdly, fatally undermining any further refutation I might have made.

In that moment, the last vestiges of any love I had ever borne him died. I had never hated him more than I did then as, after that ruinous, crowning blow, he turned and, fetching his greatcoat, cavalierly sauntered down the beach toward the path that looped its way precariously up the cliffs to the moors above. A red haze filmed my eyes; the blood roared in my ears; my heart thrummed so hard that I thought it would explode as, quivering with outrage, scarcely cognizant of what I did, I started to run after him, in my mind some jumbled, half-formed notion of thrashing him, killing him, wiping him from the face of the earth as though he had never existed. But without warning, Jarrett's arm shot out to restrain me, drawing me back.

"Let him go, Laura," he commanded tersely, "for assuredly, he has set his feet upon a road to destruction far more grievous than either you or I could wish right now, I fear. He will live to rue it, I suspect, though it will be too late then to change what he has done. His youth will be gone, misspent—and that will prove a punishment crueler and more bitter than any you can imagine."

Jarrett's eyes were veiled as he spoke, so I could not tell what he was thinking, though I would have given anything just then to know his thoughts. Had he believed Nicky's damning words about me? Did he despise me now and long to be rid of me? I did not know. Involuntarily, I shuddered, for if Jarrett refused to marry me now, especially with our wedding day so imminent, he would have to give some plausible explanation to our families for his rejection of me, and none but the truth would serve. I could not endure the shame of that.

"It *was* a lie, Jarrett," I insisted beseechingly, for

suddenly, it was somehow very important to me that he believe that—and, for some peculiar reason I could not define, not just so I might be spared from disgrace otherwise. "What Nicky claimed . . . it was a lie."

"Was it, Laura?"

"Yes."

He made no reply to that, but, instead, bent to pick up his discarded greatcoat, which he draped about me.

"Come," he said. "You are shaking from the cold."

Slowly, his arm clasped about my waist to steady me upon the rough shingle, he led me to a place where the cliff face had eroded from the elements, and the sea, so that, over the centuries, a small niche had been hollowed out, like a jagged-edged half-moon, in the wall. On either side, gnarled black rock extended to the ocean, guarding us from the wind, and within, the sand was smooth, strewn only lightly with pebbles. There, Jarrett released me and, to my surprise, reached out, fingers curiously gentle, to stroke back my tousled hair from my pale countenance. For an eternity, it seemed, his eyes searched mine intently; his hand caressed my cheek, wonderingly, I thought, before abruptly dropping to his side, curling into a tight ball, making his sinewy arm rigid. A muscle working in his tense jaw, he glanced away, staring out over the ocean for a long, silent minute before turning back to me. Then, not touching me, he broke at last the taut stillness that stretched between us.

"So, Nicky lied, did he?" he asked, his voice low, hoarse with feeling.

"Yes . . . yes," I whispered, hope, anxiety, and some incomprehensible yearning suddenly burgeoning within me, tangling my thoughts and emotions so, that I could make no sense of them at all as his eyes gazed darkly into mine, seeming to ferret out the innermost secrets of my heart and soul.

In that instant, my world contracted sharply to that quiet place where we stood upon the beach, as though some unknown force had magically woven it into a cocoon, enveloping us in gossamer folds, hushing the night, the wind, and the sea; though it was only that my abruptly heightened senses shut them out, became so keenly attuned to Jarrett's that we breathed as one.

"Show me, Laura," he demanded softly then. "Show me that Nicky lied."

I gasped, for I could not mistake his meaning, though what he asked was unthinkable. But how was I to convince him of the truth otherwise? I did not know; there seemed no other way. If I refused him, he might spurn me, believing me false, sullied, his brother's leavings. If this was the ransom he demanded of me, I had no choice but to pay it.

Perhaps my eyes revealed my thoughts, for no man had ever looked at me as Jarrett did then, as though he knew that, within moments, he would possess me intimately, utterly, and I would belong to him irrevocably for the rest of my days. At the thought, my breath caught in my throat, and a slow-burning sensation such as I had never before experienced began at the very core of my being and spread through my body like a fever, making me shiver with mingled fear and anticipation, for I did not know what to expect from him. Would he be gentle with me—or pitiless, as Nicky had been? Because I was ignorant of the answer, the pulse at the hollow of my neck fluttered jerkily; my mouth went dry. I believed that if he touched me, I would shatter like crystal, I felt suddenly so fragile and vulnerable.

The wind stirred, kissing my lips with spindrift, so it was almost as though I had pressed them to Jarrett's flesh, licked the salty sweat of his body, tasted it strong and sharp upon my tongue. To my confusion, as the torrid image, unbidden, filled my mind, I was swept by another wave of that strange, smoldering fire, so strong and violent now that it was frightening, agonizing in its intensity. My mouth parted; my tongue darted forth to moisten my lips. A soft, incoherent cry issued from my throat, as slowly, tremulously, my body swayed against his, drawn irresistibly to him by the nameless thing that had seized me so fiercely and now inexorably pulled me down into its dark, primeval flames.

However he had compelled me to face it, I wanted this man, I realized suddenly, wanted him with every fiber of my being to wash away the taint that Nicky's lips and hands had left upon me and to leave his own mark in their place. Tomorrow, perhaps I would be filled with shame and regret that I had given myself to him. But tonight, there was only the sand and the sea, and Jarrett. . . .

Of their own volition, my hands crept up around his neck; trembling, I lifted my face to his and brushed his mouth impetuously with mine. I do not know what I expected, but it was not the oath that burst from his lips before he entwined his fingers roughly in my hair and tilted my head back, forcing me to look at him.

"Don't tempt me, Laura," he warned me harshly, "not unless you're prepared to accept the consequences, for I promise you: All that is mine, I will take, and what I take, I will hold. One way or another, there will be no turning back of the clock for you when this night is ended."

"Yes, I know." I hesitated, then cried, "Have me, then, Jarrett!—and be done with it! I do not ask for your mercy, only a little tenderness, for in truth, I am yet chaste."

"Then you will find me all that you could wish, dear heart," he replied gently, "for I love you. I have always loved you. You just never could see me for Nicky."

I was stunned by his admission; I did not know what to say. I had never dreamed he cared for me, perhaps deeply, passionately, as Nicky had not. Yet I did not doubt his words, for he need not have spoken them. I was his for the taking after all. Oh, God. All these years . . . had I really been so blind? Tears stung my eyes bitterly for that, for loving the brother who did not love me—and for knowing so little the one who did.

"Oh, Jarrett . . . Jarrett!" I sobbed. "What a mess I have made of it all!" And I turned away, so he should not see the pain and grief etched upon my face.

But he would not permit me to share that alone.

"Hush, my sweet," he crooned, gathering me into his arms, crushing me to his chest, raining kisses upon my hair. "Hush now, for I did not mean to make you weep. I but wanted you to know it was not lust or revenge that drove me to bring you here, only that I would have you as mine, now and always, and heal some of the hurt you are suffering inside.''

"But, how can you be so kind, when you know I don't lo—''

"Hush, I say!''—he stilled my mouth with his fingers—''and let me love you. It is enough for now.''

He spread his greatcoat beneath us then, and drew me down upon the silvery folds of its silk lining; and I knew no fear of him any longer, only of not pleasing him, because I was ignorant of much, and what I had learned earlier this night had been wrongly taught me. I had not been tutored, then, in kisses quick and light as a butterfly's wings against my eyelids and lips and temples, or shown how lingeringly a man's tongue could trace the outline of my mouth before probing its dark, moist secret places within. I had not known until now how slowly and softly a man's hands could slide across my bare skin, so exquisite chills tingled through my body and my nipples hardened eagerly.

Sweet, sensual lips and strong, supple hands, Jarrett had, to weave his spell upon me, and willingly was I ensorcelled, my mouth opening like an unfurling bud to his, my fingers tensed and splayed as they clutched his whipcord body, so different from mine, and felt the powerful muscles that rippled beneath his flesh. He was so tall and tough that I felt small and delicate in his embrace, as though I were a willow reed he could bend or break, as he chose; and in some dim recess of my mind, I wondered if, when the time came, he would split me just as easily. I shuddered slightly with trepidation at the thought, and he, guessing my sudden qualms, tightened his hold on me, as though otherwise, like a startled bird, I would take flight, denying him what he so desired.

Little by little, our clothing began somehow to slip away. Yet would that I had not allowed him to push aside the torn edges of my bodice, for his eyes darkened dangerously as he spied the purplish blue smudges upon my breasts, and he growled a profanity that made me realize that if I had gentled him, it was only for the moment. Still, he was not angry at me, but at the one who had left those cruel bruises upon me, and he kissed each one, as though to take away the memory of how they had been made.

"What a fool my brother was," he muttered, "to use you thus and cast you away. He will never touch you again, Laura—nor will any other man. I shall have all of you, every part, like this . . . and this; and when I am done, there shall be no room in your bed or in your heart for another, I swear it."

Time turned—and kept on turning; and still, Jarrett tasted me, touched me, his kisses growing ever more insistent, his hands bolder. His lips swallowed my breath, devoured me; his tongue stabbed me everywhere with its heat. His skillful fingers aroused in me both delight and longing, so my body ached unbearably at its secret heart, in a way I had never dreamed was possible, so little had I known, in truth, of how a man could pleasure a woman.

The mist floated in from the sea, swaddling us in a blanket white and damp and cold; the wind caressed my naked skin with icy fingers. But I did not feel the autumn chill, for Jarrett had laid my velvet cloak over us, and beneath its rich folds, he warmed me with his body. I reveled in the feel of him. The dark hair that matted his chest was fine as down beneath my palms and against the sensitive tips of my breasts; his broad back was smooth as satin; his thighs were like iron. He smelled of bay rum and brandy and tobacco; tasted of brine borne on the wind, and musk. Avidly, I discovered him, explored him, mapped each line and every curve of him, and staked my claim upon his body, as he did mine.

And then, at last, he came to that virgin ground no other man had trodden, for he had spared me that; and crying out, I felt the sharp, sweet pain that makes of a maid a woman, and of a man, a conqueror. His black eyes widened fleetingly, then closed with satisfaction as he thrust hard and deep again into me; so I knew he had doubted me before, if but a little.

I could forgive him that.

Together, then, we lay, breast to breast, thigh to thigh, Jarrett's hands beneath me, arching my hips to meet his own until a thousand stars fell from the sky; while beyond, the sea rushed in upon the wild shore.

Chapter X

Of Lost Youth and Partings

Revenge is a dish best served cold.

—*Les Liaisons dangereuses*
Pierre Choderlos de Laclos

The moon dipped behind midnight clouds; the stars winked into nothingness, and outside the sheltered niche wherein we nestled, rain began to drizzle. The surf beat against the black rocks, and spume rose high into the air. Yet we lingered, loath to admit how the night slipped away, too quickly, with too many words left unsaid; for in the heat of our desire, we had not thought of blind, relentless time ticking on. But now, as I rested my head quietly upon Jarrett's chest, basking in the afterglow of our lovemaking, he spoke.

"So many times I have dreamed of this moment," he told me, "since I was old enough to understand the ways of a man and a woman, I think. You were yet a child then; but even so, I used to watch your dark braids flying, their golden streaks gleaming in the sun, and I would think: Someday, when Laura is grown, I will unbind those braids and run my fingers through that glorious mane . . . like this,'' he said, and showed me, grasping handfuls of my hair, burying his face in it, wrapping the long tresses about his throat. "So long have I loved you, dear heart. . . .''

How strange to hear him speak those words—he, of whom, despite what we had shared this night, I yet knew so very little. Still, had I given myself to him freely and felt the richer for it, with no regrets. He had indeed been all I could ever have wished for in his taking of me, tender in his fury, gentle in his possession, so different from what I had envisioned. I did not love him; but that, too, would come in time, I thought, would grow from the seed of this night's planting if I but nurtured it in my heart. And so, eagerly, when he reached for me once more, did I open myself to him.

I did not know, then, where his mouth ended and mine began; we were as one, no space between, urgent lips and tongues and hands unstill until strong he swelled and surged into me, bringer of exquisite torment—and its sweet release. His cry was piercing as the call of the gulls that nested in the cliffs; dulcet, it mingled with my own when at last I felt the long, hard length of him shudder against me, and trembled fierce with passion in his arms.

There was no time for more.

Cursed be that night, then, so short and swift. Yet I

would not trade it for another, for sweeter was it than any I had ever known before—or would ever know again with the innocence and wonder of that first time. In my heart, it held ever a precious place.

We rose and dressed. In silence, we walked back to the Heights, the rain showering upon us, the torches along the ancient manor's walls hissing and sputtering in the distance to light our path. The winding track was steep and treacherous in the rain and darkness—it seemed an endless climb—and in the wet and cold, harsh reality set in, so the magic of the night was lost. Little by little, doubt crept in to haunt me. I had lain with a man; how could I have done such a thing when he was not yet my husband? I did not know. But the deed was done; I could not undo it now. Besides, it did not seem such a terrible crime; we were to be married after all. Determinedly, I quelled my faint uneasiness, forced myself to concentrate on ascending the cliffs, carefully refraining from glancing down to where the precipice fell away sharply into the obsidian ocean crashing against the rocks below.

Aeons later, it seemed, the Heights loomed before us. Yet I dared not go inside, for how could I explain my disheveled appearance, the knowledge that should not have shone in a virtuous young woman's eyes, like those of a wakened bride? To the gatehouse, then, Jarrett took me, where he roused his father's old lunatic caretaker, Renshaw, who was too addled to notice aught amiss, and bade him go to the stables and harness a team to a carriage. Then, while I sat shivering in Renshaw's slovenly abode, trying to warm myself by his meager peat fire, Jarrett left me to fetch Clemency from the ranks of abigails attending their mistresses at the twins' engagement party.

He was gone some time; and though I never knew what he said to her, when finally he returned with my maid, her face was white, as I had never seen it, with two high spots of color in her cheeks, and her eyes could not meet mine. When I spoke to her, it was "Yes, Miss Laura" this and "Yes, Miss Laura" that, with more respect than she had ever shown to me before and never a hint of the state in which she had found me; so I knew, relieved, that somehow Jarrett had put the fear of God into her and that I need not be afraid her saucy tongue would wag about this night.

Renshaw, who, though mad, could comprehend things better than one might have supposed, arrived at last with the Chandlers' calash, its top pulled up against the rain, its lanterns glowing softly in the blackness. Shielding us with his greatcoat from the drizzle, Jarrett handed Clemency and me inside; then he took the whip and reins from Renshaw, who scuttled away, like a cockroach, back to his untidy gatehouse. After that, with a loud crack of the whip, Jarrett lashed the horses forward. Slowly, the carriage jolted down the drive onto the dark, sodden road.

"I told Uncle Welles and Aunt Sarah that you'd got a migraine, Laura," he informed me as he expertly guided the team over the shadowed, sweeping moors toward the Grange, "and had been lying down in Angel's room, but that as you were no better, I was taking you home. Since, fortunately"—his eyes flicked to my mute abigail—"Clemency vanished from her assigned post for a considerable length of time as well this evening, it will be assumed she was attending you, and the story of your having a headache should satisfactorily account for your disappearance from the party.''

How exceedingly clever and resourceful Jarrett was, I thought, relieved yet again at his enterprise and conveniently forgetting how, some months previously, I had indignantly condemned those very qualities in him. But in truth, I had not known how I should explain my long absence from the Heights or how I should return home without Papa and Mama seeing me and resolutely interrogating me about my disarray. Jarrett, however, had smoothly solved all; and not for the first time tonight was I grateful for his intervention. Then I remembered Nicholas and bit my lip anxiously.

''But what if Nicky—''

''Leave my brother to me, Laura,'' he insisted grimly. ''One way or another, I shall deal with him. Besides, he will hardly want *his* actions this night known!''

''No,'' I agreed, and, seeing Clemency's hands twist convulsively in her lap, wondered briefly if Nicky had gone to her, as he had that evening in the gardens, and had from her what he'd not had from me.

Well, she was welcome to him, I thought, grimacing, as was Elizabeth, if she could get him; for he meant nothing—less than nothing—to me now, and had I wed him, he would have made me miserable, as Angelique had once warned me. I pitied Lizzie if she married him—though, in truth, he was no less than she deserved.

How unkind was that thought, I think now, in the winter of my life; crueler yet was how it was to haunt me in years to come—and haunts me still. But I cannot turn back the hands of time. I can only relate to you, by and by, what came to pass that I should so regret wishing Nicky on poor Lizzie, vain and shallow and spiteful though she was.

Presently, we reached the Grange and turned onto the drive; the calash wheels crunched upon the gravel. I hoped the tattoo of the rain would mask the sound, for it was Jarrett's plan to set Clemency and me down at the side door, where we could enter the house unobserved. This, he did, with none, to my relief, the wiser.

"Good night, dear heart," he murmured, and kissed me swift and hard before he drove away into the darkness, the mist disturbed by the passing of the carriage closing behind him like a ghostly curtain.

I watched until he was out of sight, not knowing it was the last time I was to see him for many a long day.

Morning dawned, grey and hard-edged as a knife blade, bright with a layer of solid, shining frost upon the ground, pale harbinger of winter. Shivering beneath my blankets, I awoke, a strange sense of marvel and nervousness pervading my languorous body as I snuggled deeper under the covers for warmth. I had had a dream, I thought, a dream of Jarrett pressing me down upon the sand and having his way with me, taking me to the heavens—and beyond. But the twinge of ache between my thighs was real, sharp as Jarrett had pierced me upon the shore. No dream at all, then; I was a maid no longer.

At the realization, the night came flooding back; the color rose hot to my cheeks as I remembered, my mind a cloud of shame and confusion. Had that woman who had lain so wantonly in his embrace really been I? Yes . . . and again, yes. There was no part of me he had not known, had not claimed as his.

Somehow I expected to find myself changed; but my body, when I rose, looked the same in my cheval mirror, as though I had not spent the night locked in Jarrett's arms. Only the bruises that marred my breasts gave evidence that a man had touched me. But I would not think of Nicholas, only of him who, near the edge of the wild sea, had set his own mark upon me, for now and always.

After Clemency, oddly wan and silent still, her green eyes watchful, arrived to assist me, I dressed and went downstairs, blushing when Mama greeted me good morning and, with concern, inquired about my "migraine." Evenly enough, I answered, relieved but deeply ashamed that her faith in me was such that she readily believed my lies and, smiling, hugged me close for a moment before we joined Papa and Francis in the morning room for breakfast.

"Where is Guy?" I asked, unsuspecting of the devastating news I was about to receive.

"There has been a great deal of trouble in London, I'm afraid—with the shipping line," Papa explained, his jaw taut with anger. "A message came at daybreak. That old fool Treadwell!" he ejaculated. "He's gone off his beam, that's what! I ought never to have put him in charge of the London office! He was a good man once; but ever since marrying that flighty young wife of his, he's had his head in the clouds, paid no heed to business. Imagine his notifying me only this morning that there was a problem, when the accountant, Grimsby, hasn't reported for work in over a fortnight!

"Treadwell claims he thought the man was ill. *Ill*, ha!" Papa sneered, disgusted. "He's flown the coop, that's what!—absconded with God only knows how much money, the records are evidently in such a mess. I've no doubt the rogue kept a second set of books—and has been embezzling from the company for months! It will take weeks to look into the matter, to straighten everything out, and to find that rat-faced Grimsby, who dared to rob us. Curse me! I never *did* trust the man! I should've listened to my instincts instead of that besotted Treadwell, whose silly wife persuaded him to hire the scoundrel, as he was her brother and had fallen on hard times. 'Tis no wonder either, since he has proved such a crook!

"Of course, I dispatched Guy and Jarrett to London immediately to handle the affair. They departed not an hour ago."

Of course, my mind echoed Papa's words, dismayed. Of course, he had sent Guy and Jarrett: my brother, with his financial acumen, to go over the books and figure out what had been done to them; my lover, with his ruthless disposition, to notify the proper authorities and ensure their search for the fled accountant proved propitious. No one cheated the P & C Shipping Line and got away with it. Grimsby must be located and prosecuted for his crime. Jarrett would pursue the knave like a bloodhound, conducting his own diligent inquiries and hiring private investigators, if necessary; I felt certain of that.

Still, I was hurt and disappointed that he had not postponed his journey until seeing me at least, although there *was* a bouquet of dark green-leafed chrysanthemums waiting for me on the silver salver in the hall, blooms the topaz shade of my eyes, and a plain white card upon which he'd scrawled his name in bold black letters: *Jarrett*. That was all, however; no word of love—or of last night. Had he been compelled to leave so quickly, then, that he must trust me to understand what there'd been no time to communicate? Or—doubt gnawed at me suddenly, hideously—had everything he'd said and done last night been but a lie even more vicious and horrific than Nicky's?

God help me, I was not sure, so unexpected had been Jarrett's declaration of love for me; so newly was I become a woman, as yet uncertain of my power to hold his heart. Had he truly relinquished it into my keeping, or had he merely been parroting pretty phrases, for which I, like a gullible idiot, had fallen? He was Nicky's brother after all, was he not—minted of the same Chandler coin?

You are being very foolish, Laura, I reprimanded myself sternly. *Jarrett is nothing at all like Nicky! You are letting your imagination run rampant again, as usual.*

But still, to my discouragement, that small, poisonous doubt remained, sinuous and insidious as a serpent in my heart—and would not be banished, no matter how hard I tried.

Weeks passed, and I did not hear from Jarrett—not a letter or even a few hastily scribbled lines. As our wedding day steadily approached, I grew at first angry and then distressed that, still, there came no word. Even Papa and Uncle Draco did not know where Jarrett was. He had left the London office and checked out of his hotel —on the trail of the rascal Grimsby, he'd told Guy; and my brother had not seen or heard from him since. For all I knew, Jarrett lay dead in a dark alley somewhere, with no one the wiser as to his fate—though nobody else in the family appeared to share my concern.

"Oh, for heaven's sake! What nonsense, Laura!" Papa responded when finally I ventured to express my misgivings aloud. "Really, poppet, you have been reading far too many gothic novels, I fear. Jarrett's quite capable of taking care of himself. I should not have sent him after Grimsby otherwise. Now, do stop fretting. I promise your groom will be at the church, and on time, Laura, when the big day arrives, or he's not the man I think him—and in that case, perhaps you'd better not marry him after all!"

Mama, though not as brusque, was no more comforting.

"Well, darling," she said when I broached the matter to her, "although I'm quite happy to see that you *do* care for Jarrett after all—for I confess I'd begun to believe Welles and I had made a terrible mistake in betrothing you to him; you've seemed so reluctant, this past year, to accept his invitations—I can't help but think that your father is right, dear, and that Jarrett can fend for himself. He's your uncle Draco made over in that respect, and certainly, no one I know has ever got the best of Draco—except your aunt Maggie, of course. Perhaps you would be wise to spend some time with her, Laura, before your wedding day, to learn a few of her secrets for handling a stubborn Chandler man.''

I could find no solace in these reassurances, however. *Surely*, I thought over and over, *something has happened to Jarrett, else he would have written.*

But I did not know that for certain. Perhaps he had believed Nicholas's lies, after all, and had seduced me only to satisfy his lust or his desire for revenge before casting me aside. Perhaps he had seized upon the search for Grimsby as a golden opportunity to be rid of me, and so he did not mean to return for our wedding, but to jilt me at the altar instead.

I did not want to believe these things, but still, doubt ate at me. I grew gaunt with worry; mauve shadows ringed my eyes, and worst of all, the utterly unthinkable happened: My monthly courses ceased. To my great shock and despair, I realized I was going to have a baby.

At first, I simply did not believe it, for of all the repercussions I had recognized that I might suffer for that sweet night of stolen passion, the possibility that Jarrett had got me with child had never occurred to me: Shame, humiliation, the loss of my good name and reputation, my family's outrage and disappointment . . . all these things, I had vaguely considered; though, at the time, with Jarrett loving me, or so I'd believed, and with our wedding day so close, then only three months away, I confess it had seemed highly unlikely to me that I would endure any consequences for my folly.

But now the dull anxiety that had plagued me for weeks grew sharp, and I began to panic. My menses were regular as the tides; when my flux did not come, I knew I was carrying Jarrett's baby. If, however, still determined to disbelieve it, I required further proof of the truth, it came as bouts of morning sickness, when all I need do was lift my head from the pillow and nausea would strike; and sudden spells of tiredness, so there were afternoons when I felt abruptly as though if I didn't lie down at once, I would faint. My moods swung unpredictably, from days when I was sure Jarrett loved me and would come home soon, to evenings when I burst without warning into tears at the thought that he had deceived me far worse than Nicky ever had.

And all the while, my child grew within me, and I knew not what to do, who to turn to for help. I could not bear for Papa and Mama to learn how I had failed them; it would wound them deeply. Guy was in London; my brother Francis, at fifteen, was too young still to be of assistance; and timid Granny Sheffield would only wring her hands and insist Papa be told of the affair. I should have gone to Aunt Maggie; I know that now. But she and Uncle Draco kept few secrets from each other, and as I feared Jarrett's father and thought he would be angry at what we had done, I said naught to the Chandlers. Approaching my indecisive uncle Esmond or my self-centered aunt Julianne was out of the question; and I believed my grandmother Prescott Chandler too cool and remote to concern herself with my problems, though I misjudged her in this, for she was a woman of the world and all too cognizant of human foibles.

If Jarrett failed to return and marry me, I decided I must seek a midwife to rid me of the evidence of my shame, an idea that terrified me, given the grisly stories reported in the newspapers of the butchers who, for a price, would aid such a one as I. If not that, then I would have to run away, a daunting prospect to a woman alone, penniless, and with child. My plight seemed desperate indeed.

This was my state of mind and body, then, when I nearly destroyed Nicky's life and broke Aunt Maggie's heart.

Cruel and callous as his own against me was my crime against Nicky; I knew it then, I know it now—and regret it with all my heart for the pain it brought Aunt Maggie. But the choice I was given to undo it, I did not take, and afterward, it was too late to change my mind. The deed was done.

This is what happened that dreadful day.

I had ridden over to the Heights, for the preparations for my wedding continued as scheduled, with none but I, it seemed, afraid I might not have a groom. Angelique, who was to be my maid of honor, wished me to see her bridesmaid gown, which had just that morning arrived. We had not been particularly close in our childhood, but had become good friends since she had learned I intended to marry Jarrett instead of Nicky, whom she also loved but whom she frequently referred to as a "bad seed."

"I suspect he is cut from the same cloth as my black-sheep grandfather, Quentin Chandler," she often remarked. "No doubt Nicky shall wind up drunk and dead in a ditch somewhere one day, as Grandfather Quentin would have, had not Grandfather Nigel fetched him home from London—though poor, dissolute Grandfather Quentin *did* expire in the carriage halfway to Cornwall, you know.''

Though this was indeed the truth, I did not know how she could bear to repeat the morbid tale and would tell her so. But she would only shrug and laugh, for as I had come to learn, she was possessed of a fascinatingly macabre character in some respects and derived a great deal of pleasure from likening herself to the witch Morgawse of Arthurian legend.

That day, however, Angelique was on her best behavior, flushed and excited as, wearing the bridesmaid gown, she whirled about her bedroom, chattering not only of my wedding, but of her own to Lord Greystone, which was to take place next summer.

Thus the following hours passed happily enough for me, especially when, after tentatively I mentioned to her my misgivings about Jarrett's lack of communication, she pooh-poohed my fears, exclaiming, ''Oh, Laura, depend upon it! Jarrett's probably chasing the terrified Grimsby clear across France or Italy or someplace else beyond the Channel by now, and has arrogantly assumed you know he loves you and will be back as soon as he can. Why, Oliver's few notes to me have been so curt that I don't know why he even bothered to send them! He doesn't even sign them 'Oliver'—just 'Greystone.' Ugh! Can you imagine anything so unromantic? To tell you the truth, I don't know why we should want either of them!''

I smiled as I heartily agreed with this, for we both knew we jested; and as at least Jarrett had written his

Christian name on the card accompanying the topaz chrysanthemums, I was not only considerably amused by Angelique's indignant disclosure, but cheered as well. In better spirits than I had been for several weeks, I took my leave of her.

Now, Stormswept Heights was centuries old, as I have said, and had been built originally as a fortified manor. So its layout was peculiar, with priest holes, winding stairways, secret passages, and the like; and there was in the south tower, in the room next to Uncle Draco's study, a trapdoor in the floor, which gave way to a long, underground tunnel that led to the stables. Since, as I glanced out the windows of the great hall, I could see that it had begun to snow, and I knew the wind was bitter, I decided to make use of this corridor to reach the stables.

Would now that I had never done so, for as I reached the end of the tunnel and ascended the steps at its terminal point, I heard voices raised in an ugly quarrel overhead and knew the two people I hated most in the world, Nicky and Thorne, were in the stables. Still, decidedly curious about what was happening, I slowly, quietly, lifted the trapdoor above me a crack and peeked out, my heart thumping lest they should spy me. My detestable cousins were in the loft, I saw; but engrossed in their argument, neither noticed me.

"You arsehole! You bloody Gypsy bastard!" Thorne was spitting heatedly. "I'm warning you for the last time, Nicholas: Stay away from Lizzie! I mean it, you fucking son of a bitch! I'll kill you if you don't leave her alone!"

"What's the matter, Thorne? Are you afraid your

damned worthless father will die and I might somehow get possession of Highclyffe Hall through your sister?'' Nicky jeered. "God knows, *you're* certainly not man enough to get an heir on any woman, you filthy little bugger! Does the Lady Siobhan know the way you look at me when you think no one's watching? You'd like me in your *own* bed instead of Lizzie's, wouldn't you, you sodomizing shit? Jesus! It's enough to make me puke!''

"By God, you'll pay for that, you stinking whore's cock!'' Thorne hissed. "You'll pay!''

The next moment, the two men were at each other's throats, engaged in vicious conflict, while I watched, stupefied, unable to move, even to look away, I was in such a state of shock. My ears were flaming from my cousins' foul obscenities, words I hadn't even known existed; though, much to my consternation, because of their context, I had got the vulgar gist. I was horrified, revolted to my very core by what I had heard. I had always sensed there was something wrong with Thorne. Now I knew what it was. Thorne, perverse, sadistic Thorne, was a lover of men. Without warning, queasiness assailed me; vomit rose in my throat. Unable to choke it back, I retched violently onto the stairs, dropping the trapdoor as the heaves shook me. Afterward, with a trembling hand, I wiped my mouth off and pushed the trapdoor back open, gratified to see that the two men were so immersed in their battle that they had not heard the noise of my being sick.

Thorne had learned a lot about fighting since that day in the attic during our childhood, I recognized, for he was giving as good as he got, and Nicky, though taller and heavier, was not having an easy time of it. Cursing and grunting, my cousins rolled across the loft, sending straw sailing and, several times, vanishing from view so I lost sight of what was occurring, could hear only the sharp thwacks of the punches they exchanged. It was like the brawl in the attic all over again, I thought, only more brutal; perhaps, this time, even deadly. I wondered that the grooms did not hear all the noise and come to investigate; but no doubt they were huddled around a peat fire in their living quarters attached to the rear of the stables. As the walls at the Heights were a foot thick, I surmised the grooms were probably unaware anyone was even in the stables.

Finally, there came an ominous silence, punctuated by the sounds of labored breathing, muttered profanities, and then a sudden, wicked *whoosh*. Since Nicky and Thorne had passed behind a stack of baled hay and I could not see them, I hesitantly crept up from the corridor, tiptoeing across the floor of the stables to try to get a better look.

Appalled, I saw that Thorne had grabbed a pitchfork and was bent on skewering Nicky with it. As Thorne jabbed the tool at him savagely, Nicky deftly dodged its lethal prongs, one hand whipping out to seize the wooden handle in an attempt to wrench it away from Thorne. Furiously, the two men tugged on the pitchfork, staggering and spinning about the loft, several times coming perilously near to its brink until at last Thorne lost his grip on the handle and went crashing into a loose pile of hay, set close to the loft's edge, for pitching into the stall below. The impetus knocked the top off the hay mound;

bits of straw flew through the air in every direction as Thorne tumbled backward. To my horror, he could not halt his momentum and fell out of the loft, feet first, to land hard upon the floor of a stall beneath. The stall was empty, its door open, so there was naught to shield my eyes, riveted to the scene, from the spectacle of his legs buckling on impact, so he slipped and toppled over, hitting his head upon one corner of the wooden feed trough before he crumpled to the ground and lay still, blood trickling from the gash at his temple.

"Oh, my God," I whispered, stricken, my voice rising to a scream as I began to run frantically toward his inert figure. "Oh, my God!"

Reaching him, I knelt and shoved him over onto his back, quickly pressing my ear against his chest to see if he yet breathed, if his heart yet beat. To my relief, Thorne was alive, though white as death and seemingly knocked unconscious. Shouting, Nicky came scrambling down the ladder from the loft, nearly falling himself before, several rungs short of the floor, he jumped down and raced to the stall.

"My God, Laura, is he all right?" he asked as, drawing up short at the sight of me, he swayed on his feet, clutching the doorpost for support, his face ashen, his hands shaking.

It was then that I did that monstrous deed I was to regret so deeply for the rest of my life. I did not plan to do it, though that is no excuse for my behavior. But in truth, dear reader, I had no clear thought of revenge, no clear thought at all, really, in my mind when I slowly lifted my gaze to meet Nicky's—except that I despised him for trying to rape me that night upon the beach, and for the venomous lies he had told Jarrett afterward.

"He's dead!" I spoke the words softly, coldly, compelled into saying them by some dark, twisted thing I could not name and did not want to know. Then, without really being aware of it, just knowing that Thorne, unnatural Thorne, was cunning enough to discern my game and malicious enough to play along, I squeezed his arm warningly—in case he were lucid after all—so he would keep silent and not ruin my stratagem. "He's dead, Nicholas—and *you* killed him! You *murdered* him!"

"No!" he gasped, stunned, disbelieving, as he stared at Thorne's pale, unmoving form. "No! It was an accident! It was an accident, I tell you, Laura!"

"Don't think you can lie to me, Nicky! I heard everything. I saw everything," I insisted deliberately, with a thrill of satisfaction, refusing to let him off the hook; for had he not delighted in seeing me squirm so helplessly on his own cruel barb that night? "I'm a *witness*, Nicky. You murdered Thorne, and so I shall testify in a court of law when they bring you to trial—and hang you!"

"No! You can't mean that, Laura! You can't do this to me!" he babbled, incredulous. "For God's sake! I'm telling you, Laura: It was an accident!" When I made no reply, he swore and tore at his hair, distraught. Then he inhaled sharply, clapping one hand to his forehead. "My God! Of course. What a fool I am! It's to get even with me for that night on the beach that you're saying this, doing this, isn't it, Laura? Yes, of course, it is; I can see it in your eyes. I'm sorry—sorry, I tell you! I'll make it up to you, somehow, some way; I swear it! If you'll only tell the truth about what happened here, I'll go to Jarrett, just as soon as he gets home, if that's what you want, and I'll say whatever you like to him . . . convince him that I was drunk that night, that I lied, that I never had you—''

"Shut up! Shut up!" I cried, stiffening with mortification, aware now, somehow, that Thorne was indeed conscious, listening intently to every word, placing his own interpretation, however wrongly, on what Nicky had just said. "I don't want anything from you, you bastard! You murderer! Haven't you done enough as it is?"

"All right. All right." Nicky paused for an agitated moment, then continued. "Look . . . half an hour, then, Laura? Please. That's all I ask. Just half an hour to get away before you rouse the Heights about Thorne and they send for Uncle Esmond or, worse, the dragoons; for as my near relative, and Thorne's grieving father, Uncle Esmond will hardly prove an impartial magistrate, will he?"

"No, I don't suppose he will," I agreed calmly, observing how, all the while Nicky talked, he was feverishly fetching his tack, bridling and saddling Blackjack, caring for no one and nothing but his own neck.

Given his temperament, I wondered that he did not try to do me some injury, try even to kill me so I could not give evidence against him. But in my heart, I think Nicky was not truly wicked, just wild and reckless; and he had been spurred by drink that night upon the beach. Now he led his horse from its stall and mounted up.

"Half an hour, Laura," he pleaded, "if ever you loved me."

Then he set his heels to the gelding's sides and galloped out of the stables. He had no money, I realized suddenly, beyond what might be in his pockets. He was not even wearing his greatcoat; he had cast it aside earlier in the fracas. Perhaps he would freeze to death on the moors. His parting words rang in my ears; and now, ashamed, I thought of Jarrett and his family—soon to be my own—who loved Nicky, and I decided I had punished him enough.

"Nicky, wait!" I cried, starting to rush after him.

But I had forgotten Thorne, who hated Nicky, too, and would stop at nothing to do him harm. If my Sheffield cousin had lain still and mute before, it was only because he had gleaned a meanspirited enjoyment from Nicky's believing him dead. Now, however, seeing I was about to end the vengeful game, he rose up on one elbow, badly bruised and rattled from his fall, but, except for the cut at his temple and a sprained ankle, basically unhurt. His arm shot out like an arrow from a crossbow; his hand clamped roughly around my wrist, pulling me back.

"Eavesdroppers often hear the most interesting things, don't you agree, Laura?" he inquired archly, a slow, supercilious smile curving his lips. "And sometimes find allies where they least expect them as well, uneasy and unwelcome though they may be, eh? So, now we share secrets—you and I—and, most fortunately, each just as damaging as the other's. How ironic that poor Nicholas should have been an object of desire for us both. Thus can I well understand why you played him such a vile trick, Laura, though I really must admit I'm surprised you had it in you. I make you my compliments! *Brava!*"

He applauded me lightly. "'Twas as neat and nasty a piece of work as any I might have plotted myself. How far do you suppose Nicky will get, I wonder, before he discovers that you hoodwinked him most thoroughly and that I'm not really dead at all?"

"Not far," I said coolly, "for I aim to ride after him and tell him the truth, Thorne. It was a ghastly thing to do, and I'd say he's suffered quite enough."

"Now, that, Laura, was a most unwise admission," Thorne declared, "for I have my own reasons for hoping Nicky will be so desperate to save his neck that he'll not only flee the parish, but the entire country—and never return. So, I think . . . yes, I really do think I'm going to have to detain you for a time, Laura—just until I'm sure Nicky's too far ahead to be caught by anyone so foolish as to ride after him in this weather."

Thorne had been glancing purposefully about the stables, and now, before I realized what he intended, he jerked me to my feet, dragging me over to where some thin, short coils of rope lay tossed in a corner. At first, I could not believe he was serious about tying me up, and I laughed at him, a terrible mistake. He had not changed since that day in the attic, except to grow more beastly, and his pride was stung by my amusement. Now, despite my all-too-tardy shrieks of outrage and struggles to escape when finally I grasped that he actually *did* mean to hold me captive, he bound my hands and feet securely with the rope. Then, impatiently ripping off his cravat, he wadded it up and stuffed it into my mouth, effectively silencing me. After that, he slung me over his shoulder and carried me down into the underground passage, where he propped me up against the wall.

"Does Jarrett know what a virago he's getting, I wonder?" he queried mockingly as I cursed him, a muffled invective that nearly gagged me, and I wriggled about impotently, trying to loosen my bonds. "Laura . . . Laura." Thorne shook his head, frowning. "Save your strength. You won't get free, I promise you." Then, from his vest, he withdrew his pocket watch, opened it, and checked the hour. "It's early afternoon yet, only one o'clock," he told me. "I'll be back at tea time to release you. You'll be safe here and warm enough till then; you've your pelisse after all."

And then the devious, deviant bastard left me.

Chapter XI

Aunt Maggie

Ah, yet would God this flesh of mine might be
Where air might wash and long leaves cover
me;
Where tides of grass break into foam of flowers,
Or where the wind's feet shine along the sea.

—*Laus Veneris*
Algernon Charles Swinburne

I wept to dwell on what I had done—and shivered, snow
flurrying about me like a shroud, as I stood at the edge
of the scarred headland, staring out over the long black
rocks and wintry grey-green sea far below.

Much to my surprise, true to his word for once, Thorne
had come back to free me a little while ago; and hurling
abuse at him over my shoulder, I had hurried down the
tunnel to the house to confess my crime tearfully to Aunt

Maggie—although not the reason why I had committed it—and to tell her Nicholas was gone, had fled without so much as his greatcoat, believing himself a murderer. She had listened to my tale in silence, strangely but mercifully asking no questions. Then, when I had finished, she had risen and, calling for her horse, had galloped to the Chandler china-clay mines to inform Uncle Draco of what had happened, so he could ride after Nicky, in the hope of catching him. But as Nicky had, by now, a four-hour head start, I had little hope that his father would overtake him, and I feared Uncle Draco's rage when he was forced to return home empty-handed.

Still, I could not shirk the blame for my act; though, in truth, I had not meant things to go so far, had not considered that Thorne might intervene, attempting to turn what I had intended as no more than a brief punishment into a life sentence of banishment. The fact remained: Had I not accused Nicky of murder, told him our Sheffield cousin lay dead, Thorne would not have been given the chance for his own revenge, which he had been so quick and glad to seize. None knew that better than I.

Now, as I gazed out over the ocean, it seemed to me that the night I had shared with Jarrett upon the wild shore below had been but a fleeting respite in an otherwise relentless downward spiral, starting with that day of Uncle Esmond's fox hunt, when my life's path had taken such a different turning from what I had hoped. How I longed now to retrace my steps, to have it all to do again, for there was much I would have changed. But it was too late now for that. I must live with the consequences of my decisions—or not; and that, too, was a choice mine to make.

I do not know that I was consciously contemplating taking my own life as I stood there at the brink of the crumbling cliffs overlooking the sea. It was just that the ceaseless motion of the foamy waves seemed hypnotic; like a siren, the water's cold, dark depths lured me. I knew I had but to step forward and all my troubles would be over, swept away, as I, and the child within me, would be.

It was the thought of this last that made me hesitate, for what right had I to end my baby's life before it had even truly begun? Was it not a living, breathing being, though it slept yet within my womb, dependent upon me a while longer for its survival? Jarrett's child—and mine. Until now, it had not seemed real to me, merely a thing that, unbidden, had invaded my body, sickening and tiring me. But now it seemed to cry out to me, a voice wailing upon the wind.

"Lauuuuura. Lauuuuura."

I turned. It was not my imagination at all, I realized then, but Aunt Maggie who called to me as, hard over the frosted moors, she galloped toward me, like an angel of death—or life—the mist and snow swirling about her, so she appeared to ride in shadow—or an aura of light —I did not know which.

"Laura," she said again as she reached me and dismounted, her voice sharp now, her eyes searching mine intently, made anxious by what she found therein. "What are you doing here?" she inquired as she began to walk toward me slowly, though she made no move to touch me, as though she feared that if she stretched out her hand to me, I would jump into the nothingness below. "Do you not see how close you are to the edge of the cliffs and how treacherously the ice encrusts the ground there? Come away, lest you slip and fall onto the rocks or into the sea— Or is that what you hoped, what you intended when you sought this place? Talk to me, Laura. I will understand."

"Go away and leave me alone!" I cried heatedly, with all the passion of youth; though, after this day, I knew in my heart that only youth's vestiges remained, that I was grown old of a sudden, older than my years. "What can you possibly know of my feelings, of what drove me to come here?"

"Talk to me," she entreated earnestly once more, "and perhaps you will learn. I am not so old that I have forgotten what it was to be young—and alone and afraid."

At that, tears flowed from my eyes to freeze upon my cheeks, for in truth, I had not recognized until now how lonely and frightened I really was, how desperately I yearned to pour my heart out to another human being and be comforted. There was, too, in Aunt Maggie's voice a strange ache, as of a painful memory, so that, despite myself, my curiosity was piqued and I could not help but look at her.

It was then that I broke down—such was the love and concern for me that I saw in her eyes—and weeping, I flung myself into her embrace. With heartfelt anguish and relief, she clasped her arms tight about me, crushing me to her breast, soft as my mother's when I was a child;

and seeking blindly that same solace and reassurance now as then, at Aunt Maggie's urging, I relinquished my grievous burden onto her strong, willing shoulders, sensing somehow that she would not falter under its heavy weight.

Like a floodtide, the words surged from my lips, the whole of my story, beginning with that night in the gardens at the Grange until this day. I spared myself nothing in the telling of it, and all the while I sobbed out my eyes and tale, she held me close and stroked my hair and listened quietly, without interruption.

Then, at long last, when I fell silent, drained, empty, and yet somehow oddly at peace as I had not been for many a long day, she set me from her a little and tenderly smoothed a strand of hair back from my face. After that, her hands upon my arms, she stared out over the ocean, as I had earlier, and heaved a deep, sorrowing sigh, her shoulders trembling, as though her heart were breaking inside her, and whispered something I did not quite catch, though it sounded like "The sins of the fathers . . ."

After a long time, she turned back to me. Till my dying day, she shall look always, in my mind, as she did in that moment, utterly beautiful—not with the soft, delicate beauty of my mother, but with a bold, wild beauty, strange and haunting, the hood of her pelisse fallen back to expose her poignant face, her long black hair, tumbled from its pins, streaming loose in the wind and snow, her black eyes shadowed, as though when she gazed at me, she saw a reflection of herself in my eyes.

"So you think I cannot understand your feelings, Laura, what drove you to come here, perhaps to end your life?'' she queried finally, a wry twist to her lips. ''Even now, having told your sad story, you doubt me. No, do not deny it; I can see in your eyes that you do. But you're wrong.'' She paused for a moment, as though considering, then spoke again.

''You see, Laura, I stood here once, long ago, just as you—rejected by your uncle Esmond, whom I loved, and, though I did not yet wear his wedding ring upon my finger, carrying your uncle Draco's child.'' I gasped, stunned, for I had not known this, and she nodded. ''Yes, it's true. Just as you gave yourself to my son Jarrett, so did I give myself to Draco—out of pain and longing, wanting him to take away the hurt I was suffering inside. . . .'' Her voice trailed away. She was silent for a minute. Then softly she continued, as though speaking to herself. ''So many years have come and gone since then; but still, I remember, as though it were only yesterday, that night when Draco took me in his arms . . . and pressed me down upon a moon-dark moor . . . and showed me what it was to love a man. . . . Jarrett was conceived that night—'' She broke off abruptly, recalling herself to the present. Then she cried, ''Oh, Laura, my poor, dear girl, why didn't you come to me?''

''I—I was afraid, so afraid— I didn't know you would understand. . . .''

Once more, she hugged me near, crooning to me as my tears dripped again upon her soft, consoling breast.

''Hush, Laura, hush now,'' she commanded. ''Do you really think that Jarrett won't come back, that he does not love you, as Draco loved me? Oh, Laura, dear Laura, how little you know, in truth, of my son if you believe that. Think you that we could have forced Jarrett to honor your betrothal, to marry you if he did not want to? Of all my sons, he is the one most like his father—proud, arrogant, passionate, taking what he wants, making of life what he wills. No, Jarrett loves you!—and like his father, he is a man who will love but once and forever, with all his heart. This, I know: He'll not forsake you, Laura; come what may, Jarrett will return for you, though hell stands in his way."

"Oh, Aunt Maggie, do you really believe that?"

"Yes," she answered, smiling gently now, "for am I not Draco's wife, stolen away by him to Gretna Green, when my father would have seen me dead before he saw me wed to my Gypsy cousin?" Once more, she fell still, lost again in reverie. Then she laughed a little and shook herself and said brusquely, "Come now. We must get you home ere you freeze to death. That is my grandchild you are carrying, and I would not have you lose it."

"Oh, Aunt Maggie, how can you be so kind to me when it is all my fault Nicky has run away?" I asked, bitterly ashamed. "I'm so sorry, so very sorry. Can you—can you ever forgive me?"

"Why, of course, I can, Laura. In my heart, I already have. Think you that I know naught of being injured, of wanting to strike back? I have hated vehemently in my life; never think I have not. But I have learned now to let the past go, to forgive and forget, because only then are wounds to the heart and soul healed, though the scars remain.

"You are young, Laura, and you meant no real harm," she insisted, "only to punish Nicky for all he had so wrongly done to you. That is the way of youth—to act without thinking, to seek revenge; for it is only with age that one realizes vengeance is a two-edged sword. Yet you would have called Nicky back, had Thorne not prevented you from doing so. You are not so hard, then, only foolish and tempestuous, as I, too, was once. Even more than my forgiveness, Laura, you need to forgive yourself.''

"How can I? Nicky's gone, and I don't think Uncle Draco will find him. . . ."

"No, nor do I,'' Aunt Maggie agreed, her eyes closing, so I knew she was hurt by the thought; though it was not until my own son was born that I fully understood her deep love for Nicky, regardless of his sins, and knew how badly I had broken her heart, how much she loved me to forgive me that.

"He was ever a wild, reckless boy,'' she observed quietly. "Even as a child, he tried to best Jarrett at everything. He never understood that he couldn't take Jarrett's place in our hearts—or that he had his own place there and was just as beloved.'' She paused, remembering.

Then she declared bravely, "Still, he's a Chandler—and we Chandlers are survivors. Even if Dráco cannot catch up with him right away, Nicky will manage somehow. He'll make his own way in the world; and perhaps in a few weeks or even months, when Draco does locate him and is able to tell him Thorne is not dead after all, he will return to us, a wiser man.''

"Yes, perhaps,'' I echoed, hoping for Aunt Maggie's sake that it would be so.

Neither of us knew then that Nicky would not flee to

London, and thence to the Continent, as we supposed. We never dreamed that, instead, he would set sail across the sea, would travel halfway around the earth from us, with never a word as to his whereabouts, so nearly three long years would pass before ever we saw him again.

Chapter XII

Passions, Deep and Lasting

If two lives join, there is oft a scar.
  They are one and one, with a shadowy third;
One near one is too far.

—By the Fireside
Robert Browning

As a loose thread unravels the whole of a piece of cloth, so my miserable deed rent the closely interwoven fabric of the Prescott, the Chandler, and the Sheffield lives.

Some days later, Uncle Draco returned home, empty-handed, as I had guessed he would, though I had hoped otherwise. But he was not wroth with me, as I had feared; for Aunt Maggie, having first sought my permission, soon told him all, so Uncle Draco knew I had cause, just or not, for threatening Nicky with a hangman's rope and sending him fleeing for his life. Still, even though Uncle

Draco did not blame me and, indeed, when our paths chanced to cross, went out of his way to display toward me an interest and a kindness he had shown me only absently before, I knew I had dealt him a painful blow. Always a taciturn, brooding man, he withdrew more than ever into himself; and almost overnight, it seemed, two wings of silver streaked the jet-black hair at his temples. I was deeply distressed whenever I saw him and, though I was still afraid of him, longed even so for him to reproach me, so the guilt I felt would be eased.

But such censure was not forthcoming. Even Thorne, whose neck I felt certain Uncle Draco would have wrung with satisfaction could he but have got his hands around it, escaped punishment, as usual. Thorne's strong sense of self-preservation had warned him he would not be so easily forgiven as I, and he had suddenly found it prudent to visit his fiancée, Lady Siobhan O'Halloran, at her father's Irish estate. After liberating me in the tunnel, Thorne had departed immediately from the Hall, before either his sister, Elizabeth, or Uncle Draco should learn what he had done.

An incident so serious, with such far-reaching repercussions, could not be entirely hushed up. Servants had eyes to witness riders galloping madly across the moors and to peep through keyholes, ears that listened at closed doors, ferreting out family secrets, and tongues that delighted in gossiping. Although, except for Nicky, Thorne, and me, the real facts of the matter were known only to Uncle Draco and Aunt Maggie, wild rumors soon began to circulate in the village, at their core, a kernel of truth.

Mr. Nicholas and Mr. Thorne had argued and come to savage blows, it was said, and Mr. Thorne had been felled. Then Miss Laura, who was present at the fight, had—either mistakenly or deliberately (depending upon who told the tale)—announced that, as a result of same, Mr. Thorne was dead. So Mr. Nicholas, thinking to dance a Tyburn jig otherwise, had bolted.

News of the scandal flew so thick and fast that sometimes I could hardly hold my head up for the stares and whispers I encountered. I was not the only one affected by all the talk and speculation, however.

Lizzie went about looking as though she had just sucked on a lemon and found it even sourer than she had supposed. Because she scowled so often, two small, deep vertical lines eventually appeared between her eyebrows, and her petulant mouth acquired a permanent droop, spoiling the pale, icy beauty she had inherited from our grandmother Prescott Chandler.

In the fervent hope that Nicky would wed her, Lizzie had rejected every suitor who had ever come calling at the Hall. Now, at twenty-three, past the first blush of her youth and without another matrimonial prospect in sight, she was surely condemned to a life of spinsterhood. I suspected she found it a bitter pill indeed to swallow— especially when it must have seemed Nicky was finally within her reach. I knew I had made of her a deadly lifelong enemy; for even more than she did her brother, Lizzie blamed me for causing Nicky to be snatched from her grasp and, thereafter, despised me with a passion that surpassed all previous bounds.

Clemency, too, ascribed to me the loss of her lover—

if such Nicky had been to her—and her slanted green eyes smoldered with resentment of me when she thought I did not see. Though her fear of Jarrett was such that she continued overtly to treat me with respect, she was not slow or loath to seek revenge upon me through myriad sly, underhanded, and even childish means: prying loose the heels of my shoes, so they gave way unexpectedly beneath me; weakening the lacings of my corsets, so they snapped apart without warning inside my gowns; handing me a pitcher of frigid water with which to rinse my hair when I washed it; and countless other similar, petty things. Since such mishaps could all conceivably have been accidents, it was difficult to lay the charge for them at Clemency's door; so, though I felt certain she was the culprit responsible for them, I forced myself to bite my tongue and make no complaint. I did not intend to give her the satisfaction of knowing how she angered and humiliated me; nor did I wish for her to fling caution to the winds and reveal her knowledge of Jarrett and me to Papa and Mama. I was unsure whether Clemency had guessed I was pregnant, but even a hint of the dishabille in which she had found me at the gatehouse the night of the twins' engagement party would doubtless lead to exposure of the whole.

To my relief, my parents remained blissfully ignorant of the fact that I had given myself to Jarrett, that I was, even now, carrying his child. Respecting my wishes, Uncle Draco and Aunt Maggie had not told them these secrets, or even that Nicky had tried to rape me, that I had had reason for falsely accusing him of murder. Mercifully, Papa and Mama believed I had made an honest error in proclaiming Thorne dead.

Thus I could not help but be gladdened when, the day after Uncle Draco's return, Clemency unexpectedly ran away from the Grange.

I had no idea where she'd gone, except that I suspected she thought to succeed where Uncle Draco had failed and locate Nicky, though had she asked, I would have told her this would prove an impossible task, that if Uncle Draco could not find him, no one could. But of course, Clemency did not ask me for my advice or even, to my astonishment, for a reference (for she was brazen enough to have requested one, despite her wicked treatment of me). Without giving notice, she just packed her belongings and sneaked out in the night, uncaring that the household would naturally be turned all sixes and sevens by her unexplained disappearance.

Mama was most particularly upset, but Papa said it was good riddance to bad rubbish; and indeed, he was proved right when, the following afternoon, I discovered that Clemency had stolen half the contents of my jewel box—though fortunately nothing of any great value. She had been too clever for that, correctly surmising we would not send the law after her over a handful of inexpensive gewgaws. Indeed, I was so relieved at her going that I would not have mentioned the theft to my parents at all had not Iris, one of the housemaids, been present when I learned the trinkets were missing.

Still, I had not seen the last of Clemency, as you shall hear.

* * *

At long last, a fortnight before our wedding day, Jarrett came home.

It was after midnight when I heard a faint tap at my window. At first, I thought it was only the snow flurrying against the glass, or the branches of the towering old tree that grew just outside scraping against the panes. But then, when the sound persisted, becoming steadily louder, I rose from my bed to determine the cause. After lighting a candle and shrugging into my wrapper, drawing it close about me against the chill of the winter night, I went to the window and pulled back the curtains, gasping when I saw Jarrett's dark form without. He had climbed the ancient tree and was crouched upon one of its limbs. I was so stunned by the sight of him that, for a moment, I could do naught but gape at him ludicrously. I daresay that at any other time, he should have found this amusing, but the cold had made him cross.

"For God's sake, Laura, let me in!" he demanded, rapping peremptorily against the muntined glass, impatient at my delay. "I am like to freeze to death out here!"

Jolted to my senses, I quickly set down my candle, unlatched the window, and opened it wide. A blast of wind and snow assailed me as, cursing and shivering, Jarrett clambered into my bedroom, then slammed shut the window and locked it.

"Brrrrr," he muttered, vigorously rubbing his arms to warm himself, his greatcoat flapping. "'Tis not a fit night for man or beast out there!"

"Then why are you out and about?" I asked tartly, still startled and flustered by his unexpected appearance.

My mouth felt as parched as though I languished in a desert; my heart pounded hard and fast in my breast. How could I have forgotten how tall and powerful he was—standing there, he made my large, airy chamber seem suddenly small and cramped, my gilded oak furniture too graceful and delicate to support anyone—and how handsome he was? Had his hair always been black as the midnight sea, his eyes like shards of obsidian in his face? He laughed softly; in the hazy light of the silvered moon that streamed in through the window, his even teeth flashed white against his bronze Gypsy skin.

"Is that any way to greet your long-lost fiancé, my sweet?" he inquired impudently, his eyes raking me in a way that made me all too aware of how I must look, having just risen from my bed. I blushed, my hand clutching my robe at my throat. "Frankly, Laura, I did not ride five miles in the snow and dark to be dealt the sharp side of your tongue!" he declared. "Come here, dear heart, and kiss me."

His black eyes gleamed beneath lazy lids; a crooked smile tugged at one corner of his mouth—and at my heartstrings. How I had missed him! I had not known until this moment how very much. All at once, everything seemed right in my world again; Jarrett filled its boundaries. Once, I would have been dismayed by that. Now I could ask for nothing more.

Still, I was shy of him at first. The memory of that night upon the beach was as strong and clear in my mind as though it had happened only yesterday. I could still feel his mouth and hands upon me intimately, his weight pressing me down. His every plane and angle was as familiar to me as my own. But for all that, there was much I did not yet know of him. Would he expect me to surrender to him now, as I had before? I did not know. The prospect somehow unnerved even as it excited me, for despite Jarrett's having made love to me, traces of my maidenly modesty remained.

So it was slowly, hesitantly, that I approached him, feeling as though my white flannel nightgown and wrapper, trimmed with lace, offered poor protection against him. Surely, he could snatch them away without difficulty. Even more mortifying was the realization that, deep down inside, I wished him to do so. In addition, I was terrified someone would hear him and come to my room to investigate. It was this last that caused me to say now what I ought to have said before.

"Jarrett, what are you doing here? This is really . . . most improper!"

"That's not what you said that night upon the beach," he rejoined insolently, grinning. "Are you not happy to see me?"

"Yes, of course, but—"

"Then show me, Laura."

Show me, Laura. Show me that Nicky lied.

I had no will of my own then, when Jarrett looked at me. As though in a dream, I felt myself put my arms around his neck and lift my lips for his kiss. It was not tender when it came, but hard and hungry, as though he had thought of nothing else since leaving me. A thrill of satisfaction and pleasure shot through me at the notion. He loved me! It had not been a lie. So eager, in fact, had he been to see me that he had not waited until morning to ride over to the Grange.

His tongue probed my mouth greedily, seeking its moist softness as willingly I opened my lips to him, my tongue entwined with his. My hands clasped his face, feeling the rough stubble of his beard, unshaven in his haste to come to me. Sweet was its abrasiveness for that, so I scarcely felt the pain of it as feverishly his mouth left mine to slash across my cheek, his skin scraping mine in his ardor. His fingers burrowed through my hair, loosening impatiently the single braid into which it was plaited, then spreading the heavy mass about me like a curtain. He raised my face to his once more, kissing me deeply. Then he crushed me to his chest; his heart beat in my ear, a strong steady rhythm, in sharp contrast to the birdlike fluttering of my own. Kisses rained upon my hair; I felt his lips against my ear, murmuring words of love and passion there.

He does not know, I thought, suddenly cold and sick inside. *He does not know what I have done*.

Tears welled from my eyes at that, dampening the fine cambric of his white ruffled shirt, though I tried to stem their tide.

"Why, what's this?" he asked kindly, cupping my chin and lifting my face so he could see it. "You've no cause for tears, Laura, surely, have you?"

"More than you know," I replied. "Oh, Jarrett, I have done a horrible thing!"

He sat down upon the edge of the bed, drawing me into his lap, pressing my head to his shoulder as he settled me comfortably against him. Idly, he began to play with a thick strand of my long dark hair, smoothing it against my breast, then catching the tress up to twirl it about his finger.

"Now, what could you possibly have done, my sweet, to make you quake in your slippers so?" he questioned lightly.

At length, I recounted all, dreading his reaction, for despite their differences, Jarrett loved his brother. I did not know what he would do when he learned that Nicky had fled and that I was the cause. Yet I could not bear for there to be lies between us, so I told him the truth, quietly, fearing he would turn from me in rage and disappointment, yet hoping it would not come to that.

"My fierce falcon," he uttered when at last I had finished, "what sharp talons you have indeed. Would that Nicholas had not been torn by them, though I, more than anyone, know 'tis no less than he deserved. Had you not stopped me, I think I would have killed him that night upon the beach. How, then, can I fault you, Laura, for a far lesser crime than mine?"

"You are not angry, then?" I queried tremulously.

"No. 'Tis a grievous load, in truth, that you have borne without me—Laura . . . Laura, did you really think I did not love you, that I would not return for you? Curse you for that, dear heart, for trusting me so little, though I was afraid it would be so. It was too soon, I knew, to part from you, so newly mine; and God knows, I would not have left you could I but have given some plausible explanation for my refusal to do what was needed for the shipping line."

"I know that now. But, oh, Jarrett, why did you not write to me at least?"

"At first, because I did not know how to put into words all I wanted to say, and later, because there was so little time. Grimsby led me a devilish chase, I fear, halfway across the Continent."

"Then Angelique was right in surmising that. But you caught him?"

"Yes, he's safely behind bars in London now, awaiting trial. And I am home, with you, where I belong. . . . God, I have missed you, dear heart! You'll never know how much I longed for you those days and nights when I was so far from your side—" He kissed me again and pressed me down upon the bed, the long, hard length of him pinning me to the mattress. "Will you deny me, Laura?" he asked, his black eyes glittering in the light of the lone candle I had lit earlier. "Will you bid me go . . . or stay?"

Was it my voice that answered, so soft and hoarse and eloquently pleading?

"Stay," I whispered. "Stay. . . ."

Jarrett's mouth captured mine, swallowing the word, my breath. His tongue parted my lips, sought my own and teased it until I kissed him back with a passion that matched his.

He was not gentle with me that night, but forceful as the wild wind that blew across the moors, driving and scattering the snow before it, as my senses were driven and scattered, so I could not think, could only feel as his mouth and tongue and hands swept over the peaks and valleys of my body. My robe and night rail were as wispy leaves upon the wind, whisked away with abandon; I knew not how or when. Naked, then, I lay beneath him, exposed to him as the heaths to the elements, soaking up all that he offered, bending to his stronger will.

Like heather or bracken twining about the wind, I was, my long hair a tangle of gorse, ensnaring him, drawing him down. My breasts were mounds of soft earth, molded by his palms. His breath was sweet upon their crests; his tongue was moist as the mist that drifts and curls in the hollows of the land, enveloped by the tall grass of the commons, and I enveloped him, clung to him as he clung to me. There was no part of me he did not know, nor any part of him that was untouched by me. Dark flesh melted urgently into pale; we were as one, the elements and the earth, for what was one without the other?

Outside, the snow eddied and thudded against the window. A swirl of moonbeams shone through the panes, showering us with silver and shadow as fiercely we came together. Hard and swift, Jarrett claimed me; soft and deep, I took him into me, my low cry muffled by his lips and the wind that shrieked and moaned through the night, savage, tempestuous, a breath primeval.

Chapter XIII

Stormswept Heights

They are not long, the days of wine and roses:

—*Vitae Summa Brevis*
Ernest Dowson

It was afterward, as I lay safe in the cradle of his loving arms, that I told Jarrett of our coming child. An oath burst from him at that, and sternly, he rebuked me for saying naught before, for he feared that in his roughness, he had done me or the baby some injury. But I assured him this was not so, and at last, he was soothed; and he kissed me and made love to me once more, lingeringly, as though I were a rare flower that must be tenderly nurtured to bloom. Then reluctantly, because the hour crept toward morning and he must not be found in my bed, he left me as he had come, descending the tree and blowing me a kiss from the snowy ground before fetching his black stallion from the stables and riding away.

We were married a fortnight later. Nicholas was to have been the best man; but as none knew where he was and, though we had dared to hope, he did not come home for the wedding, Alexander stood in his brother's place at the village church, and a shadow marred the otherwise joyous ceremony. Afterward, Jarrett took me away to Portugal for our honeymoon. There, upon its sandy coast, wild and beautiful in its own way as that of northern Cornwall, we filled our days with sightseeing and our nights with lovemaking; and finally, I began to know a little the man who was now my husband, and myself as well.

Much as it pains me to admit it, previously, I had not, in truth, been a very discerning or introspective woman; certainly, if I had been, I should not have made the many mistakes I had. I saw that now—now, when it was too late to undo all that I had done. But though the days of my youth were gone, never to come again, I was still only eighteen. I was not so insensible that I could not, would not learn and grow with age; though I thought, in some respects, I would always be, as Granny Sheffield and Aunt Maggie had declared I was, a woman bold and rash, more often than not ruled by my heart instead of my head. Like all of us cursed with the Chandler wild streak, I was not fashioned of the stuff that permitted one to live life tamely; rather, my nature was such that I would ever seize life with a vengeance and bend it to my will, making of it what I must, as Aunt Maggie did. It was no wonder, then, that, though not the child of her body, I was to prove, in years to come, the child of her heart.

"Seeing you is like looking into a mirror, Laura," she often said to me after I had come to the Heights, and the more I knew of her and myself, the more I understood why this was so.

We were cut of the same cloth, Aunt Maggie and I, as were the Chandler men we loved so passionately and with such reckless abandon; for as time passed, I came indeed to love Jarrett thus, with all my heart.

I saw much of his father in this iron-willed man I had wed, for he was every bit as proud, as arrogant, as intelligent, and as resourceful as Uncle Draco. Yet I felt Jarrett's character was tempered by a sensitivity and a compassion his father lacked, though, to my deep grief, I misjudged Uncle Draco terribly in this, as you shall hear. I believed Jarrett's father a hard man, and he was—but no harder than his son, who knew how to be gentle when the occasion warranted; and though each was determined to wrest from life all that he could, neither was selfish, as Nicky was selfish, thinking of no one else.

Had I recognized these things before, I should not have loved Nicky, that rebellious thief of my heart and youth, who had used me so cruelly, then callously cast me aside. Yet, like Aunt Maggie, I was a wiser woman for my scars, for now I could see Jarrett's worth and value it, as I had not done before, nor perhaps would have done otherwise. That knowledge, if nothing more, Nicky had given me, however unwittingly.

I thought of him less and less as time went by; it was Jarrett who filled my days and nights now. He crept so softly into my heart that for a long while, I did not even know he was there, and then, when I finally did realize it, it seemed strangely, startlingly, that I had always loved him, that there had never been a time when he had not held my heart.

So, discovering and reveling in each other, we were disposed to linger in Portugal; but we stayed only a few weeks, for we wished to return to Stormswept Heights before Christmas. The absence from the Chandler family of one son due to a felicitous joining could be endured with a shrug and smile, we felt; but the absence of two sons, one whose departure had been so clouded and whose whereabouts were currently unknown, would preclude a happy holiday. So, at last, Jarrett and I sailed home from Lisbon to Cornwall, no longer strangers, not just lovers, but friends.

Dusk was falling as the Chandlers' well-sprung coach, which had awaited us in Saltash, swayed through the Heights' open, ice-encrusted gates, past the snow-bedecked lodge, and lurched up the sodden drive flanked by tall, twisted trees limned with frost. Though I knew it well, I leaned forward eagerly as my new home came into sight.

Various improvements had been made over the years, especially during the reign of the Tudors and, more recently, under Uncle Draco's aegis, yet the Heights' origins as a fortified manor were still evident in its archaic structure: in the finely carved and timbered gatehouse, in the crenellated curtain wall, and in the two large, round towers at its north and south ends. More than this, I could not see until we had passed beneath the gatehouse itself into the stone courtyard formed by the curtain wall. Then was the rest of the manor revealed.

With the exception of its half-timbered additions, it was constructed entirely of granite that gleamed eerily where struck by the silvery twilight, so the stone cast in shadow seemed even darker and greyer in comparison. The house, which was three and a half stories high, counting the attic, loomed over the carriage and was dwarfed in turn by the massive twin Cornish elms that stood like sentries in the courtyard, where the paving blocks had been carefully laid to preserve the ancient trees. The tall, narrow lancet windows that lined the Heights on the two main floors appeared to stare out at us like eyes from behind the slits of a mask as Jarrett and I alighted from the coach; light reflecting off the glazed, lozenge panes made them glitter like diamonds in the dusk. An equilateral arch at the center of the manor framed the single ponderous oak door, upon which hung a brass knocker carved in the shape of a sea gull. The small, square windows of the half story, the remainder of which was below ground, ran along the bottom of the wings.

On the second floor, on either side of the stained-glass cathedral window mounted in the stone facade above the door, were the half-timbered additions. These were fashioned of heavy black beams and stucco that, over the ages, had weathered to a pale silver grey. Set into the steep front peaks of the black slate hip-and-valley roof were the round dormer windows of the attic. Square chimneys protruded from the roof itself, and at either end, the towers rose like spires to surmount the manor. Centuries ago, they had served as open watch-towers; now they were capped by turrets, and the crenels bordered twin parapet walks from which one could look out over the land or sea, as often I would do as Jarrett's wife. The north turret, encircled with windows, functioned as a lighthouse, warning ships of the dangerous black rocks far below. Even now, its beacon burned brightly.

Jarrett had sent word of our impending arrival, for the Heights was ablaze with lights and Uncle Draco and Aunt Maggie waited to welcome us home. Now, as his parents opened the door, my husband swept me up in his arms and carried me over the threshold into the great hall. There, the servants were lined up to greet me, "Mr. Jarrett's" bride, though I had known them all since I was a child. They presented me with a small bouquet of wintry flowers, and this, I accepted a trifle shyly, murmuring my thanks, before Aunt Maggie dispersed the staff and, embracing me warmly, led me away.

The great hall, as it had properly been called in centuries past and was often still, though it no longer served its medieval purpose, was the oldest and largest room in the house. Its vaulted ceiling soared to the roof, exposing the supporting rafters and curved beams, blackened over the years by the smoke of open fires, though the hearth that had once stood in the center of the hall had long since been torn out and a fireplace constructed in the west wall. Because the chamber was so cavernous, Aunt Maggie's voice, as she spoke to me, inquiring about the honeymoon trip to Portugal, echoed in the room, mingling softly with those of Uncle Draco and Jarrett, who had moved to stand before the cheerful fire. Old stone staircases, with more recent balustrades of oak, angled steeply up the north and south walls to the wings; the climb up the steps was long, and I felt slightly dizzy as I glanced down at the hall, where Jarrett and his father conversed and smoked cigars and drank the brandy that had been served to them by Mawgen, the peculiarly silent, stony-faced butler.

Jarrett's bedroom was in the south tower, and it was to this that Aunt Maggie brought me, for I was to share my husband's chamber. This did not seem the least bit odd or hopelessly out of style to me, however, for though separate quarters for husband and wife might be the mode elsewhere, they were not the fashion at either the Grange or the Heights.

"So, Laura, are you well?" Aunt Maggie asked, her anxious eyes searching mine intently. "And happy?"

"Yes . . . and again, yes," I responded, smiling and blushing a little as I thought of the many nights now I had lain in Jarrett's arms, sated with passion and contentment.

"Yes," she agreed slowly, her dark, somber eyes lightening, "I believe you are, for there is a glow about you that was not there before. My dear, how glad I am of that." She kissed me then, as though I were her own daughter; and I knew that I would love and cherish her always as I did my own mother, that she would be ever my friend. "Renshaw will be up shortly with your trunks, Laura, and Iris can get them unpacked," she said. (Iris was the housemaid at the Grange, who had taken Clemency's position as my maid.) "Then you can bathe and change for supper. Since 'tis your first night home, your family will be dining with us. We thought you'd like that, and I know they are eager to see you, too."

"How kind of you, Aunt Maggie, to think of that. I shall join everyone as soon as I can," I replied.

Once she had left me, I glanced around Jarrett's room with interest, for I had glimpsed it only rarely in my childhood, and now it was much changed, the refuge of a man, not a boy. Because it was in the south tower, it was circular in shape, and quite spacious; its contents had obviously been chosen with care. The Chandlers favored furnishings from the Tudor period, and I saw much to admire in the old and valuable appurtenances. A massive rosewood bed, with a huge canopy, a solid headboard carved with a labyrinthine design, and the distinctive melon-bulb footposts of the Tudor era, dominated the chamber. Heavy night tables stood on either side of the beautiful bed; at its foot were a closed-sided wooden wainscot chair and a sturdy, leather-bound trunk. A large, ornate clothes press stood against one wall, a writing table and a richly upholstered chair opposite. Flanking the stone fireplace, where, upon the mantel, a scale model of one of the earliest P & C ships reposed, were a washstand and a hammered-brass bathtub. A curved stone stairway led to the turret above and to the sitting room below. Mullioned windows overlooked the cliffs and the sea; the curtains were open, and the silvery light of the rising moon and the first stars of the descending night streamed through the glass panes, illuminating the chamber. A fire crackled merrily in the hearth, so the room, done in autumnal shades of scarlet and gold, glowed, warm and inviting. Outside, the sound of the breakers lapping the shore beyond was peaceful. Somehow I knew I would be very happy here.

And so my life at Stormswept Heights began, much as I had been reared to expect, with few surprises; though, of course, the old manor was not as quiet and tranquil as the Grange, where Mama's gentle temperament and soft voice ruled all and the days passed slowly and sweetly. In sharp contrast, the Heights vibrated with energy, burst at its seams with noise and life, shook with laughter and tears. It was not unusual to awaken to the sound of bubbling mirth or voices raised in heated quarrels; for the Chandlers were unbridled in their emotions. Gypsy blood ran hot in the veins of all except Aunt Maggie, endowing them, I fancied, with the wild, undaunted spirit of those dark-skinned wanderers, which made them as quick to argue as they were to embrace. But even knowing this, it was many months before I ceased to be shocked at the sight of Aunt Maggie railing at formidable Uncle Draco, wholly unafraid of his fierce temper. His grin of wicked merriment in response startled me even more, as he needled her insolently before finally giving way to her and smoothing her ruffled feathers by calling her his "Maggie love."

Even the servants, a motley assortment of misfits who, in truth, would have found places in no other respectable household but somehow did not seem at all out of the ordinary at the Heights, did not hesitate to express their opinions vocally. Yet on those mornings when Jarrett roused me from bed by tickling me so unmercifully that my muffled shrieks and laughter echoed down the corridor outside our chamber, or began a pillow fight that ended with a cloud of feathers being strewn about the room, the grumbling of the staff was good-natured. Nor, when we dallied overlong on those mornings, appearing late for breakfast, did the impassive Mawgen lift a censuring eyebrow, as might have been expected, but served us as always, although, once or twice, I thought I saw his mouth twitch with indulgent humor.

For above all, the Heights was a house filled with love, and Jarrett, its heir, held a secure place in the hearts of all. No slack, idle son was he, resting on his father's laurels, but hardworking as though he stood not to inherit a fortune and must make his own way in life. He would never whistle down the wind all that Uncle Draco had worked so hard to achieve, but would take pains to ensure it prospered.

When he did not laze away the morning with me, Jarrett rose promptly at six o'clock, and sometimes he did not come to bed at night until the wee hours, after tending the needs of the vast Chandler empire. There were fields of wheat, oats, and barley to be seen to, herds of black cattle and white sheep that bore the Chandler mark and roamed the commons, and the magnificent horses raised at the Heights. There was the P & C Shipping Line, with all its attendant vessels, cargoes from faraway places, and docks and warehouses, to manage; and the Chandler china-clay mines, Wheal Anant and Wheal Penforth, with their rough, sometimes explosive laborers, dangerous operations, and consignments to various manufacturers, to keep an eye on. When he was not busy with these enterprises, Jarrett spent many long evenings at his desk in our chamber, making copious notes to himself in his bold, scrawling black handwriting and logging detailed entries in records and ledgers. Like his father, he asked naught of those who served him that he could not, would not have done himself; of the rest of the world, he asked nothing, having learned at Uncle Draco's knee that a man must be able to stand alone, relying only on himself.

Yet somehow Jarrett found time for me, making me an intimate, integral part of his life, in a way another husband would not have done; for at the Heights, if nowhere else in the world, a woman was a man's equal, not only encouraged, but expected to stand at his side, to act in his stead when he was not present, and her word was as respected as his.

This was heady power in a day when a woman was, in truth, a prisoner as surely as though she were shackled by chains, legally bound first to her father and then to her husband or, if she did not marry, to some other male guardian. A woman could not vote, so she had no voice in the laws that governed her. She could not own property, so she must be dependent upon whatever some man chose to bestow upon her. She could be bartered away by her family, bought by and sold to the highest bidder, with never a thought as to whether the arrangement suited her or not. She could be beaten, locked away in a madhouse, or raped by her husband, and no one would lift a finger in her defense, for it was the lot of a woman to be nothing but a man's chattel, to belong to him as surely as his house, his carriage, and his port and cigars did.

Yet though Jarrett possessed me utterly, he never raised a hand to me that was not loving, and if we sometimes squabbled, there was no lack of respect in him for my viewpoint, however much he might disagree with it. He never forced himself upon me—though I daresay he might have done so if lustily provoked—but became even more considerate of my needs and feelings as our child grew within me. He seemed to understand instinctively that the larger I got, the uglier and more ungainly I felt, so I did not know how he could find me desirable; and he took extra time and care to assure me that in his eyes, I was the most beautiful woman in the world. So gentle and kind was he that I sometimes burst without warning into tears at how, in the past, I had been blind to him because of Nicholas.

Now, oddly, I could hardly recall Nicky's face, and even the memory of my love for him was so faded that it was as though I had never loved him at all or had loved him only in a bad dream, from which I had long since awakened. The peculiar impression was strengthened by the fact that it was as though the earth had swallowed Nicky up, for we heard no word from him or even of him, though Uncle Draco offered a reward of five thousand pounds for any information of him or his whereabouts.

And so the months passed until one spring day in 1843. I shall never forget that day, for in the end, it was to affect not only my own life, but the lives of children yet unborn, my own and others dear to me, in a way I would never have dreamed possible. But that is another's story, and I must tell my own. This is what happened that crucial day.

I had spent a long afternoon with Mama at the Grange; and now, in the glossy black, red-wheeled pony trap that Jarrett had bought for me since my advanced pregnancy no longer permitted me to ride, I was driving home across the moors, when a woman slowly approached and called to me, bidding me stop. I was not afraid, for she was alone, and I had a small pistol, besides, that Jarrett had insisted I carry for protection in these uncertain times; so, curious, I obediently pulled Jocko, the pony, to a halt. I could not see the woman's face clearly, for the setting sun was in my eyes. But I could tell she was badly dressed, in a thin, worn gown and dilapidated shoes, with a ragged muslin shawl tossed over her head and shoulders. At first, I supposed she must be a beggar. Yet to my surprise, she had addressed me as "Miss Laura."

Perhaps she is someone from the miners' rows, I thought, *and so knows I am Jarrett's wife*.

But this conjecture did not satisfy me, for I knew that Uncle Draco took better care of the miners and their families than this poor woman's pitiful condition led me to believe; thus I could not help but be puzzled. She was painfully gaunt, yet with a belly distended to rival mine and ankles grossly swollen from her obvious pregnancy, as though she had stood on her feet all day or perhaps even had walked many miles.

"Miss Laura"—she spoke my name again as she drew near, her head bowed, shuffling her feet like an old woman, though her soft voice sounded young. She stretched out one hand and laid it, trembling, on the edge of the trap, as though she felt faint and needed to steady herself. "Please . . . help me. Please," she beseeched. "I—I wouldn't ask, because I . . . know I don't deserve it after—after all that I did; but, oh, Miss Laura, I—I just don't . . . think I can go on."

She looked up at me then, her tattered shawl falling back to reveal her straggly red-gold hair, snarled and greasy, and filthy with lice, too, I had no doubt. Her sloe green eyes were dull and sunken, ringed with big, dark circles in her pinched white face. A bruise shadowed one sharply defined cheek; her bottom lip was split, encrusted with the scab of a healing wound. She was so changed that I almost did not recognize her.

"Dear God," I breathed, shocked and disbelieving. "Clemency."

Chapter XIV

Beginnings and Endings

Prais'd be the fathomless universe
For life and joy, and for objects and knowledge curious,
And for love, sweet love—but praise! praise! praise!
For the sure-enwinding arms of cool-enfolding death.

—*When Lilacs Last in the Dooryard Bloom'd*
Walt Whitman

I took her home with me, of course. I could do naught else. Though, at the Grange, she had treated me with malice and scorn, and stolen from me as well, I would have had to be made of stone to despise her now. I was not so hard as that. In truth, I pitied her with all my heart, for none knew better than I what, or rather who, had brought her to this sorry pass: Nicholas. He had used her as ruthlessly as he had me and abandoned her with as little care.

Little by little, as I guided the pony and trap over the

269

faint track that wended its way across the heaths, her sad story came out.

"He always had an eye for me, Mr. Nicholas did," Clemency declared haltingly, licking her lips and wringing her hands nervously, in a way that was most unlike her, "from the time he was fifteen and I but a year older."

Still, I soon gathered, nothing much more than a few hastily snatched kisses came of the attraction until that night in the gardens at the Grange, when, afraid she might lose him to me, she allowed him further liberties, enough to keep him dangling at least.

After that, they met frequently, clandestine trysts that excited them both. But each time, according to Clemency, she succeeded in holding Nicky at bay until finally he became virtually obsessed with having her. Soon he began swearing he loved her and promising to wed her; and her ambition and vanity were such, she admitted reluctantly, that they warred with her common sense until at last she convinced herself his lies were true. Eagerly enough, then, she surrendered to him when, denied my virginity that night upon the beach, he sought her out to take hers instead and, in one of those supremely ironic twists of fate, left her with child, as Jarrett had me.

Afterward, Nicky managed to fob her off with various excuses as to why he delayed in announcing their engagement (oh, how well I could hear his smooth justifications for this!); and by the time Clemency was certain she was indeed carrying his baby, it was too late: Spurred by my accusation that he had murdered Thorne, Nicky had bolted.

Still, at first, sure he loved her and would send for

her, she was only mildly dismayed, she told me. It was only later, when she did not hear from him, that she grew anxious and determined she must seek him out.

Unable to resist buying a bit of fancy lace or ribbon, she had saved few funds over the years, so she robbed my jewel box to be assured of coins in her purse. Naturally, Clemency insisted with a flash of her old defiance, she had never dreamed of taking anything valuable. Then, winsomely wheedling rides on passing wagons, she journeyed to London, and there, she pawned my baubles so she could live while she searched for Nicky.

But of course, although she spent weeks asking after him in hotels, shops, and taverns, and even interrogating passersby on the streets about him, she did not locate him. It was not, after all, to be expected that a lone, nearly penniless woman would accomplish what Uncle Draco, with all his resources and riches, had failed to do.

Now, by this time, Clemency's money was fast running out, and she was forced to find work to support herself. No respectable household would employ her, pregnant and unwed as she was, and without a reference, too; so she finally took a job as a barmaid in a tavern near the piers that lined the River Thames. The wages were fair, but it soon became clear to her that the barkeep, a slovenly brute, expected certain favors in return for hiring her. When she tried to refuse him, he viciously beat and raped her. From then on, Clemency related woodenly, he watched her like a hawk, starving her and locking her in his room at night, so she had neither the strength nor the opportunity to run away from him.

At last, however, she grew so heavy with child that

the lout found her body disgusting, and he started selling her to those of his customers who did not care what she looked like, so long as she pleased them. But there was one, she recalled softly, a young dockworker, who worshiped and pitied her (she was still vaguely pretty then, though the harsh treatment she endured daily had begun to leave its mark); and it was this lad who helped her to escape. He hid her in his quarters for a time, but recently, Clemency explained, he met with a fatal accident on the wharves; and after a few days, when the rent was due and she could pay no more, the landlord threw her out, retaining, in lieu of what was then owing, both her own meager belongings and those of the dead boy.

Alone on the mean streets of London, then, with nary a hope of fending for herself or even of acquiring another protector, no matter how brutal, she had seen no choice but to return to Cornwall. Her coming baby was a Chandler by blood, if not by marriage, she had reasoned; and she did not think that, upon learning this, they would turn her away at the Heights.

Because few people had wanted to be burdened with a plainly ill and pregnant woman, she had walked a good deal of the way from London; and the past few days, she had grown so weak with hunger and exhaustion that upon spying me, she had dared to accost me, in the dim hope that I would assist her.

Poor Clemency! She had aimed so high and sunk so low that I could not help but be sorry for her. I was horrified by her tale, for in truth, she had not deserved so wretched and ugly a lot, and I was stricken by the thought that she had half believed I would not take her up in the trap, but would drive on. Had there really been so much animosity between us? I hastened to reassure her otherwise, beset by a strange guilt over all she had suffered for loving Nicky; for deep down inside, I knew that but for Jarrett, I might have met with a similar fate. I shuddered at the notion, remembering suddenly the biblical admonition that pride goes before destruction and a haughty spirit before a fall; and silently, I vowed I *would* learn to curb my tempestuous emotions.

Finally, we arrived at the Heights. Clemency did not want any of the servants to see her, so I installed her at the gatehouse. I knew that mad old Renshaw would not bother her, that he would hardly even be aware of her presence, and that if, by some chance, he did speak of her to the rest of the staff, they would dismiss his talk as babble. Then slowly I went into the house to recount to Jarrett, Uncle Draco, and Aunt Maggie, Clemency's grim, pathetic story.

She remained at the Heights, in the gatehouse, with none of the servants aware of her presence there; for no one but Renshaw entered his domain, which had played an important role in medieval times, but no longer served any real purpose. Uncle Draco had spoken with her, and although I did not as yet know all that had passed between them, I knew he had given Clemency leave to stay, and even had Dr. Ashford, both advised and well paid to keep his mouth shut, out to examine her. Her months away from us had taken their toll. She was physically badly battered and malnourished, and mentally depressed; but she would, the gruff but kindly physician said, heal with time, given proper care and rest. This, Uncle Draco set about at once to ensure she received, for even then, he had already conceived the scheme that, unbeknown to us all, was to have such far-reaching consequences for so many, some of whom were not yet even born.

But he did not succeed in his design alone; this, I firmly believe. God works in mysterious ways; I have heard it said a hundred times and soon knew it must be true, for surely, it was only through His intervention that Uncle Draco's plan was brought so neatly to fruition, though bittersweet was its culmination. How else to explain that freak of nature that enabled all to take place as though it were ordained, when the fraud, though it was born of love and well-intentioned, might well otherwise have been exposed? For clever must the deed have been, in truth, had not God taken a hand in the timing, as I believe He did.

But perhaps I am wrong. Perhaps our destiny is written in the stars before we are born, and there is no escaping it. Yet if that is true, all hope is false, all dreams are useless, and we are indeed no more than shells upon the sand of life, powerless to change what must be. If, as I once believed, we are swept hither and yon by the omnipotent sea of fate, what is the purpose of our existence? There must be some reason for our being, unknown though it may be to us, and for our dying, too. Otherwise, I could not bear to remember what I shall speak of by and by; for the memory of it has not dimmed—the joy, the sorrow have not lessened—though fifty years and more have come and gone since then and Uncle Draco has lain dead in his grave now these ten years past.

But long before that, together, he and God wrought their will upon us.

It was late that spring of 1843, a dreary May night. I lay in my bed in the south tower, drenched with sweat, gasping and screaming with pain; for my labor, which had begun early that morning, was now in its final stages as my child struggled with all its might to push its way into the world.

Outside, rain beat down, pummeling the windows of the south tower, pelting the shutters and rattling the glass panes so violently that I thought they would shatter. The wind howled like a banshee, whining through the cracks and crannies of the manor, causing the flames of the lamps to flicker wildly and cast eerie, dancing shadows upon the walls. If only it had not been so savage a night! I think now. If only my screams had not reverberated so loudly through the house; then might another's have been heard. *If only* . . . Those are the saddest words in the world, I think.

In the beginning, I had been nervous and excited, keyed up almost to a frenzy, unable to rest. Despite the rain, Papa and Mama had driven over from the Grange; and though Mama and Aunt Maggie both had urged me to try to relax, still, I had paced the floor like a caged animal. But then, inevitably, my contractions had started to stab sharp as a knife slicing through my body, and I had doubled over with anguish, only too happy to lie down, though it had not helped. Instead, inexorably, the pain had worsened until I had begun to thrash and writhe upon the bed convulsively, like a wild thing, certain I and my baby were going to die.

I had never before known such excruciating torment; the pain had vicious talons, ripping and clawing its way through my body until now I felt as though I would be torn asunder. Although I had cried out desperately for Jarrett until I was hoarse and, coolly overriding the stern, shocked protests of Dr. Ashford, as well as Mama's flustered demurring, Aunt Maggie had admitted my husband to our chamber, I was now scarcely even aware of him at my side, his face sober and ashen. Yet I crushed his hand so tightly in mine that, later, I was horrified to see the bloody gashes my fingernails gouged in his skin. Such was Jarrett's concern for me, however, that he made no complaint, would not have done so, I suspect, had I wrenched his hand from his wrist.

Even the poor servants were terrified for me. The bolder among them had knocked so often upon the door, wanting news of my progress, that finally, exasperated, Aunt Maggie had, with the exception of Mrs. Pickering (the housekeeper and an experienced midwife), banished the entire staff from the upper story of the manor. Now, downstairs, they huddled about the kitchen table, thinking, in their ignorance, that something dreadful was wrong, for I was only six months wed. Even Dr. Ashford, when he spoke to Mama and Aunt Maggie, his voice low so I should not overhear him (although I did), stated gravely that he expected I would be delivered of a child that, if not stillborn, would be too underdeveloped to survive more than a few hours at most. For of course, no one but I, Jarrett, and his parents knew that my baby was actually full-term and not premature. At the physician's dire prediction, Mama, fearing not only for the child's life, but my own also, burst without warning into tears and subsequently became so useless that, in the end, Aunt Maggie was compelled to send her away, too. Weeping so profusely that she could scarcely see, Mama went below, to the great hall, where I supposed Uncle Draco and Papa waited anxiously, though I was wrong in this assumption, as I was soon to learn.

For this was the consummate hand that God, in His wisdom, saw fit to thrust into our affairs that fateful night: Even as I bore down strenuously again and again, at long last arduously but joyously expelling my son from my womb into the world, Clemency lay in the gatehouse, locked in the throes of labor, delirious with agony as she strained to deliver her own baby.

Had someone told me this, I should not have believed it, though truth is stranger than fiction, it is said. But few in the manor knew she was in the gatehouse; no one knew of her current condition.

In our own way, we had made the same mistakes, she and I. How was it, then, that I should be surrounded by a loving family that night, while she had nobody? So many years now, I have pondered that question. It was, I know, but an accident of birth that made the difference between us—and the love of a man. Had I not been born a Prescott, had Jarrett not loved me, it could just as easily have been I in the gatehouse that night. Even now, a chill runs down my spine at the thought; so narrow are the odds that separate mistress and maid.

They washed my son and swaddled him, then laid him to my breast. It was the proudest, happiest, most peaceful moment I had ever known. Wrinkled, chubby, crimson with rage at his inability to return to his safe, snug nest, squalling louder than the rain and wind, he was the most beautiful thing I had ever seen. Tears penciled my cheeks as I looked at him, counted his tiny fingers and toes, and stroked his patch of black hair, soft as down. Aunt Maggie cried, too, and even Jarrett rubbed his hand across his eyes brusquely, though I think he was not ashamed of his tears.

"Well, Miss Laura," Dr. Ashford uttered tartly, for he had delivered me years ago, after all, and so felt it was his privilege to speak his mind, "that's a mighty healthy specimen you've got there—six-month child or not!"

Then, eyeing me sharply and grumbling heatedly under his breath about wayward young women who risked their lives and caused others needless worry by not telling the truth about certain matters—which anybody who had ever been young and in love could well understand after all—he snapped shut his black bag and departed. I was blushing to the roots of my hair as the physician closed the door behind him, but Jarrett only laughed and said, "Like father, like son," which caused Aunt Maggie to flush as scarlet as I and rebuke him rather sharply. But to her mortification, Jarrett laughed all the harder. He knew he was a "seven-month" child and didn't care. Mrs. Pickering, however, was scandalized, though she had helped to deliver him; and she *hmph*ed loudly, mainly because she was deaf, and declared that, the good Lord willing, she was going to keep a keen eye on our son when *he* came of age. To her indignation, that sent us all into gales of mirth; and gathering up the soiled linens, she exited the chamber, saying she would warn Mama, Papa, and Uncle Draco that another Chandler rogue was about to be loosed on the unsuspecting world.

To this day, my heart breaks when I think of how, in our gladness and ignorance, we laughed and teased that night in the south tower, while poor, piteous Clemency lay in the gatehouse, torturously giving birth to her son, with no one but a lunatic to attend her until it was too late.

Had we known Dr. Ashford was needed, we would never have let him drive away, of course. But we did not know; for in his befuddled mind, Renshaw, petrified by first Clemency's moans and screams, and then her baby's thin wails of anger and fright, somehow believed he would be blamed for the miserable state of both mother and child. So he did not heed Clemency's frantic pleas to fetch his master until her life's blood began gushing from her, in a flood so forceful that no power on earth could stop it.

Uncle Draco tried. God knows, he tried, desperately. He was like a man possessed after Renshaw, wide-eyed and babbling with terror, finally came to the manor for him. Cursing, Uncle Draco shouted at Papa, who had accompanied him to the gatehouse, to ride like hell after Dr. Ashford. Then feverishly, after running back to the house to get from the storeroom what he required, he set to work on Clemency, doing all that could have been done—pouring vile herbal decoctions down her throat, binding her tightly with clean white cloths, and packing her in ice to try to halt her hemorrhaging—to no avail.

I don't know when he realized he was losing her.

Perhaps it was when Clemency, after groping blindly for his hand, pressed a delicate gold locket into his palm and closed his fingers about it tightly. It was all she had left in the world, and even it, she had stolen from me. I never learned what, though she was destitute, had made her keep it; perhaps it represented some fragile link with the only home she had ever truly known, or perhaps she had meant it for her baby all along.

"For Rhodes," she murmured to Uncle Draco, weakly indicating her son, who lay at her side. "There's a picture of me . . . inside . . . if he should ever . . . want to know. . . ." Her voice trailed away. Then suddenly she cried, "Nicky! Oh, Nicky, my love!"

"Hang on, Clemency!" Uncle Draco muttered fiercely, stubbornly refusing to recognize defeat, even when it stared him in the face. "The doctor's coming! Damn it, girl! Hang on! You can make it! God, don't do this—"

But God had given, and now He took away. Uncle Draco could not save her. Clemency died in his arms just before dawn.

Chapter XV

Lives Intertwined

Though nothing can bring back the hour
Of splendour in the grass, of glory in the flower;
We will grieve not, rather find
Strength in what remains behind . . .

—*Ode. Intimations of Immortality*
William Wordsworth

I never forgave Nicholas for Clemency's death. But most of all, I never forgave him for the look upon Uncle Draco's face when, just as dawn broke on the horizon, he and Papa came at last to the south tower, entering by its exterior door and coming upstairs to Jarrett's and my chamber through our sitting room below, so none of the servants would spy them.

Jarrett and I had long since fallen asleep, with Ransom, as we had named our son, tucked between us so he should not roll off the bed, for we could not bear to place him in his nearby cradle just yet. Earlier, Mama had come in, tiptoeing across the floor to peek at him; and to our disappointment and concern, she had explained that some emergency had arisen, so Papa and Uncle Draco had been forced to leave the house and could not visit us just yet.

No one knew what had happened, only that, mounted on one of the Chandler horses, Papa had galloped away in the rain as though the devil were hard on his heels, and that Uncle Draco was like to kill Renshaw. But still, none had dared to ask why or to intervene when, after returning briefly to the manor, Uncle Draco had hustled the madman back to the gatehouse and neither had subsequently reappeared.

Somehow I knew that Uncle Draco had lived through hell that night, for so long as I live, I shall remember his face as it looked in that moment when he wakened Jarrett and me, dark and haunted by grief, though I expected it to be filled with joy at the birth of my son. He held Clemency's child, small and helpless, in the cradle of his big, strong arms; and even then, before I knew the whole, a horrible, sharp stab of foreboding pierced my sleepy consciousness, so I came abruptly wide-awake. My breath caught in my throat, and I clutched Jarrett's hand in sudden dread.

Yet Uncle Draco spoke not of the baby he carried, and something in his demeanor warned us not to ask. Thus it was not until he and Papa had assured themselves of my and Ransom's well-being that, stricken, I learned of Clemency's tragic death. I wept for a long time after that, for strangely enough, drawn together by our pregnancies and the shared secret of her living in the gatehouse,

Clemency and I had almost become friends these past few weeks. She had been lonely and afraid; and because I, too, had known those feelings once, I had visited her whenever I could. It had helped her, I think, to talk to me. Now I could not believe that she was dead, that, by some ultimate, ironic twist of fate, her child, conceived the same night as mine, should have been born on the same night as mine also.

Lost in reverie, I had almost forgotten the others in the room, but after a time, Uncle Draco spoke, startling me back to the present. His shoulders heaving, his voice husky with emotion, he asked softly, "Do you know what it means to be a bastard, Laura?"

I knew, then, what he wanted of me, what he had intended all along, though it was only by the grace of God that Clemency's son had followed mine that night into the world, making Uncle Draco's scheme so easy to carry out. He had not known that Clemency would die, of course. He had planned to send her away, to America, with enough money to keep her the rest of her life, if only she relinquished her child into his keeping. This, for her baby's sake, so it would not be scorned as a bastard, Clemency had agreed to do. Such was Uncle Draco's resolution that her blameless child should not suffer, as he himself had suffered, for a sin not its own, that could he but have laid his hands on Nicky, I believe he would have compelled him to marry Clemency had she been alive—or murdered him because she had died. But Uncle Draco was nothing if not shrewd and determined, and since he lacked the means to legitimize the baby, he had thought of another way to protect its name.

Jarrett's child and Nicky's . . . to be reared as brothers, twins.

I shuddered at the idea, for somehow it seemed to tempt destiny. Yet Uncle Draco's dark eyes bored into mine, like windows to his soul, laid so painfully bare that I knew it would kill something deep inside of him if I refused his request. Far more eloquently than words now did those eyes speak of all that he, a bastard, had borne in his life, of all that he would spare the child fathered by Nicky, whom he had loved with all his heart, the son whom my thoughtless, accusing tongue had sent from him. How could I deny him this, then, a name for that nameless baby?

Dear reader, I could not.

From that day forward, Rhodes was my son as surely as though he had been born of my body—and who was to say he had not been? Not Dr. Ashford, who swore that after Papa had fetched him back that night for Clemency, Jarrett had learned he was at the gatehouse and had come for him, insisting that I was still in pain, that the birth of a second child was imminent.

"Twins!" Dr. Ashford pronounced the lie smoothly to one and all later that day, never batting an eyelash. "I should have suspected it when the first little rascal came so early. Women never carry twins full term, you know. Besides, they run in the Chandler family."

And so was I spared the shame of having it said I had given myself to Jarrett before our wedding night, the gossip and speculation centering instead on poor Clemency. We knew naught, those of us who *did* know adamantly maintained, except that she had appeared without warning at the gatehouse that night, badly beaten, bleeding profusely, and begging for aid. Renshaw, frightened out of his wits, had delayed in summoning his master, and so, by the time Papa had returned with Dr. Ashford, it had been too late; though it was the physician's considered opinion that he could not have helped Clemency in any event. Uncle Draco had done everything Dr. Ashford himself would have done in an effort to save her.

There had been a man, of course, the village asserted smugly, a lover who had used her, abused her, then cast her aside. But, then, what else was to have been expected? Hadn't they always said, after all, that blood would tell, that, sooner or later, Clemency Tyrrell would come to a bad end?

How I longed to scratch their eyes out!—those ignorant scandalmongers who knew nothing, as Clemency and I had known, of what it meant to give one's heart away and have it smashed to bits instead of cherished.

But there was naught I could do for her now except to ensure she was decently buried rather than laid to rest in a pauper's grave—and love her son as though he were my own. So, Ransom and Rhodes became the twins; and as they grew and thrived, Jarrett and I thrust to the back of our minds the fact that one of them was Nicky's baby. In truth, the boys, being cousins, really did look enough alike to pass not just for brothers, but for twins; for fortunately, physically at least, there was nothing of Clemency in Rhodes. He was a black-haired, black-eyed

Chandler through and through, as was Ransom, so that sometimes Jarrett and I actually did have trouble telling them apart.

I believe my husband loved me more than ever for accepting his brother's child as mine, for our life together had never before seemed so rich. Our days abounded in joy and intimacy, drawn close, as we were, by the boys. It was then, I think, that I began truly to fall in love with Jarrett.

Because the Chandler family was large, the Heights staffed with many servants, we were spared much of the usual difficulty and frustration that accompanies the birth of a baby—especially the birth of twins. There was always someone to lend a helping hand, and the nursery, under the aegis of Annie, who had been Jarrett's own nanny, was all a mother could have wished. Aunt Maggie and Mama (who had practically moved into the manor, it seemed), were always happy to rock the boys; and even Uncle Draco and Papa were frequently to be seen dandling a grandchild on one knee.

Dear Papa. He knew the truth, of course, about the twins and so had guessed, too, that Jarrett and I were lovers before our wedding night. But Papa was a man of the world, after all, and to my relief, he did not reproach me. Instead, he wickedly remarked to Jarrett and Uncle Draco that as my brother Guy had begun courting Jarrett's sister Damaris, who had just turned seventeen and was now out of the schoolroom, it was devoutly to be hoped that the Prescotts and Chandlers did not run true to form, or we would soon run out of excuses for babies that arrived too promptly. I nearly split my sides with laughter when, later, unobserved by either my husband or my brother, I saw Jarrett accost Guy and overheard the former inquire rudely just what the latter's intentions toward Damaris were.

Guy, tossing his blond head just as Papa always did, drawled dryly, "Oh, about the same as yours were toward Laura, I would imagine, Jarrett," so I knew my brother also suspected I had not been a chaste bride; and I thanked God that Mama was too kind and trusting to believe ill of anyone. Yet it was ironic that Guy should fall in love with one of the Chandler daughters, as I had once wished, thinking then that any of them would make him a suitable wife and that I would not then have to marry Jarrett.

But such are the incongruous ways of the world, as I have come to learn, for we who inhabit it are threaded with flaws and fears, and so ever spin a tangled web. But I was not unhappy now with the twist my life had taken. Indeed, as time passed, I grew more and more certain I would not have traded my lot for any other.

Life, never stagnant, moved on. That summer, my sister-in-law Angelique wed her Lord Greystone and left us, while her twin, Alexander, brought home to the Heights his bride, Lady Vanessa Dubray. Thorne, having worn out his welcome in Ireland and proceeded thence to the Continent, now judged it safe to discontinue the pretense of his "grand tour" and came back to take up residence again at the Hall. Aunt Julianne, currently weighing upward of ten stone because of her penchant for bonbons and sweetmeats, was, of course, thrilled by her darling's return. Elizabeth, however, grown sourer than ever, barely remained on speaking terms with her brother and, naturally, tendered me the cut direct whenever our paths chanced to cross, though this was not often. Guy continued his pursuit of Damaris; and my younger brother, Francis, left school and went to work as a second mate upon the *Sarah Jane*, Papa's favorite of the P & C ships. The twins grew by leaps and bounds. And sadly, one stormy autumn eve, mad Renshaw, who had never got over the shock of poor Clemency's bleeding to death in the gatehouse, hanged himself from one of the ancient Cornish elms that towered over the courtyard of the Heights. Because he had committed suicide, he could not be buried in consecrated ground, of course, much to Uncle Draco and Aunt Maggie's regret, for in their own way, I believe they loved that old lunatic.

Beyond the boundaries of our parish, the world, too, forged inexorably ahead. From the newspapers and other sources, we learned that in India, a British commander, Sir Charles Napier, in response to the refusal of the Mohammedan emirs of Sind to surrender their independence to the powerful East India Company, attacked and, incredibly, with only twenty-eight hundred soldiers, defeated a Baluch army of thirty thousand men.

In London, a statue of the late Admiral Lord Nelson was hoisted atop a tall Grecian pillar erected in Trafalgar Square, a plaza built two years earlier to eradicate the sordid courts and shoddy cookshops that had caused the area to be nicknamed ''Porridge Island.'' Soon tourists and pigeons both besieged the square, and the admiral was subjected in stone to various indignities I felt certain he had never been forced to tolerate in the flesh.

On July 19, I. K. Brunnel successfully launched the S.S. *Great Britain*, the first of the huge, screw-propelled iron steamships that would seek to dominate the transatlantic trade, cutting into the considerable profits of the P & C Shipping Line. The reaction of Papa and Uncle Draco, upon learning of the event, was not fit for ladies' ears.

The *Sunday News of the World*, a new newspaper, started publication and, unbelievably, within a year had a circulation of over twelve thousand copies per week. This figure would eventually grow to six million, the highest of any newspaper in the world.

Over the winter holidays, a museum director, Henry Cole, designed and sent out the first Christmas cards, wishing all a "Merry Christmas and a Happy New Year." We in England read for the first time Charles Dickens's *A Christmas Carol*, the heartening story of a mean old miser, Ebenezer Scrooge, and his visitation by three spirits who changed his life; while America, apparently inclined toward the morbid rather than the uplifting, quaked in its boots at the macabre tales of Edgar Allan Poe. The following year, it was a rousing "All for one, one for all," when the first edition of *Les Trois Mousquetaires*, penned by the French novelist and playwright Alexandre Dumas, was printed.

At Greystone Manor, Angelique gave birth to a girl, christened Jocelyn, born a suspicious month sooner than she ought to have been, the earl, it appeared to our amusement, also having proved an impatient groom. As he was rumored to have a temper to rival any Chandler's, however, it was deemed prudent to overlook any possible misconduct of the aristocratic couple. Lord Greystone was, of course, quite rich and so was well able to support his growing family; but others were not so lucky.

Thus, much to the relief of the common man, who was barely scraping by, rail transport of meat, fish, eggs, green produce, and milk drove down food prices in 1844, and also improved British diets. But it did not last, for a year later, the potato famine struck. All over the Continent, Britain, and Ireland, the crops failed, decimated by disease; even potatoes in storage turned black as those in the ground, foully slimed with rot. From the snows of Moscow to the mists of Dublin, two and a half million people died of hunger. The Irish were particularly hard hit. Never very prosperous in the best of times and now literally starving to death, they flocked to England in droves, a source of cheap labor, for some would work for as little as four shillings a week, practically slave wages.

Previously, since her father had come into a bit of luck at the gaming tables and she was able to stave off the many creditors dunning her, Lady Siobhan O'Halloran had appeared content to allow her engagement to Thorne to languish indefinitely. Now, however, frightened by the violence and upheaval sweeping across her country, she speedily picked a wedding day and, much to Thorne's dismay, demanded he show up at the altar or else. So, fearing to be sued for breach of promise otherwise, my Sheffield cousin reluctantly claimed his bride.

A few months later, the news somewhat startling, all things considered, Siobhan announced she was expecting a child. Remembering how Jarrett had suspected her of having wanton appetites she did not hesitate to indulge, and knowing, as I did, Thorne's sexual proclivity, I felt sure it was not, to put it bluntly, my cousin's bun that Siobhan was baking in her oven. But much to my surprise, the baby, when it eventually arrived, after a proper nine-month interval, looked just like Thorne; so I supposed he must have conquered his distaste of women long enough to get an heir on her after all.

Siobhan was not the only female to hook her man that year of 1845. Aunt Maggie's loss was Mama's gain when Guy married Damaris and brought her home to the Grange; and though we did not yet know it, hope was in sight for peevish Lizzie, too, as, in far-off Australia, a ship called the *Fancy Free* set sail, bound for England's shores.

Francis, who had journeyed to America, returned with a copy of "The Purloined Letter," from *Tales* by Edgar Allan Poe, and a report that a New York naval architect, John Willis Griffiths, had launched an improved clipper ship, the *Rainbow*, which, being the fastest vessel afloat, was capable of successfully quashing the threat posed by the iron steamships. For my brother's astuteness in acquiring this vital piece of information and his worthy suggestion that the P & C Shipping Line either begin building or purchasing these new clippers at once, Papa and Uncle Draco awarded him a raise in salary and promoted him to the position of first mate, a heady thrill for a young man just turned eighteen.

And so did the years of my life pass, quietly and contentedly for the most part, until that All Hallows Eve of October, 1845.

How well I remember that night! Strange and gloomy, it was, with an indescribable tenseness about it, a peculiar, ominous stillness, like what presages a storm, so it seemed as though the whole world held its breath, waiting.

A moonless blackness fell swiftly after dusk. Then, little by little, the wind began to rise, moaning sibilantly through the trees, rustling their branches and loosing from the boughs brittle dead leaves to hurl them away into the night. The twin Cornish elms that stood in the courtyard of the Heights creaked and swayed, like the timbers on a ship tossed at sea; and the old manor itself shuddered about me, straining and settling eerily as the wind whipped and whined and snarled its way, unhindered, across the sweeping moors, poking and prying at the tightly shuttered windows of the house, howling sinisterly when it could not get in.

The cracks and crevices of the granite tors shrieked and soughed with each violent gust; the grass and gorse of the heaths undulated wildly, flattening against the ground as though trodden upon by some titan foot. The stagnant, slate-colored pools that dotted the dismal marshes churned and bubbled, turning black as the night sky; and the bog islands buoyed up by the murky water trembled and heaved, so their sodden black tufts of weeds shook.

Beyond the cliffs at the edge of the lawn, the frothy ocean roiled and crashed against the long, gnarled fingers of rock; white-flecked spume spewed high into the oppressive air, hissing on the wind.

Somehow the night seemed even more menacing for

the fact that no drop of rain fell; lightning did not shatter the firmament; no boom of thunder rolled across the heavens. Only the wind and the sea roared their fury.

I, cringing before the fire in the great hall, felt certain that the graves of the dead had indeed opened and that their spirits walked the night, as superstition claimed took place each All Hallows Eve. The hours seemed to creep by. The gale grew steadily more fearsome until at last it succeeded in ripping loose from a mullioned window one of its shutters. Swinging by a single hinge, the shutter banged against the wall of the great hall, sounding so like some unholy thing hammering at the door, demanding entrance, that it was some time before I realized the brass knocker actually was being pounded hard against the oak portal.

Such was the state to which the night had wrought my nerves that, for a moment, I thought wildly that some specter stood without. A chill tingle of portent crawled up my spine at the notion; I did not want to answer the door. But as it appeared no one else in the house could hear the knocking, at last, reluctantly, I laid aside the book I had been trying to read and forced myself to rise and open the portal.

So strong was the wind that it snatched the door from my grasp, flinging it back against the wall to reveal the dark figure who seemed to perch like a malevolent raven upon the stone stoop outside, black greatcoat flapping like wings. As the tall form stepped from the shadows into the light, the torches set into the stout iron sconces on either side of the portal wavered wildly, erratically illuminating the face of the silhouette. I gasped and cried out at the sight, one hand flying to my mouth with shock and disbelief, for no word of warning had there been to prepare us, and I felt as though I stared at a ghost. After three long, silent years, it might well have been.

Nicholas Chandler had come home.

BOOK THREE

The Notorious
1845–1848

Chapter XVI

The Prodigal's Return

I remember the black wharves and the slips,
   And the sea-tides tossing free;
And Spanish sailors with bearded lips,
And the beauty and mystery of the ships,
   And the magic of the sea.
     And the voice of that wayward song
     Is singing and saying still:
   'A boy's will is the wind's will
And the thoughts of youth are long, long thoughts.'

             —*My Lost Youth*
              Henry Wadsworth Longfellow

Stormswept Heights, England, 1845

"Well, aren't you going to ask me in, Laura?"—he spoke, his black eyes glittering in the torchlight, his lips curved with an odd half-smile.

"Yes—yes, of course," I stammered, though, in

truth, I wanted nothing more than to slam the door in his face, to pretend I had never answered it, had never seen him standing there upon the stoop.

I felt a terrible sense of portent at his appearance, as though somehow our lives would never be the same with his return.

Nicholas entered the manor, pausing at the fore of the great hall, his eyes sweeping the vast room intently, as though to assure himself it remained the same as when he had left home. Then he turned back to me; deliberately, his gaze roamed over me, coming to rest upon my face. Color rose hotly to my cheeks at his scrutiny. My mouth went dry, my pulse raced. Without warning, the wind died, one of those strange lulls that happen now and then, as though the night itself had ground to a halt, faded away, leaving my senses focused acutely on Nicky. In the sudden silence, I stared at him, still half believing him an apparition.

He had changed. His dark Gypsy visage was harder than I remembered, etched by the fine lines of time and dissipation, so he appeared older than his twenty-four years, older even than Jarrett, and wary, as though he had learned to sleep with one eye open. He was leaner, more muscular, his stance like that of an animal alert for possible predators—or prey—senses honed to a keen edge. His life had not been easy, I suspected, since he had ridden away that fateful day, without even so much as a cloak upon his back. Yet for all his hungry, watchful demeanor, it seemed he had prospered. His clothes were exquisite, well tailored, expensive. I wondered how he had come by them, how he had lived, where he had been.

He was bold and clever. He might have turned his hand to any number of things, on any number of the world's meaner streets, for I had no doubt now that it was there that Nicky had lost himself, vanished without a trace amid the human refuse of the earth, the vagabonds, blackguards, thieves, and cutthroats who prowled the slums of every city. He had thought himself one step ahead of a hangman's noose. Where else could he have gone than where a man was asked no questions, but was accepted on the merits of his wits and skill and daring?

There, he would have had nothing to lose and everything to gain by doing whatever was necessary to survive. I would not have put it past him to have worked as a sharp or an ivory-turner, for his hands had ever been smooth—he had kept them so with a pumice stone—and deft at palming cards or switching dice, parlor tricks with which he had used to amuse me in our youth. I knew full well he was no gentleman to scruple at playing the cheat. What else he might not have hesitated to do, I could only guess—and shiver at my thoughts.

I never learned the answers to many of my questions; for later, when asked by others about his absence, Nicky was reticent, as though he did not care to speak of those three years away from us. He had traveled here and there, he said, mostly in Australia, where he had put to excellent use his knowledge of mining and ships. He had, in a leather pouch, a handful of fine diamonds as proof of his story, and in the harbor at Plymouth, a fleet clipper called the *Fancy Free* lay at anchor, registered to one Nicholas Chandler, he informed us. What more did we need to know? It wasn't much of a tale; there was a great deal, we knew, left untold. But still, little more than that was got from him; and so the village swore darkly that it was as likely he had spent those three years imprisoned for some unknown crime as it was that he had lived them sweating and toiling in the rugged Australian outback and high on the hog in the towns burgeoning in Queensland and New South Wales, as he intimated.

Now, softly, mockingly, startling me from my reverie, he asked, "Well, do I meet with your approval, Laura? Or . . . should I say . . . Mrs. Chandler? You *are* Jarrett's wife now, are you not?"

"Yes," I said, blushing uncomfortably, realizing how I had stared at him.

"What a pity," he remarked lightly, "for in truth, you are grown more beautiful than ever." His black eyes belied his offhand tone, raking me again assessingly, as though I were a slave upon a block, making me shudder with fear, and something else I could not name, though in another, I should have called it morbid fascination. "What a fool I was," he declared abruptly, his voice low, harsh, throbbing with emotion now, all pretense of casualness gone. "I ought to have married you myself when you were mine for the asking. 'Tis the one mistake I have oft regretted these past years," he said, watching me intently, waiting for some reaction, though I offered none, forcing my face to remain impassive. I was not so insensible as to fall victim to his lies again. "Did you think I would not come back, Laura?" he queried sharply when I stubbornly refused to meet his eyes. "Did you think I would not learn what a vile trick you played me—you and Thorne? Imagine how I felt . . . hearing from some Irish jackanapes of an immigrant that Thorne was idling his days away at the O'Halloran estate! Three years of my life, you took from me—you and he. By God! You owe me for that!''

At that, before I realized what he intended, Nicky grasped my chin with one steely hand, compelling my face up to his, and kissed me full upon the lips. I was so stunned by his action that I did not struggle, but merely stood there, my hands pressed against his chest, as he took what he wanted of me, leisurely, thoroughly, his tongue shooting deep into my mouth. I did not fight him even then. I think perhaps subconsciously I wished to be certain, in my mind, that nothing remained in my heart for him; and at last, when I did not respond to him, he released me.

Though he had not aroused me, still, to my surprise, he was smiling smugly; his hooded eyes gleamed at me with triumph. I could not understand why until, to my horror, looking over my shoulder, he drawled, "Hullo, Jarrett. Laura was just welcoming me home."

Frightened, I gasped and turned, thinking, hoping desperately that it was but Nicky's idea of a joke to get even with me because Thorne lived. But it was not. Jarrett indeed stood behind me, a muscle working in his taut jaw, his eyes shuttered, glinting hard as nails. Nicky had known he was there all along, I realized, my heart sinking, the pulse at the hollow of my throat fluttering with agitation as I guessed what Jarrett must be thinking. Oh, why had I ever stood acquiescent in Nicky's arms? Why hadn't I fought, screamed, done something to protest?

"So I see," Jarrett rejoined coldly, his gaze flicking

over me curtly, contemptuously, I thought, inwardly cringing at the rage I suspected must be roiling inside him, though he gave no outward sign of it. Instead, he suggested smoothly, "Laura, perhaps since you have already greeted Nicholas, you will go find Father and Mother and the rest of the household, and inform them the prodigal son has returned."

"Of course," I said, sensing that now was not the time for explanations, though I knew I must make them later and hope Jarrett would believe me.

But now I moved swiftly to obey him, glad to escape from the hall and the tension that crackled therein, as before a battle; while outside, the wind and the sea shouted like God at the devil.

I never knew what passed between the two men after I left, though it was only words, not blows. But when I came back with Uncle Draco, Aunt Maggie, and the others, Nicky was standing before the fire in the hearth, his dark visage wiped of its supercilious smile; while Jarrett lounged in a chair, smoking a cheroot, his lips curved wolfishly with grim relish, as though he had drawn first blood and savored it.

As the household gathered in the hall, there was a flurry of exclamations and embraces; but it was not, I supposed, quite the ecstatic reunion Nicky had doubtless envisioned. Uncle Draco's welcome was tempered with restraint; unbeknown to Nicky, Clemency's shadow lay between them and would have to be answered for, I knew. Nor had Aunt Maggie, highly sensitive to her sons' moods, missed the strain between Jarrett and Nicky. Though only once in her life had she been beyond the boundaries of northern Cornwall, she was a woman of the world, all too cognizant of human foibles. I suspected that the knowledge of Nicky's attempt to rape me and the results of Jarrett's intervention were uppermost in her mind. Even now, she must be wondering uneasily, as I was, what else might come of the bad blood between the brothers.

Yet for all this, we managed somehow to get through the remainder of the night pleasantly enough, Alexander and his wife, Vanessa, and Bryony, the youngest Chandler daughter and the only one left at home, taking the edge off what might otherwise have proved a rather stilted atmosphere. Still, I thought there was a collective sigh of relief when finally we heard the ornate ormolu clock upon the mantel in the hall chime midnight and, pleading tiredness at all the excitement, were able to retire at last to our respective chambers.

Somewhat to my dismay, though I don't know why it should have been otherwise, Nicky was installed in his old bedroom. Although this was in the south wing, rather than the south tower, it was separated from Jarrett's and my chamber by only a short corridor, so Nicky was virtually right next door to us.

Further racking my nerves was the fact that Jarrett had said little to me all night. Now, as we entered our bedroom, he still did not speak but, without warning, caught me roughly by the wrist and dragged me into his arms. Then, impatiently loosening the pins in my hair so it tumbled down my back, he kissed me fiercely, possessively, his strong, supple hands hurting me as he ensnarled them in my tresses, crushing me to him. I tasted blood, coppery and bittersweet upon my lower lip, before, as though suddenly becoming aware of our open door, he released me and moved to close it. As he did so, I spied Nicky down the hall, standing in his own doorway, watching us; and I knew then what had prompted Jarrett's behavior: He had known that Nicky was there; he had wanted him to see us.

"Good night, Nicholas." Jarrett spoke the words derisively, his mouth twisted in a sardonic smile of satisfaction as he shut the door firmly in his brother's face.

Then slowly, purposefully, my husband turned back to me. I trembled as he did so, for his eyes smoldered with fury, and hurt, too; and I knew his pride was stung that I had permitted Nicky to kiss me, whether I had wished him to or not. Worst of all was the doubt I sensed gnawed at Jarrett. Had I told him so little that I loved him, then? I could have wept for that.

"Now, madam, do you want to explain that touching little scene I witnessed downstairs earlier?" he asked with a sneer, his hands clenched at his sides, as though to prevent himself from throttling me.

"He took me by surprise, Jarrett," I insisted quietly, trying not to flinch in the face of his displeasure. "You must know I would hardly have allowed him to touch me otherwise. His kiss meant nothing to me, and so he discovered when I did not respond to him. He was angry at that and so sought to make you jealous, hoping to cause trouble between us. He has not changed in that respect."

"No, he has not," Jarrett agreed. Then he swore softly, "By God! If I really believed you had welcomed his advances, I would kill you! You're mine, Laura. Mine!''

At that, he enfolded me in his arms and kissed me savagely, as though to wipe away the taste of Nicky's mouth upon my own. Then he swept me up and carried me to the bed, flinging me down upon its soft mattress. His lithe, rugged body covered mine as his lips claimed my own again, hard, demanding, bruising me; but I did not care. I was his to do with as he willed, and I gloried in that, kissing him back fervently, exulting in the tide of sudden passion that engulfed me at his touch.

His tongue probed my mouth avidly. His hands tore at the hooks of my gown, jerking them free so my dress gaped open down the back. Impatiently, his fingers tugged at the lacings of my corset, breaking those that would not be unknotted as he endeavored to rid me of the garments that kept me from him. Piece by piece, carelessly, he tossed them aside, then cast away his own clothes. Naked, we lay together, warmth and moisture mingling as flesh pressed against flesh, lips and tongues twining and tasting, hands weaving their magical delight.

''Witch!'' Jarrett muttered against my throat. ''What have you done to me? I am spellbound with wanting you. As long as I live, I'll never have enough of you. Never! I'll kill any man who tries to take you from me, I swear it! No one shall ever know you like this but I. I will set my seal upon you for all time, like so . . . and like so,'' he murmured, kissing and caressing me where he willed. ''Touch me, dear heart. See how I desire you? Open yourself to me. . . . Ah, yes, Laura, love. Yes . . . yes. . . .''

His palms glided across my breasts, my stomach, my thighs. Sparks of pleasure erupted everywhere he stroked me, radiating through my body; in their wake, his tongue seared me with its heat, intensifying the swirling fires that flared within me. I was like a catherine wheel set aflame in the night, spinning, burning, spiraling down into a dark and timeless place of atavistic ache and longing. There was no one and nothing for me but Jarrett. Breathless, I touched him, tasted him, wrapped myself around him wantonly, my long, dark hair a silken snare with which to bind him to me. His breath blew hot against my nape; my back arched and tingled as he trailed fiery kisses down my spine, about one hip, along the insides of my thighs. I quivered, molten with desire, as he drank from the hot secret well of me until I moaned low in my throat and strove against him blindly, desperate in my need.

Strong and fierce, Jarrett took me then, wild as the sea in his passion. Sweet as he pierced me was the cry that issued from my lips; on the wings of the soaring wind, it flew, a lone note that echoed in the night, then faded gently into silence.

Chapter XVII

Triangles Within Triangles

They looking back, all th' eastern side beheld
Of Paradise, so late their happy seat,
Wav'd over by that flaming brand, the Gate
With dreadful faces throng'd and fiery arms.

—*Paradise Lost*
John Milton

The following morning, Uncle Draco summoned Nicholas to the study, where they remained closeted together for over two hours. Nobody ever fully learned what passed between them, but the upshot was that Nicky sold his ship, the *Fancy Free*, and stayed on at the Heights, an invidious serpent in my Eden. To set my mind at rest, however, Uncle Draco informed me that he had given Nicky strict orders to leave me alone, that there was to be no trouble between him and me, or him and Jarrett. Further, Uncle Draco said, Nicky had received an edited version of Clemency's death, and the penalty he paid for his part in her downfall was dear: Uncle Draco, however wrongly, kept from him the truth of Rhodes's parentage. Jarrett and I need not fear that Nicky would take our son away from us.

What my husband thought of this decision, I was not sure; I suspected his feelings were mixed. Because he loved the boy, he did not want to lose Rhodes, I knew. But I could not help but think he must also have considered how he would have felt if someone had kept from him the knowledge that Ransom was his son, and so I supposed he believed Nicky was done a great injustice. I, however, could only be grateful for Uncle Draco's judgment; I loved Rhodes as surely as though he were my own child, and how, at this late date, we would have explained otherwise, especially after our elaborate ruse to protect his name, I did not know. Yet even so, I must admit I, too, felt an occasional twinge of guilt for Nicky's sake, however quickly I suppressed it.

Still, I did not think he would be a very good father, for sowing his seed did not guarantee that a man would love or even be interested in the harvest reaped from it: Witness my granduncle Nigel's attitude toward his only daughter, my aunt Maggie. She had told me he had disliked her intensely and treated her abominably, preferring his stepchildren, Papa and my aunt Julianne, to his own flesh and blood. Nicky's behavior toward the twins was no less stern or more indulgent. Indeed, whenever they came down from the nursery, he eyed them disapprovingly, as though they were piskies from some other world, and generally ignored them unless they somehow specifically attracted his notice. Then he was quick to chastise them, although whether this was because he believed them both Jarrett's children, I cannot say.

I remember that once, when Rhodes was particularly annoying (for by now, the twins had reached the stage where "no" was their favorite word), Nicky pronounced him a "frightful little monster" and, after yelling at him, spanking him far too hard for his age and making him cry, insisted Nanny Annie, as we affectionately called her, take him back upstairs immediately. After that day, both Rhodes and Ransom seemed to go out of their way to avoid Nicky, and I did not feel so bad about keeping Rhodes's parentage a secret. Jarrett, when he learned of the matter, was livid, and he informed Nicky frostily that henceforth any discipline to be meted out would be done so by the boys' father; so I presumed his guilt about hiding Rhodes's parentage had also been mitigated by Nicky's conduct toward the twins.

Other than these periodic contretemps, however, life soon, to my vague surprise, settled again into its rather predictable pattern. Nicky took up his old role in the family businesses (he was involved primarily with the china-clay mines and the horse breeding); and somehow we all managed to rub along well enough that Aunt Maggie breathed a sigh of relief, hoping bygones were now bygones.

But though Jarrett and I were warily content to bury the hatchet with Nicky, Thorne was not; and his ire knew no bounds when, that following year of 1846, it was seen that with the arrival of the *Fancy Free*, Elizabeth's ship had at last come in. Though they hardly appeared the ideal match, she and Nicky took up where they'd left off when he'd fled from the Heights, as though three years had not passed since last they'd laid eyes on each other. Lizzie was as enamored of him as ever, apparently; and although I suspected Nicky did not in the least return her love, I had come to realize he was the sort of man who would not long go without a woman. Bored, seeking amusement, and frustrated at making no headway with me, since I took care never to be alone with him, he turned to Lizzie, determined to use her to gain his own ends, I had no doubt.

In all honesty, though she was possessed of a certain animal cunning, Lizzie was not really very bright, and her vanity was considerable. Further, Nicky could be highly charming when he chose, as well I knew; so I guessed she had no inkling of the fact that he was not truly besotted with her. Revelation was to prove disastrous when it came.

But once more, I get ahead of myself. I must tell you now how, after a whirlwind courtship and an all-too-short engagement (for after all these many long years, she was not disposed to let him wriggle off her hook at the last minute), Lizzie somehow, to my astonishment, actually succeeded in coaxing Nicky to the altar.

I never knew why he married her, though I suspected a number of reasons. Not the least of these, I thought, was the fact that he wanted to get back in Uncle Draco's good graces and felt that if he at least gave the appearance of settling down and starting a family as Jarrett had, his father would be more inclined to favor him. There was, too, Nicky's desire to punish Thorne and to get his hands, some way, on Highclyffe Hall if he could, even though Siobhan had just given birth to her baby, a beautiful little boy, christened Philip, whom no one, even I, could possibly doubt was Thorne's son and heir. But perhaps Nicky hoped to prove otherwise or believed the child, who was small and delicate, would not survive. I don't know. Whatever the cause, he decided to abandon his footloose ways and tie the knot, a circumstance that raised in me a dreadful presentiment, as though a goose had walked over my grave. I believed with all my heart that nothing but ill would come of the marriage. But there was no way of stopping it.

Though Uncle Esmond was none too happy with Lizzie's chosen groom, still, being of an idealistic nature, he was glad for her sake that she was not to remain a spinster, after all, and so made little attempt to dissuade her from the match. And though Aunt Julianne was positively mortified at the idea of a "Gypsy heathen," as she called Nicky, becoming her son by marriage and took to her bed with the vapors, sniffing her vinaigrette at every opportunity while loudly bemoaning the notion that she was suffering a decline and that Lizzie would be the death of her, she accomplished naught with her histrionics. Lizzie was, by now, twenty-seven years old and needed nobody's consent to marry; so, like the rest of us, there was nothing Aunt Julianne could do to halt the wedding. In the end, forced to accept the unpalatable inevitability, she rallied (to no one's surprise) with laughable speed after receiving the sharp side of Grandmother

Prescott Chandler's tongue about the duties of a bride's mother and sourly threw herself into the preparations for the event.

The marriage took place on a cool autumn day of that year, in the village church that had served the Hall for centuries. Much to Jarrett's and my relief, Alexander and Angelique stood up as the best man and matron of honor. Uncle Esmond gave Lizzie away, while Aunt Julianne wept copiously into her lace handkerchief, bewailing the fact that she was losing her only daughter.

Long afterward, I was to think how prophetic that lament was.

It was soon after Nicholas and Elizabeth's wedding that the trouble at the china-clay mines, Wheal Anant and Wheal Penforth, began, though it is only now, looking back, that I realize that was when it all started; for at first, the incidents were small, easily explainable as everyday mishaps. So much heartache, we would all have been spared, if only, at the time, we had comprehended otherwise! But it is futile now to think of that, to wish we had been wiser, more perceptive. What is done, is done; and none of us can go back and change the past, though often we may yearn to do so. In truth, that is what the old mean when they say they wish they could be young again: They long not only to have their youth back, but to know then what they know now so they will not make the same mistakes; for to be young is to be filled with passion and to run headlong toward folly, as we at the Grange, the Heights, and the Hall did in our impulsive youth, and even after, as you shall hear.

But first, I must tell you about the china-clay mines, those hideous, sprawling blots upon the moors, where the soft white, chalky clay used to manufacture fine, delicate china and porcelain was wrested from the earth. The proper word for the mineral is "kaolin," which comes from the Chinese "kauling," meaning high hill, which is where, in China, the clay is usually found. Thus we English have always called it "china clay." It has been mined and used since the eighteenth century, most notably by Josiah Wedgwood, one of the Chandlers' better-known customers.

The mines came into the family when they were purchased by my great-grandfather Sir Simon Chandler, for he was an astute man, farseeing enough to realize that progress would come, no matter how much the aristocracy fought against it, and that, in some distant future, the landed gentry would be no more. He had bought the mines as insurance against that day, when the rights of the common man should prevail over those of the privileged class, and the baronetcy of Highclyffe Hall would need more than just a title to sustain it.

Upon Sir Simon's death, his eldest son, my granduncle Nigel, inherited the mines; and upon his death, they by rights should have gone to Granduncle Nigel's nephew and heir, my uncle Esmond. But the affairs of the Chandlers were in a very peculiar state at that time. Uncle Draco, who, under other circumstances, would have been Granduncle Nigel's heir, could not inherit because he was illegitimate. Still, for his own reasons and in spite of the fact that he had hated Uncle Draco vehemently, Granduncle Nigel had willed him the mines, thus removing them from the assets of the baronetcy and thereby subverting Sir Simon's original purpose in buying them.

The mines were responsible for a good deal of Uncle Draco's wealth, and the loss of their income was one of the reasons Uncle Esmond had such a hard time making ends meet at the Hall; though I daresay he could not have operated the mines properly anyway. The rough men who toiled at them needed a stern taskmaster in charge, lest there be constant upheaval: laborers demanding better wages, shorter hours, and such, which, if granted, would eat into the revenues, making it no longer profitable to run the mines at all. Somehow men with families to feed could not seem to understand that. Rudely educated, if at all, they supposed (and often rightly so) their selfish masters to be garnering a fortune from the sweat and blood of honest, hardworking yet impoverished men, who received naught but a pittance in return. In fact, for decades now, the common man had been in revolt against his lot.

Quite simply, the working class and the poor were, more often than not, ill-clothed, cold, and hungry; and when people were so downtrodden that they could barely scrape out an existence, they began to band together and rise up to commit rash acts against those who oppressed them. In 1795, food riots had swept across England. For several years afterward, the situation had been exacerbated by a series of bad harvests, and then the Corn Laws, which prohibited the importation of cheap foreign grain, thus assuring the landed gentry of a profit from their own fields and causing the price of bread to escalate to exorbitant rates.

With progress had come machines as well, which could be run by women and children, who worked for lower wages, displacing men who could then find no other jobs to support their families; and of course, increasingly, especially after the terrible potato famine, England had been swamped by masses of Irish refugees, who would take any wage rather than starve.

Jobless, and soon homeless as well, destitute men in greater numbers than ever now flooded the workhouses in the cities and wandered the roads of the countryside. In years gone by, some had taken to the high toby, robbing the rich at gunpoint, while others had become smugglers, leading the dragoons a perilous chase. Others, their ears filled with the talk of liberty and equality brought home by England's redcoats who had fought the French during the time of Napoleon Bonaparte, had fomented rebellion, inciting the common man everywhere to stand up and demand his rights, violently if necessary.

In the end, these insurgents proved the most dangerous, of course. At their urging, for decades now, mines had been blown up, the windows and machinery of factories smashed, textile mills torched. Frequently, the ringleaders and followers alike of these seditious groups were caught and tried for their crimes. But although countless men had been hanged or transported, the blows against tyranny continued to be struck, in the form of unions, strikes, destruction, and bloodshed.

In June that year of 1846, things got so bad that Parliament was finally forced to repeal the Corn Laws, reducing and soon virtually eliminating the duties on imported grain. Also decreased were the duties on imported cheeses, butter, and other foodstuffs, while the duties on imported live animals were abolished. As a result, the large landholders in Ireland, most of them absentee landlords, quit growing wheat and turned to raising cattle, throwing tenants off the land so it could be used for pasturage. Soon these wretched, dispossessed Irish flocked, too, to England's teeming, troubled shores.

But despite all this, I could not think those who labored at the Chandler china-clay mines had much cause for complaint. They were better housed, better clothed, better fed, and better compensated than most. Uncle Draco knew what it meant to be poor and cold and hungry. Consequently, a fair day's wages for a fair day's work was paid to all employed by him; and if there were those who insisted on still more, who could not grasp the principles of economics, the laws of supply and demand, and so were shown the door, well, such were the hard times in which we lived.

No one could say that mining china clay was safe or easy; it was a moiling, grueling job. Kaolin is fashioned when feldspar, especially in rocks such as granite, with which Cornwall is abundant, decays. It must be dug from the ground, washed into pools at the bottom of huge, deep pits, and then separated from the quartz waste. After that, it must be brought to the surface, washed again, filtered, and dried. Because, in Cornwall, the china-clay deposits are funnel-shaped, with the narrow end submerged far beneath the earth's surface, the pits cannot be backfilled as they are excavated. So, in places upon the heaths, like eerie white mountains, piles of pale quartz residue stretch and rise, while among them lie the vast pits themselves and standing pools tinted a peculiar, muted shade of green, from minerals, I suppose, though I cannot say for sure.

Accidents happen. Because the once-hard granite has turned to a soft, crumbly mass, it slips and slides like sand through an hourglass. A man can be buried alive in a sudden avalanche of that heaped quartz waste, a cave-in of that treacherous chalky clay, running back into the ground like a sinkhole or desert quicksand; a man can drown in those strange, silent green pools; and machinery poses its own hazards. Since Uncle Draco's time, the safety records of Wheal Anant and Wheal Penforth had been good. But now, as I have said, oddly, little things began to go wrong, nothing serious at first, but occasional, though not wholly unexpected, difficulties that were a nuisance and that caused expensive delays.

Yet I confess I listened with only half an ear to Uncle Draco, Jarrett, Nicholas, and Alexander at the supper table, as they discussed the problems at the mines. With the coming of the new year, I discovered, to my delight, that, at long last, I was again with child; so I was wrapped up in the changes taking place in my body, the preparations for my baby's birth, and with the twins, who, upon learning they would presently no longer have me solely to themselves, badgered me with constant questions. I had, too, my own irritants to deal with. Upon marrying Nicky, Lizzie had, of course, come to the Heights to live, and she was a continual thorn in my side. I think that even then, all was not well between her and Nicky. God punishes us by granting our wishes, I have heard it said; and certainly, attaining her heart's desire had not proved a joy to Lizzie. She was unhappy, sick and bloated as an overinflated balloon with her own pregnancy. As Lizzie's size increased, her tongue grew more and more waspish as well, for she loathed her heavy, awkward body and resented the baby that had robbed her of her health and looks. Nor, at the Heights, was she pampered and petted, as she had been at the Hall; and this, too, gnawed at her ferociously.

At night, in our bedroom, Jarrett and I often overheard her and Nicky quarreling, and sometimes, the following morning, Lizzie would come down to the breakfast table, an ugly bruise marring her cheek beneath the powder she applied so carefully. Though she always managed to have some other plausible explanation ready if anyone remarked on her appearance, we felt sure Nicky had hit her. Dark mauve circles ringed her eyes, doubtless from the many nights she must have spent lying awake, waiting for Nicky to come home and tormenting herself about his whereabouts. Often, he left the Heights shortly after supper and did not return until the wee hours of the morning.

"Trouble at the mines," he would say, excusing himself, eager to be gone. "I've got to go back. Don't wait up for me, Lizzie, darling."

But later, Jarrett and I would hear him cursing and stumbling down the corridor to his chamber and know he had been carousing instead of taking care of business. That Nicky was unfaithful to Lizzie, I did not doubt; and once or twice, I spied him riding upon the moors with Siobhan, something that caused me considerable uneasiness. How like poor, dead Clemency, she was, with her fox-red hair, her pointed face, and her emerald-green eyes! Why had I never noticed the resemblance before?

Now that I was no longer an ignorant, green girl, I understood the sort of appetites Jarrett had once accused Siobhan of having—base, lusty, insatiable appetites that I did not suppose perverse Thorne sated, having done his duty and got an heir on her. Jarrett had been right, I mused, in surmising that Siobhan had had her reasons for wedding Thorne, that it had not been only lack of money that had prompted her to accept his proposal, but the fact that too many other men had known or suspected she was no blushing, inexperienced virgin and so had not offered her marriage. Being a woman of the world, then, she had surely by now guessed or learned for certain the truth of her husband's sexual proclivity. Was it any wonder, then, that she should find virile, handsome Nicky attractive? Or that he, saddled with puffy, pregnant Lizzie, who grew more peevish every day, should be drawn to willowy, wanton Siobhan? It boded ill, I thought; no good would come of it, these triangles within triangles among us, this tangled web we had woven of our lives.

I felt as though we were sitting on a powder keg, that, sooner or later, someone would light the fuse and a horrible explosion would occur.

As the months passed, the incidents at the mines continued, worsening steadily; and now explanations for the mishaps were not so easily found. Eventually, someone—we did not know who—started a rumor that the mines were haunted; after that, in the miners' rows and in the village, talk of phantoms and piskies abounded, made worse when one of the workers toppled down a quartz pile and broke his leg. Afterward, he swore an apparition had pushed him, though it was more likely he had been careless or drinking on the job. Another laborer tumbled into a pool, narrowly escaping drowning. He, too, claimed to have been shoved by unseen hands, though it had rained earlier that day, so the ground was slick. This was only the beginning, however. Soon equipment started to disappear as well. Never located, it was as though it had vanished into thin air, adding fuel to the fire of ghost stories.

While not so foolish as to believe the tales of evil spirits and malicious sprites, Uncle Draco suspected sabotage by disgruntled unionists, and he posted armed guards at the mines; each man had orders to shoot first and ask questions later should any interlopers be sighted. After that, the accidents and loss of costly machinery ceased; so it seemed it was live culprits we must fear after all.

Life went on, though not more smoothly. Late that summer, Lizzie's child was born, a son, christened Winston. Her hips were narrow, her delivery was difficult. She almost died. After that, to Lizzie's secret relief, Dr. Ashford cautioned against her ever having another baby; and it was then that she made a monumental mistake in her marriage: She turned Nicky out of her bed.

The resulting argument was heated and bitter; not for the first time did I wish their chamber were not so close to Jarrett's and mine.

"You frigid bitch!" I overheard, from down the hall, Nicky curse her a few nights later. "What makes you think you can deny me my marital rights?"

"'Tis not my fault," Lizzie insisted sulkily. "You heard what the doctor said, Nicky: It is likely another child would kill me."

"There are ways of preventing pregnancies, Lizzie— French letters, for one. But I don't suppose you have thought of that! No, I can see you have not, for indeed, what do genteel ladies like you know of such things?" he sneered.

"Nothing!" Lizzie spat. "Though no doubt you have learned plenty from the whores you frequent, Nicky! Do you think I don't know that you are unfaithful to me?"

"Well, and what if I am?" he shot back cruelly. "Did you believe you had only to surrender your maidenhead and I would be satisfied, my dear? Jesus! An iceberg has more passion than you! Rather than scorn them, you ought to take a few lessons in whores' tricks yourself; at least a whore is clever enough to pretend some interest in the man who pays her."

"How dare you speak to me in such a fashion?" Lizzie shrilled. "'Tis filthy, disgusting, and insulting! I'm your wife, Nicholas, not some cheap trollop who sells herself on a street corner!"

"What's the difference? I've bought and paid for you, too, haven't I, my pet? Admit it: You wouldn't have looked twice at me if I hadn't had two pennies to rub together! No, you sold yourself to me in exchange for all those servants now at your beck and call, all those fancy clothes I've put on your back, and all those chocolates you love so well and that I provide," he jeered. "So, wife or not, in truth, you *aren't* any better than a whore, madam. Worse, for now you say you won't keep your end of the bargain!

"My God! I must have been mad to wed you! But, then, you were not so cold before you got my ring on your finger, were you, Lizzie? No, you were eager enough to spread your legs for me then! Well, I could force you to open them now, if I wanted, and no one would raise a hand to stop me. But I won't. The world is full of beds, and those beds are full of willing women. So, keep your thighs closed tight, you prim prude! See if I care. I'll take my pleasure elsewhere, and be damned to you, Lizzie!"

At that, their bedroom door slammed shut with a bone-jarring crack, so I thought the frame must have splintered from the impact. Shortly thereafter, from the courtyard came the sound of hoofbeats as Nicky galloped off into the night, while next door, Lizzie wept into her pillow, wrenching sobs that aroused my sympathy for her, despite the fact that she hated me and would have disdained any comfort I might have tried to offer.

But it was little Winston for whom I felt sorriest. As the weeks passed, Nicky, annoyed by his son's constant, loud crying, scarcely paid him any heed; while Lizzie, appalled by his spitting up and wetting all over her gowns, was only too glad to turn the poor mite over to Nanny Annie and a wet nurse, and wash her hands of him. Alexander's wife, Vanessa, was too shy to interfere in the nursery, except when matters involved her own daughter, Blythe, born the year before. So, in the end, it fell to me to instruct Nanny Annie and Nurse when there were decisions to be made about Winston's welfare;

and thus it was that he, too, like his half brother, Rhodes, became in his own way my son.

It was early that autumn that my own child was born, a daughter, whom Jarrett and I named Isabelle, in honor of one of Granny Sheffield's long-dead sisters, as I was called after one of her long-dead brothers, my granduncle Laurence. Isabelle proved a delightful baby, gay and gurgling, with never a hint of the temper Ransom and Rhodes had displayed, though I suspected she would soon grow as spoiled and willful as they; for Jarrett was quite the doting father where his darling daughter was concerned.

"She looks just like her beautiful mother," he said proudly, making me blush.

After five years of marriage, his desire for me had not waned; nor had he ever sought another's bed, but was as fiercely faithful to me as Uncle Draco was to Aunt Maggie.

What friends, we were, she and I—and quiet, gentle Vanessa, too. It was only Lizzie who held herself aloof, alone in her misery, detesting me utterly and having been poisoned by her mother against Aunt Maggie. Aunt Julianne had slyly stolen Uncle Esmond away from Aunt Maggie when they were young; and now, like her daughter, having got what she wanted, Aunt Julianne was dejected by her lot in life and blamed everyone but herself for her misfortune.

She abhorred Uncle Draco and resented his riches, which she felt ought to have been Uncle Esmond's; and she frequently accused Uncle Draco and Aunt Maggie of somehow altering Granduncle Nigel's will so they could get their hands on the Chandler china-clay mines. No one except Thorne paid any heed to this patently false allegation, however. Even Lizzie firmly rejected it as being untrue; for most of Nicky's income was derived from the mines, and of course, she did not want to lose that. In his heart, Thorne did not really believe it either, I felt sure.

But I was wrong.

Chapter XVIII

Faithless Hearts and Fury

Heav'n has no rage, like love to hatred turn'd,
Nor Hell a fury, like a woman scorn'd.

—*The Mourning Bride*
William Congreve

Quiet are the tears of age. Soft as rain, they slip down my cheeks as I remember the days of which I shall speak by and by, sad days, dear reader, though I would have had them otherwise. But there is no joy without sorrow, as I have come to learn and accept, for life is a rose, in truth, its stem bearing many thorns. Many times have they pricked me and left their wounds, healed now, though the scars remain, as Aunt Maggie once told me they would. In my youth, I would have dashed my tears away, ashamed. But now I know it is no weakness to weep, and there was much to cry for in those bittersweet days that are no more.

How did it happen that we came to be as we were? What forces and events shaped and molded us into what we became? I do not know. Perhaps, in the end, it was as I have often thought, that we ourselves chose to be what we were and so determined the course of our lives.

If Nicholas had not been so wild and reckless, if Elizabeth had loved him more—or not at all—if Thorne had been as other men, if Siobhan had not given herself so freely, all that happened would never have happened.

How strange to think that from childhood, when those four first realized they had minds of their own and began to use them, their lives had been leading up to this moment. How strange to think, as well, that as a tiny pebble tossed into a pond causes ripples that reach to the water's farthest limits, so do the lives of others touch and change our own, and ours, theirs, whether any of us wishes it or not.

On a late-November morning, grey with drizzle, Thorne came unexpectedly to the Heights to talk to his sister, Lizzie. I was surprised to see him, for he rarely visited the manor, deeming it prudent to avoid as much as possible the Chandlers, who disliked him intensely. Further, he and Lizzie had hardly been on speaking terms since her marriage to Nicky. Thus I, sitting before the fire in the great hall, could not help but shiver when Mawgen admitted Thorne. I felt certain in my bones that he brought bad tidings; and as I remembered the sight of Nicky and Siobhan riding together upon the moors, some dim inkling of what my Sheffield cousin intended to reveal to his sister pervaded my mind. Yet I had only my speculations; I did not know for sure what he meant to tell her, and in the end, the news was even more shocking than I had supposed.

Upon being summoned, Lizzie came downstairs; and since she and Thorne went into the library, where they could be private, I never learned all that passed between them, though now I can piece together much of what must have been said. But my worst fears were confirmed when, less than an hour later, Thorne reappeared, on his face such a supercilious smirk of satisfaction that I knew he felt he had at last evened the score with Lizzie for wedding Nicky.

After her brother had left, Lizzie walked slowly out of the library, dumb and disoriented, like a person who has received a stunning blow. There was such a pallor to her skin that I was afraid she would faint, and I hastened to her side, begging her to sit down and tell me what was wrong. But she did not seem to hear me and, when I persisted, shook off the hand I laid upon her arm, hissing and scratching at me like an angry cat. I was so appalled that I drew back, my cheek streaked with red where her fingernails had raked me. She did not apologize, but swept past me, going upstairs to her bedroom.

Do we ever really know people? I wonder and think perhaps not, for I never would have believed Lizzie capable of what she did after that. To this day, I wonder what thoughts were chasing through her mind as, like a puppet, woodenly, she stripped off her gown and donned her riding habit and cloak. What cold fury was in her heart as deliberately she took from Nicky's desk drawer his small silver pistol and, after checking to be certain it was loaded, as she must have done, dropped it into her pocket? I will never know. But I shall never forget her face, white and grim and determined, when she came downstairs and called for her horse to be brought around to the courtyard.

Afterward, Dr. Ashford said she was suffering from the unexplained depression that often strikes a woman after she has given birth; it had been only four months, after all, since Winston was born. Perhaps the physician was right; but in my heart, I shall always think that Lizzie was in the grip of some sudden madness, that she had stood all she could and so just snapped.

Mounted upon her flaxen-gold mare, she galloped wildly out of the courtyard. Such was my feeling of dread, then, that I, too, hurried to change—faster than I had ever done in my life. Then, calling for my own horse, I set out after her, though she had, by now, almost a twenty-minute head start. But Black Buccaneer was swift as the wind, and he did not fail me now. Across the moors, we flew until finally I spied Lizzie in the distance and knew she was headed toward the china-clay mines. Lashing Black Buccaneer forward with the trailing ends of my reins, I bent my head low over his neck, feeling the wind, damp with spindrift and drizzle, tear ruthlessly at my hair. But I did not care. I was driven by foreboding to reach Lizzie, as though if I did not, something terrible would occur. Heedlessly, I raced over the heaths, but Lizzie was as reckless as I, riding as I had never seen her ride before, seeming not to care how her mount slipped and stumbled upon the wet earth.

Now the mines were in sight, the tall white peaks of

the quartz residue looming like massive ghosts over the commons in the rain. Like a specter, Lizzie disappeared into their midst, and I knew, with a sinking heart, that I was not going to catch her in time, that I would be too late to prevent whatever she intended. But still, I rushed on, following the trail of her mare's hoofprints, which wove between the piles of quartz waste, heaped high. Sodden clumps of the chalky dust churned beneath Black Buccaneer's hooves, filming his coat and my mantle. I gagged and coughed, as though inhaling a cloud of flour, but pressed the gelding on, though not so quickly now as we sank into the soft, crumbly quartz residue, and the ground shifted and slid treacherously beneath us.

Then at last the edge of one of the vast, sprawling pits lay before us. Now, for the first time, Black Buccaneer balked, whinnying and prancing nervously as he eyed the rim that fell away beneath us. But still, with all my strength, I compelled him down the steep, sloping wall of the pit, gasping as the loose, soaked clay gave way under his hooves, trembling lest we topple to the earth far below.

Lizzie cantered rashly across the pit's floor, toward the deep, muted green pool at its center, where Nicky stood, giving orders to some of the men who worked the mines. Long hoses twined like sinuous serpents across the ground; from one, held by several of the laborers, water gushed in a powerful stream, spraying the china clay so it swirled into the pool. As Lizzie drew near, Nicky glanced up, stunned by the sight of her. He shouted a warning; but still, Lizzie refused to slacken speed, shrieking at him, the wind ripping the words from her mouth and whisking them away, so I could not hear them above the roar of the pumping water.

Finally, however, she jerked her mare to a halt. Then, to my horror, she withdrew from her cape pocket the gun I had not known until this moment she carried. As I watched, my heart in my throat, she aimed it at Nicky and pulled the trigger. The pistol exploded with a deafening bang. The shot went wild, the bullet whining across the pit to bury itself in the china clay and startling her mount into dancing crazily, nearly unseating her. Terrified as they realized what was happening, the men wielding the hose dropped it and ran, scattering in all directions as they scrambled for their lives up the walls of the pit.

Nicky was not among those who fled, however. Swearing and bellowing with rage, he started purposefully toward Lizzie instead. Threateningly, she raised the gun once more, pointing it straight at his heart; but still, he strode toward her, undeterred. I do not think that, even then, he grasped the fact that she truly meant to kill him. Her hand must have wavered when she fired, however, for as the hideous report sounded, I saw Nicky, staring at her with disbelief, grimace and clutch his arm, blood spurting between his fingers. Horribly, Lizzie pressed the trigger yet again; but to my utter relief, the pistol had only two chambers, and both were now spent.

Recognizing that the gun was useless to her now, she hurtled it at Nicky, narrowly missing his head. Then savagely she yanked her mare around and galloped off. Setting my jaw, I whipped Black Buccaneer forward.

"Are you all right?" I yelled at Nicky.

"Yes, 'tis only a flesh wound, thank God!" he replied. "Ride after her, Laura! Hurry! I think she's lost her mind, and there's no telling what she may do next. I'll follow just as soon as I can."

Even as he spoke, he was hauling his shirttail from his pants, tearing from it a strip of cambric to bind his arm, his dark Gypsy face ominous as he called for his horse.

Hard after Lizzie, I rode, to no avail. She was like a woman demented as she slashed her mount brutally with her riding crop, so that, even from a distance, I could see the gashes she left upon the poor mare's flaxen-gold hindquarters, welling crimson before the blood was washed away by the rain.

"Lizzie!" I shouted desperately. "Lizzie, wait!"

But she ignored my cries, urging her mount to an even more dangerous pace, her grey pelisse billowing about her like a shroud. It had begun to rain harder now. The downpour plastered my hair to my head, dripped into my eyes, and chilled me so, that, for a moment, cursing Lizzie, I was sorely tempted to return to the Heights. But I did not, forcing myself to go on instead. The moors were like a black muddy marsh as we left the mines behind, striking out toward the Hall, which, in Lizzie's heart, was still home and must have represented sanctuary to her then.

She never made it. A hedgerow loomed before us, and she did not slow down, but continued toward it at a dead run. Stricken, I watched as, at the last minute, her mount refused the jump, crashing into the thorny bramble and sending Lizzie sailing from the saddle, over the hedge-row.

Frantic then, my heart thumping so hard that I thought it would burst, I sped toward the disastrous scene, hoping, praying soundlessly in my mind that Lizzie was alive. The mare thrashed amid a tangle of smashed bramble, squealing unbearably, one leg curled at a peculiar angle. The limb was broken, and the horse would have to be destroyed. Lizzie lay sprawled on the soggy ground, her body unnaturally still, a smear of mud upon one cheek, blood trickling from the corner of her mouth.

I knew, even before I reached her side, that she was dead.

Chapter XIX

The Dark Before Dawn

Ah, love, let us be true
To one another! for the world, which
seems
To lie before us like a land of dreams,
So various, so beautiful, so new,
Hath really neither joy, nor love, nor light,
Nor certitude, nor peace, nor help for
pain;
And we are here as on a darkling plain
. . .

—*Dover Beach*
Matthew Arnold

The morning of Elizabeth's funeral was cold and grey, made bleak and bitter by a biting wind that had brought with it a lowering sky and flurrying snow. A thick blanket of mist drifted in from the rough sea to cover the moors, where the heather and bracken had turned black and sodden as the marshes with the dismal weather; even the graves in the cemetery a short distance from the village church looked straggly and overgrown.

We buried Lizzie where countless generations from the Hall lay at rest, some in what had once been the Chandler family vault but that now belonged to the Sheffields, I supposed; others in the ground, with granite tombstones at their head. Lizzie had been just twenty-eight years old—like Clemency, too young to die. But still, she was dead, her neck broken, her body shut up in a box now for all time.

Nicholas had been wrong about his wife, I thought as I stood there in the swirling snow, listening to the funeral service: She had not been without passion; in the end, it had run as hot and high as that of any of us cursed with the Chandler wild streak—and proved just as fatal.

"Unto Almighty God we commend the soul of our sister departed, and we commit her body to the ground; earth to earth, ashes to ashes, dust to dust . . ." the vicar, Mr. Earnhart, intoned.

I watched as Nicky laid a large bouquet of lilac chrysanthemums upon the coffin; the blooms and leaves shivered in the wind as the pallbearers lifted the casket to carry it down into the vault. Nicky's dark face was set and shadowed; his eyes were hooded, so I could not tell what he was thinking, whether he blamed himself at all for Lizzie's death. But Thorne, who must surely have known it was his callous revelations that had sent her galloping toward the mines, pistol in hand, had tears in his eyes; so I knew that, in his own way, despite their

differences, he had loved his sister and must be eaten up
with guilt over the part he had played in her demise.

Uncle Esmond appeared to have aged twenty years
overnight; I had never seen him look so old and ill, and
I knew by the expression on Aunt Maggie's face that her
heart ached for him. He was silent in his sorrow, as was
Grandmother Prescott Chandler, her beautiful but grieving face hidden by a black veil. In sharp contrast to them
was Aunt Julianne, who moaned and wailed hysterically
until finally, near the point of collapse, she had to be led
away, taken home, and sedated. Thus, of all those from
the Hall, only Siobhan stood dry-eyed, unrepentant, her
chin held high, her mourning gown cleverly cut to conceal her burgeoning body.

I did not know how she had dared to show her face at
Lizzie's funeral; for now, in my heart, somehow I knew
with certainty what Thorne had told his sister that awful
day in the library at the Heights: Siobhan was pregnant
with Nicky's child.

The holidays that winter were restrained; nor did the new
year of 1848 promise to be any better, bringing with it
a resurgence of the trouble at the mines, though now,
however, there was no attempt to conceal the deliberate,
malicious vandalism and theft. Someone was wickedly
stealing Chandler property and wantonly destroying what
could not be easily carried away. Because, during the
most recent attack, the pumps had been permanently put
out of commission, both mines were forced to close until
replacement machinery could be shipped to northern
Cornwall.

Yet even so, and despite the armed sentries Uncle Draco once more posted to patrol the mines, someone managed to set fire to the stone building that housed the offices and records. Because there were no pumps to obtain water to douse the blaze, buckets had to be carried from the pools in the huge, deep pits, and the edifice, which had stood for a hundred years and served as the Chandler China Clay, Ltd., headquarters since my great-grandfather Sir Simon's time, burned to the ground. Fortunately for the business, Uncle Draco kept a duplicate set of books at the Heights, but everything else the offices contained was lost. Still, as Aunt Maggie often said, the Chandlers were survivors. In no time at all, it seemed, a tiny wooden structure was erected as a temporary head-quarters, while work on new stone offices that were to be an exact copy of the old began.

Early wildflowers sprouted on the graves in the cemetery; the world and life moved on. My brother Guy and his wife, Damaris, had their first baby, a son, christened Fletcher; in London, Angelique and her husband, Lord Greystone, were blessed with an heir, too, named Lucius and titled Viscount Stratton. My brother Francis was promoted to captain of his own vessel, the *Misty Maiden*, one of the P & C Shipping Line's fleet clipper ships; and young Bryony, the last of Aunt Maggie's daughters, announced her engagement to the Honorable Richard Tamarlane. The twins would be five this year and were growing like weeds, promising to be handsome young men someday; Jarrett had bought each a pony, and Will, the head groom, was teaching them to ride. Blythe, Alexander and Vanessa's daughter, was a pretty two-year-old, sweet and shy, like her mother; Winston and Isabelle were sitting up and learning to crawl, and according to Nanny Annie, what one didn't think of, the other did!

Siobhan grew heavy with Nicky's child. Surely, he must have realized it was his baby she carried. But of course, neither he nor she said aught of the matter; nor, to my surprise, did Thorne. Banding together for once to protect their own interests, he and Nicky had firmly clamped a lid on most of the unsavory gossip that arose as a result of Elizabeth's mad behavior the day of her death. Though many guessed that Nicky had been unfaithful to Lizzie and that Thorne had brought her proof of her husband's infidelity, thereby setting off her rampage, Siobhan's name was never dragged into the affair. I don't think anyone but I ever suspected that her daughter, called Katherine, who was born later that year, was not Thorne's child.

With the coming of spring, the new pumps for the mines finally arrived, and after the installation of the machinery, work at the pits started up again—as did the attacks, although the guards Uncle Draco kept on duty helped to mitigate most of the damage and robbery. Still, the culprits responsible went unapprehended; and at last, one night at the supper table, Jarrett and Nicholas suggested that perhaps no one was ever seen or caught because it was not a group of violent unionists bent on destroying the mines, after all, but a single man with a grudge against either the china-clay company or the Chandlers themselves.

"Maybe you're right." Uncle Draco nodded thoughtfully. "What, then, do you propose we do?"

"Get rid of the sentries for a while, Father," Nicky urged, "and let me start patrolling the mines alone. That way, whoever is doing this won't know I'm there and so perhaps will come out into the open to do his dirty work."

"All right," Uncle Draco agreed slowly. "We'll try it your way for a few weeks, Nicky."

So the guards were removed, to no avail. Night after night, Nicky kept watch, sometimes riding or wandering furtively about the pits, at others, hiding in the small wooden building that was temporarily serving as the offices. But whoever was responsible for the attacks must have suspected a trick and so did not venture near the mines.

It was early summer when Angelique wrote to say she and Lord Greystone would be descending upon us within a fortnight, bringing their two children. Aunt Maggie grew quite excited and, as, with the exception of Nicholas, we were no longer in formal mourning for Elizabeth, planned a small party to welcome Angelique home. Vanessa and I helped with the invitations and preparations, and when the evening of the soirée at last arrived, everything was ready.

The grey towers of the ancient manor gleamed like quicksilver as the dazzling light from the hundreds of candles in the chandeliers of the great hall streamed through the sparkling casement windows, whose lozenge, lead-glass panes had been polished until not a single smudge remained. The night rang with gay laughter and the ripples of melodious music that wafted through the open windows. The stringed instruments of the quartet Aunt Maggie had hired for the occasion harmonized prettily with the plaintive calls of the sea gulls and the sweet cries of the curlews in the distance. The gentle clink of the punch-bowl ladle as it filled and refilled crystal glasses was accompanied by the low sounds of the servants' voices as, laden with silver trays, they moved among the guests in the great hall, making certain no one wanted for anything.

A long buffet table set up at one end of the room groaned under the weight of its heavy burden: plates piled high with slices of roast beef, venison, pheasant, and partridge; parboiled potatoes flecked with parsley, French green beans with slivered almonds, buttered carrots, and squash cooked with onions; hot rolls and thick slices of crusty bread. Everything was kept warm by squat candles lit beneath elegant silver chafing dishes. There were fruits and cheeses, and cakes and candies, too: grapes and strawberries dusted with sugar, sharp cheddar and Brie that melted on the tongue, rich German chocolate cakes and scrumptious petit fours, meringues and rum balls.

"Well, what would you like, Laura?" Jarrett asked as we perused the table.

"Everything, of course!" I exclaimed, smiling.

"As always, your wish is my command, dear heart."

Accordingly, he heaped my plate with a little of this and a little of that, then filled his own. Seeing no chairs, we sat down upon the stairs leading up to the south wing, talking softly and laughing as though we were young lovers and not about, this year, to celebrate our sixth anniversary.

After we finished dining, we downed our champagne, then danced together. For some reason, it reminded me of the first time I had ever felt Jarrett's hands upon me, the night of my coming-out party, when we had waltzed in the ballroom of the Grange. I had worn a white gown, not unlike the ruffled pink silk frock I had on tonight. Had seven years really passed since then? I wondered. It hardly seemed possible. Perhaps my husband recalled the first time he had held me, too, for his arm tightened around my waist, and his eyes glittered as he smiled down at me.

"You're even more beautiful than you were that night at the Grange, Laura," he whispered huskily, so I knew I was right in thinking he was remembering also, "and just as enchanting when you blush, my sweet."

He kissed me lightly upon the lips; then the music stopped, and the spell was broken. As he led me to a vacant chair, Jarrett's eyes swept the great hall intently, as though he were looking for someone; a puzzled frown knitted his brow.

"Do you see Nicky, Laura?" he queried.

"Why, no," I answered. "But 'tis only eight months since Lizzie's death, Jarrett," I reminded him, "and he's still in half mourning. Perhaps he just wasn't up to a party."

"No, I don't think so. Thorne's gone as well," he observed quietly.

"Thorne? What's he got to do with Nicky's leaving the party?"

"I'll explain it later," he said abruptly. "Right now, I've got to get to the mines."

"The mines?" I cried softly, bewildered and concerned, a prickle of portent suddenly crawling up my spine.

"Yes, make my excuses to Mother and Angel, would you?" he called over his shoulder.

And then he was gone, swallowed up by the throng as he made his way unobtrusively toward the south tower and the trapdoor that opened onto the long tunnel leading to the stables. For a long, hard minute, I stared after him anxiously, biting my lip. Wasn't that just like a man—to tell you just enough to worry you and no more? Well, I wouldn't stand for it, that's all. My jaw set determinedly, I rose and followed my husband to the south tower. There, I raised the trapdoor and descended the steps to the passage below, my palm cupped to shield the flickering flame of the candle I had taken from Uncle Draco's study and now carried as I hurried toward the stables.

A cool breeze assailed me as I exited the corridor, climbing the stairs at its end up to the stables. Setting down my candle and crooning to reassure the horses, who snorted and nickered at my appearance, I took a bridle from the tack room and approached my handsome Welsh pony, Jocko. Normally, he pulled the trap, of course. But as he was small and broad-backed, he would be easier to mount and ride astride, without a saddle, than Black Buccaneer; and I did not want to disturb the grooms, for I did not know how I should explain why I wished to leave the Heights in the dead of night, alone, with a rout going on and I dressed in a fancy party gown.

Quietly, I entered the pony's stall and coaxed a bit between his teeth. Then, after glancing out the stable door to be certain I was unobserved, I led him outside. Once I was away from the yard, I flung myself onto his back, hitching my skirts up about my knees, and set off at a rapid trot toward the desolate gatehouse. After I had passed beneath its small, empty loft overhead, I kicked Jocko into a gallop, riding like the wind across the moors.

Though I reckoned it was by now close on midnight, the night was not dark. A full moon had risen earlier, and it lighted my path, as did the stars twinkling in the clear, inky sky. It had not rained for many a week now, and the heaths were baked hard, as they were always in the hot summers of northern Cornwall, when the sun parched the grass to the pale gold color of champagne and sucked every last drop of moisture from the earth. Jocko's hooves rang sharply against the dry ground; he was sturdy and surefooted, and did not slow or stumble as I urged him on. He reminded me of my childhood pony, Calico Jack, long since put to pasture now.

The wind whispered across the commons; it seemed as though the heather and bracken breathed as they stirred and rippled, bowing gently with each sough of the breeze. I could almost imagine they were alive, as a person is alive, watching me with a thousand eyes as I passed by. Some people might have found the idea unnerving, but I loved the moors, as Aunt Maggie loved them; and so, though I was alone, I was not afraid, only apprehensive about what Jarrett would do when he discovered I had followed him. He would be furious, I thought, blanching at the notion, for his temper was as wicked as ever, though seldom directed at me. Now, at the realization that it almost certainly soon would be, I nearly turned back to the Heights. But then I thought of Nicky and Thorne, whom, for some reason, Jarrett had obviously expected to encounter at the mines, and I pressed on soberly.

Why the two men should have left the soirée to go to the china-clay pits, I did not know. But it augured ill; of that, I was sure. Nicky and Thorne each had spent far too many years at the other's throat for any amicable meeting to be taking place tonight. Jarrett suspected something. I did not yet know what; but if my husband were riding into danger, I intended to be at his side. I loved him with all my heart; only death would keep me away.

At last, the mines came into view, the mountains of quartz residue pale and eerie in the moonlight, like spectral titans crouched upon the heaths, misshapen giants, white and silent as the grave. I shivered as I approached, frightened now, for such was the thick, floury consistency of the quartz waste that it was like masses of cotton muffling all sound, soaking it up so the commons were hushed, breathless, it seemed. Between the peaks, the wind sighed and wended, catching up the chalky dust and blowing it softly, like swirling clouds or mist—or spirits—into the darkness. I had rarely ever in my life seen the mines at night—and never from this proximity. Now it was easy to understand how the ghost stories about them had started. They might have been haunted, quiet and mysterious as they were, uncanny, with only that coarse white powder billowing across the moors and, every so often, the rippling sound of water when some insect or other creature disturbed the stagnant pools.

It was all I could do to force myself to nudge Jocko forward. As I entered the shadowed chain of mounds, they seemed to loom over me menacingly, as though, with each step of the pony, they sidled stealthily closer, intent on smothering me with their soft, alabaster dust and stillness. I felt as though I were suffocating, as I had felt that day in the attic when Thorne had locked me in the trunk. But that was long ago. Why should I think of it now? I did not know. Yet I could not thrust the similarity from my mind. I eyed each pinnacle nervously, as though some unseen thing lurked there to swoop down upon me, as Nicky had that night upon the beach, forcing me down onto the sand. . . .

When finally I reached the edge of one of the immense pits, it looked to me like some strange, unworldly crater, like those I have heard are on the moon and so make the silvery globe appear as though it has a man's face. So did the bottom of the pit seem, too, where showered by moonbeams, for hoofprints and wagon tracks and other markings I supposed came from some sort of machinery or perhaps the long hoses used in the mining process snaked across the floor, and I could imagine I saw in them a man's face.

Carefully, I skirted the rim of the pit, making my

way toward the small, temporary building serving as the offices, for it was there I hoped to find Jarrett. As I drew near, I observed that the door was open, swinging gently on its hinges, creaking weirdly in the breeze. A light glowed from within, and to my relief, Jarrett's horse, Blackfire, stood without. Slowly, I dismounted and, holding fast to Jocko's reins, lest he should bolt, walked toward the wooden structure, softly calling my husband's name. There was no response.

Timidly, I peeked inside, but I could see by the wavering lamp set upon a littered desk in one corner that no one was there. Where could Jarrett be? I wondered. And Nicky and Thorne? I turned to go, and as I did so, my eyes fell upon a chair on which a fine oak gun case reposed, beautifully carved, polished until the burnished wood gleamed. I recognized the gun case at once as belonging to Uncle Draco. Someone had taken it from his study and brought it here. It was open; I could discern clearly the indentations in the plush red velvet, where Uncle Draco's long, black-barreled dueling pistols usually lay. They were gone. My mouth went dry at the implications; my heart beat too fast in my breast.

Swiftly, I whirled and mounted Jocko, setting my heels to his sides. I must find Jarrett. *I must!* But I did not know where to look; the mines were sprawling, Wheal Penforth almost a mile away from Wheal Anant. But surely, my husband was here at Wheal Anant. His stallion was here; the gun case was here. Nicky and Thorne must be here as well. At any rate, Jarrett must have believed so.

And then, startling me, I heard his voice—not far away, I judged—raised in anger.

"This is madness!"

The words echoed through the piles of quartz residue and the china-clay pits, so that, at first, I was not quite sure whence they had come. But then finally, as my husband continued to speak, I got my bearings and turned Jocko toward the sound. A few moments later, I spied all three men.

"This is madness, I tell you!" Jarrett reiterated. "Utter madness! Dueling is against the law! If one of you is killed, the other will be hanged!"

"Shut up, Jarrett—and stand back!" Nicky hissed. "I'm warning you: I'll shoot *you* instead if you don't. This is none of your affair. 'Tis between Thorne and me, and you're not stopping it. This time, he's going to get what he deserves if it's the last thing I ever do!"

Butt out, Jarrett, or I'll make you sorry you didn't! This . . . snotty whelp is finally getting what's . . . long overdue him, and you're not going . . . to stop me from giving it to him!

How odd that Nicky's words that day in the attic during our childhood should come back to haunt me now as, from the foot of a quartz-waste heap, I stared down at the broad pit below, where the three men stood, as they had once stood as children in the storeroom. The French have a term for what I felt then: *déjà vu*—already seen. It was a nightmare I had lived through before. The pit was like a Greek amphitheater; I could hear every word, clear as a bell. I should have ridden away, but I was unable to tear myself from the scene. Slowly, as though in a trance, I slid from Jocko's smooth back, hunkering down upon the ground, so the men would be less likely to notice me.

"Those are brave words for a filthy, sneaking cheat, Nicholas!" Thorne sneered. "How I shall enjoy killing you—as you killed my poor sister!"

"*You* did that, you son of a bitch, going to the Heights and whining your dirty lies—"

"Lies, Nicholas? Come now. We both know that puling female pup Siobhan whelped is your bastard!"

So it was true. Jarrett's head jerked up sharply at that; he hadn't known, then, hadn't even suspected. . . . It was sheer chance, I thought, that I had seen Nicky and Siobhan together and so had added two and two, and got four.

"And whose little bastard is Philip, Thorne?" Nicky gibed. "Or did you manage to conquer your distaste of women long enough to spread your wife's legs at least once, you foul sodomizer? Jesus! No wonder Siobhan had no stomach for you!"

"Do you think I care? She's a *whore*, Nicholas! My wife and your lover, a whore! How does it feel to know the mother of your daughter gives it away to any man who asks—and doesn't even bother to charge them for it—or did you think you were her one and only?"

"No. 'Twas merely that she desired a *real* man in her bed for a change, and I'll admit I took a certain pleasure in cuckolding you, Thorne!" Nicky paused, and when he spoke again, his voice was deadly. "Start the count, Jarrett. Our cowardly cousin's played for time long enough, trading insults with me."

"I won't do it, Nicky," Jarrett insisted, his jaw taut with rage. "It's madness, I tell you! We know now that Thorne is the culprit responsible for all the trouble at the mines. We need only turn him over to the law and press charges against him."

I gasped at this revelation, stunned. But of course, I realized now, it followed that Thorne, who resented the mines being willed to Uncle Draco and who knew they were the source of most of Nicky's income, should strike a blow where he calculated it would hit the Chandler men the hardest.

"You're a fool, Jarrett, if you believe that Father will agree to such a thing," Nicky declared. "There've been enough scandals in the family as it is. Do you really think he'll consent to washing any more of our dirty linen in public? Do you honestly believe that Uncle Esmond will prosecute his own son or see him turned over to the dragoons to be imprisoned or transported? No. Thorne will get off scot-free, just as he always does. But not this time. I mean to see to that. Start the count, Jarrett."

"No."

"Then I'll do it myself. Stand aside, Jarrett, lest you get caught in the cross fire. Back to back, Thorne. Twenty paces, then turn and shoot—or are you too hen-hearted to go through with it after all?"

"Ask me that when your life's blood is draining away,

you lousy whore's cock!'' Thorne taunted boldly, though I thought he must have been scared even so.

Jarrett and Nicky both were crack shots; they could drill the pip out of a playing card at fifty feet. But I guessed Thorne's pride was so great that it would not permit him to back down, and for all I knew, his skill with a gun had improved drastically over the years. Perhaps he truly believed he could kill his opponent.

"Say your prayers, you disgusting bugger," Nicky jeered. "You're about to meet your Maker—in hell!"

Stricken, I watched as though in a dream as each man pivoted, so they stood back to back, right hands raised, pistols pointed skyward. I could not believe that this was happening, that they actually intended to duel with each other, that Jarrett did not somehow prevent it, though, in truth, I confess I do not know what he could have done to halt it. Nicky and Thorne were both grown men, after all, and determined on their chosen course of action.

"One. Two. Three . . ."

The ominous count rang out through the night, shattering the silence. I bit my lip so hard that I drew blood to keep from crying out as slowly, purposefully, the two men began to step off the paces. In the black-velvet firmament, the moon shone like a lustrous pearl; the stars glittered like diamonds, illuminating the pit and the men's faces—Nicky's, dark and grim; Thorne's, pale and sheened with sweat. From a distant marsh, a lone curlew called, piercing the night.

"Seven. Eight. Nine . . ."

I licked the blood from my mouth, ran my tongue nervously over my dry lips to moisten them. My pulse raced; my heart pounded so violently that I thought it would explode in my breast. I felt as though I had run a very long way and now could not get my breath. Their whole lives—Nicky's and Thorne's—had been building up to this disastrous moment, I thought. In seconds, perhaps one of them would be dead. . . .

"Fifteen. Sixteen. Seventeen . . ."

To my utter horror, I saw Thorne spin about without warning, his gun held at the ready. He had turned early—the cheat!—before the count was finished. It was then that I began to scream, shrill, terrified cries that reverberated through the quartz-waste hills, the empty pits. Even as Jarrett flung himself at Nicky, Thorne aimed, cocked the hammer of his pistol, and fired. The brothers fell to the ground, rolling, so much alike, so similarly dressed in the black evening clothes they had worn for Angelique's party that I could not distinguish between them.

Only one man got up.

I went crazy then, staggering and sliding down the steep, sloping wall of the pit, crying and screaming hysterically because I did not know which brother lay sprawled upon the earth—or even if he lived. The one who was standing glanced up at me, shocked at the sight of me stumbling to the bottom of the pit. Then deliberately he lifted his arm, pointed the gun in his hand at Thorne, and coolly pulled the trigger. For a moment, Thorne just stood there, so I thought he was somehow miraculously unscathed. But then he swayed on his feet; his body began slowly to crumple downward, looking like an organ-grinder's pleated music box collapsing.

He was dead before ever he struck the ground.

Chapter XX

The Last Good-bye

Dear as remembered kisses after death,
And sweet as those by hopeless fancy feign'd
On lips that are for others: deep as love,
Deep as first love, and wild with all regret;
O Death in Life, the days that are no more.

—*The Princess*
Alfred, Lord Tennyson

It was Nicholas who killed Thorne. In my heart, I knew that it was so even before I reached the brothers and saw that it was Jarrett who lay stretched upon the floor of the pit, blood pouring from a wound in his shoulder, staining the white china clay scarlet in the moonlight. Thorne never could shoot straight; even though he had been aiming at Nicky, his bullet had passed through Jarrett. But my husband lived; I thanked God for that. His injury was not serious; he would survive.

Quickly, I knelt and began tearing strips from my petticoats with which to staunch the bleeding and bind Jarrett's injury, ignoring the fact that, through gritted teeth, he cursed me roundly for following him to the mines. If he hadn't wanted me to come, I told him tartly as I divested him of his jacket, waistcoat, and shirt, then he should not have made those cryptic statements and then just left me hanging, burning with curiosity and anxiety about his welfare—and only look what had happened to him!

By then, of course, I was crying so hard that I could scarcely see to wrap the makeshift bandage around him, and Nicky had to complete the job, fashioning a crude sling for my husband's arm, so his shoulder would not be subjected to too much strain.

"I suppose Thorne's dead," Jarrett said finally, his voice somber.

"Yes," Nicky replied. He paused. Then slowly he remarked, "You saved my life, Jarrett—and risked your own in the process. Why? After all I've done to you and Laura—"

"You're my brother, Nicky. I love you. But I don't guess you ever quite understood that."

Nicky glanced away, then back, swallowing hard, as though there were a lump in his throat, choking him, his black eyes suspiciously bright in the moonlight as he struggled to master his emotions.

"No," he admitted at last, on his dark visage a queer, heartbreaking expression. "I was always too damned busy competing with you, trying to best you, Jarrett— just as Thorne was me. I see that now—now, when it's too late." His voice was bitter and filled with regret. "I'm finished here in England, you know. I'll have to get away before anyone learns that Thorne is dead and that I killed him; else they'll set the law on me, and I'll surely hang. I know how much our good Queen Victoria frowns on dueling. She's as stern, straitlaced, and unforgiving as they come, that fat old cow who sits on England's throne."

"Then why'd you do it, Nicky?" Jarrett queried. "There were other ways of handling Thorne."

"But none so sure as the one I chose, was there? I'd been suspicious of him for a long time, you know. He'd always believed Aunt Julianne's silly accusations about Father and Mother amending Grandfather Nigel's will so they could get their hands on the china-clay mines. Thorne really thought Wheal Anant and Wheal Penforth ought to have belonged to Uncle Esmond, and since they didn't, and he had no means of obtaining them besides, he decided to ruin them—and me, as well, in the process.

"I figured he'd come here tonight, with no guards posted and everyone else at the soirée. So, as soon as I spied him leave the Heights and slip out to the stables, I took the dueling pistols and followed him. I knew if I caught him in the act of sabotage and threatened to expose him and turn him over to the authorities for prosecution, he'd just laugh in my face. But a challenge . . . well, that's something a man with any kind of pride at all just can't walk away from; and Thorne's ego was supreme. I knew that he wouldn't back down, that we'd be rid of him for good."

"But you might as well have murdered him, Nicky,"

Jarrett pointed out quietly. "You knew he could scarcely tell one end of a gun from another."

"Maybe so, but that doesn't mean he might not have killed me just the same; he stood as fair a chance as anyone else would have. Still, I prefer to think it was a kind of wild justice for the three years of my life he stole from me—Laura would have called me back and told me the truth if Thorne hadn't tied her up, Mother said —justice for the mines, and justice for what he told poor Lizzie that day at the Heights. She was always too high-strung, and it sent her over the edge. We killed her, Thorne and I. I owed her something for that. She was my wife, and she loved me. She deserved better than what I gave her, and Thorne deserved to pay for all he'd done. He never would have gone to gaol. Father, Uncle Esmond, and Uncle Welles would have seen to that; you know how they are about protecting the families however they can. So now Thorne's dead, and the slate's wiped clean at long last."

Nicky fell silent then; for a moment, all three of us were still, thinking of those days gone by, those days of our misspent youth that were no more. Which of us had ever dreamed then that we would come to this? That wayward Clemency would bleed to death in the gatehouse at the Heights? That Lizzie would try to shoot Nicky, then break her neck, flying over a hedgerow? That Thorne and Nicky would duel, that one of them would lie dead, killed by the other, not twenty-five feet from where we now sat?

As I said at the beginning of my tale, we had thought that the world could be had for the taking, that we had only to reach out and make it ours. Rash and defiant, we had seized life with a vengeance and made of it what we willed, a mosaic ill fashioned and much mended, the cracks showing ever after, the pieces fragmented, poorly placed; for what do the young, in their ignorance, really know of harmony and grace? So little. So very little.

The hour was late, and so finally we rose.

"Well . . . I guess this is good-bye," Nicky said, his voice raw with sudden emotion. "Jarrett—" He broke off abruptly, hugging his brother close for a long minute, the loving gesture speaking for him the words he could not say. Then he turned to me. "Kiss me, dear Laura— for old times' sake, for our lost youth, and for those halcyon days we shall never know again. I don't think Jarrett will mind, just this once."

No, somehow I knew he would not—just this once. Slowly, I lifted my lips for Nicky's kiss, and as his mouth met mine, I was a girl of seventeen again, in the gardens at the Grange, loving him. There would always be a place in my heart for him, I realized now, tucked away in a corner with my innocence and youth and girlish daydreams. No matter what he was, what he had done, Nicky had been a part of my life; he would always be a part of my memories. Reluctantly, he released me and stepped away, one hand reaching out to smooth back from my face a strand of hair that had tumbled from its pins.

"I did you both a great wrong once—that night upon the beach," he stated. "It was a lie, what I told you that night; Laura was never mine."

"I know," Jarrett said.

"I'm glad," Nicky answered. He paused. Then he

uttered, "Look after Winston and Katherine for me, will you? Poor little tykes. I don't expect I ever would have been much of a father to them anyway."

Such was the remorse in his voice for that, that I was suddenly glad, so very glad that we had never told him about Rhodes, that Nicky must not leave with that burden, too, upon his shoulders.

"Where will you go?" I inquired softly.

"Back to Australia, I reckon. Tell Father and Mother I'll send them word this time, when I can. I never was much of a letter writer." Nicky whistled for his horse, which idled nearby, along with Thorne's, and mounted up. He smiled a cocky grin as he gazed down at us, though his black eyes were sad, I thought. "Whenever you get to wondering or worrying about me, if you ever do, just think of me lazing by a billabong—that's a stagnant pool—somewhere, in the shade of a eucalyptus tree," he teased with a touch of his old arrogance, so I knew he would be all right after all.

Then, setting his heels to his gelding's sides, Nicky galloped up the wall of the pit and rode away into the darkness.

"Is he taking your heart away with him, Laura?" Jarrett asked in the hush that enveloped us, his voice uncertain, aching with need and wanting.

"Oh, my love," I whispered, tears starting in my eyes, "after all this time, do you still doubt me? He took my youth long ago, yes, and that, he shall ever carry with him, I think. But not my heart, no, never that. It lies where it has always lain these many years past now, Jarrett: safe in your keeping."

He put his good arm around me then and kissed me deeply; and I knew that I did not regret losing Nicky, that I would never again regret losing him. He had been a dream, while Jarrett was reality, solid as the black rocks of the Cornish coast, his love for me just as enduring.

Across a Starlit Sea
1848

Chapter XXI

Now and Forever

Now lies the Earth all Danaë to the stars,
And all thy heart lies open unto me.

Now slides the silent meteor on, and leaves
A shining furrow, as thy thoughts in me.

Now folds the lily all her sweetness up,
And slips into the bosom of the lake;
So fold thyself, my dearest, thou, and slip
Into my bosom and be lost in me.

—*The Princess*
Alfred, Lord Tennyson

Stormswept Heights, England, 1848

We buried Thorne next to his sister, Elizabeth, in the cemetery that lies just beyond the village church. I don't think Uncle Esmond ever recovered from the shock of losing both his children so close together and so young.

He was like a clock with a broken mainspring, withdrawing even farther into his dreamy, isolated shell. Only little Katherine, as the years passed, ever truly managed to draw him out. Then he would smile and seem almost his old self, and it was easy to understand why Aunt Maggie had once loved him, as I had Nicholas.

Aunt Julianne was so stricken by grief at Thorne's death that she went into deep mourning and never came out, dressing always in black and keeping the Hall so like a tomb that soon scarcely anyone went there anymore. Gradually, with time, the moors crept ever nearer, encroaching on the park; and the ivy clung ever more thickly to the walls of the manor.

We never saw Nicholas again. In the beginning, now and then, a letter would come, a few hastily scrawled lines, badly written. But eventually, the time that elapsed between the missives grew longer and longer until finally they stopped arriving altogether; and in the end, we did not know if he was alive or dead. So now, as I sometimes do, whenever I get to wondering and worrying about him, I just picture him lazing by a billabong somewhere, as he advised, in the shade of a eucalyptus tree; and somehow, in my heart, I feel he survives, wild and reckless as ever, though sadder and little wiser. Sometimes, I walk along the coast at night and look out across the starlit sea; I imagine I can see Australia's distant reefs, and Nicky's laughter comes to me on the wind, though it is only in my mind.

But it is Jarrett who holds my heart, who chases away the shadows of the past when they grow too dark and haunting, who sometimes takes me to that small, secluded cove upon the beach and presses me down there, upon the sand, as he did that first time when I was yet half woman, half child and he showed me what it was to love a man. It is for Jarrett I yearn when the nights are long; in his strong arms, I am born anew.

Those bittersweet days of youth are gone forever now. But our love remains, like the wind that blows across the sweeping moors, or the sea that rushes in upon the wild shore: boundless, everlasting.

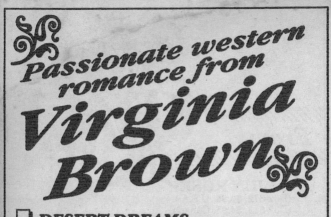